Nicole Conway

Published by Month9Books
Cover design by Beetiful Book Covers © 2015
Dragon head design by Nicole Conway

Month9Books

To my grandmother-in-law, Evelyn Conway.
I can never thank you enough for all that you do for us.

PRAISE FOR AVIAN

"An INCREDIBLE second book." - Natalie at Book Lovers Life

"An exhilirating read." - Grace Fonseca

"Great fantasy book. I read it with my son and he really enjoyed it." - Jennifer Harless-Smith

"Five stars. Can't wait for the next one." - Rita B.

"I hope there is another one soon." - Regina

"You need to read this." - Sharlane Collins

"I really enjoyed this second book in the series. The characters are easy to identify with, and it was very fun to read." - Catherine Schoder

"I love this series. I think this author is so creative and the characters are great. Can't wait for the next book to come out." - RT

"Can't wait for the third book. Couldn't put it down." - Ken Hall

one

Not everyone can be a dragonrider. Not everyone can handle the stress or the physical demands of having the most dangerous job in the king's forces. My mentor, Lieutenant Sile Derrick, once told me that dragonriders are not born—they are made. He said that they have to be hammered, shaped, and baptized in fire, just like when a blacksmith molds a lethal sword out of a hunk of raw metal. Blybrig Academy is where all dragonriders are made. It's our forge. Never in a hundred years would I have guessed I would find myself there, facing the furnace of my destiny. But destiny has a funny way of picking you when you least expect it.

There was snow on the mountains when I left Blybrig behind for the three-month interlude in my training as a dragonrider. I hadn't been back home to Mithangol in almost a year. I wish I could tell you that I was looking forward to seeing my father, stepmother, twin half-sisters, and older half-brother again. But I wasn't. In fact, I was absolutely dreading it. The very thought of living with them put painful knots of anxiety in my stomach.

I looked into the cold wind from the back of my dragon, Mavrik, who stretched his wings out wide to catch the updrafts. He soared like a magnificent blue-scaled eagle. I was sitting between his strong neck and powerful wing arms in a saddle made of finely crafted leather. He could sense my uneasiness. Every now and then, he flicked a glance back at me with one of his big yellow eyes, making curious clicking and chirping noises.

"It'll be fine." I tried to sound confident. "I'm sure things will be different now."

In fact, I knew they probably wouldn't. If anything, now they would be much worse. My father had never liked me. He had never even wanted me to begin with. But after my mother passed away, there was nowhere else for me to go except maybe a prison camp. I'm pretty sure that's where I would have ended up if my mother hadn't left behind a letter that named Ulric Broadfeather as my biological father. That letter made him my only living relative, so he was duty-bound to adopt me. It was a law in Maldobar, so he couldn't refuse even though I was a halfbreed. It would have looked worse to abandon me than for him to have a halfbreed for a son.

Far below, tucked into the crevices of the Stonegap Mountains, I saw Mithangol. That was where Ulric and his real family lived, and where I'd been an unwelcome guest since I was twelve years old. It was the dead of winter now, so all the roofs of the houses and shops were covered in a thick blanket of clean white snow. I could see the steep slopes dotted with dark fir trees and smoke rising up from all the chimneys.

I'd lost all track of time while I was in Blybrig Academy. It was close to the coast and cut off from the world by mountains on all sides, so the seasons practically stood still. It was always warm, dry, and sunny there. After spending so many months in the constant warmth of the desert, I'd forgotten what the winter cold felt like. I shivered hard, and Mavrik made an unhappy grumbling, growling sound. I guess he didn't like the cold, either.

Since I was sure no one at home was expecting me, I wasn't in any hurry to get back there right away. Besides, there was someone else I had to see first. Mavrik circled around the outside of the small city looking for a good place to land. Finally, he cupped his wings and lurched toward the ground, stepping awkwardly into the snow and growling as he hunkered down long enough for me to jump down out of the saddle. I took my bag off his back, and gave him a good scratch behind the ears.

"Go find a good spot in the sun," I told him. "At least until I can figure out how to fit you in the barn." I wasn't sure Ulric was going to allow that—especially since there was a good chance Mavrik might eat the horses. The only thing more dangerous than a hungry dragon is a bored dragon.

Mavrik blinked at me, snorted, and took off into the sky again. I stumbled back as the rush of wind off his wings hit me hard, making me lose my balance for a moment. I stood ankle-deep in the snow, watching him soar upwards and disappear into the low clouds. Even if I couldn't see him, I could still feel his presence like a buzzing warmth in the back of my mind. It gave me comfort as I started hiking through the thin line of pine trees.

I knew Mithangol like the back of my hand. I'd spent a lot of a time avoiding my family, and even more time getting into trouble with Katalina Crookin. Katty had been my best friend until I went to Blybrig, and so I started for her house right away. I still considered her one of my closest friends, even if I hadn't seen her in almost a year. Knowing that I'd be standing in her house soon, getting hugged and force-fed by her mother while I told them about my training, put a smile on my face. I was so excited to finally see her.

I walked down the side of the road that led past the Crookin's home. Further down that same road was Ulric's house, but I wasn't going to let myself think about that yet. Katty's father was a blacksmith, and I knew by the smell of scorched metal in the air that he must have been working in his forge. The sun was just beginning to set as I came up the drive toward the front of their house. I saw lights burning in the windows, and smoke puffing out of their chimney. The place looked cozy, and exactly how I'd remembered it.

I knocked on the front door, my stomach churning and doing excited back flips while I waited. I wanted to see Katty, and at the same time, I was so nervous. I wondered if she had changed since we last saw each other. I was fairly sure I hadn't grown at all, despite my best efforts. Finally, the handle lurched, the door opened, and I held my breath.

It wasn't Katty.

Mrs. Crookin stood in the doorway wiping her hands on her apron. When she saw me, she started to smile. Her eyes got bright, and she grabbed me before I could even remember to hold my breath. She always hugged me so tight I thought I might suffocate.

"Jaevid!" She crooned at me, and started kissing my cheeks. "Look at you! So handsome in that uniform! Katty told me you were taken in by the academy. Training to be a dragonrider, is it?"

I blushed as she held me out at arm's length. I was still wearing my fledgling uniform with the king's golden eagle stitched onto the chest. I hadn't bothered putting on my armor, though. It was still packed away in my bags. "Yes, ma'am."

"Oh she's going to be so excited to see you. She read your letters over and over." Mrs. Crookin started wiping dirt from my face with her apron. "She's out at the forge, dear. You should go surprise her."

Katty had told me in one of her letters that she was going to be an apprentice for her father and learn to be a blacksmith, too. I knew that would definitely make her happy. She had always talked about wanting to learn her father's craft. It was her dream.

I left my bag in the doorway and started out across the snow toward the barn where Mr. Crookin had built his own forge and bellows. Black smoke belched out of the stone stack, and I could see the bright red glow of the fire inside shining from the crack under the door.

My stomach was doing more aerobatics than ever as I started to pull on the handle. I opened it just a little, barely enough to peek inside and see what she was doing. All of a sudden, my heart hit the back of my throat like someone was choking me. It hit me so hard I couldn't even think. I couldn't breathe. All I felt was a burning, angry heat in the pit of my stomach like I'd swallowed a mouthful of dragon venom.

Katty was there, and I didn't see her father anywhere. But she wasn't alone. She was standing with a boy who looked like he was eighteen or so—a lot older than I was. He was a lot taller than me, too, with coal-black hair pulled into a short ponytail. He was wearing a blacksmithing apron just like she was, and they were laughing together. I didn't recognize him, which bothered me the most. Mithangol was a very small city. Most of the younger men had bullied me at one time or another while I was growing up, so I knew who they were. But I had never even seen this boy before.

She giggled at him while he teasingly smudged ash on her cheeks, and when she turned around to start working again, I saw him put a hand on the base of her back. It made that angry fire in my gut burn all the way up through my chest. I couldn't even see straight.

They hadn't noticed I was standing there, so I shut the door and backed away. I went back to the house with my heart hammering in my ears. When I got inside, I picked up my bag and got ready to leave.

"Wasn't Katty working out there?" Mrs. Crookin sounded worried. She was leaning in from the kitchen, looking me over for an explanation.

I couldn't meet her gaze. I was sure if I did, she'd see how upset I was. "Yeah. But she's busy. I'll just come back some other time," I lied.

Mrs. Crookin didn't try to stop me as I gathered my bag and left. When the cold air hit my face, I realized just how angry I really was. I didn't even understand why seeing her with that boy made me so upset. But it did. It felt like some kind of betrayal, even if I had no justification for it. Katty and I were just friends. We'd always been just friends. I had no right to be upset about who she flirted with. None of that mattered right then, though. I was so furious I was seeing red.

In my mind, Mavrik sent me an image of him burning the barn to the ground with Katty and that stranger inside. I shook my head, and looked up to the darkening sky. "Don't bother," I muttered.

I knew he would hear me even if he were ten miles away. We were linked now in a way I didn't understand. While I was at Blybrig, I'd discovered I had a unique ability to call out to animals. They could understand me. But so far, Mavrik was the only one who could communicate back to me. That was our secret.

I dragged my feet through the snow as I walked down the road toward Ulric's house. My thoughts were clouded and confused. I wasn't even worried about seeing my family anymore. All I could think about was that stranger and how he'd touched Katty, smiled at her like that, and made her laugh. It made me so annoyed with her, and even more furious and frustrated with myself. I was so caught up that when I turned the corner to walk up the steep, muddy drive toward my family's home, I didn't notice the house.

Then I looked up.

There were no lights burning in the windows, and the house was completely dark. It was getting kind of late, though. Maybe everyone had already gone to sleep? Still, it was strange that there was no smoke coming from the chimney. As cold as it was, Ulric would have normally lit the fireplace to keep the house warm all night.

I hurried up the drive toward the porch, noticing that the garden was dead and covered in snow. My stepmother, Serah, usually covered the ground with pine straw to protect the plants from the cold until spring. Cupping my hands around my eyes, I peeked in through the front window to see if anyone was still sitting up in the parlor. Sometimes Ulric sat at the side of the dying fire to smoke his pipe until really late.

What I saw put another hard, painful knot in my throat. I ran to the front door and started beating on it. To my surprise, the door just swung freely in. It wasn't even locked.

The house was empty.

For a few minutes, I could only stand there in the open doorway while the cold winter wind howled past me. I stared through the darkness into the parlor and kitchen in front of me. There wasn't a stick of furniture anywhere. Judging by the dust gathered on the kitchen counters and windowsills, they hadn't been here for months.

Slowly, I began to realize the truth: they had left me. Ulric had taken his whole family, moved, and never said a word to me about it. Maybe it was naïve to expect him to tell me, but it still left me stunned.

"Jae!" I heard someone call out to me, and I recognized who it was right away. But hearing *her* voice didn't give me comfort like it usually did. I didn't turn around. I just kept standing there, staring into the empty house, wondering what I was supposed to do now.

Katty ran up behind me with ash still smudged on her cheeks. She was flushed and out of breath, wearing a dark gray dress and blacksmithing apron that were both covered in scorch marks. "Jae?" she said my name again.

I was going to have to face her eventually. At least now, she wouldn't know I was upset about what I'd seen with her. I had bigger problems. "They left," I muttered back, finally looking back at her.

Katty had grown. She looked different, and not in ways I necessarily felt comfortable with. The boys in town had always teased her and called her ugly because of her wild, frizzy curls and scrawny build. Her golden, curly hair was longer and it wasn't frizzy at all. It framed her round face and made her look ... very, very beautiful. Her wide blue eyes glittered in the darkness, but I had to look up to see them because she was taller than me now. All her freckles were gone, and now her skin looked smooth and soft. She had adult shapes to her body now that were almost hidden by her thick leather apron.

She looked a lot more grown up now. And for some reason, that made me more angry and frustrated than ever. Katty was only a few months older than I was, so I had always felt better about my lack of size because she wasn't all that big, either. But now I knew for sure that I was doomed to be a tiny scarecrow forever. Even girls were outgrowing me.

"I know," she said softly. "I came by a week ago to see if you'd come back yet, and they were already gone. This was left for you. I found it slipped under the front door. It's from your brother. I hope you don't mind, but I read it already. I wanted to know why they left without saying anything." She reached into her apron pocket and pulled out a wrinkled envelope.

I took it from her, scowling at it as I crammed it into my own pocket. Why they'd left didn't matter to me right then. All I cared about was that now I was alone here, in a big empty house. I didn't have any furniture. I didn't have any clothes other than my uniforms. I didn't even have food.

"Don't worry, okay?" Katty reached out to put her arms around my neck. She hugged me, but it didn't make me feel any better. In fact, it just felt awkward and wrong—like she was comforting a little kid. "We'll help you. We'll bring you anything you need."

"Thanks." I couldn't make myself say anything else. I was too upset. My jaw locked up and I clenched my teeth.

"I'm so sorry, Jae." She hugged me even tighter. "I've missed you so much."

For some reason, I didn't quite believe her. She'd obviously had some company to keep her from being lonely without me. "Yeah," I managed to answer dryly. "Well, I'm back now for three months."

"You can come stay with us tonight," she offered.

I backed away from her a little, looking into the empty house and trying to decide what to do now. Finally, I shook my head. "No, but thanks. I'll be fine."

She arched a brow at me suspiciously. I could see confusion in her eyes. "But Jae, there's nothing here. You can't possibly—"

"I'll be fine," I repeated. "Please leave me alone."

This definitely wasn't the welcome home I'd expected. Oh sure, I'd anticipated getting the cold shoulder from Serah and my siblings, being forced to sleep in the loftroom again, and maybe even getting a beating from Ulric just for old time's sake. This had caught me completely off guard. I felt so lost.

Katty nodded a little, and started to look sad. "Okay, if you're sure. I'll come by tomorrow with something to eat. We'll catch up." She gave me a hopeful smile.

I couldn't smile back at her. I tried, but the ability wasn't there. As she turned to leave, I lingered in the doorway of the empty house and watched her walk away. I waited until she was far away, too far to see me through the darkness, to let my feelings show.

A few tears blurred my vision and left warm streaks

down my face. I wiped them away quickly. Maybe if I were a normal-sized, halfway healthy looking young man like that stranger she'd been giggling with, Katty would have noticed me first. But I wasn't. And I never would be. I swallowed my feelings quickly. No matter what happened, I was a dragonrider now. Dragonriders didn't cry.

It started snowing again. Fat white flakes swirled in the air around me when I turned back toward the house again. There really was no point in going inside. Not tonight, anyways. So I shut the door and started for the barn instead. I called out to Mavrik, telling him to land, as I pushed open the heavy barn door. All the horses were gone. So was the wagon, and most of the tools Ulric had kept on hand for his work as a tackmaster. There was old hay still piled on the floor, and it still smelled like the oils he used to season the leather for the dragon saddles.

The earth flinched under my boots as Mavrik landed, and I heard him chirp at me worriedly as he crawled my way. The barn was barely big enough to squeeze him in. He had to curl up into the smallest dragon-ball I'd ever seen. He laid down with his snout on his tail and his wings folded up tightly against his sides. If he stretched at all, he'd take out a wall or the roof. It definitely wasn't as comfortable as the Roost, but at least it was safe from the wind.

I rolled the door close again, and started looking around for anything left behind that I could use. I found a few half-burned candles and an old quilt that smelled like it had been used as a horse blanket. Using the piece of flint I kept in my saddlebag, and a hunting knife I'd stolen from a farmer a few months ago, I lit the candle and wrapped myself up in the blanket.

As I leaned back against Mavrik's side, I finally took out Roland's letter and held it up to the candlelight. His script was small, and it was hard to read, but what it said left my head spinning worse than ever.

Roland had officially joined the ground infantry about the same time Ulric and I had left for Blybrig last spring. He'd gone to training in Halfax, and been given a post as a cavalryman. Ulric and Serah had told him about their decision to move only a few weeks before they actually had. Apparently, Ulric had gotten an offer to buy a bigger house with a better workshop near Westwatch. They'd given this house to Roland to live in when he wasn't away with the infantry, but he didn't want it. So he was offering it to me, instead. He wrote that if I wanted it, it was mine, or I could try to sell it. He didn't plan on ever coming back to Mithangol if he could help it. I didn't blame him for that.

At the very bottom of the letter, in what looked like a last minute scribble, he wrote that he was being sent to the frontlines at Northwatch. He said that if I ever made it that far, I should try to find him. When I read that, I exchanged a wide-eyed look with Mavrik. Roland had never wanted anything to do with me before. He had always acted like I didn't exist. I wasn't sure what to think of that.

I read the letter over and over to be sure I hadn't missed anything. All the while, my mind was racing with the question of what to do about the empty house. I didn't know if I could sell it and leave Mithangol like he had, or if I should try to stay and make some kind of a temporary life for myself here. I only had three months. For a long time, I sat there staring at the letter while Mavrik purred himself to sleep. I scratched at his big ears and rubbed his scaly snout.

Finally, I folded up the letter and blew out the candle. There wasn't anything I could do tonight. I was tired from traveling, and my mind was foggy with so many confusing emotions. I curled up closer to Mavrik's warm side, putting my head against his neck and closing my eyes. I listened to him breathing as he slept.

I knew I couldn't express to him with words how glad I was to have him there. Still, I knew he'd probably be able to sense my emotions the same way I could sense his. He probably knew I needed him now, when I had no one else to turn to. He wasn't just my mount; he was my friend, my partner, and my greatest ally. Whatever happened to me now, I knew he would be there. I would never really be alone.

two

I woke up the next morning feeling stiff. It was still cold outside, but I was warm where I lay, snuggled up beside Mavrik under the old horse blanket. I wasn't eager to get up and face the day, or the winter weather outside.

It was easy to feel hopeless. It was easy to look at my situation and want to give up. I could just go live with my best friend Felix for the interlude, like he'd wanted. He was the son of a rich duke, so I would have plenty to eat, a nice warm bed, and lots of time to train if I went to stay with him. The only reason I'd bothered coming back here was to see Katty, and now that was completely ruined.

Then it hit me.

It hit me so suddenly, I glanced at Mavrik to make sure that he hadn't put that thought in my mind, but he was still asleep. I'd spent too much of my life feeling sorry for myself. I wasn't going to make anyone proud moping around. I was done taking the easy road, and sitting back wishing things would get better. I hadn't just spent a year in training to be a dragonrider to let something like this defeat me. This was an opportunity to show everyone else that I wasn't helpless, that I could fend for myself, and I intended to seize it. For me, nothing was ever going to be easy. The only thing I had control of was how I handled it.

I got up, brushed the straw off my clothes, and started pushing the heavy barn door open to let the morning light stream in. Usually winter days in Mithangol were overcast and bleak, but today the sun was shining through the thick cloud cover. It sparkled over the freshly fallen snow, and a blast of cold wind cut me right to the bone.

Behind me, Mavrik growled sleepily as the morning sun filtered in. He squinted, snorted, and rolled over to face away from the light. Apparently, he wasn't ready to get up yet. It had been hard enough to pack that much dragon into this small barn to begin with, so I decided I would let him sleep. There wasn't much he could do for me today, anyway.

"I'm going to get things cleaned up," I told him as I tied my cloak under my chin. "Don't eat anyone, okay? And don't burn down anything, either. We're keeping a low profile."

He just flicked the end of his long tail and started snoring again.

The house didn't look any less bleak or empty even with the sun shining through the windows. I decided to go in and see exactly what I had to work with before I started cleaning. Ulric and Serah hadn't left me much, though. I opened all the doors and windows to let the cold wind blow through. It made it freezing inside, but I had to get rid of the musty smell.

I hadn't spent all that much time inside the house itself before, so it was weird to be standing in it alone. Serah had never liked me touching her things, and she had forbidden me to be inside without her supervision. It wasn't a big house, and it wasn't fancy at all. The floors were bare wood, and the walls were covered in old plaster that was chipping in places. Downstairs there was only a small parlor with a fireplace, a kitchen with a wood stove, and a single washroom with a big copper basin for bathing.

There was basically nothing left in all the kitchen cabinets except a few old breadcrumbs and some old empty jars. There were a few split logs stacked up beside the stove, but I had a feeling I was going to have to learn to cook for myself now. I had never cooked anything before in my life. I didn't know how to make bread, or anything like that. This wasn't going to be easy. I knew I had a lot of learning to do.

Up the narrow staircase were the three bedrooms. They were all about the same size, and I had never slept in any of them. I was surprised to find that they left all the bed frames and old, lumpy mattresses behind. There was a fireplace in the room that used to belong to Ulric and Serah. It also had the biggest bed and a window that overlooked the front drive. I decided I would take that room for myself, since this was going to be my house now.

The second room had been Emry and Lin's. There were two much smaller beds set on either side of the space, with a window in the middle of the far wall. The rest of the furniture was gone. The only trace of my horrible twin sisters left was a hole in one of the walls leftover from when Emry had thrown a fit, accused me of stealing a pair of earrings from her, and hurled a jewelry box at me. She'd missed me, thankfully, but managed to put a big dent in the plaster. Naturally, that had invited Ulric's wrath down on both of us—well, mostly on me.

Roland's room had the only other decent sized bed. Since they were expecting him to be living here from now on, it still had a lot of his stuff left in it. His bed still had all the sheets and pillows on it, and his armoire still had his clothes inside. They were all bound to be way too big for me, but at least now I had the option of something to wear other than my academy uniforms.

I had never been inside his room before, and it was weird to be standing there with his belongings. He had sounded very sure in his letter that he wasn't coming back, though. I guess none of this stuff mattered enough to him to come back for it.

At the end of Roland's bed was a large wooden trunk with iron clasps and hinges. The old padlock on the front wouldn't budge, no matter how I picked at it. Considering there was no one here anymore to beat me senseless if I broke into Roland's private property, I didn't waste any time using my hunting knife to pry the hinges off the back of the trunk and open it.

Inside, buried under an old blanket, was a collection of things I knew must have been special to him—things he hadn't wanted anyone else to touch. Lying on top was an old scimitar that looked like it must be some kind of heirloom. But as far as I knew, our father had never been a soldier, so I didn't know where Roland would have gotten a blade like that. I didn't remember ever seeing him carry it around.

I picked it up, feeling how light it was in my hand. The more I looked at it, the more I realized what a beautiful weapon it truly was. It had ivory and silver inlaid into the hilt with designs that looked like the head of a stag. The curved blade needed to be sharpened and polished, but it was slender and had a beautiful shape. It looked like it had probably been a very expensive blade whenever it was originally forged. Even the scabbard was covered with a sheet of hammered bronze that had the same engraving of a stag's head on it.

I'd never seen such an ornate weapon before. All the weapons we used at the academy for training were blunted or made out of wood so we didn't accidentally kill each other. None of them looked like this. None of them had been crafted so carefully, with such attention to detail and beauty.

I grasped the leather of the grip and took it out of the sheath, holding it firmly. I had practiced with lots of different weapons at the academy in the past year. None of them suited me well. I fumbled clumsily with the swords that were too heavy or too big, struggled with bows that I didn't have the strength to draw, and made all the instructors look at me like I was a dead man walking.

But this scimitar was different. I could feel it right away. Something about the way it fit into my hand, even if it was still way too big, just seemed right. It felt comfortable in my palm, and I liked the way the light danced over the unique curved shape of the blade.

I put the scimitar back into the sheath, and set it aside to keep going through the trunk. Roland had been keeping his savings from working odd jobs around the city in a leather purse. I counted out twenty gold pieces, ten silver, and fifteen coppers. I had never seen that much money in my life. As wrong as I knew it was to take his life's savings without asking, I needed to buy food. I would have to pay him back later. Eventually, though probably not anytime soon, I would start getting paid for my work as a dragonrider.

The only other item buried in the trunk was a leather-bound book. I untied the strings that held it closed, and discovered it was a journal. Immediately, I closed it and put it back into the trunk without reading a single word. Maybe I'd borrow his savings, and keep the scimitar, but I drew the line at that. I wasn't going to rifle through his personal thoughts. It felt wrong to even hold the thing.

Picking up the purse of coins and the scimitar, I shut the trunk again and looked around the room. I couldn't shake that eerie feeling I got from standing in there. Roland and I had never been close. We'd only exchanged a handful of words in three years. We were basically strangers, but he must have found some reason to reach out to me. He was the last person in the world I had expected that from. It was a humbling surprise to know that he even thought about me.

I turned around to leave the room with my new treasures in my hand, and almost smacked right into Katty. She was standing in the doorway watching me. She hadn't made a single sound. It scared me to death.

"What are you doing here?" I asked, doubling over to recollect my nerves. For a moment, I'd thought she was Ulric or Serah about to catch me going through Roland's stuff.

She had her arms crossed, and her golden curls bounced around her face when she shrugged. "Momma sent some food for you. I told you she would last night." Her tone was sharp, and I noticed she was scowling a little. I was about to ask why, but she beat me to it. "I know you saw me with Bren last night. Momma said you went out to the shop, so I know you saw. Don't try to deny it. Tell me the truth, is that why you're acting so weird?"

That caught me off guard. I stared up at her, since she was now several inches taller, and fumbled for words. "I'm not acting weird."

"Yes, you are. I've seen you hurt, sad, and upset because of your family plenty of times. But you've never been this way toward me." She took a demanding step in my direction. "You've never not wanted me around. So why don't you go ahead ask me what I know you want to ask?"

I frowned hard. "There's nothing I want to ask."

She matched my firm look with an even angrier one of her own. "Fine. Be stubborn, then. I'll tell you, anyway. My father took Bren on as an apprentice at the same time I started. We've been working together every day since then."

"Great," I growled back through clenched teeth. I was starting to feel that furious heat rising up in my chest again. "I'm sure he's a swell guy, too."

"He is!" She snapped. "And it just so happens that I like him!"

"Good!" I yelled as I stormed past her. I was so angry my hands were shaking. I wanted to get away from her. I stomped down the stairs to the kitchen and started heading for the front door. I'd almost made it there when she grabbed me by the back of the shirt and yanked me to a halt.

"Jaevid, talk to me about this!" She started shouting, too. "I know you're jealous. But can you blame me? He's going to be a blacksmith, too. He'll be able to help me take over my father's business. He comes from a good family. And he's—"

"—not a scrawny little halfbreed," I finished for her. I was losing my ability to keep my anger under control, so she got a full-forced glare when I turned back to face her.

Her expression went totally blank, and I saw her blue eyes go wide. Anyone who didn't know her well would think she was just surprised, but I'd been around Katty long enough to pick out those faint traces of guilt in her expression. I'd hit the nail on the head.

Even if I wasn't puny-looking, I doubted she would ever see me as more than a friend because I was a halfbreed. She was willing to be seen with me, to associate with me, but only as a friend. She had drawn the line at that, but had failed to let me know about that little detail. I'd never be anything more to her, and I was just now figuring that out.

I took a few seconds to breathe. I was trying to keep my temper in check as best I could before I said anything else I'd probably regret later. It didn't work.

"Well, I'm glad we've finally cleared that up. Now I know where I stand. Just get out, Katty." I growled at her again.

Her eyes went steely, and she recoiled a little. I guess she was waiting for me to reconsider or apologize because she kept standing there, staring at me.

I couldn't stand it. I hated knowing that every second we had spent together was basically a fraud. I already had to fight to earn any acceptance and respect from the other riders at Blybrig; I wasn't about to do the same thing for her attention. If she wanted Bren so badly, then she could have him.

I left o. .he front door without saying anything else. I already felt bad for letting my true feelings show. I hated that I knew how she really felt about me now. I felt like a fool for ever thinking I had a chance with her.

Katty didn't try to talk to me again. I caught a glimpse of her storming toward her house as I ducked into Ulric's workshop. I'd known her so well before, or at least that's what I thought, but now she looked like a stranger. It felt like the Katty I used to know was gone … and I'd never even gotten to say goodbye.

I didn't know what else to do with my frustration, so I went to work. There was a lot left to do, anyway. Ulric's shop was basically empty. There wasn't anything left downstairs except for some scraps of leather and a pair of wooden sawhorses. It still smelled like the oils and hides he'd worked with, and I couldn't shake a sense of tension in the air as though his presence had left an invisible stain on the place.

My stomach was churning as I climbed the ladder up to the loftroom where I had lived like a stowaway for three long years. All the old crates and boxes being stored up there were still sitting around, right where they had been before. My cot was there, too, with the same old quilts piled on it and a candle burned down to a nub. It was drafty and cold because of the cracks in the walls, and as I stood there staring at my old room, I started to think about my mother. So many nights I had lain awake in that bed, missing her. Now, she felt further away than ever. My memories of her were beginning to fade. I couldn't remember her smell anymore, or the sound of her laugh. It chilled me to the bone.

There were rusted old garden tools, rakes and shovels, and old scraps of wood leaned up against the walls in the loftroom. Long-forgotten pieces of furniture were pushed into corners and covered with sheets. One by one, I started going through the storage crates. They were stuffed with moth-eaten clothes, a set of cast-iron pots and pans that looked like they were several generations old, and odds and ends that were probably worthless to anyone else. But these were my treasures. They were the only things in the world, except for the clothes on my back, that actually belonged to me.

What interested me more than anything else I found was an old carpenter's toolkit in a solid, handmade wooden box. I had known Ulric was a craftsman, from a family of craftsmen, but I had never seen anything like that before. There were tools for boring holes, saws of all shapes and sizes, files, chisels, a hatchet, and a hammer. I held each one, and wondered how you could use such simple instruments to make things like tables and chairs. Something about it made me want to give it a try, just to see what I could do.

After emptying the loftroom and moving my new housewares onto the front porch, I went to close all the windows and doors again. I brought some firewood from the stack behind the barn and started a fire in the downstairs hearth, and in the kitchen stove. Using one of the big iron pots I'd found, I melted down buckets full of snow and used an old shirt as a rag to start washing the down windows, floors, and walls. I washed away months of dust, years of bad memories, and all my anger.

When everything was clean, I started moving the old pieces of furniture in. There hadn't been much, but it was enough to get me by for three months. There was a rocking chair that must have been for a nursery because it was made from the same color of wood as an old baby crib I'd also found in the loftroom. I'd left the crib up there, but the chair I put in the parlor near the fireplace.

I put an old washstand up in my new room, and stacked the iron cooking ware in the kitchen cupboards. It took me almost all afternoon to push Roland's big armoire from his bedroom, down the hall, to my new room. I stripped down the sheets, blankets, and pillows from his bed and put them on mine. Then I took his trunk, too, and put it at the end of the bed. Among the knickknacks left behind in the loftroom were a few old oil lamps that I put in my bedroom and down in the kitchen.

By the time I finished arranging everything, it was already dark outside, and I was absolutely starving. I finally sat down on the floor in the parlor, warming myself in the light of the fire, and unwrapped the food Mrs. Crookin had sent. She had packed up a big wedge of cheese, roasted meat, fresh loaves of bread, and some dried fruit in paper packages—enough to last me a few days if I rationed it. So I ate all I dared, and put the rest away in the kitchen.

When I went back out to check on Mavrik, he was gone. He had squeezed himself out of the barn door somehow. Under the moonlight I could see faint silhouettes of dragon-shaped footprints in the snow. I wondered where he went. I had been so busy all day; I hadn't even stopped to check up on him.

The image of Mavrik chopping happily on the leg of a freshly killed deer flashed into my mind. It made me gag a little, hearing the sounds of bones crunching between his teeth in my mind like that. I glared up at the sky and called out to him, knowing he'd hear me no matter how far away he was, "Keep that kind of stuff to yourself next time, will you?"

I left the barn door open for him whenever he decided to come back, and stomped through the snow back to the house. It was warm inside now, and even though there wasn't much in the way of furnishings, it still felt cozy to me. I took the liberty of barring the front door with the big wooden beam Ulric had left leaning in its usual place. When I locked myself inside, I finally felt safe.

I shoveled some logs and embers out of the parlor hearth into the iron pot, and carried them upstairs to start another fire in my bedroom hearth. It was strange to be alone in an empty house, and yet at the same time it made me feel calm. It was a lot better than sleeping in the barn or the loftroom. It was actually the nicest place I'd slept in so far.

I settled down under the mound of old quilts I'd borrowed from Roland's bed, and watched the fire cast flickering shadows on the ceiling. There was still a lot left to do. I had to find some way to feed myself. It would have been a whole lot simpler if the garden weren't frozen solid. My mother had taught me a lot about how to grow all kinds of things, but there was no way I would be able to grow anything to eat in the dead of winter.

I was hoping that if I carefully budgeted the little bit of money I had, I could make it last until training started again without having to find a job somewhere in the city. I could buy cheap grain, and try to set snares or hunt for squirrels and rabbits in the woods. Mavrik might even let me steal a few scraps from his kills, since he clearly didn't have a problem finding his way to a deer when he wanted one.

One way or another, I knew I would make it. I had to hold out for three months. Until then, I would learn to survive on my own.

three

Before I left for the interlude, Lieutenant Rordin had insisted that I keep training during our three-month break, even though I wasn't at the academy. I knew he was right. I was doomed to be smaller than all the other riders, so I was going to have to work a lot harder in order to keep up. I was going to have to train more than everyone else. So every morning, I did.

The minute my feet hit the floor, I did as many push-ups and sit-ups as I could until I was soaked with sweat. Then I layered up in three or four shirts and two pairs of pants before braving the cold to run. I didn't have a good gauge of how far I was going compared to how far we were running at the academy, so I just ran until I was too tired to go on. When I finally staggered back to the house, I ate a quick breakfast from my stores of food while I heated up water in the copper basin in the washroom. Then I bathed, changed into fresh clothes, and started the rest of my rigorous morning routine.

Over the weeks, I set up a network of snares in the pine forest around the house. Since I was determined *not* to run into Katty, I avoided their property altogether. I baited my traps with little piles of seeds, or pieces of dried fruit, and was lucky enough to get a couple of rabbits or some squirrels almost every day. That paired with the big sack of dried apple chips, three wheels of cheese, and sack of grain I'd bought in the city made for good eating. After some vague instructions from the baker in town, I could even stagger through making crude loaves of bread. They didn't taste great, not like the heavenly bread Mrs. Crookin made, but they were at least edible.

During the day, I took up learning woodworking and carpentry. Those old tools I'd found in the loftroom became my friends, and I spent hours in Ulric's workshop learning how to use them through trial and error. I learned to chisel, to shape wood, to craft whole pieces of furniture without having to use any nails. It wasn't easy, and my hands blistered from handling the tools. I managed to cut myself a few times and bust my knuckles open with the hammer, but I was determined. I wasn't giving up.

My first few creations were pretty awful. I made a table with one leg that was shorter than all the others, so it wobbled and was basically useless. The first chair I made fell apart the minute I sat down in it. But I kept practicing. I loved it, even if I wasn't good at it yet. I worked every day, and savored every second I spent shaping something useful out of raw pieces of wood. Eventually, my chairs didn't fall apart. I could add extra details to the pieces I made, like intricate carvings, or claw-like feet to the bottoms of chair and table legs.

I sold my first rocking chair to the baker in the city. It took me forever to carry it there on my back, but I didn't want to risk anyone seeing me on Mavrik. That was a whole lot of attention I didn't need. Once I got the chair to the bakery I was careful not to say that I was the one who'd made But the baker's wife was thrilled with it. She insisted on buying it the second she saw it. So I sold it for two silver pieces. It was the first time I felt like I'd done anything worthwhile, except for saving Sile's life a few times the year before.

Selling something I'd made boosted my confidence. I started making things that were more complex, and buying better pieces of wood to use with the money I made. I bought nails, new hammers, and sanding tools. I spent all day drenched with sweat, creating new projects in my father's old workshop. My hands got rough, and they got stronger and tougher every day. But as soon as the sun began to set, I knew it was time to get back to reality.

At dusk, I saddled up Mavrik and took off to fly drills. I didn't want anyone to see us, sweeping low over the mountains, flying patterns, and diving along the steep cliffs, so we always waited until dark. We flew for hours, until I was too tired to keep my eyes open anymore. Then we landed, and I went inside to eat dinner before I went to bed.

I fell into a routine. The days ran together. The only thing that kept me conscious of the time was how often I bumped into Katty—which happened less and less. I saw her a few times in the city, and of course, she was always with Bren. She stared at me from afar like she was waiting for me to do something. She always managed to look angry and sad at the same time, like she wanted to choke me until I apologized to her. But I never spoke to her. I never went near her, or even waved. There was a distance there I didn't think I could breach. It still hurt to think about her, and seeing her only made it worse. It was like there was a big, rotting hole in the middle of my chest. I knew I missed her, but I couldn't decide if it was because she'd been *that* special to me, or if I just hated being alone.

I was working on a new kitchen table for my house. Right away, I knew it was going to be one of the nicest things I'd made so far. I was taking my time, smoothing out the top with a big strip of rough sandpaper, when I heard a horse whinny outside. Immediately, I put my tools down. I wasn't expecting any visitors, and I knew how a horse would respond to the sleeping dragon curled up in my barn if Mavrik decided to get curious. Horses and dragons didn't get along.

"Stay put," I murmured to Mavrik, knowing he would hear me.

I pushed the workshop door open and went out into the snow. The wind was frigid, and the snow was so deep it came up to my knees. Mithangol was not a great place to be in the winter months.

A mail courier was riding up the drive toward my house. It had been weeks since I had even seen one carrying letters past my house, and none of them had delivered anything to me. When he saw me, the courier stopped and started rifling through his saddlebags. He was waving a letter in the air by the time I met him.

"From Saltmarsh, outside of Southwatch," he said as he handed me the letter. "Anything for delivery?"

I shook my head and took the letter from him.

The courier didn't waste any time. He turned his horse around and trotted off back down the drive.

Looking down at the weathered envelope, I saw the address scribbled onto the front. It didn't say whom it was from, though. I knew where Saltmarsh was only because I had to memorize very detailed kingdom maps as part of my training at the academy. It was a small port city about ten miles to the west of Southwatch, along the coast. I didn't know anyone living there, though.

I had some hopes the letter would be from Roland or Felix as I opened it. But as I unfolded the thick parchment, I got a sick feeling in the pit of my gut. All it said was:

I need you. Come quickly. — B.D.

The message was vague, but I still knew who it was from right away. I only knew one person in the whole world with those initials, and I didn't think she would go to the trouble of sending a letter like this if wasn't an emergency.

Beckah Derrick was the daughter of my former sponsor at the academy. She was one of the smartest and bravest people I knew, and she was also one of my best friends. If she needed me, then I wasn't about to hesitate.

"Looks like we're taking a trip," I muttered as I stood there in the snow, staring at the letter.

Mavrik came crawling out of the barn, yawning and making curious chirping noises. He leaned his big head down to look at the paper, too. His hot breath blasted past my head as he snorted, and sat back on his haunches.

I scratched his chin, making him purr and flick the end of his tail. "Don't worry. I bet you'll like Southwatch. It's probably a lot warmer there."

It didn't take me long to pack because I didn't have much to take. I gathered up enough rations of food to last a few days, some of Roland's old clothes that were still several sizes too big for me, my armor, and my hunting knife. Once I had everything tied down to the saddle, I locked up the house, closed the barn, and climbed onto Mavrik's back.

We leapt into the sky just after midmorning and headed south along the coast. It was freezing cold, and I hunkered down as close to Mavrik's neck as I could to keep out of the wind. He was warm, and it kept me from freezing to death, but my teeth were chattering until we finally got out of the mountains.

As we soared past the last few peaks, I got my first look at the ocean. A blast of salty wind filled my lungs, and made me smile. The whole horizon was covered in blue, as far as the eye could see. Down below, the waves lapped at white sandy beaches. I could see fishermen dragging nets out of the surf. We passed little cities and towns nestled right close to the coast, rolling green farmland with cattle grazing, and huge marshes. In the distance, I could see the tiny dark shapes of ships going in and out of the ports. The cool wind didn't bother me anymore, not with the warmth of the setting sun on my face.

We followed the coastline, flying low and fast as I kept an eye out for Saltmarsh. My internal map was telling me we should be getting really close. Just as the sun was about to set over the ocean to the west, I saw the lights of a city down below. There was a big port stretching out into the ocean, with three-mast ships docked. I knew it had to be Saltmarsh. It was supposed to have one of the biggest shipping ports for goods going in and out of Maldobar, second only to Southwatch itself.

I urged Mavrik to swoop lower, keeping a lookout for a good place to land. He let his wingtips brush the ocean, roaring happily as we swept over the beach and stirred up flocks of seagulls and pelicans. As we cruised the outskirts of the city, I picked a good spot on the open beach to touch down, and Mavrik started to flare his powerful wings to slow us down. He stretched out his hind legs, ready to grip the sand.

Suddenly, I got a queasy feeling in the pit of my stomach.

Something wasn't right. It hit me full-force, and sent a swirl of panic through my body like a cold shiver. Mavrik felt it, too, and he faltered in his landing. It was rough, and I had to cling to the saddle to keep from being thrown over his head.

A dark shadow passed over us. I heard a sound; a deep thundering roar that made my heartbeat stop for a few seconds. I knew that roar, even though I'd only heard it once before. It was the kind of sound you never forget.

The earth flinched as Icarus landed right in front of us. He bared his jagged teeth, his broad wings spread wide, and his red eyes burning like fiery coals. He flared his spines, puffing out angrily and making himself even bigger than the humongous beast he already was.

The king drake was every bit as terrifying as he had been the first time I saw him. He was like a monster that had crawled right out of someone's nightmares. His scales were as black as volcanic glass, and he was at least twice Mavrik's size. I had watched him devour his own rider, the Lord General, in a fit of fury only a few months ago. But I had no idea why he was here now. Apparently we had some unfinished business.

Mavrik snarled back at him, slicking his ears back against his skull and letting the spines on his back and tail raise up like hackles. He flared his wings and hissed, snapping his jaws threateningly at the king drake. In my mind, I saw the flickering image of myself getting out of the saddle. Mavrik wanted me to escape.

I squeezed the saddle handles. "No way," I growled through my teeth. "If it's a fight he wants, then he'll have to take on both of us. I'm not leaving you."

Mavrik let out a thundering roar, but Icarus wasn't afraid. Why should he be? He was bigger and definitely stronger. The king drake bellowed back, and started to lunge for us with his jaws open wide.

I yelled out in anger, and Mavrik spat a column of burning venom right in Icarus's face.

It made the king drake hesitate, and gave us just enough time to get back in the air. I knew we'd have the advantage there. Icarus might have been stronger, but we were faster. No one was faster in the air than Mavrik.

Icarus started chasing us. His wing beats sounded like claps of thunder, and I could feel his eyes on us. I was too scared to look back and see how close he was. Mavrik poured on the speed, zipping through the air and giving us enough space to whip around and make a calculated attack dive.

It seemed like a good idea at the time. We had a brief window, a speck of leverage, and one shot to use it. But my training in aerial combat like this was ... well, I hadn't gotten *real* training yet. I was going on instinct and prayers. Neither were enough.

Icarus was ready for us. As a king drake, I had no idea how many battles he had already fought in, or how many riders he had crushed like twigs. As soon as we got close, he swirled out of our path, and reached around to clamp his jaws onto one of Mavrik's legs as we zipped past.

Mavrik shrieked. I could feel his panic and pain like it was my own. It made me cry out with him. Icarus bore down with his teeth, and flung us toward the ground like we were a scrap of meat.

Mavrik tried to recover. He tried to flare, to brace for an emergency landing, but there wasn't enough time. We had only seconds before we hit, and he used that time to make sure I wasn't crushed under his weight. He landed on his side, skidding across the sand. It hurt, and at that moment, I wasn't sure which was his pain or mine.

When we came to a halt, Mavrik tried to get up. His leg was bleeding. The punctures were painful, but it didn't look li' ` any bones were broken. We were lucky, so far. He str... gled, growling and whimpering. Quickly, I started unbuckling myself from the saddle.

Another loud boom made the ground shake again as Icarus landed not far away. Burning venom dripped off his jaws as he started prowling toward us slowly, watching us with those horrible glowing eyes. He was taking his time, deciding how best to tear us both to shreds.

I scrambled off Mavrik's back as soon as I got the last buckle undone. I grabbed the hunting knife from my saddle, and started running headlong for the king drake. Mavrik howled in protest, floundering and limping as he got back to his feet.

"Stay back!" I yelled, brandishing my knife. "If you want to kill him, you'll have to get through me, first!"

Icarus seemed to consider that. I probably looked like a good appetizer to him. He canted his head to the side, his nostrils flaring as he breathed in my scent. Behind me, I heard Mavrik snarling and roaring desperately. He was not in any shape to fight a king drake.

Icarus stood over me like a towering black demon. He roared so loud it made my teeth rattle. I could smell the venom on his breath. I saw my death in his bottomless red eyes. This was it, I guessed. He wasn't going to let

Mavrik and I get away with challenging him. You didn't challenge a king and walk away unharmed.

Suddenly, I heard a scream. It wasn't a dragon scream. It definitely wasn't me, either. It came from down the beach, and sounded a lot like a girl. All three of us stopped, turned, and looked in surprise.

Beckah Derrick was running as fast as she could over the sand, stumbling and tripping all over her white nightgown. Her dark hair was tied into two long braided pigtails that whipped behind her as she sprinted toward us. She waved her arms, screaming at Icarus at the top of her lungs. The huge black dragon regarded her with a snarl, and I prepared myself to fight to the death to save her and my dragon—a fight that probably would have lasted about two seconds.

But all of a sudden, Icarus started backing away from me. He lowered his head and hissed, still growling and glaring at me like he wanted to finish me off in one bite. Beckah was yelling at him like she was scolding a naughty puppy. She walked right up to the huge black dragon and swatted him on the snout. It made him flinch, hiss, and turn his head away like he was ashamed. He wouldn't look her in the eyes.

Speechless didn't even begin to describe how I felt. Shocked. Stunned. Completely blown away—those were a little more accurate. I exchanged a wide-eyed look with Mavrik. He looked like he couldn't believe what he was seeing, either.

"I told you that is a no-no!" She said with her hands on her hips. "You can't just eat people. It's not nice. Those are my friends! Stop being such a bully!"

Icarus hunkered down in the sand, making himself as small as a monstrous black king drake could. He curled his long spiny tail around his legs and snorted at her in frustration. But when she started rubbing his neck and snout … he actually started to purr. His red eyes closed, and he pushed his nose against her affectionately.

At that point, I was pretty sure my heart had stopped beating entirely.

Beckah turned to look back at me with a big grin on her face. My mouth was hanging open, and not just because she was petting Icarus like he was an overgrown housecat. She had grown, too. The last time I'd seen her had been almost six months ago. She had looked like a little kid then, and I had thought of her like she was the little sister I needed to protect. But apparently everyone else in the world was growing up except me.

Beckah walked toward me with the wind in her hair. Her fluffy bangs puffed over her face, and the light of the setting sun made her green eyes the same color as the ocean. She was as tall as I was now, and so beautiful it made the back of my throat feel like someone had punched me in the neck.

When she put her arms around my waist to hug me like she always did, I hesitated. I wasn't sure if I was allowed to touch her anymore. I almost forgot who she was. That is, until she squeezed me so hard it made me choke.

"I knew you'd come," she said.

I smiled in spite of myself, and hugged her back. She smelled really good, like a mixture of the ocean and flowers. "Of course I'd come." I studied Icarus from over her shoulder, who was still glaring at me like he wanted to eat me. "I guess this is what you were talking about?"

She leaned back to look at me with a big, happy smile that put dimples in her freckled cheeks. "You don't know the half of it, Jae."

four

Beckah had started building a little campfire with pieces of driftwood further down the beach. It was about a mile away, and we walked there together with our shoes off, letting the waves lap at our bare feet. I carried my boots and socks in one hand, and she held onto my other one tightly. Whenever I looked down, I couldn't tell which fingers were hers and which ones were mine. It gave me a strange feeling.

When we got to her campfire, I helped her drag up more pieces of driftwood to burn, and spread out a quilt she'd brought from her house on the sand. I used the flint stone in my saddlebag to start the wood burning while our dragons settled in, curled around us like a living wall of scales and wings.

Mavrik was licking his wounds, and he didn't look happy at all that Icarus was so close to us. Every now and then he'd snarl at him a little, like he was warning him not to try anything. Icarus ignored him. I was just glad they weren't trying to kill each other anymore.

"He's been following me ever since the prison camp," Beckah said as she sat down on the quilt. "I don't know what to do about him, Jae. He won't leave. I've told him to go at least a hundred times. You have no idea how hard it is to hide a dragon."

I laughed as I sat down next to her. I tried not to blush when she scooted over closer to me and leaned her head against my shoulder. "Does your dad know about him?"

She shot me an exasperated look. "Absolutely not. Can you imagine what he'd do? You know girls aren't allowed to ride dragons."

"You already have," I reminded her.

Beckah sighed. "That was different. It was an emergency. Momma and Daddy were so furious about all that. If they knew about this, it would be much worse. But I can't keep him a secret for much longer. Some of the people in the city are already talking about a big black dragon that's been swiping cattle. Sooner or later, they're going to find out."

She looked up at me, and the light from the fire made her green eyes sparkle. It made me nervous. "Can't you talk to him?" she asked. "You know, like you did before? Please, Jae, just tell him to go away. I can't keep him, and I certainly can't ride him." She was telling me one thing, but I could see something completely different in her expression. She didn't really want him to go—she was afraid of what would happen when her parents found out.

"I'll try," I promised.

She put her head back against my shoulder. "There's so much I want to tell you, Jae. I don't know where to start."

"You mean more than being followed around by a king drake?" I asked.

It made her giggle a little. "I'm so glad you're here."

"Yeah, me too." Talking about everything that had happened since I'd gotten back to Mithangol was hard. None of it was easy to admit. I mean, being abandoned by your entire family isn't exactly something to be proud of. But she didn't make me feel embarrassed when I started explaining it to her. I told her about everything except for what had happened with Katty. For some reason, I didn't want Beckah to know about that. It really was embarrassing to think about, let alone tell her about it.

"Well, at least your brother left you a letter," she said with a sour look on her face. "I just can't believe what they did. How could they leave like that? It's horrible."

I shrugged. "It's over and done, now. If I hung onto every bad thing anyone's ever done to me, I'd be dragging around a lot of extra weight."

She was quiet for a few minutes. Then scooted away a little, far enough to turn around so that she was facing me. She grabbed my hands and started looking at them in the light of the fire, tracing her fingers over my palms. "So all this is from the woodworking?" She asked, rubbing her thumb over one of the thick calluses on my hand. "I noticed it before."

I tried not to think about how soft her hands were. "Yeah. Maybe I'll make you a chair or something."

She grinned at me. "I'd *love* that!"

I blushed so hard I couldn't even look at her. "How is your dad doing with retirement? How's his arm?"

I should have known better than to bring that up. She let my hands go and her expression fell. She sat back some and stared at the fire with a far-away look in her eyes. "That's the other reason I asked you to come here. Something is wrong with him, Jae. Something he isn't telling anyone about. He's so nervous ever since that whole mess at the prison camp. It's almost like he's afraid someone is watching us. He's always been a little paranoid, I guess. But never like this. It's scaring me."

"What do you mean?" Hearing that made me worried.

"We used to live in Southwatch, you know. He moved us out of our nice house in the city as soon as we got back. Momma was furious, and they argued about it for weeks. He wasn't going to take no for an answer," she said. "Now we're living in a much smaller house out here in the middle of nowhere. We weren't allowed to tell anyone where we were going. He's going to be so mad when he finds out I told you, but I didn't have a choice."

I took her hand again and squeezed it a little. "I won't tell anyone, Beckah."

She smiled at me weakly. "I know. I trust you more than anyone."

The silence got awkward as we sat there, staring at each other in the light of the fire. I got this weird feeling like I should do something, but I wasn't sure what. She was looking at me like she was waiting for something to happen. It put nervous knots in my stomach and I didn't understand why.

"We'll figure it out," I promised her. It seemed like whenever I was around her, I started making promises like that.

She looked a little disappointed, and sighed as she

looked away back toward the fire. "I hope so. Maybe you can talk to him about it. He trusts you, too, you know."

I wasn't sure what to think about that. I knew how much I respected and admired her father, Sile Derrick It was hard to believe that he thought of me as anything more than a scrawny kid he'd had to protect from being pummeled by the other students while he was my sponsor and instructor. Sure, I'd saved his life a few times, but I didn't consider that to be anything other than my duty as his student. I didn't expect any praise or respect because of that. If anything, I still felt like I owed him for all the time's he'd stuck his neck out for me.

"I want to understand why, Jae." Beckah whispered. The emotion in her voice surprised me. I noticed there were dark circles under her eyes. She looked haunted, and her voice trembled when she spoke. "I don't believe what they told us, that it was just some kind of plot by the Lord General. They didn't choose my daddy at random. It was planned. There's a reason they tried so hard to kill him twice. If it was only a plot to use him as some kind of a sacrifice, they could have picked anyone. They could have plucked someone else off the street and no one would have even noticed. They came after him for a reason, and now I think he's afraid they'll try it again. I think that's why he moved us like this. I think he's trying to hide from them."

I could tell she'd been beating herself up over this. I couldn't imagine what it had been like for her, but I wanted to make her feel better. I put an arm around her shoulders and pulled her toward me to hug her again. "I don't believe what they said, either. It'll be okay. Your father is the best man I've ever met. You have to trust that he knows what he's doing."

Beckah hid her face against my shoulder. "I've felt so alone," she whimpered. "I've missed you so much."

My face burned and I was glad she couldn't see it. No one had ever said that to me before. Not like that, anyway. It made me blush until the tips of my ears felt like they were on fire.

"What about Felix?" I have no idea why I even said something like that. It was stupid, and I knew it the moment the words left my mouth. I regretted it immediately.

She pulled back and looked at me strangely, like I'd suddenly grown a third eyeball. "What about him?"

I swallowed hard. "Well, I mean he was there with us through everything. Do you miss him, too?"

Beckah frowned. "That's different."

I opened my mouth to speak, but I didn't get a chance. She grabbed my chin and kissed me on the cheek.

It seemed like the world was moving in slow motion. I just sat there, staring at her. At first, I wasn't sure what to think. But as the seconds passed, I realized I liked it. I *really* liked it.

"We should go back to the house," she said as she stood. She offered me a hand to help me up, and then started folding up the quilt. "Momma's probably already gone to bed, but Daddy will still be up. We have to tell him you're here." She sighed shakily and looked at Icarus. "Do you think you can get him to leave me alone?"

I was still having a hard time thinking about anything except that kiss. But I looked at Icarus, and he shot me another disapproving dragon glare. "I'm not sure. I guess we'll try to discuss it in the morning, though."

I took my one bag off of Mavrik's saddle and followed Beckah across the grassy dunes. The moonlight was bright enough to see by, and the wind was strong coming in off the ocean. In the distance, I could see the lights of the city a few short miles away down the coast.

The Derrick's house wasn't small, like Beckah had made it sound. At least, not to me. It was two storeys tall, made out of dark stacked stone, and there were a few candles burning in the arched windows. I could barely make out a stable behind it as we walked up the sandy drive toward the front door.

I started to get nervous because I wasn't sure how Sile was going to react to me being here. I was anxious to see him and talk to him about what had happened. I might even get some real answers this time. But at the same time I knew he might slam the door in my face and tell me to mind my own business. Beckah also looked nervous as she opened the front door and let me go in ahead of her.

The house was nice and cozy on the inside. There were pictures on the plaster walls, and rugs on the floors. A narrow entryway led into the parlor where Sile was sitting with his feet propped up by a smoldering fire in the hearth. He didn't even look back at us as we stood in the doorway.

"I've told you about sneaking out, Beck." He grumbled.

"I'm sorry," Beckah muttered back. "Daddy, we have a guest."

He turned and looked back then, his piercing glare hitting me full force. At first, I was definitely afraid he was going to come at me swinging. When he saw it was me, his expression changed into confusion and frustration. He seemed annoyed that I was here.

He shot Beckah a punishing look. "We talked about this."

She cringed and looked way. "I know, Daddy, but—"

"Go back to bed. Right now," he growled at her.

Beckah nodded, gave me a worried smile, and hurried away up the stairs.

The silence was uncomfortable. I stood in the doorway for a few minutes, wondering what I was supposed to do or if I should even stay. Maybe these were valuable minutes he was giving me as a head start before he forced me out the door. Then I heard him sigh, and he settled back into his chair to stare at the fire again.

"I was hoping you would have at least grown an inch by now," he muttered.

I was instantly humiliated. "S-sir, please don't blame Beckah for—"

"Sit down," he cut me off.

I shuffled across the room and sat down in the chair across from him. His expression was unreadable and intense. He had the same dark circles under his eyes Beckah had, like he'd sat up every night just like this, waiting for someone to come pounding on his door to take him away again. I noticed his arm wasn't wrapped up in a cast anymore.

"She thinks I don't know about the dragon," he said darkly.

I was too surprised to answer.

"I may be old and retired, but I'm not stupid. I've been around dragons longer than you've been alive. I know when there's one stalking around my house." He glanced at me again, looking me up and down like he was searching for any sign of growth since last year when I'd started training. "Well, there's a little more meat on you, at least. Not enough, though."

My face burned with embarrassment again. "I've

been training every day."

He nodded. "Good."

"She asked me to come here because she wants me to ... tell Icarus to go away." I blurted. I sincerely hoped Beckah wasn't hiding outside the room eavesdropping on us. I felt like I was betraying her by telling him everything.

"He won't listen to you, boy. Maybe you can talk a king drake into rebelling against a rider he didn't choose, but when a dragon picks its companion the way Mavrik picked you, there's nothing you can do to change it. It's like fighting gravity."

Sile always had a way of teaching me things even when he didn't mean to. I'd never questioned Mavrik's attachment to me, much less tried to understand it. Hearing that Icarus, the most powerful drake in the world, had picked Beckah—that was amazing news.

"She's a dragonrider," I whispered under my breath.

He shot me the same punishing glare he'd given her earlier. "No. She's a girl. Women are forbidden to join the brotherhood of dragonriders. You know that."

"But ... I thought you said that being chosen automatically made someone a dragonrider, regardless of who they are," I argued. "What if she wants to be one? How is it any different than when Mavrik chose me?"

"Because there are some things women are not meant to see, let alone experience," he snapped angrily. "You really want my daughter, my precious little girl, holding a sword and riding into a line of enemies that want to slaughter her? As her father, I am supposed to protect her. That is my duty as a man. It's not something a boy can understand."

I bit my tongue. He was right. The idea of her doing something like that, something that would most likely get her killed, cut me right to the core. I didn't want anything to happen to her. I wanted to protect her, too.

"Things are the way they are for a reason, Jaevid," he said. "They may not be fair, but we must choose our battles wisely. We have to do what we can to protect what matters most."

I got the feeling he wasn't just talking about Icarus anymore. Everything Beckah had said to me about how he'd moved them here in secret started nagging at my brain again. "What are you protecting them from?" I asked. "Beckah said she thinks you're hiding out here—that you're afraid someone is looking for you."

He flicked me another irritated glance before he reached over to a table beside his chair and started filling a pipe with tobacco. "You know everything you need to know right now," he answered coldly. "You should be less worried about my affairs and more concerned with the training that awaits you this year. The avian year at the academy is the most difficult, and it's the year when the weak or stupid often die. Everything they do is to prepare you for what might happen when you step on the battlefield. They will beat you hard because war is going beat you even harder."

Felix had said something similar to me about what lay ahead in our avian year. He had mentioned that we'd have to endure interrogation training and how to survive in Luntharda if we found ourselves stranded behind enemy lines. That put a hard knot of anxiety in my chest as I sat there, staring down at the tops of my shoes.

"I was hoping you'd have at least gained an inch or two, or a few more pounds of muscle. Maybe then you'd be less of an easy target for them during the interrogation portion." Sile sighed, shaking his head some before he started to light his pipe and puff rings of gray smoke into the air. "They're going to come for you, Jaevid. You're the weakest link. You need to start asking yourself if you're ready for that."

I clenched my hands into fists. "I've been the weakest link my whole life, sir. I can handle it."

He snorted, and I saw the corner of his mouth twitch at a smile. "That's why I like you, boy. You're brave to the point of insanity. You'd walk into the abyss without a second thought."

I wasn't sure if I should take that as a compliment or an insult. It kind of sounded like both. "I just do what I think is right, sir."

Sile looked at me then, and there were a thousand thoughts in his eyes that I could sense, but I couldn't understand any of them. Somehow, it made me feel very small. There was a lot he knew, a lot of things he wasn't telling me. And when he looked at me like that, it made me wonder what would be waiting for me back at the academy.

"Sometimes what you know is right isn't what everyone else wants to do," he said. "Then you have to ask yourself if you're willing to live with the consequences of doing what you know is wrong just to keep the peace."

I swallowed hard. "I couldn't do that."

He smiled darkly. "Is that so? Why?"

I tried to square my shoulders and look more confident than I was. "Because I'd rather be seen as a traitor by everyone else than betray myself like that."

Little by little, the edges of his grim smile began to fade, and I saw those hundreds of thoughts come rushing back like an ocean tide. "I hope you always feel like that, Jaevid," he said softly and turned away to look back at the fire again. "There's a guest room upstairs. Third door on the right."

"S-sir?" I hadn't expected him to ask me to stay.

"I suppose it's good to have someone as idiotically brave as you are around now and again. If anyone can change that dragon's mind, it's you. We'll address it later." He wafted a hand at me, waving me out of the room. "Goodnight."

I started for the doorway with my bag in my hand. My head was still spinning like a top after everything he'd said to me. I was almost out of the room when he cleared his throat to get my attention again.

"And if I catch you sniffing around my daughter's room, I'll pull those pointed ears right off your head."

five

Being in Sile's house was weird. He had never talked about his family to me before, so everything I knew about them had mostly come from Beckah. I wasn't sure what I was allowed to touch, or where to go, but I found the guest room right where Sile had told me it was. The room was spacious and a lot better decorated than my house. There were curtains on the windows, a big bed with comfortable looking blankets, and a soft wool rug on the floor.

I shut the door behind me as quietly as I could, and put my bag down on the floor at the foot of the bed. The two tall windows faced the front of the house. In the distance, I could see the ocean glittering in the moonlight. I cracked one open to let the cool, salty breeze flow in. The house was so quiet that I could hear the surf. It was a beautiful sound that slowly lulled me to sleep.

The lonely cawing of seagulls woke me up early the next morning. I rolled over, squinting at the beautiful view of the sea over the dunes ... and that's when I realized I wasn't alone. I saw a few locks of golden hair peeking over the blankets in the bed next to me. Suddenly, I was aware that there was a very warm, very alive *something* sleeping next to me.

I bolted upright in bed. Before I could figure out what had happened, I was sitting nose-to-nose with a big shaggy dog. He looked at me with warm brown eyes, and swiped his slobbery tongue right up my face.

From the doorway, I heard someone giggling. I looked to see Beckah standing there, watching us with the bedroom door cracked open. She whistled and the dog bounded off the bed, trotting to her with his tail wagging. She ruffled his ears as he went past.

"I forgot to warn you last night," she laughed. "Eddy can open doors ... and he also really likes to sleep on the bed."

I laughed. "Smart dog."

Beckah shrugged a little and started twirling a lock of her dark hair around her fingers thoughtfully. "So Daddy talked to me this morning. He told me he knew about the dragon already. And he's going to let you try to convince him to leave."

"Yeah," I admitted. "We sort of discussed that last night."

She stood there quietly for a moment, still twirling her hair, and finally looked up at me with a hesitant look in her eyes. "I'm not sure I want him to go."

I was afraid of that. Icarus had chosen her. He listened to her. They had the potential for the same kind of bond I had with Mavrik. And for me to step in and try to drive them apart, well, it felt wrong. I wasn't sure I could do it, or if Icarus would even listen.

"What do you want me to do?" I asked her.

She sighed shakily and nibbled on her bottom lip. I could see that she was struggling with this. For her to keep Icarus was definitely counterproductive to Sile's efforts to keep his family hidden. People were already talking about the king drake in the city. He was sure to attract all kinds of attention. Not to mention the fact that she was a girl, and girls weren't allowed to be dragonriders. But at the same time, I couldn't think of any better protection than an angry dragon. Icarus wasn't going to let anything happen to Beckah—not if he could help it.

"Daddy took Momma to see the doctor this morning. She was having pains all night," she said finally. "So I have a little time to think it over. They probably won't get back until late this afternoon."

I nodded. "Okay."

"I thought we could go to the beach." She smiled a little and came in to plop down on the edge of the bed. "So hurry up and get dressed!"

I noticed she was already wearing something she could swim in. It was a white cotton dress that came to her knees with no sleeves and little purple flowers stitched on it. She had sandals on her feet made out of knotted strips of cloth, and her long hair was hanging in two loose braids down her back.

I threw off the blankets and started rummaging around for my shoes. I didn't have anything to wear other than what I had on. I definitely didn't have anything that was made for swimming, but I figured I could make it work.

While I was hurrying through lacing up my boots,

Beckah came crawling across the bed. Before I knew it, she was braiding my hair. I could just imagine what Felix would've said if he could see me sitting there with a girl fixing my hair.

"It's gotten so long," she said. I could hear the smile in her voice.

It made me really nervous to have her touching me like that. She'd always seemed fascinated by my hair. Human men usually kept their hair cut short, and mine had gotten very long over the past few months.

"My mom wanted me to keep it like this." I told her.

She kept tugging on my hair, winding it down into a long braid before she finally tied it off on the end. "Is that something all gray elves do?"

"Yeah," I said as I looked back at her. "Having long hair is one of their sacred traditions. Different tribes do different things, like weave beads into it for every year of life or major accomplishment. It's a symbol of pride."

She smiled at me and gave my braid a playful yank. "Okay then, Mr. Pride, let's go to the beach."

I helped Beckah carry a quilt, a bag of snacks, and a few towels back down the winding path that led across the dunes toward the beach. Eddy went with us with his tail wagging the whole way. He ran on ahead and barked like crazy wh he chased flocks of seagulls.

The sun was warm on my back as we worked together to spread out the quilt. We anchored down the corners with rocks so the wind wouldn't blow it away. The sand was so soft and clean that it literally squeaked when we walked on it. We sat together on the quilt, taking off our shoes, and talking about everything that had happened since we'd last seen each other. I was so busy telling her about all the new pieces of furniture I wanted to make that I didn't notice she was packing together a ball of sand in her palm—until she threw it and hit me right in the face.

Beckah took off running into the waves, laughing wildly, and I chased after her. We spent all day in the surf and sun, chasing crabs and the little fish that darted in around our legs. She showed me how to make sandcastles by squeezing watery sand through my fist, and I let her bury me up to my waist. Beckah was a great swimmer, and she taught me how to dive down and find seashells in the deeper water. It was the most fun I'd ever had in my life.

When lunchtime came, we went back to sit on our quilt and eat some of the food she'd packed. She'd brought some leftover biscuits from breakfast stuffed with blackberry preserves, some pieces of cheese, and four huge, juicy peaches. We talked while we ate, leaning back on our elbows with our feet in the sand. Eddy was still running around, digging holes and begging us to throw a stick so he could retrieve it.

We talked about anything and everything. She wanted to know about my mom, and for once, it didn't hurt so bad to think about that. I asked about her parents, things I knew Sile would never tell me even if I had the nerve to ask him.

"So is she going to be all right?" I asked. "Your mom, I mean. You said she was having pains."

Beckah took a big bite out of a peach. "I don't know. Daddy said she's having a hard time with this baby. She's supposed to have it any day now, but she's been like this the whole time. She barely eats, barely sleeps, and she says she feels sick all the time. The doctor says there's nothing more he can do. She just has to stay off her feet as much as possible and hope for the best."

I looked down at the half-eaten peach in my hand. "I'm sorry, Beckah."

"It's okay. Momma's strong. She can make it." She got quiet for a moment while she chewed, and I could tell she wanted to change the subject. "So where are the dragons?"

I had wondered the same thing. Mavrik flashed an image of himself and Icarus sunning themselves in a grassy field, preening their scales, and basking in the warm air. I guess they'd worked out their differences, for now. "They're close by. I think they've finally called a truce."

I caught Beckah staring at me with a weird look on her face, like she was amazed. "Can you really talk to him with your mind? What does he say to you? What does he sound like?"

"He doesn't *say* anything." I blushed. "It's more like pictures. He shows me things, sort of like I'm dreaming only I'm not asleep."

"Will I be able to talk to Icarus like that?" she asked.

I shook my head a little. "I don't know."

Slowly, a big grin started to inch across her face. "That is *so* awesome!"

I rolled my eyes at her and laughed. "I'm glad someone else thinks so."

She took another bite out of her peach as she lay back on the blanket. For a few minutes, she didn't say anything and we sat there together listening to the roar and crash of the surf. It was peaceful, and I felt so calm. I didn't want to go back to Mithangol. I didn't even want to go back to Blybrig.

"I don't want Icarus to leave," she said as she lay there,

wiggling her toes in the sand.

I turned to look down at her. I had sort of been expecting this, but it was still surprising to hear that she'd made that decision so suddenly. "What changed your mind?"

"You," she said matter-of-factly. "You always make me feel braver. And I can't help but feel like he chose me for a purpose. Maybe there's something I'm supposed to do for him. He wouldn't choose me for no reason, would he?"

She got quiet then, and I wasn't sure what to say until she sat back up and nudged me with her elbow. "When you're at the academy, do you ever get afraid? I mean, I know they do some terrible things to you during training. I've heard Daddy and his friends talk about it. Does it scare you?"

I had to think about that. I had been through a lot during my first year of training, a lot of new experiences and challenges I hadn't been sure I would survive. Now everyone was telling me the worst was yet to come.

"Yes," I answered. "But when those times come, I just try to think about something good. Good memories always give me hope—like the times I spent with my mom when I was little."

She reached over and took my hand. Her fingers were still sticky from peach juice, but when she looked at me and smiled, it was like seeing the sunrise for the first time. There was so much warmth and hope in her eyes.

"When things get tough this year, when you start to feel afraid, I want you to think about today," she said.

"I will," I promised.

We packed up our stuff and started back for the house. Being in the wind and sun all morning had worn me out, even though it was the first day in months I hadn't gone straight from bed to a grueling workout routine. My arms and legs felt heavy, but my heart was full. I'd never smiled this much before in my life. It made my cheeks hurt.

"Look! Momma's home!" Beckah pointed excitedly to where a horse and carriage were parked in front of the house. She went running on ahead of me, tripping over herself with her braids flying.

I could see Sile helping a very fragile-looking woman out of the carriage. I had never seen his wife before, but it didn't surprise me that she was pretty. Or at least, she might have been. Now I understood what Beckah had said about her pregnancy being hard on her.

Her belly was hugely swollen, and she was so petite that it looked like might cause her legs to break under the weight. She had dark, reddish brown hair and soft blue eyes. Her skin looked almost ashen, and her cheeks looked sunken. Sile handled her like she was made of glass, easing her down the steps from the carriage to the ground.

When she saw me, Mrs. Derrick paused. Our eyes met, and I wasn't sure what to do. I didn't know how she'd react, or how much Sile had actually told her about me. She leaned a little closer to her husband and whispered something, Sile nodded, and then, very slowly, she started to smile.

It made me stop because when she smiled, even though she basically looked like she might collapse at any moment, I could see how much Beckah favored her. They had that same familiar gentleness in their eyes. She curled a finger at me to call me closer.

I went toward them hesitantly, not sure if I was

allowed to talk to her. Sile was eyeing me over again like he was still looking for some sign of growth. I hated to keep disappointing him.

"He's absolutely darling," Mrs. Derrick said. She had a very soft, breathy voice.

"It's good to meet you, ma'am." I stopped a few feet away from her, and was about to bow ... but she took a few hobbling steps toward me and put her hands on my cheeks. They felt cold to the touch, which was a little disturbing.

"Aren't you just the cutest thing? Like a little lamb," she crooned. "Such good manners. You should thank your mother for that every night in your prayers. Only mothers teach such good behavior to their little boys."

I was beyond embarrassed. Out of the corner of my eye, I saw Beckah giggling at me, and Sile was rolling his eyes.

"Don't patronize him, dear. He's seventeen now, right? Not a kid anymore," Sile said. He was at least trying to defend my masculinity. I couldn't thank him enough for that.

"A-actually, I'm sixteen, sir," I stammered.

"Sixteen is hardly a grown man, Sile. Look at him. Such a sweet little boy." Mrs. Derrick gave my cheeks a tug before she let me go. "It looks like you've both had too much sun this morning. Beck, dear, you're as red as a cherry. Come inside and help me get settled. We should make a good supper for our guest tonight, don't you think?"

She started trying to walk to the house, and I realized then why Sile was so intense about helping her. She could barely take a step without shaking. Her body looked incredibly weak. It was worrisome to me, and I'd only just met her. I couldn't imagine how it must have made him feel to see her that way.

Gently, Sile took his wife by the arm and helped her up the front steps into the house. As I stood there watching them go, Beckah came up beside me and nudged me with her arm.

"I knew she'd like you." She winked at me. "Don't take it too hard, little lamb. It's because she's got babies on the brain. She talks to everyone that way."

I couldn't help but laugh. "Well, I guess I've been called worse."

We followed them inside and Beckah took all our things to put them away. It took Sile a long time to get Mrs. Derrick settled in a big chair at the head of the dinner table. The chair was covered with blankets and cushions so she was comfortable, and he wrapped her up in a quilt carefully. I watched him kiss her forehead.

There was love between them—I could sense it. But I could also sense a lot of tension and frustration. There was something distant in their eyes when they looked at each other. I didn't understand why. He regarded her like she was an artifact to be preserved. There wasn't much tenderness in his expression whenever he gazed at her. It was like he was just going through the motions, doing what he knew he should because he didn't know what else to do. And when she looked at him, it was like she wanted to say something, but didn't know where to begin. She just seemed so lost.

Sile started making dinner while Beckah helped him. They were washing and peeling vegetables, stoking the cooking fires, and working together like a well-trained unit. They'd obviously done this before. I wasn't sure what to do with myself. I felt like I should be helping, too.

"Come have a seat, dear." Mrs. Derrick was smiling at me as she patted the chair next to her at the table. "Your name is Jaevid, isn't it? Beckah told me all about what you did for my husband. You must be a very brave little boy."

"He's not a little boy, Lana. He's about to start his avian training. He'll be a war-hardened soldier this side of next year. Quit babying him." Sile growled. His tone was harsher than it should have been for talking to someone as fragile as she was, but his wife didn't seem to pay him any attention.

"You know, of all Sile's students I've met, I think you must be the first one that's ever come to visit," she said as I sat down next to her. "You'll make such a handsome little soldier. Honestly, those no-good rich boys that take up dragonriding these days could stand to learn a thing or two from you. They've never had to do an honest day's work in their lives! They can't appreciate how hard others have to work to get where they are."

I wasn't sure if it was safe to answer. Sile kept shooting us glares out of the corner of his eye. "Thank you, ma'am." I decided that was the safest thing to say.

She reached out to brush some of my hair out of the way, just the same way Beckah had when we'd first met. She touched the pointed tips of my ears with her cold fingers. "Fate was cruel to have cursed you with mixed blood. Look there, dear, and hand me my stitching."

She pointed to a basket sitting near the fireplace. I brought it to her and she started to take out little pieces of soft fabric, needles, and thread. While she talked to me, Mrs. Derrick sat beside me sewing baby clothes by hand. I recognized the same stitched flowers that Beckah had on her beach dress.

"You shouldn't be worrying with that," Sile grumbled as he filled a pot with water. "We can afford to buy clothes, Lana."

She frowned down at her work. "Things like this should be made with love—not that you care to understand anything that's important to me." The sharpness in her tone startled me a little. It made things awkward immediately.

Sile glared at her, but he didn't say anything back. It was uncomfortable. I caught Beckah looking at me with a hopeless look on her face while she was chopping carrots. She seemed so sad. It must have hurt to see her parents acting that way.

"Beck is learning to stitch, too, you know," Mrs. Derrick said. "Someday, she'll be able to make her own dresses for her children. She might even get a good job at a tailor's shop in the city. The city's a much better place to meet husbands. Like a good merchant, or maybe a grocer. Wouldn't you like a grocer, dear?"

Beckah's cheeks got so red you couldn't see her freckles anymore. "Momma!" She squeaked in protest.

Mrs. Derrick smiled at her affectionately. "You'll have to practice, though. No one wants knots in their embroidery. Fine men want polished wives, so they look for that sort of thing. Details always matter."

Beckah blushed even harder and turned her back to us to start stirring a big pot of stew. I heard her mumble, "I'm not even good at stitching."

Sile set the table for us with bowls and spoons. He helped Beckah bring over the bubbling pot of thick vegetable stew. It smelled so amazing it made my mouth water. I hadn't eaten this good since I was at the academy. We had freshly baked bread with fruit preserves, and the leftovers of an apple pie from the day before with big glasses of milk.

I didn't say anything to them about it, but that was the first time I'd had a family meal with anyone since my mother died. I was never allowed to eat with Ulric and his family when I lived with them. It always upset his wife for me to be sitting at the table with her *real* children. Even Mr. Crookin had seemed uncomfortable with it whenever he caught me eating at their table with Katty. I'd never been welcomed at anyone's family table until now.

Even though Sile didn't say much during dinner, we still had a good time. Beckah and I told them about what we'd done at the beach all morning, and Mrs. Derrick teased us about our matching sunburns.

I felt something warm and wet on my leg, and looked down to see Eddy sitting at my feet. He was drooling all over me, watching me take every bite. When I noticed him, he licked his lips hopefully. I snuck him a few little pieces of bread.

After dinner, Sile started helping his wife upstairs to their bedroom while Beckah and I cleaned the kitchen. We cleared the table, wrapped up the leftovers in paper, and started doing the dishes. Beckah passed me the freshly scrubbed dishes so I could dry them with a towel. I stood beside her, trying not to think about what her mother had said about merchants and grocers. I couldn't figure out why that bothered me so much.

"How long can you stay here?" she asked.

I didn't want to think about that. I was having such a good time here with her, the last thing I wanted to do was go back to the bitter cold in Mithangol and sit by myself in an empty house. "As long as you want me to, I guess.

Until I have to go back to the academy."

"I wish you didn't have to go." Beckah's voice sounded sad.

"I'll come back," I said.

She sighed. "I know."

Neither of us said anything else as we stood there, finishing up the dishes and putting them away. I was realizing how hard it would be to leave. I knew Sile probably wouldn't like it one bit, but this place had already begun to feel like home to me. It was warm and comfortable, and it was filled with people I cared about. I didn't feel unwanted here, which was definitely a first.

"I'm scared to talk to Daddy about Icarus," Beckah said. She looked at me with worry in her eyes. "He won't understand. He'll tell me I can't keep him because I'm a girl. You know how he is. It's impossible to argue with him once he's made up his mind about something."

I smiled at her. "I think he'll understand better than you expect. Besides, you have to try, right? Icarus is counting on you."

She smiled back a little, and for a few moments, we stood there and stared at each other. Once again, I got that nagging feeling in the pit of my stomach that I should do something. I just couldn't figure out what.

A loud scream from upstairs made us both jump.

Our eyes went up to the ceiling, hearing the thumping of someone running over the floorboards overhead. Sile started shouting for us at the top of his lungs. Maybe it was what had happened to us last year at the prison camp, or maybe it was my training finally starting to sink into my subconscious, but I grabbed Beckah's hand right away and started dragging her up the stairs as fast as I could.

six

I had never seen so much blood before in my life. It started at the doorway to their bedroom and made a slippery trail all the way to the bed. Mrs. Derrick was lying on her back, clutching her belly in pain, and screaming at the top of her lungs. Sile's hands were covered in blood, and there was no color at all in his face. He stood there looking absolutely terrified. He appeared too shocked to know what to do, which definitely didn't make me feel any better. If he was panicking, then I should be petrified.

"It's the baby," Sile stammered. His voice was broken and I could see desperate grief on his face. Not even he was trained for something like this.

Beckah was pale. She looked like she might collapse at any moment. "We need the doctor!" she managed to cry out.

Sile grabbed her by the shoulders suddenly, forcing

her to look at him. "Go downstairs. Get as many towels as you can."

"B-but, Daddy! The doctor!" She started to sob.

"There's no time. It takes two hours just to get to the city. She won't last that long." He told her firmly. "Go! Do as I tell you!"

Beckah ran out of the room crying, and I was left standing there staring at Mrs. Derrick as she writhed in pain. When I looked at Sile, I knew something was seriously wrong. This wasn't the way it was supposed to happen. Her life was in danger.

Sile went to her bedside and held her hand, whispering to her softly as she whimpered and sobbed. I could see his hands shaking, and I could have sworn I saw tears in his eyes. It hurt to see him like that, but I didn't see how I could do anything except get in the way. I had no medical training when it came to things like this.

From outside, I heard a roar like thunder. The house shuddered under a sudden blast of wind. Too late, I realized what was happening.

I ran to the window, looking out just in time to see Icarus sailing into the darkness toward the city with Beckah clinging to his back. She was going to get the doctor. For a few seconds, I couldn't breathe. I watched her disappear into the night with the sounds of Icarus's wing beats fading in the distance.

"I have to go after her!" I started for the door. "She doesn't even have a saddle!"

Sile caught me by the back of the shirt, yanking me back into the room. "Even if she finds the doctor, he won't make it here in time!" He yelled right in my face. "I know *you* can fix this. So do it! Save her!"

I stared up at him in terror. I had no idea what he

was talking about. What could I do? I wasn't a doctor! I'd only had a little bit of training when it came to treating wounds—and he was the one who had taught me all that stuff in the first place!

Behind us, Mrs. Derrick screamed in pain again. It made Sile tighten his grip on me.

"She told me what you'd be able to do," he growled furiously. "I won't let my wife die. Heal her!"

I raised my hands up in surrender. I tried to speak, but all I could do was choke on my words. Sile pushed me toward the bed and grabbed my wrists. He forced me to touch his wife's face, putting my palms on her forehead. He held me there with all his strength no matter how much I struggled.

"Do it!" He shouted again, right in my ear.

Mrs. Derrick looked up at me through her tears. She was trembling, and I could see the pure panic in her eyes. She grabbed my arm and squeezed it hard.

"P-please," she sobbed.

I was at a loss. Sile was looming behind me, ready to rip my head off if I didn't do something. She was looking up at me pleadingly. And I was just standing there with my hands on her face, trying to figure out what they wanted from me. This woman was going to die right in front of my eyes and they were both acting like I could somehow stop it.

I did the only thing I could do: I thought about my own mother. Seeing Mrs. Derrick like that brought back those horrible memories of watching my mother slip away, lying in her bed with her body burning up with fever. I'd never felt so helpless before … until now.

Tears started to run down my face. I didn't want to watch anyone else die like that—like their life was slipping right through my fingers.

Then it started like a tingling warmth in the back of my mind. Just like the first time I'd called out to Mavrik, I felt that twinge of pressure in my chest. Unlike all the times I had felt it before, this time it began to spread. It grew and grew until I could barely breathe. All around me, the sounds of Sile yelling and Mrs. Derrick crying seemed to fade away to white noise.

My ears were ringing. Everything got fuzzy. Time seemed to slow down to a crawl. I could feel my palms getting hotter and hotter until it was like my hands were stuck into red-hot coals.

All of a sudden, the room was spinning out of control. I heard a sound like a concussive boom, but I couldn't tell if it was real or only in my head. Something inside me snapped. I couldn't breathe at all anymore. I couldn't think. I could barely even feel myself falling.

Before I knew what was happening, I was lying on the floor while the ceiling spun above me. I still couldn't hear anything except a high-pitched ringing in my ears. I didn't know how long I lay there. It felt like hours, but I really had no idea. My body felt like a slab of lead. I couldn't move my arms or legs. My lungs started to ache, and I realized I still couldn't breathe.

Suddenly, Sile crouched down over me. I could see his lips moving and the worry on his face, but I couldn't hear anything he said. He picked me up like a ragdoll and started carrying me out of the room.

I managed to catch a glimpse of Mrs. Derrick before we left. She was propped up in the bed cradling a squirming bundle of cloth in her arms. There were still tears in her eyes, but they were tears of joy now. She was smiling, kissing her newborn baby. Seeing her like that gave me a little hope. I figured if I was about to die from whatever I'd done, at least I was able to help her somehow. At least she would be happy and her baby would be safe.

Then my air ran out. Darkness swallowed me before I knew what was happening. It felt like drowning in black water. It was quiet, so quiet. About the time I started to wonder if I was dead, I sputtered awake again. Sile was leaning over me, pumping my chest with his hands and forcing his breath into my lungs. He saw me stirring and started smacking my cheeks to try to wake me up.

I choked, taking in as much air as I could. For an instant, I was relieved. I thought I was going to be okay. I could finally breathe normally again. I could hear, even if things were still a little fuzzy. And then I realized I still couldn't move my arms and legs.

Pain hit me so suddenly that at first, all I could do was scream. As it got more intense, though, I couldn't even do that anymore. White-hot agony shot through me like someone had rammed a dagger right between my eyes. My skin was on fire. My blood boiled. It took everything I had to grit my teeth and bear it.

"Jae!" I heard Beckah's voice call my name, but I couldn't will my eyes to open long enough to see her. The pain was too much.

"Where's the doctor?" Sile asked her. He was sliding his arms under me again to pick me up off the floor.

"H-he's on his way. He promised he'd hurry. Daddy... w-what happened?" I could hear Beckah crying. She was following him, whimpering my name pleadingly. I couldn't see her, but I could sense her nearby. I wished I could move, or at least open my eyes and look at her.

"Go and see to your mother, Beck," Sile ordered as he put me down on the bed. He pushed a hand against my forehead, and that was when I realized I was burning up. His hand felt really cold against my skin. He pulled my eyelids open with his fingers, and I could see him looking down at me with concern.

"But, Daddy—" she started to protest.

"I said go!" he yelled.

I couldn't see anything when he let my eyelids close again, but I could hear the sound of footsteps leaving the room. The bed flinched, and I could hear Sile's ragged breathing near me. It almost sounded like he was ... crying.

"The gods will never forgive me," he whispered shakily. "I gave her my word and now I've failed her."

Time passed with those words echoing across my mind.

The pain didn't let up for an instant, although I seemed to get used to it enough that I could think through it somewhat. I wanted him to explain. What had I done? And how had he known I could do it? Would I even survive this? I had so many questions, and no way to ask them. The pain sizzled over my body like someone was skinning me alive. It even made my bones ache right down to the marrow.

Once, I thought I heard another voice nearby. It wasn't anyone I recognized, though. It sounded like an older man, and I could vaguely feel him poking at me, like he was examining me.

"Sixteen you said?" I heard the stranger ask. He must have been the doctor. "A bit late, but I've seen this before. These halfbreeds are a strange sort. It's that elf blood, you see. It throws off their growing patterns. The gray elves don't mature slowly like normal human children do. Instead, it happens all at once. As best we can tell, it's much like an insect bursting from a cocoon. Sudden, rapid change that takes an incredible physical toll. Just imagine every part of you being stretched at once."

There was an uncomfortable silence. The room felt heavy. Even though I couldn't see, I could sense everyone was looking at me.

"Those gray elves are a notoriously tough breed, though," the doctor continued. "Their bones are like metal, and wounds to their flesh tend to heal much faster. So their pureblooded offspring can handle such a radical change. But having human blood in the mix weakens these halfbreeds too much. Think about it. How many adult halfbreeds do you see walking around? Not many at all. So few of them survive this."

"Is he going to be okay?" Beckah's voice asked. It sounded like she was sitting very close by. Vaguely, I could feel her hand holding tightly onto mine.

There was another tense silence. I wanted so badly to answer, to sit up and assure everyone that I was fine. I just needed to rest and then everything would be okay. But I couldn't.

"Lieutenant Derrick, you're a good man, so I'll be perfectly honest," the stranger answered. "I've only ever witnessed this once before. So few of them even survive to adolescence at all. His body probably won't be able to stand the pain. But even if it could, he is starving for nutrients as we speak. All children need food to grow, and what he's going through is basically years of physical maturity packed into a very short amount time. He's already thin and has obviously suffered from some malnutrition. He will probably starve to death in the next day or so. You should … make the necessary preparations. I can send word to the minister for you.

He doesn't like presiding over the burial rites for elves, but in your case, I think I could convince him to make an exception."

Beckah started to cry. I wanted to yell in protest. I was alive. Couldn't they see that? I wasn't even dead yet and they were already planning my funeral!

"Isn't there anything we can do?" Sile sounded determined.

The stranger sighed. I heard footsteps going toward the door. "You could try forcing him to eat, though in his current state, I'm not sure it would help even if he ate constantly over the next few days."

"Thank you, doctor." Sile and the man kept talking as they left the room. Soon I couldn't make out anything else they said.

Suddenly Beckah put her arms around me. She buried her face against my neck and I could feel her shaking as she cried. "I won't let you die," she said. "So don't you dare give up, you hear me?"

She got up and left the room, and I was left there wondering what was happening to me. I had always hoped and prayed that I would grow some. I had anticipated getting a little taller, especially since my father was practically a giant compared to most other men. I had expected my voice to get deeper, or that I would at least fill out to look less like a skeleton. But nothing could have prepared me for this. Now, I was just hoping I would survive.

Each day that passed felt worse than the one before it. Instead of getting better, the pain seemed to get worse and worse. Everything ached. My stomach felt like it was grinding against my spine. I was so hungry I couldn't think, and so thirsty that it hurt to even breathe.

Every time I started to lose my will to go on, Beckah was there. I always knew it was her because I could recognize the feel of her hands. She forced me to eat by prying my mouth open and pouring something like soup down my throat. I don't know how often she did it. It seemed almost constant. And each time she finished, the effects were immediate. I felt a little better for a few minutes. My stomach didn't ache so badly, and I got some relief from the agony in my bones. Then the pain would return with a vengeance.

I was living in a nightmare. The doctor's words kept gnawing at the back of my mind. He had said I wouldn't survive this. He even told Sile to go ahead and prepare to bury me. I didn't want to die. Not yet. But it was getting harder and harder to remember anything other than suffering.

As more time passed, my mind started to fray. My thoughts were less clear. I couldn't tell who was touching me or feeding me anymore. I couldn't feel anything except the pain.

Mavrik gave me some relief in my darkest moments. He sent me images of us flying at the academy; memories that sometimes found me in that dark place. I could sense his concern, and it brought me comfort to know that he hadn't left me to go through this alone. After a while, though, I couldn't even make myself focus on that either. I was numb inside and out. I started to lose my will to go on.

I started to hope I would die, just so the pain would finally stop.

seven

It was peaceful when I opened my eyes. At first, I thought I might be dead. I could faintly hear the sound of the surf in the distance. I could smell the salty ocean wind coming through the open windows. The air was cool against my skin, and everything felt calm.

The pain was finally gone.

At first, I just assumed I was dead. It was the only thing that made sense. That is, until I realized I could take a deep breath, and nothing hurt. I could wiggle my fingers and my toes. Slowly, I started trying to raise my head up to look around. My body was stiff and sore all over, like I'd been run over by a herd of horses. There wasn't a single part of me that didn't ache. My joints felt like someone had poured sand into them. My head throbbed when I looked into the glare of the sunlight.

But I could do it—I could move. I could think. And

even that intense soreness was nothing compared to the pain I had been in before.

Then I saw Beckah curled up on the bed next to me. She was slumped back against the headboard, sound asleep, with a half-finished bowl of soup in her hands. I could tell by the look on her sleeping face that she was exhausted. There were dark circles under her eyes and her hair was frazzled. She probably hadn't let herself rest in days. Or had it been days? I wasn't sure. My sense of time was distorted. Everything had felt like one long nightmare.

I sat up slowly, and reached out to carefully slip the bowl of soup out of Beckah's grasp so she didn't spill it in her sleep. Suddenly, I noticed my hands. I stared at them, and it was surreal.

They were … huge!

Or at least, they were a lot bigger than they had been before. I started wiggling my fingers to make sure they were actually my fingers, and not some kind of illusion.

A surge of adrenaline made me forget all about Beckah and the soup. I got out of bed and almost fell flat on my face. My legs were still weak. I could barely walk, so I leaned against the bed as I staggered across the room toward the mirror.

The young man looking back at me was barely recognizable. I didn't believe it really was me until I saw him moving whenever I did. It just didn't seem possible. It couldn't be real.

The man in my reflection looked a lot like my father, with a squared chin and piercing pale blue eyes. His hair wasn't black, but it wasn't white like a gray elf's either. It was somewhere in between, like the color of ash. All traces of boyhood were gone from his face, and when he narrowed his eyes back at me … his gaze was disturbingly piercing. It made my skin prickle because it was the same harrowing, fierce look my father had on his face almost constantly.

Slowly, it started to sink in. That was me. I wasn't a puny, half-stuffed scarecrow anymore. I actually looked older than I was, maybe nineteen instead of sixteen. I didn't look like a kid, I looked like a man!

I must have grown out of my clothes because I was basically just wearing underwear and they definitely weren't mine. I guessed I was borrowing some from Sile, which was kind of embarrassing and awkward. I didn't dare take them off, though. I wasn't wearing anything else.

I looked down at my arms, my legs, and it actually got me choked up. I wasn't a skeleton. Well, at least not as much as before. I was still lean, still skinny compared to someone like Felix who was all brawn, but now I looked mature. I looked healthy. I was so grateful for every single ounce of muscle I could get. I still wasn't totally convinced this wasn't some kind of dream. It seemed too good to be true.

"Jae?" Beckah said my name.

I turned to see her sitting up on the bed, wide-awake, and staring at me with eyes as big as saucers. She almost looked scared of me. I tried to speak but it came out as a bunch of excited sounds.

"Is that really you?" she asked shakily.

"I-I'm not sure," I stammered as I glanced back at the mirror to make sure. My voice sounded different, too. It was deeper. "I think so."

She put the bowl on the nightstand and started creeping toward me cautiously. When I turned to face her, she jumped back a little. I noticed she was looking up at me—way up. I was a lot taller than her now. She was trembling a little as she eyed me up and down.

"Beckah." I hated to see her be afraid of me. I wanted her to know it was still the same me. On the inside, I didn't feel any different than before. "It's okay."

She didn't look convinced, even as she started to inch toward me a little. At any moment, I half expected her to bolt out of the room screaming. I could see her looking me over, like she was searching for traces of the scrawny little Jae she'd known before. When she finally met my eyes again, the corners of her mouth were twitching at a smile.

"Well, you're definitely not a lamb anymore," she said uneasily.

I smiled, and before I could think about it, I hugged her. Probably not the best idea since I wasn't exactly wearing much in the way of clothes. But I knew she was the reason I was still alive and breathing. I had survived because she never gave up on me. I knew I would spend the rest of my life trying to find some way to repay her for that.

She didn't seem to mind if I was mostly naked or not; she put her arms around my waist like she always did and hugged me tight. She wasn't strong enough to choke me anymore, though. The hug was a lot different from before. I was so much bigger than she was now. Her head only came up to my chest, and I could easily swallow her up in my arms. She felt so fragile.

Her angry-looking father definitely minded the hugging, though. Sile was standing in the doorway. He arched a brow at me and cleared his throat, narrowing his eyes into lethal slits. Somehow, it reminded me of the way Icarus glared at me. I knew that was probably going to be my only warning. I had about two seconds to let his daughter go before he made good on his promise to rip my ears off. Growth spurt or not, I was well aware that Sile could still beat me within an inch of my life without ever breaking a sweat.

We jumped apart immediately. Beckah was blushing as she hurried over to pick up the bowl of soup. She skirted around her dad as she went out of the room like she couldn't get away fast enough.

"Oh by the way, he's awake," she added quickly.

Sile gave her a hard look as she disappeared into the hallway. "I can see that," he grumbled. When she was safely downstairs and out of earshot, he curled a finger at me to follow him. "You can't walk around naked in my house, boy."

I followed him to his room, keeping a hand on the wall because my legs were still wobbly. They tingled like they had been asleep for a long time. As I walked behind him, I noticed I was taller than he was now. That startled me a little, and it made me want to shrink down some. I didn't feel like I deserved to be taller than Sile.

"They're going to be too short," he said as he opened his armoire and started throwing clothes in my direction. "But they'll do for now. Figures you'd inherit *his* stature."

I pulled a green tunic over my head and stepped into a pair of pants. They were definitely too small. The shirt was tight across my chest and back because my shoulders were bony, but broad. The pants were so short they came up above my ankles. The waist was a little too big for me, though, so I kept pulling them up until Sile finally tossed me a belt. When I finished dressing, I noticed Sile was still standing there with his arms crossed, sizing me up like he always did.

"You feeling all right?" he asked.

His concern caught me off guard. "Yes. I'm a little sore. It's already getting better, though."

I met his gaze. For a few long, uncomfortable minutes, we just stood there staring at each other. His brow was furrowed, and he was frowning like he wanted to yell at me. I wasn't sure why.

"You know I had to buy a coffin. It's leaning up against the side of the house outside." He snapped. He acted like I had forced him to do that.

I didn't know what to say. I wondered if I should apologize or not. I wasn't sure what I'd be apologizing for, though. Almost dying?

"Don't do that to us again," he warned.

I nodded, even if I wasn't completely sure what he was talking about. "Yes, sir."

He snorted and looked away, scratching at the back of his neck uncomfortably. "I suppose I should thank you."

"For what?"

He started toward me, and I couldn't tell if he was about to hug me or punch me in the face. I cringed because both options seemed uncomfortable. When he got close enough, he put a hand on my shoulder. "It was my fault. I forced you to do something you weren't ready for, and it almost cost you your life. But what you did—"

Like a bolt of lightning, the memories of what had happened burst into my head. His wife had been dying right in front of my eyes. Then Sile had insisted I do something about it. And … I *had* done something, I just didn't know what. I couldn't stand it anymore; I had to know.

"What did I do?" I interrupted.

Sile smirked at me and shook his head some. "Why don't you go downstairs and see for yourself?"

Sile followed me as I went down to the first floor. The more I walked, the steadier my legs got. I was stiff, and parts of me were sore, but it was getting better by the second. The more I moved, the better I felt.

I could hear singing coming from the kitchen, and I thought I recognized Mrs. Derrick's voice. Something smelled fantastic, like freshly baked pie. It made my mouth water.

As I started to peek around the corner, Sile gave me a shove from behind. I came stumbling into the kitchen, almost tripping and falling on my face. Beckah was sitting at the table with her sewing tools spread out around her. She smiled at me, but I had a feeling she wasn't practicing her sewing because she wanted to.

"Jaevid!" Mrs. Derrick's voice sang my name.

When I turned around to see her, I barely recognized her. Her eyes were shining and her skin was glowing. She looked healthier than all of us. There was rosy color in her cheeks, and she had more meat on her bones. She looked ten years younger, and her smile was so bright that it made me blush.

There was a squirming lump cradled against her chest in a sling made out of soft pink fabric. I didn't even notice until I heard it whimper and start to cry. It was a tiny, wrinkly baby. She patted and stroked it, cooing softly until the baby became silent again.

Mrs. Derrick looked up at me and smiled again. There were tears in her eyes, but she didn't look sad. Before I could smile back, she started hugging me. She kissed both my cheeks until they were wet, and combed her fingers through my hair.

"What a beautiful gift fate has given you, my lamb," she whispered.

I blushed because I didn't know what she was talking about. I couldn't figure out how I had caused any of this. How had I saved her? What gift was she talking about?

Mrs. Derrick seemed to notice my confusion. She put her palm against my cheek and stroked my face with her thumb. "Someday you'll understand. In the meantime, sit down! Look, I've been baking all morning. There's a blueberry pie just for you. Go on!" She basically shoved me into a chair across from Beckah.

Before I could protest, there was a piece of pie and a fork in front of me. It distracted me immediately. Who can argue with pie?

I was too shocked to start eating, though. Mrs. Derrick was … better. Much, *much* better. I didn't know if that was my fault, or just because she'd finally had her baby. I looked at Beckah for answers, but she only grinned shyly and went back to her sewing.

"He can eat later," Sile said. He was leaning in the doorway watching us with a strange smirk on his face. "I need to talk to him outside."

Mrs. Derrick swatted at her husband with a wooden spoon teasingly. "He hasn't had anything but soup in nearly two weeks! Let the poor child have a bite or two! Look at him, still as skinny as a rail. He needs some meat on his bones."

Sile rolled his eyes, but he never quit grinning.

"I'll get you a piece, too," she crooned to him. It must have worked because he grabbed her spoon and pulled her in close enough to kiss her on the mouth.

Watching them made me blush, and suddenly I had

a good reason to stare down at the steaming hot piece of pie in front of me. Looking at it made it impossible to think about anything else except how hungry I was, so I started eating.

"Now see what you've done?" Beckah whispered.

I looked up with a mouthful of food in my cheek. She was kidding, I guess, because she winked at me and grinned.

Warm, solid food felt amazing in my stomach. I ate four slices of pie and two pieces of berry cobbler before I finally felt full. Mrs. Derrick wanted to keep feeding me, but thankfully Sile waved her off.

"Let's go outside," he said to me with a dark twinkle in his eyes.

I started to get nervous. That was same look he got at the academy whenever he was about to force me to do something unpleasant in the name of training.

"But I don't have any shoes," I protested. My old boots were definitely not going to fit anymore.

"You won't need them." He pointed to the front door. "Hurry up. You don't realize it, but you're due back at the academy in two weeks. Time is running out, and there's still a lot you need to learn."

Sile was right. I would have to go back early and have new armor made. Probably a new saddle, too. No way my stuff from last year was going to fit me now. I wondered if I'd have to come up with the money for all that myself, or if Sile was still going to be my sponsor. My new instructor, Lieutenant Jace Rordin, was about as nice as anyone could expect from a war dog that had just been dragged off the frontlines. He didn't act like he hated me. But I seriously doubted he was going to buy me any new equipment. Armor was expensive. The little bit of money

I had saved up from my carpentry work wasn't enough to even buy myself a new helmet.

I followed Sile out the front door and toward the little stable behind the house. I tried not to look at the coffin that was still leaning up against the side of the house. He had said it was supposed to be for me. I couldn't help but notice that it would have been way too small now. Still, seeing it gave me a creepy feeling.

Sile opened the stable door and disappeared inside. While I waited for him, I tried to get a grip on my nerves. I needed some answers, and I knew Sile was holding out on me. He knew more about me than I did, apparently. I needed him to tell me what I'd done to his wife to heal her like that, and how he knew I could even do it in the first place. I had a feeling he wasn't going to just throw up his hands and confess everything. He had been keeping these secrets for a long time, and there had to be a reason.

Sile came out of the stable with a long wooden carrying pole and an old, banged up helmet. He smirked at me as he dropped them at my feet and went back inside to bring out two fifty-pound bags of grain. I watched him tie the bags to each end of the pole, and then he snapped his fingers and pointed at the ground.

I knew what that meant. I squatted down and braced myself as he put the carrying pole over my shoulders like a yoke. Once upon a time, a few weeks ago, those bags of grain would have weighed more than I did.

"There's a pier for local fishermen three miles down the beach to the east. There and back twice. The sand near the surf is firmer. Try not to fall and ruin the grain, if you don't mind." he said as he picked up the old helmet and mashed it down onto my head. "And I better not catch you walking."

"Yes sir." My answer was automatic. It was easy to fall back into the state of mind I had been in during training. Even though Sile hadn't been my instructor for a while now, I knew better than to argue with him. He didn't like excuses.

Sure, I had kept up my own workout regiment every day since I left Blybrig, but that didn't help me at all. Running down the beach with a hundred pounds on my back was more than exhausting. I wasn't used to my new body, and all my joints ached. My muscles were still sore. Every step hurt.

It was nearly dark by the time I finally finished, and I was exhausted and starving again. I dropped the pole and bags back outside the stable before I sat down to catch my breath. I was dripping sweat and my feet were throbbing. All I could think about was food. I really hoped there was some pie left.

"Here." Sile appeared behind me with a big piece of fresh-baked bread and a canteen in his hand. He tossed both of them to me. "Took you long enough."

"I *have* been training," I insisted as I took off the helmet and gulped down big bites of the bread. "I'm still weak. I'm not used to this body yet."

"That's not going to be an excuse at the academy. You know that," he said, walking around me to pick up the bags and carry them back into the stable. When he came out again, he had two wooden practice swords in his hands like the ones we used in training. He dropped one of them at my feet and nudged it toward me with the toe of his boot. "Get up."

"Sile," I protested. "I have some questions."

He turned his back to me and walked a few feet away, spinning the sword over his hand with expert speed. I seemed to recall hearing him say that the arm injury he had gotten at the prison camp last year would keep him from ever being able to hold a sword again. That didn't seem to be the case. He was whipping the practice sword around like there was nothing wrong with his arm at all.

"There'll be time for questions later," he growled. "Besides, the answers aren't important."

"They're important to me!" I couldn't keep myself from lashing out at him. It was one thing for him to brush me off, but he was keeping things from me on purpose and trying to make it seem like none of it mattered. It did matter. It mattered a *lot*. "How do you know so much about me? How did you know I could heal your wife like that? What's wrong with me?"

When Sile turned around, he had a dangerous look in his eyes. It actually scared me a little. He pointed his sword at me threateningly. "What should be important to you right now is learning how to survive because what is coming your way will, in all likelihood, kill you. Now get up."

I obeyed, snatching up the sword as I stood. But I didn't take my eyes off him; I wasn't backing down yet. "Saving your life last year almost killed me. I think you owe me a few answers."

I saw his jaw tense and his knuckles turned white as he gripped his sword more tightly. "I didn't ask you to save me," he growled through clenched teeth.

"You didn't have to," I growled back. "Beckah did. And she suspects that you've moved them all here because you're trying to hide from someone—and I think she's right. It's all connected somehow, isn't it? I'm not stupid, you know. I know it wasn't coincidence that you stuck your neck out for me so I could become a dragonrider.

No one else would have done that for a halfbreed. Not even my own father cares about me that much. So why won't you tell me what's going on?"

Sile lunged at me so suddenly I was caught completely off guard. I almost fell backwards as he brought his sword down toward my face. I moved to block, and the impact rattled my teeth. So much for that "crippling injury" he was supposed to have. He still hit like a hammer.

But I had changed some since the last time we'd crossed blades. I was stronger, and I could hold off his attacks. My own strikes were faster, steadier, and I could see him having to focus harder to keep up. He couldn't toy with me like before.

Something had definitely clicked in my brain. The sword felt good in my hands. I stepped easily through parries and strikes that had been so difficult for me last year because I lacked the size to match my opponent's reach. It didn't feel like a struggle anymore.

I could sense that Sile was getting more and more aggressive. His attacks came faster, and he was using tricks that he'd never used before. I thought I had him on a downward swing, and he locked his hilt with mine, and twisted the blade out of my hand. Before I could even process what happened, there was a boot in my chest. Sile kicked me to the ground.

Suddenly I was lying on my back with both swords pointed at my throat. I was forced to tap out in surrender.

"Why won't you tell me?" I glared up at him. "It's my life. I have a right to know."

"Because I promised her I wouldn't," he snapped.

"Who?"

I saw the rage in his eyes. He'd said too much. "I told you, it doesn't matter!"

While he was busy being angry with himself for giving something important away, I used a leg sweep to knock him down. I didn't give him a chance to recover. I threw myself at him and tried to get him into a grappling hold.

It was a good idea, in theory. But I was very rusty on the grappling maneuvers. I had been so terrible at hand-to-hand combat before. I was basically just a practice dummy for Felix. I had no good experience to go on.

Sile pinned me with a knee across my neck in a matter of seconds.

"Quit worrying about answers and focus on what you have to do to survive." He bore down with his weight so hard I could barely breathe. "And don't tell anyone about what you can do. I mean no one. Not even Felix. Don't even try to do it again. You can't tell anyone what you can do."

Part of me really wanted to punch Sile in the face—maybe even break his nose for good measure. But I was having a hard enough time staying conscious as he crushed my windpipe. All I could do was nod, and he finally let me up.

I sat up coughing and rubbing my neck. I was so furious I couldn't see straight. I already knew better than to tell anyone about what I had done to his wife, just like I knew better than to tell any of the other riders that I could talk to Mavrik with my thoughts. I was starting to collect a lot of big, dangerous secrets. "And what exactly am I supposed to survive? Felix already told me about the interrogation stuff. So they'll use me as a punching bag for a few weeks? Big deal. It's not like I'm not used to that already."

Sile cracked a smirk and rolled his eyes, offering me

a hand to pull me back up to my feet. "Felix is a good friend to you, however not even he can fully appreciate what's about to happen. I've done everything I can to protect you. But when you exposed yourself last year and risked saving my life, everything I've done in that regard became pointless. Now there's nowhere you can hide, and I can't be there to protect you anymore. You should try growing some eyes in the back of your head."

Something about the way he said that made me very uncomfortable. "You mean someone's going to try to kidnap me now? For some kind of immortality ritual?"

Sile glared at me like that was a stupid thing to ask. It made my face feel hot. I was embarrassed and frustrated because I didn't know what questions I should be asking. Most of the ones I did ask, he refused to answer.

"Go inside, get some dinner, bathe, and go to bed," he commanded, picking up both swords and starting back into the stable. "Be back out here at first light. Your vacation is officially over."

eight

There was a sense of urgency in the way Sile trained with me every day. I was running out of time. He pushed me harder than I had ever been pushed before, and still wouldn't tell me exactly why. He didn't give me a spare minute to question him, either. I barely even had enough time to think.

Sile got amazingly creative coming up with ways for me to build up my strength, which frankly hadn't exactly blossomed like I'd hoped it would. At first, it was a struggle just to make it through one exercise. But after a few days, I could already feel myself getting stronger. I could run further and faster without getting tired. He had me doing pull-ups and chin-ups on an exposed beam in the stable. I did push-ups with those bags of grain piled on my back, and sit-ups until I felt like I was going to puke.

We sparred for hours, practicing with swords, scimitars, and drilling through grappling techniques. He even tied me to the family carriage and had me pull it around the house in circles a few times. All that work made it hard to keep track of time, but I could tell his intensive training was starting to work. Even if I hadn't gained much muscle, I was getting more and more comfortable in my new body every day.

I felt bad for how much I was eating. I knew I was costing them a lot of extra money. But I was starving all the time. My appetite was out of control, and I couldn't do anything about it. It made the training Sile was putting me through show with quicker results, but it also meant I was eating them out of house and home. I could eat more than the rest of the family combined. Mrs. Derrick teased me about hiding it under my chair, because even though I could eat a whole roast by myself, I never gained a single pound.

While we trained, Beckah brought us water and food regularly. I could tell by the look on her face that something was wrong. She seemed nervous just to be around me. I wondered why. I wanted to think that my sudden growth spurt wouldn't change anything between us—but it already had. She was right there in the same house with me, and I missed her like she was a thousand miles away. We didn't talk much, and she barely made eye contact with me.

After a week and a half, I knew my time with Sile's family was up. As much as I hated the idea of going back to Mithangol, I needed to do a stopover at my house to check on everything. Then I had to get to the academy in time to have more armor and a new saddle made. My legs were way too long for the one I had now. Sile had wrestled with it, trying to find a way to rig it so I would fit without looking like a man trying to squeeze into a baby's highchair, but it was a lost cause.

"Just take it off," I told him. "I can ride without it. It's only a day's flight."

Sile frowned. He obviously didn't like that idea. "It's dangerous to ride without a way to anchor yourself to him. If he banks too steeply you'll slide off. I've already demonstrated for you what it's like to fall off a dragon's back."

"Lucky for me, I can talk to him. Besides, Beckah did it and she's never even had training. I'll be fine," I countered. Mavrik chirped with agreement, and I started unbuckling the saddle from between his neck and wing arms.

Sile was strangely quiet as I removed the saddle. He stood back and watched, rubbing his chin and following me with his dark eyes. "You need to start a fight," he said at last.

I stopped and stared at him. "A fight? With who?"

He shrugged a little. "It doesn't matter. The bigger the better, though. That way they can't say you were just using your new size to pick on someone smaller."

"But why?" I'd spent most of my life avoiding fights because of the guarantee that I would be crushed. The idea of starting one on purpose was not something I was excited about.

Sile moved around to Mavrik's other side and started helping me unbuckle the saddle. "At survival training, they always target the weakest link and use him to exploit and antagonize the rest of the class. They want to get a reaction. Unfortunately, there's only one other person in your class who cares what happens to you. And trust me, the last thing you want is to put the spotlight on him. So you need to prove that you aren't the weakest link anymore. You don't have much time to do it, though."

"And the best way to do that is to get into a fight?" I didn't like the sound of this at all.

"Yes. And I would strongly encourage you to win." He gave me a meaningful look over Mavrik's back.

"What am I supposed to do? Walk up and punch someone?" I tried to think of a good reason to do something like that. There wasn't one.

"I'm sure you'll come up with something. You were essentially a doormat for most of your peers last year. Surely there's someone you'd like to get revenge on," Sile said as he hoisted the saddle away and flung it over his shoulder.

I stood there thinking about that while he carried my old saddle away into the stable. Mavrik got up and shook himself. We exchanged a glance, and a vision of Lyon Cromwell flashed across my mind.

"I'm not going to punch Lyon for no reason," I told him.

Mavrik made an irritated grumbling noise and stared preening his scales. I knew what he was thinking, and not just because he started showing me images of the fight at the prison camp last year when Lyon abandoned us. I had plenty of reasons to do more than punch Lyon. He was not my friend. He hated me, and he had spent a lot of his spare time bullying me in the past. I would have been lying if I told anyone I didn't resent him for that, but that was a far cry from wanting to go out of my way to pick a fight with him.

"Forget it. We'll think of something else," I grumbled.

Mavrik yawned and started crawling away, looking

for a shady spot to stretch out for a nap. Sile came back and followed me to the house. I still had to pack up my stuff and say my goodbyes. I was hoping to get back to Mithangol after nightfall. If I could get in and out of there without anyone seeing me, I would be happy.

It was awkward to eat my last lunch with them. Or at least, it was awkward for me because Beckah wouldn't even look up from across the table. She sat there, swirling her fork in her food, and didn't say a word. It was killing me. I needed to talk to her before I left for this year of training. She was the only person who gave me any confidence in myself.

Mrs. Derrick was caught up with her new baby girl. The chubby little thing was wrapped up in layers of pink blankets. She squirmed in her mother's arms, making strange baby-noises. Every now and then, though, Mrs. Derrick would look up at me and smile again, reminding me to eat as much as I wanted. I decided that was probably her way of thanking me.

Sile was uncomfortably quiet, too. He looked like he was lost in thought, or maybe even worried about something. I hoped it wasn't me. I wasn't small anymore. I could survive. I wasn't doomed to be the weakest link everyone would prey upon. At least, that's what I was hoping.

After dinner, I went up to the guest room and packed up the few things I'd brought. Mrs. Derrick told me to leave my old clothes and boots, since none of them fit now. I didn't have much else to take. My belt, vambraces, helmet—none of it would be any use to me anymore. So I tried to fold it all up neatly and put it on the dresser. Sile had bought them all for me, so it only seemed right to give them back now.

The door shut behind me suddenly and I almost jumped out of my skin. I half hoped it was Beckah, but instead Sile was standing there with his arms crossed. He was looking at me like he had something to say. Immediately, my stomach started to squirm nervously.

"I've decided to let the dragon stay," he told me. "Icarus, that is."

I swallowed hard. "I think that's a good idea."

He frowned. "Because Beck wants to keep him?"

"No," I answered quickly. "Because if you want to keep something around for security, a king drake is the best guardian anyone could hope for."

He snorted and looked away again. "I kept hoping Valla would come back. But I'm a fool for even expecting that from her. She didn't choose me the way Mavrik chose you. I was a taskmaster to her, nothing more. Despite all we've been through, she's better off without me. She didn't even look back."

"You let her go?" I wasn't all that surprised. Sile had mentioned before that his dragon wasn't bonded to him like Mavrik was to me, or Icarus was to Beckah. He'd also said he was going to let her go, since he wasn't a dragonrider anymore.

"I owed her that much," he said. "Look, Jae, regardless of what's been said and done, I do owe you an apology."

I froze and stared at him. I was beginning to suspect I might be hallucinating. "For what, sir?"

"For keeping these things from you. For pushing you too far and almost getting you killed." He looked at me uneasily. "But I'm a man of my word, and I gave someone a promise that I'd only tell you what you needed to know. This isn't the right time. You'll have to trust me about that."

I did trust him. But that didn't make me feel any better right then. I was starting to get nervous. Just thinking about going back to Blybrig had my stomach tied up in painful knots.

On the one hand, I wanted to see Felix again and get back into the saddle. I wanted to start training like I had been before. Then on the other hand, I dreaded what was coming. I hated the discriminating way everyone looked at me, and knowing that I basically had no allies there other than Felix and maybe Lieutenant Jace Rordin. We were all supposed to be brothers at arms, and yet I knew I was still an outsider. That would probably never change no matter what I did.

"I'm still trying to believe that I can do this," I told him. "I knew it wouldn't be easy, but it's hard enough trying to have faith that I'll make it to the end of training."

Sile walked toward me and put a hand on my shoulder like he had before. It was still strange to be able to look at him eye-to-eye now. "Faith won't make things easier for you, Jaevid. But it will make them possible."

He reached into his pocket, taking out a small leather bag. I could hear coins jingling around inside as he handed it to me. "For your new armor and saddle," he told me. "There should be enough there to get you fully outfitted."

"Sir," I started to protest. I didn't want to take any more of his money. He'd already paid for the equipment I'd used last year. He'd volunteered to sponsor me because my father wouldn't, and I knew there was no way for me to ever pay him back.

Sile shoved the bag into my hand anyway. "Just shut up and take it."

We exchanged an awkward moment of silence, staring at one another. I had an eerie feeling we were both thinking about the same thing: what was going to happen to me this year at training? Was I going to be able to survive it? Sile acted like there was something greater at work here—something I was supposed to be a part of. If I didn't make it, if something went wrong, what would happen?

I cleared my throat, put the coins into my pocket, and picked up my nearly empty bag. "I should get going." I paused on my way out the door and looked back. "Where's Beckah? She's been avoiding me, hasn't she?"

Sile scowled at me. "Still sniffing around my daughter, are you?"

I felt my ears start to burn with embarrassment. "S-she's my friend, sir."

"She was headed to the beach, last I saw her," he grumbled at last. "She doesn't like goodbyes."

He sounded like he knew that firsthand. It made me think about all the times she'd had to say goodbye to him as he left for training or war. She never knew if she'd see him again every time he left. Now, it was starting to be that way with me, too.

Then I realized why she might be acting so weird.

After thanking Mrs. Derrick for all her good food, I left the house and headed for the beach. Overhead, Mavrik was wheeling in slow circles with his blue scales sparkling in the sunshine. The salty sea air blew in hard from the water, and the sun was warm on my skin. As I came over the last grassy dune, I could see the dark shapes of ships on the horizon, the powdery white sand stretching along the coast, and the glittering waves crashing against the shore.

Beckah was standing near the water with the wind in her hair. Icarus was crouched beside her, his huge body compacted up like a crouching cat, and his long tail wrapped around him. It looked like they were having a secret conversation. They both looked back at me at the same time when I got close. That's when I noticed that Icarus was wearing my old saddle—the one I'd grown out of. It didn't look like it fit Icarus very well, after all he was a lot bigger than Mavrik, but it was probably about the right size for Beckah.

"You're angry at me, aren't you?" I asked her. "For leaving, right?"

Beckah frowned. "No."

"Then it's the way I look now? You don't like it?"

She didn't answer right away, and I got a sick feeling in my stomach that maybe I'd been right. I could handle her being upset with me for leaving. But if she was shutting me out because of how I looked—I wasn't sure I could stand going through that again. It wasn't something I could change. I couldn't help the way I looked.

Finally, she turned back toward the ocean and let out a loud sigh. "I'm not angry at all, Jae. It just seems like the war and the academy both keep taking away the people I care about the most. There's never anything I can do to stop it. I wish you weren't going. I wish you'd stay here with us. And at the same time, I wish I was going with you," she confessed. "I feel like I *should* be going with you. I can't explain it. But ever since Icarus chose me, I've had this feeling that there's something I'm supposed to be doing. It's getting stronger and stronger, and I'm afraid. No one's going to accept me as a dragonrider because I'm a girl."

"You told me once that it didn't matter what anyone else thinks," I reminded her. "You said that if it was somethi͏ I really cared about, then nothing else mattered."

Beckah started to fidget. I could see that she was thinking hard about this, and that she was obviously worried. It was a big chance to take. I still wasn't comfortable with the idea of her riding into battle or trying to become a dragonrider, but I wasn't going to try to hold her back. If she wanted to fly, I knew nothing was going to stop her.

"It is weird to see you this way now," she mumbled. "I know it's silly, but it makes me wish I could look more grown up, too. Maybe then you wouldn't forget about me, or think of me as a little kid anymore."

"Forget about you?" I put my bag down and went to stand next to her. She flashed me a stubborn look, but all I really noticed was how her eyes were the same sea-green color as the ocean.

"I'm still the same person, you know. I don't feel any different on the inside. And besides, I like the way you look." Admitting that made me blush. "I'll come back, Beckah. You'll see me again. I won't forget."

She reached down into the pocket of her apron and took out a square piece of thin, white cloth. It was handkerchief. When she put it in my hand, I saw that there were two dragons stitched on it. One was blue like Mavrik and the other was black like Icarus. They were flying together with their necks and tails intertwined and their wings spread wide.

"Momma says that in the old days, ladies would give knights tokens for good luck to carry with them into battle," she explained. "I know the stitching isn't very good.

I guess Momma's right, I should have practiced more."

"You made this for me?" I smiled at her, and took her hand. "It's amazing."

She grinned back at me, and her freckled cheeks looked slightly more rosy than usual. "Keep it with you, okay?"

I nodded. "Of course."

"Please be safe," she said earnestly. I felt her squeeze my hand.

Something stirred in me, seeing her that way. The urge to protect her shot through my body so suddenly, it was startling. Just knowing that I would be at the academy, too far away to do anything for her if something happened, was now unbearable.

"If anything goes wrong, tell your father to go to Mithangol," I said.

She canted her head to the side like she was confused. "Why?"

"My house is empty now, and no one would think to look for you there. Sile knows where it is; he's been there before. My family won't be coming back, and yours might need a place to hide. You'd be safe there. You'll tell him, won't you?"

Beckah nodded, but I saw sadness in her eyes. She squeezed my hand again before she let it go. "Goodbye, Jae."

Behind us, Mavrik landed and started making insistent chirping sounds as he tossed his head. It was time to go. By the time I finally thought about hugging her one last time, I was already sitting on Mavrik's back, trying to find a good way to hold onto his scaly hide. It was way too late then, and I cursed myself all the way back to Mithangol for not thinking of it sooner.

nine

It was dark when we landed in Mithangol. I was sore and exhausted from hanging onto Mavrik's back for dear life the whole way. Dragon scales are not built for comfort at all. I was definitely not looking forward to another long ride without a saddle. The sooner I got some new equipment, the better.

The house looked the same as I'd left it—dark and basically empty except for the furniture I had made myself. As soon as I got inside, I built a fire and started cooking a quick dinner. I ate alone at my kitchen table and thought about Sile and his family the whole time. It was so quiet. There was no life, no happiness in my house like there had been in theirs. No baby noises. No sounds of laughter. It made me miss them a lot. The time I'd spent with them was the first time I'd ever really felt like part of a family. Now that I was by myself again, I realized how alone I felt in this house.

After a hot bath, I started going through Roland's old clothes in his room. His clothes had once been enormous, but now they fit me just right. I was relieved to finally have a decent pair of boots that weren't uncomfortably tight.

I packed up several extra changes of his clothes, belts, and socks into my bag, along with the coins Sile had given me. I took out Beckah's handkerchief and looked at it again, running a thumb over the stitching of the two dragons. It made me smile and think of how much I already missed her. Carefully, I folded it up and tucked it back into my pocket.

It was late by the time I settled into bed. The fire burning low in my bedroom hearth put long shadows across the room. Even though it was peaceful and I was warm and comfortable, I had a hard time falling asleep. Something made me feel restless and uneasy. Then I finally did start to drift off, and I had the worst nightmare of my life.

As soon as my eyes closed, the dream pulled me under like someone had yanked the rug of reality out from under me. It didn't start out bad right away. I dreamt was sitting at the kitchen table in my mother's old house in the war refugee ghetto in the royal city of Halfax. The smell of flowers, plants, and warm fresh earth filled the air and took me back to the only time in my life I had ever really been happy. The rush of familiar sounds and smells made my head spin.

My mom was standing there with her back to me, preening a plant that was growing out of a big clay pot on the kitchen counter. It was a weird-looking plant, not one I'd ever seen growing in Maldobar before. There were huge red and yellow blossoms on it that were as big as my palm. Mom's silver hair was tied up in a braided knot, and I could hear her singing in her native language. It had been so long since I had heard her voice. It put a sharp pain in my chest like someone was twisting a knife in my heart. When I was little, I would have given anything for a dream like this—just so I could see her one more time.

"M-mom?" I tried to speak but my voice cracked with emotion.

She turned around like she was surprised to see me sitting there. Then she smiled, and it left me reeling. I'd missed her so much. Even though I knew it wasn't real, seeing her face was like taking a breath after holding it for all these years.

"Jae? Spirits and Fates! You've gotten so big!" She beamed at me as she wiped her hands on her tattered apron.

I tried to get up. I wanted to run to her and put my arms around her, but I couldn't move. Something held me in place like I was sinking in quicksand. It was a reminder: this wasn't real. It was a dream. It wouldn't last for long.

Her smile started to fade some, and I saw traces of sadness in her eyes. She came closer, just out of my reach, and sat down at the table across from me. "I know it's been hard for you, dulcu."

She spoke with the same heavy accent she'd always had. My mother had struggled with learning the human language, so she'd always mixed in elven words whenever she couldn't remember human ones. She had called me "dulcu," which was like calling someone "sweetheart" or "darling," all the time. I couldn't believe I had almost forgotten that.

There was so much I wanted to ask her. But right then, all I could do was stare at her and try to drink in every detail. I didn't want to forget again. She had her bangs tucked behind her long, pointed ears, and there were little wrinkles in the corners of her diamond-colored eyes. Her heart shaped face was aged, and still beautiful and ethereal looking.

"I'm very proud of you," she said. "You know that, don't you?"

I finally managed to speak. "But I'm a dragonrider now. I'm learning to fight—to kill your people—for the humans. How can you be proud of that?"

She looked sad again. "Some things are not simple because they aren't made to be that way. That is you, too, dulcu. You were not made to be simple, so things will never be easy for you. I'm very sorry for that. I wish I could be there to help you."

Mom stiffened suddenly, and her eyes got wide. She glanced back as though she could hear someone whispering in her ear. I got an extremely bad feeling, like someone was breathing down the back of my neck. It made my skin prickle.

In the corner of the room shadows were starting to gather in a big, boiling mass. They grew larger and darker, growing to climb the walls like inky black vines. The bigger they got, the more the tension in the room rose. It was like someone was dragging their icy fingertips up my spine.

"He knows," my mother whispered. When she looked back at me, I saw fear in her eyes. "You must keep learning, Jaevid. Don't be afraid of what you can do."

"But, Mom," I protested. Somehow I could sense that the dream was about to collapse on itself. "Will I ever see you again? Like this?"

My mom just smiled gently. It was one of those looks only mothers can give.

The dream shifted as the black vines spread, consuming the room and choking out all the light until there was nothing except darkness. I was cold and lost, not sure which way was up or down. It was scary, but what came next was much, much worse.

When the darkness cleared, I was standing on a muddy road in an open valley. At first, I was relieved. After all, the place was beautiful. The sun was shining over rolling hills covered in a blanket of clean, white snow. There were huge mountains crowned with snow on either side of the valley, but they were miles away.

Before me, I could see what looked like a huge forest with a dark tree line that marched off in both directions for miles and miles. It was like standing on the boundary of two completely different worlds. The trees were enormous—about three times the size of a normal tree. The road I was standing on wound away into the distance, snaking along the backs of the snowy hills until the dark forest swallowed it up.

Suddenly, I heard the shrill whinny of a horse. I looked back as a company of horsemen came trotting down the road. There were sixteen of them dressed in shining bronze armor, carrying the banner with the king's golden eagle on it. They rode surrounding a beautiful gilded carriage that was drawn by four white horses with blue ribbons woven into their manes and tails.

They were heading for the forest with their banners fluttering. I tried to step out of their way, but once again, I couldn't move an inch. My feet were stuck and I braced, expecting the carriage and horsemen to plow right into me.

Instead, they blurred right through me like I wasn't even there. All I felt was a slight chill. As real as it all seemed on the surface, I realized this was just a dream as well.

The company went on, leaving me behind without a second glance. It was like they couldn't see me at all. I caught a glimpse of one of the guards as he passed— something about him seemed vaguely familiar. I couldn't be sure because his helmet covered most of his face.

As soon as they got past me, a shout went up. The company came to an abrupt halt. From where I was standing, I couldn't clearly see why they'd stopped. I only caught a few glimpses of what looked like a man in a heavy brown cloak, standing right in the middle of the road. Had he been there the whole time? I didn't remember seeing him there before. Immediately, the mere sight of him gave me a cold feeling. The hood of his cloak was pulled down to hide his face, and he didn't move at all.

"Stand aside for his majesty, the King of Maldobar, who seeks peaceful court with those who dwell in the wild forest!" The leader of the guards announced.

I heard a raspy voice begin to chuckle from under the stranger's hood. It gave me a pins and needles sensation in my arms and legs. All my hair stood on end. I didn't know that voice, I was sure of that. But something told me I *should* know it.

"Peaceful? You don't even know the meaning of the word." The stranger sneered. "You human fools. You're all so ignorant, and yet so sure of what you think you know. It's your greatest flaw. But it could be useful. Yes, you will be very useful to me."

I could sense the tension rising. Some of the guards were touching the hilts of their swords. Their horses shifted uneasily.

"Stand aside!" The guard tried again.

The next thing I heard was screaming. Chaos erupted all around me. Horses shrieked in panic and threw their riders off, galloping away in all directions. I saw the shadow of something streaking down from the sky as fast as an arrow. It was huge, although not as big as a dragon. I had never seen any dragon move that fast. The creature was too quick to even be seen clearly, and it made a terrifying screeching sound like the piercing cry of an eagle.

I could smell blood and hear swords clashing, but I was helpless to do anything about it. I couldn't move. I finally saw the man in the brown cloak as he butchered two of the guards through with a sword that looked like it was made out of white wood. The hood covered most of his face, so I only caught a glimpse of his features as he turned past me. I saw his diamond-colored eyes flashing with anger, and a few locks of his platinum-colored hair. His lips curled into a brutal snarl.

He was a gray elf.

Just meeting his eyes put a stabbing pain in my chest that made me choke. A smothering sense of chaos started bubbling over my brain, twisting my thoughts and making me furious. But as soon as he looked away, the feeling subsided.

The way he fought was unlike anything I had ever seen before, even at Blybrig. He moved like a ghost. Every stroke of his strange white sword was smooth and effortless. In a matter of seconds, he was the only one left standing.

The gray elf warrior stepped over the broken, slashed-up bodies of the guards with no sign of remorse. He wrenched open the door to the carriage. All I could do was watch in horror as he started dragging out the people hiding inside. The king, a middle-aged man with graying hair, came out fighting. But he didn't last any longer than his guards did.

Panic surged through my body, turning my blood to ice when the gray elf rammed his sword into the king's chest. The warrior watched the king gasp and die with a burning look of malice in his color-changing eyes.

The warrior dropped the king's dead body into the mud, kicking it aside and going back into the carriage again. I watched him do the same thing to the young queen and her two small children, leaving them all piled there in the sludge as though they were nothing but trash. I had witnessed plenty of horrible things in my life. This was different. This made my whole being cry out for revenge. Nothing about this was right. It was murder—senseless murder!

Then I heard a sound that made my heart stop cold.

One of the guards was back on his feet. It was the one that had looked so familiar to me, though I still couldn't figure out who it was. It seemed like his face was intentionally skewed to hide his identity, but I could still tell that he was fairly young. He stood shakily with his sword in hand, shouting out a challenge to the murderous gray elf that had just slain the whole royal family in cold blood.

The guard was the only one left alive, and he was bleeding from a deep gash on his leg. His bronze armor was spattered with blood. He could barely stay on his feet. A sense of comradery thrummed through my chest like a surge of heat and energy. More than anything, I wanted to step in and stand beside him. We could both fight and die together, side by side.

The gray elf warrior turned around slowly, his face still mostly hidden underneath his hood. I could see his mouth. He was smiling wickedly. He spun his white blade over his hand again and again with expert speed, taking slow steps toward the lone guardsman. I was no master swordsman, and even I could tell he was toying with the guard. This wasn't going to end well.

"Aren't you brave?" he hissed with pleasure, like this was all amusing to him. "Tell me, little soldier, just how brave are you? What would you do to save your own life?"

The two men squared off, preparing for a final fight. I could feel my pulse racing. Dread was building up, like hot stones were being stacked on my chest until I could barely breathe.

Something important was about to happen. I didn't understand how, but I *knew* it. The gray elf started to take his first step, his sword drawn back to strike …

I bolted awake.

I sat up in bed with my mind racing and my pulse still hammering in my ears. I was soaked in a cold sweat. Immediately, I felt sick. I barely made it to the big iron pot by the fireplace before I threw up. When my stomach was empty, my thoughts finally started to clear.

For a long time, I just sat there leaning against the wall. The heat from the coals smoldering in the fireplace was warm against my face, but I was still shivering. I tried to remind myself that it was only a dream. It didn't help at all.

It was so early in the morning that the sun wasn't even up yet. The air was bitter cold, and there were snowflakes falling from the dark sky. I was more exhausted than ever, and I knew I'd never be able to go back to sleep—not with dreams of gore and bloodstained snow still burning in my mind. I needed to get up, move around, and do anything to keep my mind off of that stuff. I couldn't afford to get distracted by nightmares now.

I started to get dressed, pulling on a pair of Roland's old boots and vambraces, two thick wool tunics, heavy canvas pants, and a belt. I clipped my hunting knife to my hip, tied my hair back, and clasped an old traveling cloak around my shoulders. It didn't take me long to pack up the rest of my gear, including the old scimitar I had found in the Roland's trunk. I tucked Beckah's handkerchief into one of my vambraces where I knew it would be safe, and started downstairs.

The snow was falling heavily when I came outside. Mavrik was growling about the cold and flicking his tail as I pushed the barn door open. He stayed hunkered down in the hay, his wings and legs folded up close to his body, watching me as I looked around for something to use as a makeshift saddle. I found a length of rope and I used it to tie my bag onto his back, but there wasn't much else to work with. My safety would depend on Mavrik. It made me extremely anxious. We would be flying higher and further to reach the Devil's Cup, a small crescent-shaped valley where Blybrig Academy sat looking to the western seas. I would have to ride carefully and take things slowly.

It took a few minutes of coaxing to get Mavrik out of the barn. He hated the snow, not that I blamed him. We hadn't been in Saltmarsh for very long, but I was already missing the warmer coastal temperatures, too. Unfortunately, that wasn't the only thing I missed about Saltmarsh.

Once we took off, soaring above the heavy clouds that smothered Mithangol in winter, the air was much clearer. In the distance, the sun was just beginning to rise, and it turned the tops of the clouds a warm pinkish golden color. It looked like a sea of color spread out before us, breaking against the peaks of the Stonegap Mountains that stuck up through the clouds like castle spires. The air was still chilly, and it cut right through all the layers of my clothing. Still, it was good to breathe in the clean, free air.

"Ready to get back to business?" I asked as I gave Mavrik's scaly neck a pat. Even over the rush of the air humming past us, I knew he would hear me. "I bet Nova's already there waiting for you."

He canted his head to the side some so he could look back at me   h one of his big yellow eyes. He gave a trumpeting roar, and beat his wings harder. We lurched forward with more speed. It made me smile and lean down against his neck. After months of dreading what was waiting for me at Blybrig, now that I was finally going there … I just couldn't wait.

ten

We were already making good time. I used the peaks of the mountains as markers, so I knew exactly which way to fly as we made our way toward Blybrig. As the day wore on, the temperatures on the ground started to rise and the clouds began to clear away. I could see the cliffs and steep ravines dotted with fir trees far below. Everything was still covered in snow. It reminded me of the long, grueling journey through the mountain pass I had made with my father last year. I was more than happy not to be on foot again this year, let alone traveling with Ulric. He wasn't exactly good company.

"I wonder if Felix will even recognize me," I wondered out loud. The air rushing by was so loud I could barely hear my own voice.

Mavrik snorted, and glanced back at me again. In my mind, he showed me an image of when Felix and I had parted ways last year, awkwardly exchanging a few friendly punches on the arm. Felix had been so worried about letting me go back home by myself. He had also spent a lot of time sticking up for me last year, and making sure none of the other students beat me to death when the instructors weren't looking. Boy, was he in for a surprise.

Suddenly, Mavrik's body shuddered underneath me. He went completely tense, all the muscles in his body becoming as solid as stone. I barely had time to brace myself before he snapped his wings in tight against his body and started a frantic dive straight down.

"Stop it! What are you doing?" I shouted at the top of my lungs. I pulled on the knobby spines that ran down his back with all my might, trying to get him to level off again.

Mavrik ignored me. He started making swift, jerking twists to avoid cliffs as we rocketed down toward the earth. Fear burrowed deep into my gut like a cold knife, but I clenched my teeth and tried to flatten out against his neck. Without a saddle to anchor me down, it took everything I had just to hang on.

Then an image flashed across my mind. It was garbled and hazed with frantic color, but I saw it clearly for an instant. I saw the faces of Katty, Bren, and Mr. Crookin, all pale with terror. I saw blood on the snow, and something big closing in for the kill.

Then it made sense. They must have been somewhere far below us on the Stonegap Pass, making their way to Blybrig as well. Mavrik could smell them, even from a few miles away. I felt like an idiot for doubting him. He showed me another flurry of images, and this time I saw the knife in my belt, the scimitar, and the maneuver he wanted to try.

"All right," I muttered as I reached down to pull out

the hunting knife. "Get me as close as you can."

Mavrik spun downward, bursting through the last layer of clouds that hugged the lowest parts of the mountains. Rocks and steep cliff sides seemed to appear out of nowhere, so close that a few more inches would have taken my head off.

I saw them a few hundred yards away. Mr. Crookin's wagon was stuck in the deep snow on the side of the road. It looked like it had a broken axel, and the horses were panicking, pawing the air and bucking against their harnesses. Katty was huddled over her father, who was lying motionless on the ground. The snow around them was stained red with blood. Bren was still on his feet, holding a sword at arm's length to keep three big wolves at bay. The wolves were pacing and snapping, looking for the right moment to strike.

Mavrik's thoughts raced across my brain, showing me scenarios and where the other wolves were. He smelled eight in all. I tightened my grip on my knife. The scimitar was old. I wasn't confident it would hold up in a fight, so I decided only to use it as a last resort.

We burst through the heavy fog, and Mavrik let out a bone-rattling roar. It startled the three wolves who were squaring off with Bren, sending them scurrying to the thickets on the side of the road. I knew they would be back.

I gathered my courage, and waited until the very last second. The ground rushed up, and Mavrik flared his wings in the blink of an eye. He stretched out his hind legs, touching down for only a flash of a moment before kicking skyward again.

As Mavrik touched the earth—I jumped off his back. I hit the ground and dropped into a roll so that the impact didn't break my legs. When I got up, my head was spinning and it took a second to get my bearings.

Someone behind me shouted, "It's a dragonrider!"

I spun, spotting Bren first because he was standing closest to me. He was still armed with a sword. Then I locked eyes with Katty. It only lasted a second or two, but the minute she saw my face, I knew she recognized me.

"Look out!" Bren shouted again.

I turned around, just in time to see fangs flashing in my face. A wolf lunged at me, and I didn't hesitate. All that training with Sile clicked into my brain instantly. I dove, spinning to dodge the wolf's attack, and swinging around to drive my hunting knife into the back of the animal's neck. The wolf yelped, whined, and collapsed onto the snow.

"On your left!" Bren was standing with his back up against mine, giving us a circle of protection to watch on all sides.

The mountain wolves closed in, emerging from the thickets like ghosts. There were seven in all, each one easily two hundred pounds. They encircled us, pacing around to look for the perfect opening to make an easy kill. They were wild with rage, lashing out recklessly like they were rabid. Something about it didn't seem right. I had never heard of wolves acting this way, and when I looked them in the eyes, I got a sick feeling that scrambled my thoughts. It made it impossible to try to speak to them like I had with other animals.

Bren caught one in the leg with his sword, and jumped on it quickly to drive his blade through its ribs before it could get away. I had the smaller weapon, so I knew I would have to get up close and personal. I was prepared for that.

A big wolf lunged at my front while another came from the side. I managed to throw my knife, hitting the first one right between the eyes. It dropped to the snow immediately and didn't move again. The second one hit me like a brick wall. I felt its jaws clamp onto my thick leather vambrace, beginning to jerk and flail like it wanted to rip my arm off. Its teeth couldn't touch my skin because of the thick leather, and I quickly reached for my scimitar.

The instant the blade left the sheath, it filled the air with a metallic humming sound. I was only barely aware of it, like a faint chime on the wind. But all of a sudden, the wolf let me go. Immediately it started backing away with its ears pressed back, whining like it was in pain. I was stunned, staring at the cowering creature.

Then another wolf hit me from behind. I felt its jaws on my shoulder, tearing at the layers of my clothes to get to my skin. Immediately, I threw myself backwards with all my strength and hit the ground so my weight bore down on the wolf, pinning it underneath me. I spun the scimitar in my hands, jabbing it backwards and catching the beast in the stomach. It shrieked in pain and finally went limp.

Looking up from where I was sitting in the snow, I saw the eyes of three big wolves still standing. They started closing in. Bren was right next to me, shaking like he was terrified but still holding his sword. He kept looking over at me as though he expected me to give him orders.

Suddenly, an image flashed across my mind.

"Get down!" I yelled at the top of my lungs. I threw myself at Bren, grabbing him from behind and wrestling him to the ground a second before it hit.

I heard Mavrik's roar, the wind buzzing over his scaly hide, and the sound of him breathing flame. I felt the heat of it on the back of my neck, singing a few hairs as he passed right over us. When I looked up again, Mavrik had disappeared back into the fog, but the wolves were nothing but three mounds of burning fur in the middle of a big puddle of sticky venom.

It was over. Everything was strangely quiet, except for the popping of the flames. The wolves lay motionless all around us, and I let Bren up as I staggered back to my feet. He stared at me with a mixture of shock, horror, and surprise. I was about to explain, but another sound made us both turn. We raised our blades, ready to fight.

But it wasn't a wolf this time.

What came out of the woods looked like some kind of cat. It was huge, as big as a fully-grown bear, and covered in shaggy silver fur. It had a bobbed tail, big muscular legs, and two long fangs that dripped down below its jaws. It stalked toward us with its head low, snarling with rage.

"W-what is that?" I heard Bren whisper from beside me.

I was too stunned to answer.

Its blue eyes were focused right on me, like it was looking right into my soul. When I looked back, it was as though I could feel chaos boiling inside the creature. It was the same feeling the wolves had given me, and I couldn't figure out why. It was a wild, angry, primal chaos. It didn't have any sense of right or wrong. It only craved violence and blood. I knew I had experienced this kind of reckless fury before, I just couldn't remember where. I didn't have time to think about it then.

Slowly, I reached a hand out toward Bren. "The

sword," I said. "Give it to me."

Bren didn't argue. I felt him put the hilt of the sword in my hand. I squeezed it hard.

"Now move away. Don't look into its eyes," I told him, keeping my own gaze fixed upon the huge silver cat. I couldn't explain why, somehow I knew it was only interested in me. This was personal.

I stepped toward the beast, meeting it in the snow with Bren's sword in one hand, and my scimitar in the other. I gripped both weapons and squinted into the cold mountain wind, watching as the animal moved with me. It stepped when I did, and smelled the air. I could feel it looking me over, searching for a weakness.

I got no warning. The cat charged before I even had a chance to try to speak to it. I wanted to talk it down, to settle things without spilling any more blood, but now that option was completely off the table. The cat sprang toward me as fast as a bolt of lightning. I saw its jaws opened wide, rows of jagged fangs ready for the kill. There wasn't time to hesitate. I had one chance, and one plan.

I dove toward it.

Behind me, Katty screamed.

My body moved, acting on pure instinct. I wasn't even afraid. I ran toward the cat and dropped to my knees, skidding under its body and swinging both blades out wide to strike its legs.

The beast howled in pain. I felt the impact as the cat's huge body collapsed into the snow. It flailed around on the ground, snarling and snapping as I got back on my feet.

Even when I stood over the cat, it was still trying to get to me. It couldn't even move its hind legs anymore, since I'd nearly cut them off, but its rage was so intense that it wouldn't surrender. For whatever reason, the cat *needed* to kill me. It was like some kind of crazed sickness. I could feel that boiling wrath starting to leak into my own mind, just by looking at the cat. Something about it disgusted me beyond words.

I jabbed my scimitar into the animal's heart. Immediately, it went still and that sick feeling of fury drained out of the air. I stood there, watching the last few breaths of life leave its body, and I realized today was the first time I had ever killed anything with my own hands. I wasn't necessarily proud of that. I didn't want to kill anything, but there wasn't any other choice.

Everything was quiet again. Slowly, I turned around to look at Bren and the others. They were all staring back at me with wide eyes. Even Mr. Crookin looked completely dumbstruck. I bowed my head some, and sheathed my scimitar.

Behind me, I heard the sound of wing beats and felt the ground flinch as Mavrik landed. He let out a deep growl, and sent an image into my mind that made my hands curl up into fists. He was reminding me that these people might not be my friends.

I looked straight at Bren. He looked about eighteen. His black hair was pulled back into a short ponytail like before, and his features were soft and almost babyish. His dark eyes stared at me with a mixture of awe and relief. He wasn't very tall, but he was stocky and must have been pretty strong. He was a blacksmith's apprentice, after all.

I thought about what he had done during the fight. He'd obeyed my every order, and fought bravely at my side. It was strange, but out of the three of them, I got the feeling he was the one I could trust the most.

"It's all right," I said. "He's fine."

Bren blinked as though he were trying to make sure he wasn't dreaming. "Y-you sure about that? He's snarling at me."

"I wasn't talking to you." I glanced back at Mavrik, who was still swishing his tail angrily. He hadn't forgotten what had happened the last time I saw Katty and Bren together. Seeing them flirting with each other had filled me with anger and confusion before. But when I looked at them now, something was different. Without speaking, I tried to tell him that.

I locked gazes with Katty again and I felt … nothing. No pain. No resentment or anger. I wasn't sure if that was a good thing or a bad thing.

"The dragon understands you?" Bren still looked amazed.

I nodded and handed Bren his sword back. So much for keeping my special ability a secret. "Usually he listens to me. I'm not making any promises, though. You might want to keep your distance."

Strolling over to one of the dead wolves, I put my boot on its neck and pulled my knife out of its head. That simple hunting knife was turning out to be awfully handy. It had saved my life more than once now. It was like a good luck charm.

I could feel Katty staring at me as I walked toward where she was sitting in the snow. She was holding her father's head in her lap. It was hard to tell if she was happy, sad, angry, or just confused. Maybe she was trying to process the situation. Or maybe she was trying to figure out how I had grown almost two feet taller in a few weeks.

Mr. Crookin was conscious, but I could tell he was in a lot of pain. I saw right away where he had been bitten by one of the wolves. The bite was deep, and his leg was bleeding badly. I used my knife to cut away his pant leg to get a better look. Even though my medical training wasn't very extensive, I knew I could treat something like this. At least, I could make sure he wouldn't bleed to death before they made it to Blybrig.

"Get me a belt, or a strap. Something to stop the bleeding," I ordered.

"Right!" Bren ran off obediently.

I tried to smile at Mr. Crookin, who was staring at me with a glazed look in his eyes. He had snowflakes in his bushy beard, and even from that distance I could smell the scent of scorched metal on his clothes. It brought back memories of being in the forge when Katty and I were younger.

"I'll get you fixed up. You can be back on the road by morning. They'll be able to see to it properly at the infirmary," I told him. Then I looked at Katty. It made her flinch, as though she were afraid of me. "Try to get him into the back of the wagon. We need to move away from here. The smell of blood might bring other predators."

She stared and didn't say a word. It was really uncomfortable.

I left them to retrieve my bag from Mavrik's back. He snorted at me when I came close, flashing me a look that I understood even without the visual aid in my mind; an image of the last time I'd talked to Katty. We had argued, and it hadn't ended well. I wasn't the sharpest person when it came to girls, but even I could tell things still weren't okay between us.

"I know, I know," I muttered as I slung my travel bag over my shoulder. "I'm not exactly thrilled about it either, you know. But I can be civilized. Hopefully she can, too. Besides, I'm not going to let Mr. Crookin bleed to death. So just stay close, okay? Make sure we don't get any more surprise guests. And don't eat Bren."

Mavrik chirped at me and took off, stirring up the snow as he went. When it settled, I found myself staring at the huge cat's dead body again. All my life, I'd heard of animals like this living deep in the mountains. This was the first time I had ever actually seen one, though. Even when I traveled on the same path through the mountains alone with my father last year, we hadn't seen anything like this. Ulric always kept a fire going when we made camp. He'd told me once that fire and the smell of humans was enough to keep anything dangerous away. These kinds of animals weren't used to the smells and sounds of people.

I stared down at the cat's body and remembered the sense of chaos that had come off of it. Something about it wasn't right. I just couldn't figure out what.

When I climbed into the back of the covered wagon, Mr. Crookin was talking quietly with his daughter. I couldn't hear exactly what he said, but I know I heard him mention my name a few times. As I approached them, they both went silent and stared up at me. It made things even more awkward.

Katty helped her father into one of the small beds, and started taking his boots off. She scooted as far away from me as she possibly could when I came over and put my bag down. I tried not to pay her any attention. In such close quarters, it was difficult. She was acting like I might decide to hit her or something, even though I had never once tried to hurt her in my life. I knew better than to ever raise a hand against a girl. I'd seen my father do it enough times to understand no good came of it.

I took out my small first aid box, and carefully laid out all the tools, gauze, and salve I would need. I didn't have much. This kit was supposed to be for emergencies. I wondered if I should try healing him the same way I had healed Sile's wife. But I quickly shook those thoughts from my mind; I'd already revealed one secret today. I wasn't even sure I could trust these people anymore. And compared to talking to dragons and animals, healing someone with my touch was bound to raise a few eyebrows. It might even get me in serious trouble if someone at Blybrig found out.

"Bring hot water," I told Katty. "I have to sterilize the needle before I can start."

She still didn't speak to me. She got up, and left the wagon without a single word. Even though I wanted to ignore her, I couldn't help but watch her go. She had changed so much since last year. Sure, she was beautiful, but her personality was totally different. I wasn't sure I liked it. She was like a stranger to me now.

"She's a stubborn girl," Mr. Crookin said in his gruff voice. I guess he felt bad about the cold way she was treating me.

"It's fine." I started inspecting his wound, trying to wipe away the blood so I could see where I needed to stitch.

Mr. Crookin made a snorting noise. "Well, it seems you haven't changed much after all," he said. "You know, you might do better in life if you got angry every now and then. Especially when people deserve it."

I didn't answer.

Bren came in suddenly, holding a leather belt out to me. "Here. This is what you wanted, right? We got a small fire going outside using some of that dragon venom. We should have hot water soon." He sat down nearby, and I noticed that he couldn't even look at the wound without his face getting pasty white. The sight of blood must have made him sick.

I used the belt to make a tourniquet. When Katty came in lugging a pot of steaming hot water, I sterilized the needle and used a wet washcloth to clean the wound. Then I started sewing it shut. I have to give Mr. Crookin some credit for being a tough old man. He didn't flinch even once. When I finished, I smeared some smelly herbal salve over the wound so it wouldn't get infected. Finally, I wrapped it in a few layers of gauze.

"That should hold you for a few days." I smiled at Mr. Crookin as I finished bandaging his leg. "Sorry if it hurt. This was my first time treating a real wound."

Mr. Crookin nodded in thanks. "You did fine, boy."

"I checked the axel, Master Crookin." Bren piped up suddenly. He was looking better now that the bloody part was over. "It's not broken. It came out of line. If we can readjust it, then we could get back underway."

"I'll help you. He shouldn't move around too much. It might pull the stitches out." I offered as I packed up my first aid kit and put it back in my bag. "Then I'll be out of your way."

Bren frowned like he was disappointed. He looked toward Katty as though he hoped she would say something to stop me. She didn't. She still refused to speak while I was there.

"At least let us feed you a meal before you go," Bren insisted. "You saved our lives. Those wolves came out of nowhere. I've never seen them attack a wagon like that."

I shook my head. "Neither have I."

"And then the mountain cat." Bren was starting to

sound nervous. "It's just like those guards said … "

"Guards?" I asked.

Bren's expression was grim. He fidgeted with his hands while he started to explain. "We passed a few guardsmen as we were leaving Mithangol. They warned us to be careful. There are rumors spreading throughout the kingdom of wild animals going crazy like this. They're attacking people for no reason. And not only predators like wolves and mountain cats. Peaceful animals like deer are doing it, too."

His story sounded a little too unbelievable. I couldn't visualize a herd of deer attacking anyone. Deer were supposed to be peaceful, timid animals. Still, my mind kept racing back to that feeling of chaos I'd felt from the wolves and the huge cat. If the deer were possessed by that same kind of rage, then they might actually do something like that. It was terrifying to think that it might really be some kind of sickness that was spreading through the kingdom. I dreaded to think of what would happen if people started getting infected.

"I'll help you fix the wagon," I decided out loud. "And stay for dinner, if you're sure that's what you want."

Bren smiled and stood. "Okay!" He still had a lot of energy for someone who'd just been in a fight for his life.

I left my bag in the wagon and went out into the snow with him. While he unhitched the horses, I looked around for a good, sturdy tree branch we could use to lift the wagon long enough to reposition the wheel axel. Lucky for us, the wagon wasn't very big. It was heavy, though, thanks to all the tools and supplies inside.

Once the horses were clear, Bren crawled under the wagon and got ready to move the axel back into place while I used the long branch to wedge under the wagon and lift it. It was incredibly heavy. My arms were shaking as I pushed down on the branch and tried to keep it steady. Thankfully, it only needed to be raised a few inches. Bren wiggled the long metal axel back and forth, trying to position it.

Then something cracked.

Bren yelled as the branch snapped in half and the weight of the wagon started to collapse down on top of him. I reacted in the blink of an eye. I grabbed the wagon right under the wheel and lifted with all my strength. My arms ached. My back creaked. The full weight of the wagon seemed to be bearing down on me, but I couldn't let it fall or Bren would be crushed.

"Hurry and get out!" I yelled. My fingers were starting to slip. I could feel the wood scraping on my skin, setting my palms on fire. It was like trying to hold up a small house with my bare hands.

"No!" Bren shouted back. "I-I've almost got it!" I heard him frantically trying to wiggle the axel again.

"You idiot! Do you want to die? I can't hold it!" I started to yell again. My fingers were definitely sliding. I knew I had maybe three more seconds left before I lost my grip.

Suddenly, the load lessened. Katty appeared right beside me out of nowhere, helping me hold the wagon up. She was a girl, but she had always been tough. Apparently now that she'd been working with her father in the forge, she was even stronger. She helped hold the weight of the wagon long enough for me to get a better grip.

"Got it!" Bren immediately scrambled out from under the wagon. I dropped the weight back onto the axel, and the wagon settled with a groan.

"You almost got crushed, you know." I grumbled, trying to catch my breath and watching as Bren dusted the snow off his clothes. My fingers were still throbbing.

"Lucky for me you caught it, huh?" He smiled cheerfully. I was starting to wonder if he was dumb or something. "Anyway, we can hitch the horses back up now. Good work!"

I glanced sideways at Katty. She was actually smiling back at him. Seeing her in a good mood caught me off guard. Bren strolled away to fetch the horses, and she stood there beside me, shaking her head.

"I know what you're thinking," she said. I was stunned that she was actually talking to me. "No, he isn't stupid. He's just a happy person. Nothing ever gets him down. And I like him that way."

I crossed my arms and shrugged. "Stupid or not, I suppose he does seem like a nice guy." I couldn't help but smile a little myself.

"Are your hands okay?" she asked. "You could have broken your back like that, you know."

Her concern surprised me even more. I glanced down at my fingers. "Sore. Maybe a little bruised. But fine."

She was quiet again. I watched as she helped Bren fasten the horses back to the wagon. We worked together again to get the heavy wagon out of the snow and back onto the side of the road. It took almost an hour because of how far into the deep drifts the wagon had gone. But eventually, we got underway.

Katty and Bren sat on the driver's seat next to each other. From inside the wagon, I could hear them talking and laughing together. I sat on the floor beside some crates of raw metal slabs, feeling awkward and out of place again. I didn't like Katty that way anymore, but I still didn't like the feeling I got when I saw them together. It reminded me of how she had dismissed me because I was a halfbreed. That still hurt to think about. In fact, it hurt way worse than being rejected just because she didn't like me that way.

"I hear that instructor of yours, Sile Derrick, has been relieved of his duties as a dragonrider." Mr. Crookin was lying on his bed. Hearing his voice made me jump a little because I thought he was asleep.

"Yeah," I answered. "He got hurt last year. He can't ride anymore."

"Convenient. But it's a good thing." Mr. Crookin made a thoughtful, grumbling sound like a sleepy old bear. "Rumor is that he's a dead man walking. Any man who goes into that wicked forest and comes back alive and unharmed must have some kind of dark magic in him. That kind of thing always ends in bloodshed. It's better if he doesn't take anyone else down with him."

I sat up a little. "What do you mean? Wicked forest... are you talking about Luntharda? Sile has been there?"

Mr. Crookin let out a throaty, coughing noise. "Yes, well, that's the rumor. It was years ago, not long after the war first began. They say he deserted his fellow riders on the eve of battle and went into the forest alone, only to return three days later completely untouched. Either he has the luck of the gods, or there is something wicked in him, as well. Luntharda takes no prisoners. It wouldn't simply let a human man go like that."

I was so surprised that I sat there, staring at Mr. Crookin while the wagon jostled and bounced. Sile had never said a word about this to me before. I wondered if Felix even knew about it.

Thoughts were still racing through my brain when

Mr. Crookin added, "I worried he might be trying to work a bit of that dark magic on you. It's strange that he took such a liking to you. That forest has already fouled your blood, but you do seem to have a decent heart in spite of that. My wife insists that you're a good boy."

I still couldn't say a word. My brain was stuck on the news that Sile had gone into Luntharda all alone and yet somehow he'd survived. Last year, I had done a lot of reading about Luntharda. There were more horrible things in that forest than I could even count. Imaging that Sile had gone into the forest alone and survived—let alone walked away from it without a single scratch—didn't seem possible. It had to be a rumor.

"Do you love my girl?" Mr. Crookin asked suddenly.

I snapped out of my daze. "S-sir?"

"Katalina. My daughter. Are you in love with her?" he asked again.

I swallowed uncomfortably. Mr. Crookin had never spoken to me this much before, and how I felt about his daughter was the last thing in the world I wanted to discuss with him. Still, I decided it was best to give him an honest answer. "No. Maybe I did love her once, a little. But not anymore." My throat was stiff with embarrassment.

Mr. Crookin was quiet then. I thought maybe he was trying to decide what to say, or that he might be offended by my answer. Then I heard him start to snore. I slumped back against the side of a crate, and let out a sigh of relief.

I glanced back toward the front of the wagon where Katty and Bren were sitting side-by-side on the driver's seat. I couldn't help but wonder why Mr. Crookin had asked me that all of a sudden. Just by the way she blushed and smiled at Bren, it was obvious that she liked him, not me. She'd never been that way around me. At least, if she had, I'd never noticed it before.

The fact that Bren wasn't such a bad person was still sinking in. Part of me had been hoping he would turn out to be a jerk because then it would be a lot easier to hate him. He was so cheerful all the time it seemed like he might have brain damage. I could tell he liked Katty a lot, too. They seemed happy together, and that didn't upset me like it had before. I didn't love her. She was just a memory. If they could be happy together, then I could be happy for them.

For some reason, the only person I could think about at that moment was Beckah. I reached into my vambrace and took out the handkerchief she'd made for me. I ran my fingers over the stitching of the two dragons, a black one and a blue one. Mavrik and Icarus. The more I thought about her, the more I realized I missed her. It made me smile.

Then I noticed Katty was turned around in her seat. She was staring right at me. Her eyes were locked on the handkerchief I was holding …

… and for whatever reason, she looked absolutely furious.

eleven

We stopped after nightfall and made a small campfire. Mr. Crookin was sound asleep. He wasn't running a fever, so for now it seemed like he would be all right. Bren and Katty were worried about him, and I tried my best to assure them that he was probably exhausted from so much blood loss. It was better to let him rest for now.

Bren and I sat by the fire while Katty prepared food for us. She threw together a simple stew with dried meat and vegetables in a big iron pot. It smelled so good, and I was starving. I didn't hold back my appetite. After three big bowls and a small loaf of bread, I finally sat back and sighed.

"You were hungry, huh?" Bren chuckled.

I blushed. "Yeah, I guess so."

"You know, I had a totally different picture of you in my head." Bren kept talking between bites of stew. "You don't look at all the way Katty described you. It's great to finally meet you."

I saw Katty's shoulders flinch slightly, but she didn't look up at us. She kept staring straight down into her own bowl.

If this conversation was making her uncomfortable, Bren was totally oblivious to it. "You're so tall! I swear, you look like you should be in your twenties."

"Actually, I'll be seventeen soon," I answered.

"Geez! I can't believe you're younger than me!" Bren laughed and grinned. "And you're a dragonrider. That is *so* awesome. I'm jealous! I bet you get a ton of love letters, huh? I swear, if anyone even mentions dragonriders, girls swoon all over the place. It must be nice to be so popular."

Immediately, the atmosphere became tense and awkward again. Out of the corner of my eye, I watched Katty. She had stopped eating, and was squeezing her spoon in her fist until her knuckles were white.

I swallowed hard, and looked down at the tops of my boots. "Not exactly."

Bren looked confused. "Why not?"

I didn't want to answer. How could he not know? Was he really that dense? I was a halfbreed—it didn't matter what job I had. Women would continue to treat me the same way Katty had. I would never be good enough. I would always be disgusting to them. I couldn't believe Bren didn't realize that.

"Ah, I get it," he said suddenly, like it was all clear to him now. "You're old fashioned! The romantic type, right? So then there's just one special girl. What's she like?"

For some reason, I was blushing like crazy. I kept staring down at the ground, trying to decide how to change the subject. I didn't know how to describe to anyone else how Beckah made me feel, and I didn't want to try. Not in front of these people.

Before I could answer, Katty stood up. "You're both idiots. This is a stupid conversation." She slammed her bowl down on the ground and stormed away from the campfire. Without another word, she disappeared into the back of the wagon.

Her sudden reaction left me in shock. For a few minutes, Bren and I sat there in stunned silence. Katty hadn't even finished her dinner. It didn't look like she was coming back for it, either.

"Sorry about that," Bren mumbled with a concerned frown. "I always do that."

"Do what?" I wasn't sure what he meant.

He sighed. "Say stuff without thinking. I guess I shouldn't bring that kind of thing up in front of her. I know you two had some kind of a relationship, right? She always told me it was nothing. She said you were more like a little brother to her. I didn't think she would care."

Even though I was totally embarrassed, I tried not to let it show. I shrugged, and forced a smile. I didn't want him to feel bad. It wasn't his fault, anyway. "It's okay. Don't worry about it."

"I should have told you already," he said. "Thanks for saving us today. I can make swords all day long, but when it comes to fighting ... I guess I've never been good at that kind of thing. I was so relieved when you showed up."

Bren reached over to shake my hand, and I caught myself hesitating. People didn't thank me for stuff like that very often. Even Sile, after going through so much last year to save his life from being sacrificed by the Lord General, had just growled angrily that I shouldn't risk myself for his sake.

"It's my duty as a dragonrider to fight and protect citizens. You don't have to thank me." I finally shook his hand, and we exchanged a smile.

"That reminds me." He perked up suddenly, pointing to the scimitar at my hip. "Can I see your weapon? I noticed it before, but I couldn't get a good look."

I unbuckled the scimitar from my belt and handed it over to him. "It's pretty old and beat up." I almost felt like I should apologize for that, since he was a blacksmith. He was bound to notice how worn and dull it was. It probably looked like I hadn't taken care of it.

"Wow," he breathed in awe as he looked over the scabbard. I saw his eyes grow wider. He handled it carefully, looking over the details on the hilt and blade. "I've never seen anything like this before."

His reaction confused me. Sure, it had an intricate design on it, but it was so beat up you'd barely notice. "What do you mean?"

Bren scooted a little closer so he could show me. "Well, look here. The shape of it means it was definitely made by a human. Humans always make blades in this style. They're straight and slender. You can see the blade is only slightly curved, right?"

I nodded. It was definitely a scimitar, but the curve was gradual and elegant, rather than severe and dramatic.

"Elves always make their blades leaf-shaped. And they never put cross-guards on it, like this one. So whoever made this blade was definitely a human." He turned it over, brushing his fingers over the faded designs on the hilt and pommel. "Look here, you can see words used to be engraved on the blade itself. Humans rely do that. Not unless it belonged to a very important family. And the stag," he hesitated. "The stag is the emblem of the gray elf royal family. Kind of like our king uses the eagle as his symbol. I've never seen the stag on a blade before. Elves are very possessive of their weapons, you know. Very few of them ever fall into human hands."

I hadn't noticed the words engraved on the blade itself before. They were so faint, almost rubbed down until they were completely gone. I couldn't make out what they said. The more he talked, the more I started to understand why he was so amazed by this scimitar. It was stranger than I'd ever realized.

"So maybe it was a human blacksmith that made this scimitar." Bren was almost whispering now. "But it looks like it was made it for an elf. Why else put that stag on it? I've been studying weaponry and armor my entire life. I've studied every style and method of making all kinds of weapons, and I've never heard of a blade like this before. Look at all the details and effort they put in to make it look like the perfect blend of human and elven design. It's incredible! Where did you get it?"

I cringed. I didn't want to tell him I'd taken it from my brother's belongings. "Well, I think it's some kind of family heirloom. I found it buried at the bottom of a trunk in my father's house."

"It's a shame you don't know anything else about it. I bet it has quite a history." Bren started to hand the scimitar back to me. Then he stopped. His eyes met mine directly. "Let me fix it for you. You know, as a way of saying thanks for saving my life today. I can repair the damage and make it look like new again."

"I-I can't let you do something like that for free," I stammered. "That kind of thing is usually expensive, right?"

"I want to!" He started insisting. "Besides, I haven't made a name for myself as a blacksmith yet, so I need all the practice I can get. And I promise, I'm very good with swords and armor. I won't mess it up."

His mind was made up, and I decided it was probably best not to try to talk him out of it. He seemed determined. So I smiled and nodded in thanks. "I appreciate it."

Bren grinned from ear to ear. "Great! I'll have it finished for you before we leave Blybrig, I promise."

"I'd ask about hiring you to make me some new armor, but I don't want to cause any more problems between you and Katty," I said. "Seems like she's had enough of me to last her a lifetime."

His smile faltered a little, and he sighed loudly again. "She's hard to understand sometimes. It's too late for me, though. I'm already in love with her."

I didn't know what to say. He was so honest about everything; it was kind of intimidating. I shifted uncomfortably, and looked up at the dark sky. "I should get going before the sun rises."

"You're sure you don't want to rest here for the night?" Bren gave me a concerned look. "It's late. You've got to be tired after what happened today."

Honestly, I should have been about to drop. I hadn't slept well in days. Instead, just knowing I was this close to Blybrig made my head buzz with energy. And thinking about what Mr. Crookin had told me about Sile didn't help either. I was restless. I knew I wouldn't be able to sleep now, even if I tried.

I smirked at him and gave him a thumbs up. "I'm fine. See you in a few days. Try not to get eaten by anything."

Bren smiled back at me, and gave me a thumbs up in return. "May you have safe travels, dragonrider."

I gathered up my bag and left the camp as quickly as possible. Mavrik and I took off into the midnight sky, leaving the ground far below. Once we broke the cloud cover again, the heavens opened up overhead. The moonlight was so bright. It washed over everything, making the world seem like it was made out of platinum. We chased the shooting stars, skimming the tops of the clouds and racing toward the dawn.

As the sun began to rise and turn the horizon soft shades of pink, I got my first look at the Devil's Cup since last year. It put a big smile on my face right away. I could sense Mavrik's excitement, too. He let out a booming roar as we started our descent down toward the valley.

It was early in spring, but all the prickly plants and cacti were already in full bloom. They brought an unnatural amount of color to a place that was usually nothing but hot, arid desert. In the very middle of the crescent-shaped valley, Blybrig Academy stood proud. I could see the sunlight glinting off the roof of the breaking dome, the place where I had first met Mavrik. I saw the Roost, crowded with dragons and riders like always.

I was so busy looking down I forgot to look up. A sudden roar almost made me have a heart attack. Nova swept in beside us, chirping a greeting to Mavrik. She was the big, beautiful female dragon that belonged to

Felix. Her coppery colored scales gleamed with patterns like a jungle snake.

Her saddle was empty, and I reached down to pat Mavrik's neck to get his attention. "Where's Felix?"

Mavrik chattered to Nova, who roared in reply and veered away, sailing through the sky down toward the academy. Mavrik sent me a mental picture of the student dormitory. I guessed that Nova was just out exploring while Felix was getting settled into our room.

"Well, let's hurry then!" I patted his scaly neck again, and he growled in agreement.

Mavrik was eager to join Nova. When we finally landed outside the academy, he barely gave me enough time to untie my bag from his back before he was taking off again to chase her through the clouds. The burst of wind off his wings made me stagger back. I tripped over my own feet and landed on my rear end. Mavrik didn't care. He was too busy nipping playfully at Nova's tail.

"Flirt!" I yelled after him.

He didn't answer.

I got up, dusting the dirt off my pants and slinging my bag over one shoulder. Suddenly I heard a familiar voice from behind me.

"Riding in bareback. That's a first." My new instructor, Lieutenant Jace Rordin, was standing right inside the academy's front gates in full armor. By the way he was glaring at me, anyone else would have thought he was about to chew my head off ... but that was the way Jace looked at everyone. I'd never seen him smile.

"Trying to show off?" he growled.

I stopped and saluted him by putting a fist across my heart and bowing slightly. "Almost dying every time he decides to take a steep turn isn't showing off, sir."

Jace snorted. His eyes scanned me over from head to toe. That's when I realized he actually had to look *up* to meet my gaze now. I was taller than him. He still had a much stockier build, but this was definitely new.

"What happened to you?" I could sense him still sizing me up.

I shrugged, and it was hard not to smile. "A lot. It's kind of hard to explain."

"Humph." He just scoffed and turned away, walking ahead of me into the academy. "Well, at least I won't have to worry about someone accidentally stepping on you during morning drills anymore. I was getting tired of scraping you off the bottom of everyone else's boots."

"Yes, sir." I decided this was probably Jace's attempt at being happy for me.

"Go ahead and get settled into your room. Third floor this time. That sidekick of yours already picked up your books and maps." He started barking orders at me right away. "See that you get all your equipment on rush order. You need to be fully outfitted when training starts."

"Yes, sir," I repeated.

"Morning drills start at dawn on the first day of training. You don't have a saddle, so I don't expect you to fly drills until then. But I better see you working on your ground combat maneuvers. Have that friend of yours help you." He went on and on. For some reason, it was a huge relief to have someone breathing down my neck, growling orders at me again. It was familiar, and it put my nerves at ease.

"Yes, sir. Thank you, sir." I stopped to salute him again.

He gave me a cold look. "What are you thanking me for, avian?"

"I-I guess for not treating me any differently," I stammered. "You know, because I look like this now."

Jace frowned. "Why would I treat you any differently? I don't care if you have six eyes and hooves for feet. You better have your butt in that saddle as soon as possible, understood? No excuses."

I nodded and turned toward the dormitory. Once I had my back to him, I couldn't keep from smiling anymore; it was *so* good to be back. The world made more sense here. I knew what I had to do, where I was supposed to be, and what was expected of me. That was the best kind of therapy a man could ask for.

I walked past the armories on the way to the student dormitory. Some of the blacksmiths and tackmasters were already there, heating up their forges and taking orders for saddles and gear. I knew I needed to get back there soon and place my orders so my equipment would be ready before training started. I didn't have any time to waste.

I tried not to look for my father. He'd moved to a different city, but I knew he would still come back to Blybrig for spring. It was when he usually made most of his money. Thankfully, I didn't see Ulric anywhere as I passed. It made me nervous to even think about running into him. I wasn't sure how he'd treat me now that he'd basically disowned me.

Groups of other boys were hanging around outside the student dormitory when I walked up to the door. They were fledglings, I guessed, and they stared at me with wide eyes as I went by. I was used to being stared at like that, but it almost seemed like those boys were actually afraid of me. Beckah had seemed scared of me, too, at first. I wondered if Felix would act like that.

The dining hall on the first floor was just how I remembered. It always smelled like fresh bread in there. I made a mental note to stop back by for a late breakfast as soon as I could. As I went up the stairs, I passed the second floor where I'd shared a room with Felix last year. There were more fledgling students clamoring in the hall, looking for their names written on the doors. It brought back a lot of memories.

The third floor was much quieter. Only a few other avians were hanging out in the hallway, but I didn't recognize any of them. They were wearing a different style uniform than I had worn last year, and some of them had golden stripes stitched onto their shoulders. I wondered what that meant. I'd never noticed it before. Last year, my only focus had been survival, so a lot of things had just passed right under my nose.

My stomach started twisting into nervous knots as I walked down the hall, looking for my name on the placards that were nailed to all the doors. Each one had the name of an instructor and the names of his three students below it. Last year, we had only been in pairs of two. The avian class was much bigger, so I assumed each instructor probably had to take on an extra student.

When I finally found the placard with my name, I stopped dead in my tracks. Shock hit me like a brick to the temple as I read the names carved into the placard over and over:

6
Sn. Lt. Rordin
Jaevid Broadfeather
Lord Felix Farrow
Lord Lyon Cromwell

All I could do was stare at it for a minute or two. I blinked and leaned closer to the door. I was seriously hoping my eyes were playing tricks on me. That couldn't be Lyon's name. Lyon Cromwell was going to be teamed up with us? Was this some kind of sick joke? Lyon had betrayed us not once or twice, but *three* times last year. He was a coward and a traitor. He'd also used me like his personal punching bag a few times. I wasn't even sure how he'd managed to get away with his betrayal and still be in the academy at all. He'd vanished right after he abandoned us to be mauled by Icarus and the Lord General, and as far as I knew, no one had said a word about where he went.

I started to get queasy and angry all at the same time. Then the door opened and smacked me right in the face. I dropped my bag and staggered back, holding my nose.

"Whoops!" A familiar voice was laughing from the other side of the door.

Felix stuck his head out of the room, grinning from ear to ear the same way he always did when he was up to something. "Sorry! Didn't see you there, man."

I stared at him. He hadn't changed much at all. His hair was a little longer, but it was still that same dark golden color. His wavy bangs swept across his forehead, and his light brown eyes glinted with mischief. He was looking back and forth down the hall like he was waiting for someone.

"Hey, if you see a little halfbreed coming this way, let me know, will you? Just whistle or something. I've got a bucket of water set up over the door and—"

"Felix!" I put my hand down and glared at him.

"Do I know you?" I watched him blink at me like he was confused. He didn't recognize me. Slowly, he started narrowing his eyes and tilting his head to the side a little. Then his mouth fell open.

"J-Jae!" he yelled.

I scowled and crossed my arms. "Seriously? You didn't recognize me at all?"

Felix punched me in the shoulder so hard it sent me rocking onto my heels. That's when I realized he'd been going easy on me last year whenever we sparred together. Really, *really* easy, apparently.

"You jerk! Why would you do that?" I yelled back at him as I clutched my shoulder. "That hurt!"

"You ruined my welcome home present!" He reared back to hit me again.

"Present?" I dodged his swing as he tried to punch me in the face. "You were going to drop a bucket of water on my head! What kind of stupid present is that?" I grabbed his arm as he swung at me again, stepping in close to throw off his balance before I slung him down onto the ground.

"I worked hard on it!" He was laughing as I tried to wrestle him into a headlock on the ground.

It didn't work. I was taller, but he was still much bulkier and a lot stronger. He jabbed another punch into the pit of my stomach. Immediately, I couldn't breathe. While I was choking for air, he flipped us over and pinned me to the ground with a knee in my back.

"Well, it's definitely you," he chuckled. "You're still terrible at this."

"Get off!" I rasped. I could barely talk because my stomach was throbbing from where he'd hit me.

"Fine, fine. But you lose." He stepped off, grabbed the back of my tunic, and tried to pull me back to my feet. He had a much harder time managing that now that I was taller than he was. "Seriously, though. What happened to you? You look like a twenty-year-old! Did you find a witch to cast a spell on you or something?"

I was still rubbing my stomach and my shoulder. I couldn't even stand up straight. "I finally hit puberty, I guess," I wheezed. "Do I seriously look *that* old?"

"Hit puberty?" Felix laughed loudly. Other students in the hall were staring at us now. "You didn't just hit it. You mugged it in a dark alley and left it to die. What are you now? Six foot three? Six foot four?"

I blushed and snatched up my bag. It was embarrassing to have him making a scene in the middle of the hallway. The other avians were staring at us like we were crazy. "I haven't measured," I grumbled as I hobbled toward our room.

"Your hair is different, too. Is that because of your gray elf blood?" He started poking me in the back as he followed. "Too bad you couldn't manage to bulk up a little more, huh? Then someone might actually mistake you for a dragonrider this time around. But no one can have everything, I guess. Look at you, you're so lanky— like a flag pole."

I knew he was teasing me. No one liked watching me squirm more than Felix Farrow. And if I fought back, it would only make things worse. The teasing never stopped once he knew he had some leverage that embarrassed me. I'd already made that mistake last year when he found out I was writing "love" letters to Katty.

"Shut up! It's not that big of a deal!" I grabbed the doorknob and started to go inside.

Felix tried to stop me. "Hey wait a min—"

It was too late.

The bucket fell from where he had it balanced over the

door, landing right on my head. Ice-cold water splashed everywhere, drenching me from head to toe.

Felix was laughing like a maniac.

I sputtered and pulled the bucket off my head so I could throw it at him.

"It's not my fault! I did warn you." He grinned, grabbing my shoulder and giving it a friendly shake. "By the way, welcome back."

twelve

My boots and socks were still squishing with water as I walked out of the dormitory. Felix was hot on my heels, and he hadn't stopped talking since I hit the doorstep. I could feel him staring at me. Every now and then, he poked at me again like he wasn't sure I was real or not. Finally, I couldn't take it anymore.

"Would you stop that? It's getting annoying," I growled in frustration.

Felix looked up at me with amazement still written all over his face. "Sorry. It's kind of hard to believe this is really you. I keep expecting to blink and suddenly you'll be back to your old scrawny self again."

I could feel my face starting to get hot with embarrassment. "Tell me about it. I still don't recognize my own reflection."

"And you honestly don't know what did this to you?"

he asked. "Are you going to come back looking like an old man the next time we get a break from training?"

I shot him a glare. "I don't think so. Look, it's not like I know all that much about gray elves either. You know I wasn't raised in Luntharda. I was a kid when my mom died, and she had sheltered me from everyone my whole life—including other gray elves. I only know what I heard the doctor say, and who knows how much of that is even true."

"And what did the doctor say?" He looked interested.

My memories of what had happened were blurred because of the pain I'd been in. It was like trying to remember a dream, so I just told him what I could. The gray elves all grew that way, apparently. They grew fast, in short bursts, instead of gradually over time. All I knew for sure was that it had hurt—a *lot*—and I wasn't looking forward to it ever happening again.

"I can't believe your mother never mentioned any of this to you." Felix sounded skeptical, like he didn't quite believe me.

"I was twelve when she died, Felix," I snapped at him angrily. "We were just trying not to die of starvation. We didn't exactly have the time to discuss my future."

Felix raised his hands in surrender. "Geez. Relax. You're kind of cranky now, you know that? Did all that growing give you mood swings or something?"

I scowled and elbowed him in the ribs. "I'm not cranky."

We walked together toward the armories where craftsmen were hard at working making armor, saddles, and weapons. I had Sile's bag of coins in my hand, and I was trying to ignore the way the other students and instructors were staring at me as we passed. It was bad enough to have them look at me that way; Felix could have at least been a little more sensitive about it. It made me irritated that he was being this way. I wanted things to go back to normal.

We went to the blacksmiths' side of the armory first, and I looked for the same old man who'd made my armor last year. It seemed like a good idea to stick with someone who'd already worked with me before. At least I knew he wasn't going to intentionally compromise my equipment. I'd seen last year how badly things could go if something on a saddle broke during flight.

On our way, we passed another group of avian students. Once again, I didn't recognize any of them, but I did notice they looked a little older than us. They were also wearing those same golden stripes stitched onto the shoulders of their uniforms.

I leaned over to Felix. "What are those stripes for? Do they outrank us?" I still wasn't familiar enough with the order of power amongst the dragonriders to know who outranked me. I just assumed I had to salute everyone except for fledglings and other avians.

"Hah! They'd like you to think so. Don't let them talk down to you." Felix smirked. "We get four tries to pass this year in training. Didn't you know that? If you fail the battle scenario, or you don't perform well in interrogation training, they give you a stripe and you get to try again next year. After three stripes, they put a circle on your shoulder, and that means it's your last chance to pass. Trust me, you do not want to get a circle. They always give those guys the hardest time."

"Does anyone pass on the first try?" I asked. I had to wonder. There seemed to be a lot of avians walking around with stripes on their shoulders.

Felix shrugged. "Sure, I guess some do. But it's not the end of the world if you don't. The whole point of this training is to learn how to hold up under pressure, so the more you endure, the stronger you are."

I let that sink in as we walked the rest of the way to the blacksmith's shop set up in one of the small forges. So even if I messed up this time, I could try again next year? Hearing that left me puzzled. Sile had always made it sound like this was the only chance I'd get.

The blacksmith from last year didn't seem to even notice that I had basically doubled in size since he measured me before. Or if he did, he didn't say a word about it. He worked, grumbled, and scratched at his beard while he jotted down my information.

When he started fitting me for a helmet, I noticed that there were a lot of different styles. Last year, all his samples had been plain and basic. Fledglings didn't need nice armor for training. Each one of these helmets had a different shape and design. He picked them up one by one, taking his time to fit it onto my head, and then examine carefully how it looked. Finally, he seemed to settle on one he liked. It fit my head snugly, and the glass slit for my eyes was a little wider, so I could see more.

"Going traditional?" Felix asked. I could see his expression through the glass eye-shield, and he didn't look happy. "The style seems a little old-fashioned to me."

The blacksmith made an annoyed, barking sound as he yanked the sample helmet off my head. "Bah! What do you know? Who is the armor master here, you or I?"

"It's okay." I didn't want Felix to start an argument over something like that. Maybe he didn't realize how personally these craftsmen took their work. After years of watching Ulric make dragon saddles, I knew better than most not to question them like that. "Traditional is probably best. I stand out enough already as it is."

Felix frowned like he didn't agree. "At least do some engraving. Otherwise, I might as well just loan him my grandfather's armor."

The blacksmith made another angry sound, like a mixture of a growl and a cough, but he didn't answer. Instead, he went back to work. When he finished, he held up his notes for me to see.

"Sign there. Then pay up," he ordered, jabbing a gritty finger at the bottom of the page.

I scanned over the notes. I couldn't read his jumbled writing at all, but I signed my initials at the bottom anyway. When I counted out his payment, I ended up handing over a third of the coins from the stash Sile had given me. It made me anxious about how much money I was costing him. How long did it take to earn this much? Shouldn't this money be spent on his own family?

"Never seen anyone jump from a si three to an eight in a year," the blacksmith muttered. It caught me off guard. Even though he probably didn't get many halfbreed customers, I'd assumed he didn't remember me. He crammed the coins in his apron and waved me off. "It'll be ready in two days."

It took a little longer to find the tackmaster who had made my saddle last year. After we did, and got Mavrik to agree to being fitted with the wax mold again, the exchange went basically the same way. I picked out a more basic, traditional design made out of black leather, and Felix complained that it was too plain. Apparently, I was expected to have a more ornate saddle since this would be the one I used in battle someday.

In the end, I insisted on sticking with the most basic

style. I still couldn't shake off my guilt about spending all Sile's money that way. It seemed like a waste. I didn't really need all the frills and details that Felix kept insisting on. They were just for decoration.

"It's fine," I told him. "It probably took Sile a long time to earn this money. I can't blow it all on stuff I don't even need. I'll get the basics, and send whatever money is leftover back to him. He's got a family to feed, you know."

"He gave you that money so you *could* blow it on outfitting. A rider's saddle is supposed to be his pride. It's a mark of accomplishment." Felix crossed his arms stubbornly. He didn't get it. He was the son of a powerful duke, so I knew money was probably never an issue for his family. But I had experienced first hand how much difference a little bit of money could make. It could mean the difference between eating or going to bed hungry.

I rolled my eyes and paid for the plain saddle anyway. "It's just a sa ' e, Felix. My bond with Mavrik is my pride. It's all I need. Anyway, I haven't exactly accomplished anything yet, have I?"

Felix couldn't really argue with that, but he sulked the whole way back to the dormitory. When we sat down in the dining hall, he slammed a tray of food down between us. There were two big plates piled high with food. For the first time since my weird growth spurt, I didn't feel guilty about eating as much as I wanted. I didn't waste any time diving into the fresh baked bread and roasted meat.

"You're different now." Felix was still glaring at me over the huge leg of turkey he was holding.

"How so?" I asked.

"I don't know. I can't put my finger on it. Something's

definitely changed, though," he answered with a mouthful of food. Then, in the blink of an eye, his sulky demeanor vanished like he'd forgotten all about the saddle and armor. He started grinning at me with that mischievous twinkle in his eyes again. "So. How's your girl? I bet she was surprised to see you like this, eh? Did you finally kiss her?"

"No." I'd given up trying to explain to him that Katty and I had never been a couple a long time ago. He assumed that because we'd written letters to each other. I just decided to go with it. "She basically dumped me right when I got back."

"Aw, that's rough." He looked genuinely sorry for me. "Did she say why?"

"Not exactly. I sort of came home and found her with someone else." It still stung to admit that. Not because I had any feelings for her anymore, though. "She's here with him, now. They're both working for her father as blacksmith apprentices."

Felix sat straight up in his chair, and looked like he was about to choke on his food. "You're kidding! She's here? Why didn't you say so before? I want to get a look at her."

I shook my head. "No way. She doesn't want me anywhere near her."

"What about the new guy?" he pressed. "Why don't you try to fight him for her? You'd probably win now that, well, you're practically a giant."

I frowned down at the half-eaten loaf of bread in my hand. "Because he's actually a nice person. It wasn't his fault. She told him I was like her little brother." My pride took another hit.

Felix cringed. "Ouch."

"Yeah. Tell me about it." I took a big bite of bread and chewed while I thought it over. "I'm not that upset, though. I was before. Now I think it's better this way."

He looked stunned. "Seriously?"

"Yeah." I shrugged.

Felix started eyeing me suspiciously. I could see the wheels turning while he tried to figure out why I wasn't more upset over being rejected like that. I'm sure anyone else would have been. But whenever I thought about my feelings, or girls, or any of that stuff ... it wasn't Katty's face that came to mind.

I could feel the lump under my vambrace where the handkerchief Beckah had made for me pressed against my forearm. It reminded me of the last time I'd seen her, standing on the edge of the ocean. I did *not* want Felix to know about any of that. I knew if he ever found out, the teasing would never end.

"So what about you? How was your time at home?" I changed the subject before he could start interrogating me.

Felix's eyes got dark, and he started picking at his food. He stabbed at his boiled potatoes like he was trying to murder them. "Terrible, as usual. I don't want to talk about it."

I was speechless. Felix had never shut me out like that before. But when it came to my personal life, I knew he would never let me dodge questions like that. I wasn't about to let him get away with it, either.

"You might as well just say it," I said. "I'm not going to let it go. So talk."

His lip curled some, like he was fighting back a snarl, and he stabbed another potato. I could see rage burning in his eyes. "Seriously, leave it alone."

I was willing to call his bluff. I leaned forward and stole a potato off his plate just to spite him. "Talk," I demanded again.

He shot me a dangerous look and stayed silent for a few minutes. I didn't say anything, either. Finally, he let out a loud sigh and surrendered. "Dad's got some kind of nervous illness. He won't even come out of his room. My mother tells me he's sick with worry that I won't uphold my duties as his heir, or that I'll be killed in battle and there'll be no one left to take over the estate. She says if I acted more like an adult and took more responsibility, he might get better."

I hoped I was hearing that wrong. "You mean, they're saying it's your fault he's sick?"

Felix didn't look up. His expression was so bleak, I barely recognized him. I'd never seen him look like that. "Jae, it's always my fault when it comes to them. Dad was furious when I chose to become a dragonrider instead of staying home and learning to run our estate. If I wasn't their only child, I know he would have already disowned me. He's told me before he doesn't think I can handle being duke."

"I'm sorry." I didn't know what else to say.

He shook his head. "Don't be. I'm not giving this up. I've worked too hard. It feels wrong not to be here, you know? Dad can disown me, if he wants."

I couldn't help but frown. "You're giving up being a duke? Just to be a dragonrider?"

"Of course not. He won't *actually* disown me. I'm the only heir to my family's name. When my dad dies, there's no one else to take over except me. If I don't take his place as duke, our estate will have to be broken up amongst our extended family. Sooner or later, I'll have to retire as a dragonrider and take his place. In the meantime, I'm going to do what I want. And I want to be here." He said it like it was nothing, but I knew giving up being a dragonrider was a big deal. I had seen the effect it was having on Sile.

I thought about that while we finished eating. It was hard for me to see Felix as a noble. We had been through a lot together last year, and he'd never acted like someone with a lot of power or influence. Looking at him from across the table, I tried to decide if I could even picture him as one of those fat, rich men wearing fluffy silk shirts, fur cloaks, and lace.

No. I definitely couldn't picture that.

As we left the dining hall to go back to our room, Felix brought up the dragonrider ranking system again. He was amazed that I still didn't know anything about it, and started rattling off information faster than I could follow.

"Once we pass our avian year, we'll be sworn in as lieutenants," he explained.

"You mean like Sile was?" It didn't seem right for me to be the same rank as Sile and Jace yet. They had both fought in the war and served as instructors for years.

"Hah! No, of course not. They were *seasoned* lieutenants. That's different. It means they've fought in combat more than five times, or have done something worthy of being promoted," he said. When we got to the door of our room, he paused to show me where the placard had the abbreviation "Sn." before Jace's name.

"And that stands for seasoned?" I hadn't paid much attention to it before.

He nodded. "Although, most people just call them lieutenants anyway. They like to group us all together because generally we are the ones who do the most fighting. It takes a long time to get promoted past seasoned lieutenant, and once you do, it means less time on the actual battlefield."

Felix went on tell me about the other ranks. After seasoned lieutenants came captains, colonels, and then there were only three higher ranks a dragonrider could achieve. Those were the most prestigious offices in all of the king's forces.

"The two sky generals are in charge of all the forces north or south of the royal city," he went on as he opened the door. "But really, they're basically glorified errand boys. They spend most of their time behind a desk, and answering to the lord general when something goes wrong."

We both fell silent when he said that title. We'd met the last lord general, and it wasn't something either of us wanted to talk about where someone might overhear.

When I looked at Felix, I could see the frustration on his face. I wondered if he had the same concerns and suspicions I did. I knew for sure that none of what Academy Commander Rayken had told us last year was true. Of course, I had no real proof of that. But anyone with holes for eyes could see that it was some kind of a cover up. Someone was working hard to keep the truth hidden about what the Lord General had been doing with that god stone.

I started thinking back to when I first saw that stone. Commander Rayken had called it the god stone. I didn't know what that meant, or anything about the stone itself, but I could remember clearly how looking at it had made me feel. Just one glimpse of it had pulled me into some kind of weird trance. It still gave me chills. Thankfully,

Sile had been there to clamp a hand over my eyes and drag me away.

"So, what about being an academy commander?" I asked as I tried to shake those memories from my mind. "Where does that fall in the rankings?"

Felix shrugged as he wandered across our small room to flop down on his bed. "It's the same as captain, but there's only one academy so there's only one commander. The king hand-chooses the new academy commander himself. He usually gives it to a dragonrider who's shown good leadership in combat, or who's been injured such that he can't fight anymore. I'm actually surprised Sile didn't get it. It's not the most glamorous job in the world. I mean, he's basically a glorified babysitter for all of us, right?"

I got a sour taste in my mouth. Immediately, I remembered the rumor Mr. Crookin had told me while we were in the mountains. Thinking about Sile going into Luntharda made me forget how to walk. Before I realized it, I was standing in the doorway staring into space.

"What's wrong?" Felix was looking me over like he was concerned.

I wasn't   e how much I should tell him. Sile had warned me about saying too much. But I needed to know if the rumor was true or not.

"I saw Sile during the interlude," I finally admitted.

He frowned at me suspiciously. "What do you mean? He went to Mithangol?"

"No." I shut the door behind me before I dared to say anything else. "I got a letter from Beckah. She wanted me to come visit. They're living in Saltmarsh now. That's where I was when this growth spurt hit."

I started to explain as we went into our room. Our new dorm room wasn't that much bigger than the last one. It was more like a closet with three beds crammed into it, and a skinny window on the far wall. Felix had picked the bed in the middle, and I knew why without even having to ask. He wanted to put himself between Lyon and me in case our old enemy tried anything suspicious.

But now Felix was glaring at me like he might reconsider that. "You've been holding out on me," he said accusingly.

I winced and shuffled to sit on the bed next to the window. "Sile didn't want me to tell anyone. You know how he is." I knew that wasn't a good excuse.

"So what's going on?" he demanded.

It took a while for me to tell him about what had happened during the interlude. I didn't go into too much detail about how my family had abandoned me. That didn't even bother me that much; they'd never felt like a family to me, anyway. I was way more concerned about what had happened at the Derrick's house.

I told him everything about Beckah and Icarus, and how Sile didn't seem like he was wounded at all. He had been plenty capable when he sparred with me. I told him about my suspicion that someone was still after Sile. Whoever it was, Sile was running scared, and he had a lot to lose if they ever caught up to him. It had to be more than some dumb plot about an immortality ritual. I'd never even heard of a god stone, or whatever they called it.

I kept the details about what had happened with Sile's wife to myself. I didn't want anyone to know about how I had somehow healed her. I wasn't sure how it happened, or if I could even do it again. I wasn't ready to talk about it. I needed answers first. I knew if I said anything now, Felix would probably give me that weird look again—like I was transforming into some kind of monster right before his eyes. I hated it when people looked at me like that, but it hurt even more when Felix did it.

I told him about what had happened in the mountains, and how I couldn't talk to the wolves or the big mountain cat that had attacked me. I repeated everything Bren had told me about other animal attacks that were happening throughout the kingdom, but when it came time to ask him about the rumor ... I choked. I didn't know how to ask. It sounded like an accusation, and I didn't want to be the one pointing fingers at Sile's back.

"So," Felix sounded overwhelmed. He paused to take a breath. "Basically Beckah's a dragonrider, the animals are all going rabid, and Sile is still being hunted by some unknown enemy who wants to murder him and his family?"

I couldn't answer. It was a lot to think about, even when he summed it up like that.

"And you seriously thought you could handle all that by yourself?" He laughed, but the atmosphere was still tense. "Well, I don't know anything about crazy animals attacking people. I haven't heard anything about it. Sile's probably right about you getting too involved in his personal affairs. You'll get distracted from what you should be focused on. We're here to train. This is what's most important now, right? Just forget everything else. If you're constantly worrying about something a hundred miles away, you're liable to get killed by something two feet in front of you."

He did have a point. I already had so much on my

mind. It was hard to keep my eyes on my goal when the rest of my life felt like it was spinning out of control. Somehow, I had to get it together. I had to focus.

"Besides," he said. I could hear the mischievous grin in his voice without ever having to look at him. "You were holding out on the most important detail of all. How long did you think you could hide it from me?"

"Hide what?"

He chuckled wickedly. "That you're in love with Beckah."

I wanted to deny it. I also wanted to punch his lights out. But I couldn't do anything except look away with my ears burning like they were on fire.

Felix saw my reaction, and it made his eyes gleam dangerously. "You're not even denying it!"

"What's the point?" I tried to deflect. "You'll tease me about it no matter what I say."

He wasn't listening. He'd already launched into harassing me, and I knew nothing would stop him now. "You know, I kind of feel bad for telling everyone you weren't stupid. You should know better than to go after an instructor's daughter. Do you have a death wish?"

"I'm not going after her," I snapped. It wasn't a lie, but I wasn't necessarily proud of that. I kind of wished it had been.

"Yeah, right." Felix rolled his eyes. "Take a little advice from someone who actually has experience with girls, okay? Stay away from her. Sile will literally kill you if he ever catches you two together. And considering how many friends you have in the world, it'd probably be best not to lose the one who's paying for all your stuff."

thirteen

I still couldn't figure out how to ask Felix about the rumor. After he fell asleep, I couldn't stand to stay cooped up in our room either. I was restless, and listening to him snore wasn't helping at all. So I laced up my boots and went down to the dining hall to swipe a few spare beef bones from the trash bins. Then I started for the Roost.

The night air was cold, and the moon was so bright it put shadows on the ground. All the other students and instructors were closed up in their rooms, resting for the next day. The craftsmen had already put away their tools and shut down their work for the night. I caught a glimpse of the red-hot coals still smoldering in a few of the forges as I passed the armory. It made me wonder if Mr. Crookin and the others had ever made it here.

When I arrived at the Roost, a few avians were still doing the cleaning detail rounds. As fledglings, we'd gotten away with not having to do much in the way of care when it came to our dragons. But according to Felix, this year would be different. We would have to take turns cleaning all the stalls and lugging around big buckets of raw meat to feed the hungry dragons. We would have to oil our own saddles, and clean our own weapons.

None of the other avians paid me any attention as I made my way to Mavrik's stall. It wasn't a very large room, but it was just big enough for a dragon to nest in. The floor was covered with soft hay, and there was a trough of water along one of the walls. The Roost was built like a giant honeycomb, with no walls on one side so the dragons could fly in and out. Through the opening in Mavrik's stall, I could see the whole academy shimmering in the night. I could see the moonlight shining off the snowy mountain peaks in the distance, and thousands of stars.

Mavrik was curled up like a mound of blue scales. His wings were folded up tight, and his snout was resting on the tip of his tail. When I came in, he opened one of his big yellow eyes and studied me. I saw an image of myself sleeping in my bed flash through my mind.

I smirked and gave him a shrug. "I tried. I can't sleep. You know how Felix snores. It's like listening to a bear try to cough up a hairball."

He made a grumbling sound and closed his eye again.

I tossed the cow bones right in front of his nose as I sat down in the straw next to him. Immediately, his big nostrils puffed open wide as he smelled the scraps of meat and cartilage still left on the bones. He opened his mouth lazily, snaking out his long black tongue to twist it around one of the bones and drag it into his jaws. The sound of his teeth crunching the big bone into splinters made me cringe.

"You're welcome." I shuddered and looked away.

Leaning against his scaly neck, I could feel him breathing and moving as he chewed. It made me feel calmer, like I could finally hear myself think, and I didn't have to hide anything anymore. Mavrik knew all these secrets and rumors were beginning to smother me. I couldn't hide anything from him.

"Being back here like this reminds me of when we met," I murmured.

Mavrik made a few low, clicking sounds as he crunched on another bone. The image of our meeting, of when I first came into the breaking dome and saw him, came into my mind. It was bizarre to see myself from his perspective. I had looked so terrified, small, and pathetic. My face was covered in bruises from the beatings I'd taken. But for whatever reason, Mavrik had chosen me.

"I'll keep my promise," I told him. "When this is over, maybe we'll both be free to find our own peace somewhere."

Mavrik started to push his big snout up against my arm, insisting that I rub him. He purred as I scratched at his snout and ears, resting his big head on my leg. It was so heavy it started to cut off the circulation, but I didn't want him to move. Being so close to him made me feel safe.

I took out Beckah's handkerchief and rubbed my thumb over the embroidery of the two dragons. I wondered where she was. Maybe she was standing on the beach with us again, or talking to some grocer about how well she could stitch.

"A girl gave that to you, right?" An angry voice hissed at me suddenly.

When I looked up, I was shocked and a little relieved

to see Katty was standing in the stall's doorway. After what had happened with the wolves and the mountain cat, I was concerned about what would happen if they got attacked again.

Katty didn't look happy at all to see me, though. Her arms were crossed, and she looked every bit as furious as the last time she'd caught me staring at that handkerchief. I quickly put it in my pocket.

"You look at it a lot." Her nose wrinkled up like she had smelled something terrible.

Behind me, I felt Mavrik's side vibrate as he growled. He lifted his head off my leg to look at her, showing his teeth and twitching the end of his tail. Apparently, he still hadn't forgiven her.

I put a hand against his snout to try to calm him before I answered her, "Yeah. Why does that matter to you?"

She blinked like someone had spat in her face. I saw her cheeks start to get red, and she dropped her hands to her sides. The rage on her face finally broke, and she started to look sad. Tears welled in her eyes. I wasn't expecting that.

"I made a mistake," she whispered. It sounded like she was clenching her teeth. "You're not like a brother to me. I don't know why I said that. It's not true."

I was starting to get uncomfortable. "Katty, it's fine. I lost my temper, too. But everything's okay now. We can still be friends."

She started to get angry again. Her hands curled up into fists. "That's not what I mean," she snapped.

Before I could ask her what she was talking about, Katty came stomping across the stall and dropped down onto her knees in front of me. She grabbed my face in both of her hands, and glared at me like she was expecting me to do something. When I didn't move, she made an annoyed huffing sound and started leaning toward me.

Alarm bells were ringing in my head like crazy. Nothing about this was right. I couldn't go through with it. Before she could kiss me, I put a hand against her shoulder to stop her. Our noses were only a few inches apart.

"What are you doing?" I demanded.

Her eyes popped open like she was stunned. I could feel her breath on my face. "Don't you want to kiss me? It feels good. You'll like it, I promise."

"No." I slowly pushed her back away from me. "You know this isn't right. What about Bren? I thought you liked him?"

She scowled. Her chin started trembling. "How can you reject me like this? Like I'm nothing!" Her voice was shaking, and her eyes were glaring right into mine. It felt like I was staring into a churning black abyss. It felt like chaos. "You think just because you're some big shot dragonrider now, you can toss me aside and have any girl you want? You think the girl who gave you that handkerchief cares about you?"

"What are you talking about?"

I didn't understand where all this anger was coming from. I was so bewildered by what she was saying; I didn't notice she was rearing back to hit me until it was too late. She slapped me hard across the face. "You're wrong! I'm the only one who will ever care anything about you. It doesn't matter what job you get, what you look like, or where you go. You'll always be a halfbreed. No girl will ever love you like I do. You'll never have anyone. It's me or no one."

She started to slap me again, but I caught her wrist.

Behind me, Mavrik was snarling again. His ears were slicked back, and he was sending me mental images of how he wanted to bite her head off—literally. I wasn't sure how long his patience was going to last.

"Katty, stop it!" I held onto her wrist tightly as she started to fight me.

She was strong because of her work as a blacksmith's apprentice, and it didn't take long for her to pry herself away from me. She stood up and started trying to hit me again. I had to use a few sparring moves to hold her off so I could get to my feet.

I didn't want to fight her, but this had to stop. When she started to attack me again, I spun her around into a grappling hold with her arms pinned behind her back. I made sure I did everything I could to hold her still without hurting her. She started cursing at me as I forced her to walk out of the stall. Once we were in the hallway, I let her go and took a step back.

"Go back to your father," I growled at her. "I don't know what made you change like this, but you're not the Katty I used to know. Whatever you've become, I don't like it. Stay away from me. Don't come see me ever again."

For a few seconds, we just stood there glaring at each other in the darkness. I knew by the look on her face that this wasn't over. She was still angry. She wanted to hurt me. I didn't understand where all this was coming from. She'd already picked Bren instead of me! Wasn't that supposed to be the end of things between us?

Finally, Katty spun around and ran. When I heard her footsteps going back down the stairs, I could finally breathe. My cheek was stinging from where she'd slapped me as I returned to the stall and sat down again.

Mavrik was still growling. The very tip of his tail

twitched back and forth, and he was staring at me with his cat-like eyes glowing in the moonlight. He sent me another image of himself snacking on Katty's head.

I cringed and pushed the image away. "Quit that. It's grossing me out."

When I sat back down against his side, his growling started to fade. He sulked and refused to look at me. "I always do that, huh?" I asked as I scratched him behind his ears and horns. "You try to stick up for me, and I tell you no."

Mavrik made an annoyed, grumbling noise like he agreed.

"It's not that easy, you know. You can't eat people every time they make you upset." The more I scratched, the more I felt him start to relax. Soon I had him purring again, and his big yellow eyes started to close.

I tried not to think about the things Katty said about girls never caring about me. I knew Beckah wasn't like that. She cared about me. But doubt started creeping in anyway.

Beckah was growing up. Even I could see that. She might start to change. She might meet a grocer ... or a Bren. And then I might become like a little brother to her, too.

I had forgotten all about my nightmare. I was so exhausted, it didn't even dawn on me that this was the first time I'd gotten to sleep since that night. But as soon as I felt myself starting to nod off, leaning against Mavrik's side, I got a jolt of panic. I didn't want to have that dream again.

Unfortunately, I didn't have a choice.

As soon as I dozed off, I could feel it coming. I fought it as hard as I could, but the dream held me under. I could feel the cold of the wind. I could see the giant trees of Luntharda looming before me as I stood on the muddy road. I saw the king's company coming toward me, heading for the forest with their banners fluttering in the sunlight.

The scene played out just like before. The gray elf warrior emerged, cutting through the ranks like an angel of death. He butchered the king in cold blood. And then that single guard rose up from the bloodstained snow, barely able to stand, to fight him.

My heart was pounding in my ears. I knew it was a dream. Even so, I couldn't force myself to wake up no matter how I tried. I didn't want to see what happened. I was afraid and angry because there was nothing I could do to intervene. My body was stuck in one spot. All I could do was watch.

I saw the gray elf take his fighting stance, sneering at the guard and beginning to advance. The guard's hands were shaking so badly he could barely grip his sword. They started to lunge at each other, and I tried to look away. I didn't want to see what happened next.

Then the dream started to fall apart again. I was sinking into the earth, being swallowed by the darkness. I never saw who struck first. My last glimpse of the dream was the gray elf and the guard running toward each other, prepared to fight to the death.

All of a sudden, I heard my mother's voice. It seemed to be coming from everywhere at once, booming like thundering in my mind.

"Return it."

It was so clear, and so loud, that it made me bolt awake. I was drenched with a cold sweat, and my mind was racing. I felt sick immediately, but I was determined not to throw up this time.

I sat against Mavrik's side, gasping for breath and trying to calm down. Mavrik was looking at me, and I could feel his big puffs of hot breath blasting against my face. He started chirping with concern as he pushed his snout against my chest. He sent worried colors of blue and yellow swirling into my thoughts.

Without thinking, I reached to close a fist around my mother's necklace. I was used to feeling it around my neck, but when I touched it … it felt like it was on fire. It burned me, and I jerked my hand away from it. I'd worn this necklace for most of my life. It had definitely never done anything like this before. It was a piece of carved bone.

Mavrik and I exchanged a stare. My hand was red and throbbing where the necklace had burned it. Since I could see his thoughts trickling through my brain like a shower of worried blue color, I knew we were both thinking the same thing: what the heck was going on?

Jace found me on my way back to the dormitory. It was still dark outside, but I knew the sun would be rising soon. I hadn't intended on spending the night in the Roost. I was stiff from sleeping upright, and cold because my clothes were damp with sweat. All I wanted to do was take a hot bath and try sleeping in my bed for a few more hours.

But when I saw Jace, it stopped me dead in my tracks. I knew I was busted.

"Where have you been?" he demanded.

I winced. I knew students weren't supposed to be outside their rooms after dark. Technically, training hadn't started yet. I also knew better than to think Jace would give me a pass because of that. "I'm sorry, sir. It won't happen again."

Jace narrowed his eyes like he didn't believe me. "It better not. Four extra laps this morning might help you remember."

I nodded. "Yes, sir."

"Go on. You have plenty to keep you busy, avian." He brushed past me on his way out of the dormitory. I turned to watch him go. Jace was a hard man to read. He never made any expression except for that grim, sour-looking frown he wore all the time. I honestly couldn't tell if he was grumpy, angry, or just bored out of his mind.

Felix was already getting dressed when I got back to our room. He was hopping around, trying to wedge his foot down into one of his tall riding boots. "Well, you look awful. Busy night, I take it?"

"I don't want to talk about it." I sighed and sat down on the edge of my bed.

"Your old girl came by here last night. She's pretty, but man, she's gotta nasty temper," he said. "Apparently, she thinks someone gave you a love token. She was demanding to know who it was from."

"Katty came here?" I frowned. Apparently, I'd been right about her not letting it go. This was getting out of control. I leaned forward and rubbed my face. My head was throbbing from my nightmare, and my skin was sticky from sleeping in sweaty clothes. "What am I supposed to do?"

Felix slapped a hand against my back. He was laughing. "You're supposed to get ready for morning drills, dummy. Get your priorities straight. Work first, girls later."

I groaned. He was right. There was nothing I could do about it now, anyway. Felix kept laughing at me right up until I told him about the four extra laps I'd earned us by sneaking out of the room after dark. For some reason, he didn't find that quite as funny as my lousy love life.

He shot me a dirty look on our way out of the dormitory. "You seriously need to figure out how to keep a low profile. Remind me not to stand too close to you during the mock interrogation."

I punched him in the arm for spite.

It might have devolved into another sparring session, but we had work to do. As the twilight turned the horizon purple, we started running. We ran laps around the academy's outer wall until we were staggering with exhaustion. Then we started repetitions of push-ups, sit-ups, and grappling holds.

Jace met us armed with wooden practice swords. He shouted at us, giving commands to demonstrate parries, strikes, and disarming techniques until it felt like my arms were going to fall off. I'd never felt more confident in my life. I was still skinny—like a flag pole even—but

I wasn't the weakest link anymore. This was my chance to prove it.

Our morning drills went on until way past breakfast. Official training hadn't started yet, so there was no call to arms to signal the start of the day. Jace could hold us hostage as long as he wanted. Finally, after four long, grueling hours, he called us to a halt. My hands were buzzing with energy. My heart was pounding. Sure, I was starving and completely exhausted, but I hadn't felt this alive in months.

"Well, it seems you haven't forgotten everything from last year. But it's not good enough," Jace growled as he walked around us. I could feel him sizing me up again. He never looked at Felix that way, which was annoying and unfair. I knew it was probably because I was a halfbreed. "Go clean yourselves up. I've signed you both up for tack detail until training starts. You'll be checking every saddle, oiling every scrap of leather, and polishing every bit of brass. Understood?"

"Yes sir!" We both shouted in unison.

Jace dismissed us, and Felix and I glanced at each other. Tack detail didn't sound very fun. It could have been worse, though. I was more than happy to take the smell of oil and polish over the stench of dragon manure any day.

We ate breakfast without talking at all. I was too exhausted to say anything, and Felix was too busy shoveling as many pieces of bacon into his mouth as possible. He acted like he'd never seen food before. He always ate like that in the morning.

I took my time bathing. Every muscle in my body was sore, but it didn't bother me. I noticed that I was starting to get very distinct calluses on the palm of my sword hand. When I got out of the tub, I hurried through combing out my hair and tying it back into a ponytail. It was getting so long and hard to manage. I caught myself wishing Beckah were there to braid it for me like before.

Looking at myself in the mirror still made me uncomfortable. I hated how much I looked like my father. I'd always favored Ulric a lot more than I did my mom, but now it was like seeing his ghost in my reflection every time I looked in the mirror. It was creepy, and it made my heart skip a beat with panic every time.

I was entertaining the idea of trying to sneak in a short nap before I started tack detail as I walked back to our dorm room. Having nightmares every night was starting to take a heavy toll on me. If I couldn't get any sleep, I wasn't going to last long once our real training started. I'd almost decided it was worth getting my head chewed off if Jace found out when I walked in.

Lyon Cromwell was standing in the middle of the room. By the look of things, he had just arrived. He was still holding his travel bag in one hand, and wearing special riding gauntlets with resin palms made for gripping a dragon saddle.

He and Felix were squaring off, standing less than a foot apart, and glaring right into each other's faces. No one was saying a word, but I could sense that things were about to come to blows. This wasn't going to end well.

"Hey!" I slammed the door behind me to get their attention. "Knock it off! If Lieutenant Rordin hears about you guys fighting—"

Felix cut me off before I could finish. "He won't. It's hard to run off and tattle with a broken jaw, isn't it Lyon? Step back outside, Jae."

"That's right, rich boy." Lyon sneered. "Send your

little sidekick away while the grownups talk."

I rolled my eyes. Apparently, nothing about Lyon had changed since last year. He was still a bully. And he still hated my guts. "I'm not going anywhere. You're both being stupid. We're supposed to be working together."

Lyon shot me a glare. "Save your preaching, halfbreed. He's the one who jumped me as soon as I walked in."

"I have a name, you know." I glared back at him. "And I'm not preaching for your benefit. Felix, back off. It's not worth it."

I could see Felix thinking it over. I knew him well enough to tell that he was weighing the risk of being caught and punished by Jace against how good it would feel to punch Lyon in the face a few times. I didn't blame him for wanting to. I wasn't exactly Lyon's biggest fan. But if we were all going to have to spend the rest of the year living, training, and doing cleaning rotations together, then it was probably best not to start off by beating each other's faces in.

"We don't have to like it." I took the risk of getting caught in the crossfire and stepped between them. "We just have to tolerate one another. So let's suck it up and get through this."

Felix met my gaze. He let out a deep, growling sound and scrunched his mouth up angrily. "Fine."

I let out a sigh of relief when he turned away and left the room. For a minute there, I thought he might decide to hit me instead. He slammed the door so hard it made my teeth rattle.

"You're not winning any points with me, you know," Lyon said. "I don't need you to stick up for me. I don't need you at all. No one here does."

I'd already heard this speech from him last year. It was

old news. "Yeah, yeah. I know. Because I'm a halfbreed, right?"

Lyon fumed silently. He glared daggers at me for a few seconds. I could sense that he was looking me over with the same sort of amazement Felix had. I looked a little different than the last time he saw me. I wouldn't be easy prey for him anymore. Now I was several inches taller than he was.

"We're on tack detail," I told him as I went to drop my dirty clothes in the basket by my bed. "Jace's orders."

I didn't stick around to hear anything else he had to say. It was hard enough to stand close to him. All I could think about was what he'd done to Sile last year. I wanted to punch him myself. It wasn't worth it. Hating him and trying to make him pay for what he'd done wasn't going to get me anywhere. I couldn't let myself get distracted by those feelings right now.

When I caught up to Felix, he was throwing tack around in the Roost's saddle room like a hurricane. He still looked furious, and didn't say a word when I came in. He was stacking saddles and slamming bottles of polish onto the workbenches. His jaw was tense. I could see a vein standing out on his forehead.

"Are you gonna stand there and watch me do all the work?" he snapped suddenly.

I shook my head and started helping him stack the saddles up, moving them all onto one side of the room so we could go through and check, polish, and recheck them all one by one. "I wasn't doing that for his sake, you know," I muttered. "I know you were trying to stick up for me."

Felix didn't answer.

"Things are different this year. You don't have to be

so worried about me. I can take care of myself now." I picked up a couple of oiling rags and tossed one to him.

He paused, staring at me as he caught the rag. We studied each other awkwardly from across the room without saying a word. After a few minutes, Felix's shoulders sagged. He let out a sigh. "Old habits die hard, I guess. I had no idea if you'd even come back this year. You don't know how many nights I stayed awake wondering if that scumbag father of yours had murdered you and tossed your body in a ditch somewhere."

I smiled and started setting up three workstations for us with stools and sawhorses. "Well, now that you don't have to worry about being my bodyguard, worry about yourself for a change. Don't let the stuff Lyon says get to you. He's just trying to start a fight. By the way, do you think he'll actually come help us?"

Felix went over to the stack of saddles. He took the first one off the top of the pile and threw it at me. It was like tossing me a small cow. I managed to catch it, but it almost knocked me over.

He laughed. "Who cares? We already know we can't trust him, right? So I'm not gonna rely on him for anything. Fool me once ... "

I couldn't argue with that logic. Last time we had relied on Lyon, we'd ended up trapped in a prison camp with royal guards and a king drake standing between the exit and us. I dropped the saddle onto the sawhorses and started checking all the straps and buckles. If anything looked bent, torn, or loose it would have to be fixed before the rider could use it again.

Felix started doing the same with another saddle. As the hours ticked by, we checked each one over and over, and then cleaned them with leather oil and brass polish.

Of course, Lyon never showed up to help. By the time the sun was starting to set, there were still a dozen saddles left in the pile. My hands were aching, and I was beyond starving.

"Let's finish up after dinner," Felix grumbled. "If I look at another buckle my eyes are going to turn to mush."

I agreed and stood up to stretch. We still had a lot left to do, but I couldn't imagine starting on another saddle until I had something to eat. Thinking about some fresh, hot bread and roasted meat made my insides squirm happily.

Felix and I left the tack room and started for the dining hall. It was late in the evening, but the academy was still bustling with activity. Students were running around in groups, following instructors. Most of them were wearing their uniforms, but Jace hadn't given us our new avian tunics yet. The fledglings all looked so young to me now. It was hard to believe I'd been one of them last year. It seemed like so long ago.

The craftsmen were still working in the forges and armories, making new equipment while their apprentices ran errands. Tackmasters poured wax for saddle molds while riders struggled to get their dragons to cooperate. I still didn't see my father anywhere, but I wasn't going to go out of my way to look for him. After all, it's not like I had anything to say to him, and I knew better than to think he even wanted to see me.

I was about to take my first bite from a big piece of roasted pork when Felix drummed up the topic of the annual officer's ball. Immediately, he had a captive audience. Other avians sitting close to us scooted in closer, grinning like we were sharing in some big secret.

They were more than willing to ignore me altogether if it meant they'd get some useful information about girls. Felix apparently knew a lot about them and he was always more than happy to talk about it. He loved the attention.

Training hadn't even started yet, but Felix was already planning out our evening like the ball was tomorrow night. He rattled off the names of noble girls he wanted to dance with, and people I should avoid. None of those names meant anything to me. I didn't know any nobles except for him and Lyon, but some of the other avians seemed interested.

"Julianna Lacroix," he whispered like her name was a curse in some foreign language. "You'll know her because of her teeth. They're so big she can't say two words without spitting on everyone in a two-foot radius. If you can't avoid dodging a dance with her, at least try to hold her out at arm's length to avoid the spray."

I scowled at him. "That's rude."

Felix glared right back at me challengingly. "Says the one who's never even met her. It's like dancing with an angry camel. You'll see at the ball."

I rolled my eyes and went back to eating. The other avians were much more interested in his detailed descriptions of the noble girls. They asked him questions, and Felix went on and on about who would most likely step on their feet, try to trap them into boring conversations, or would be the most willing to fool around with a few meaningless kisses.

When I didn't join in, Felix started scolding me again. "You should take this more seriously." A few of the other students sitting near him nodded in agreement. "We're expected to interact this year. We have to make an impression."

"I'd rather not make an impression as a moron, if it's all the same to you," I growled at him. It came off a lot harsher than I meant it too. I regretted it instantly, and Felix actually looked a little stunned that I had lashed out at him like that.

He sank back in his seat, frowning at me like he couldn't decide if I was kidding or not. I shrugged and waved a hand at him to try and brush the subject away. "Look, it's not a big deal to me. No one's going to ask me to dance, you know that. So why worry about it?"

Felix pursed his lips. "You never know. Halfbreed or not, you're still a dragonrider."

I was starting to hate it when he said things like that to me. My heritage didn't matter to him, but it mattered to everyone else—especially girls. Katty had made that fact very clear. Her angry words were still ringing in my ears. As much as I didn't want to admit that she was probably right, I had to face facts sooner or later. When it came down to it, I was still a halfbreed. Beckah was probably going to end up with a grocer after all, and there wouldn't be anything I could do to stop it.

"That's the stupidest thing I've ever heard." Lyon piped up right on cue. I hadn't even noticed him coming into the dining hall. He sat down with a tray of food a few seats down from me. "Don't even get his hopes up. The noble girls will take one look at him and probably faint in terror."

I flashed a look of warning to Felix. I could see him gritting his teeth already. His shoulders were hunched up aggressively, and his biceps were bulging under his sleeves.

Lyon apparently had a death wish, because he didn't stop there. "I mean, come on. We were all told the same stories as kids. Gray elves are blood-thirsty savages squatting in the mud of that wicked forest, weaving evil magic and eating the hearts of fair maidens. That's all those noble girls will ever see when they look at him. It doesn't matter what uniform you put him in. You can't make dung into diamonds, and you can't make a halfbreed a hero."

There was silence at the table. The other avians sitting around us were looking back and forth between the three of us, not daring to say a word. The tension was so thick you could practically see it. Felix might as well have had steam coming out of his ears. Frankly, I didn't care what Lyon said about me anymore. He probably knew that, too. He was just trying to get a rise out of Felix. Unfortunately, it was working.

Anyone could have seen that Felix was on the edge. His hands were balled into fists that made the veins on his arms stand out. His jaw was locked, and his nose and mouth were twitching at a snarl. I knew we had a few seconds before he snapped and dove over the table.

Suddenly, something inside me clicked. I'm not sure what it was. Maybe I was thinking of what Sile had told me before—that I was viewed as the weakest link in the academy and the others would try to take advantage of that. Or maybe I had grown into a moody jerk with a really short temper. Either way, something came over me and I was helpless to stop it. I saw what was happening, and instead of keeping my head down for the sake of appearances, I acted.

Lyon was using me to get to Felix. That was going to stop.

I put my hands on the table and stood. All eyes turned to me. I only focused on Lyon. "You and me. Outside. Right now."

Lyon choked on his food. "What?"

"You heard me." I couldn't believe how calm I sounded. "If you've got something to say, say it to me. Don't talk like I can't hear you, or like I don't understand. I know what you're trying to do. You think you can keep using me to provoke him? Like he's my keeper or something?" I leaned down to put my face uncomfortably close to his. "Big mistake. I'm nobody's sidekick. I'm definitely not your doormat anymore. So let's go outside and clear the air, shall we?"

A chorus of *oooh's* went up all around the dining hall. I could feel the excitement rising with the anticipation of a fight. Everyone was hoping for a show.

It was a stupid thing to do. Even I knew that. But Sile had been right all along when he told me I had to pick a fight. I saw that now. I had to establish myself as a capable member of this academy, especially if I wanted to make sure Felix didn't go around swinging wildly at anyone who said something bad about me. I knew Felix would fight to the death defending me against everything and everyone. It sounded great in theory. In practice it put a huge target on his back. It made everyone look at him like an obstacle that had to be overcome in order to get to me. I had to make a stand for myself now.

Lyon sat there, glaring up at me. I could tell he was thinking it over. He probably didn't want to fight me, but I'd left him no choice now. If he backed down now, he would look like an even bigger coward.

He pushed his tray of food away and stood up to meet me nose-to-nose. "Fine," he agreed. "Outside it is."

fourteen

A huge crowd of students followed us out of the dining hall. I knew it was only a matter of time before the instructors noticed and stepped in to stop us. I had a plan. This had to be fast.

We gathered right outside the dormitory, and slowly everyone started forming a big circle around Lyon and me. Last year, Lyon had kept company with a group of lackeys who always showed up whenever he wanted to push me around. As he emerged from the crowd, I noticed that he was alone now. In fact, I hadn't seen them around him at all since our incident at the prison camp last year. Maybe he'd lost his friends?

As I started toward him, I felt a strong grip on my elbow. "Have you lost your mind?" Felix muttered furiously.

I wasn't sure how to answer that.

"Jace is going to beat your face in," he warned. "Call this off. You've made your point."

I pulled my arm away and smirked. "No, not yet. You don't get it, do you? If I'm going to survive here, and if you're going to keep being my friend, then I have to do this. Besides, what's the worst he can do? Make me run a few more laps?"

The color was draining out of Felix's face. I knew why. I joked about it now, but the chances that Jace might actually beat me for this were good.

I tried not to think about it as I turned back toward Lyon. I knew there was a lot worse Jace could do than hit me a few times. He could get me kicked out of the academy. "Yeah, like that's anything new." I muttered to myself. The fear of getting kicked out had been my driving force last year. Now, for whatever reason, it didn't scare me as much. I was trusting Sile's advice. Surely he wouldn't tell me to do something that would get me in that much trouble.

The crowd around us had started yelling and cheering as I squared off with Lyon. The realization of exactly how stupid this was started crashing in on me. Not just because it was unnecessarily barbaric, but also because I was pretty much the worst hand-to-hand fighter in the world. I couldn't remember if I'd ever actually seen Lyon spar before, so I didn't know what his strengths were. It was a safe bet to assume that whatever he could do, it was better than anything I could come up with.

I widened my stance, put up my fists, and braced for impact.

For a few seconds, we paced around in a slow circle and sized each other up. It was almost like a dance. I was studying how he moved, trying to find a weakness. Lyon was short and husky, so I knew he'd probably hit hard. I'd have to use my speed and reach to keep from taking too many blows. After all, part of my plan was to draw this out as long as I could.

Lyon lunged first. He dove at me and started swinging his fists. The crowd roared with excitement. I only heard one person cheering for me, and I didn't have to look to see who it was.

I dodged and weaved around Lyon's attacks easily. He was a lot slower than I expected. I easily darted in to jab at his face, pounding his cheeks and then jumping back out of his reach again before he could retaliate. It started to frustrate him. I could see his anger mounting. Even if his heart hadn't been in this fight before, the idea that I might beat him in front of everyone was starting to wear him down.

He started getting reckless. He lunged at me and grabbed the front of my tunic. He pounded his fist into my face so hard it made my brains feel scrambled. I was stunned, but not for long. I hooked a leg through his and drove my elbow into his gut, sending us both sprawling into the dirt.

I knew I wasn't much of a match for him when it came to grappling. My height and speed wouldn't serve me much. On the ground, he had the advantage, and he refused to let go of my tunic so I could get away. Lyon got me into a headlock from behind and started to squeeze. My vision blurred. I could taste blood in my mouth.

Through the haze, I saw Felix squatting down a few feet away from me. He was yelling at the top of his lungs, but I couldn't make out anything he said over the noise of the crowd. I tried to get my legs back under me. If I wanted to win, I had to get back on my feet somehow.

Lyon was so heavy. His arms were thick and strong, squeezing my head tighter and tighter. It was hard to move at all. No matter how I squirmed or clawed at his arm, he kept adding pressure to my neck until I could barely breathe.

Then, something inside me broke like a floodgate of anger. It wasn't anything like that sense of calm that had come over me in the dining hall. This was something a thousand times worse. I'd never felt anything like it. White-hot rage filled my veins like fire. My vision snapped into focus. My body surged with energy. The pain from being hit and choked was gone.

I went absolutely crazy.

Without warning, I slammed my head back against Lyon's. It hit so hard I heard the crack like someone snapping a tree in two. Immediately, he let me go.

Normally, I would have taken that chance to get back on my feet so I was in a better position to keep the fight going. After all, that had been my plan all along: to show the others that I could hold my own until an instructor stepped in to break things up. No one had to get seriously hurt. Worst case scenario, Jace would make Lyon and me run laps all day.

But now things were out of control ... and I couldn't stop myself. My body moved without my permission, doing things I didn't even know I could do.

I was like an animal. I dove after Lyon and whipped him into a lethal hold, bearing my knees down on his shoulders and locking my ankles under him. I saw the fear in his eyes as I snarled down at him, and drew back to begin pounding my fists into his face again and again. My knuckles were coated with blood, and I wasn't sure how much of it was his or mine.

The crowd went completely silent. All I could hear was the gory sound every time my fist met his face. Lyon wasn't moving anymore, but I kept hitting him anyway.

Someone grabbed me from behind. I knew it was Felix by the strength of his hold. He tried to pin my arms and drag me away, but I whipped around, stepping easily through complex sparring moves like they were nothing. I moved like a ghost, and not even Felix could keep up.

I had him pinned on his stomach in matter of seconds, wrenching his arm behind his back and adding pressure that would break it if he didn't surrender. But he wouldn't tap out. Felix would never surrender like that, and part of me knew it. I'd have to break his arm.

That should have been more than enough to make me stop. Felix wasn't my enemy. He was my best friend. I didn't want to hurt him. But I couldn't shut my brain off. I couldn't stop. My body kept moving, getting closer and closer to snapping his arm.

Suddenly, I felt the point of a knife at my throat.

"Let him go, demon," an unfamiliar man's voice boomed at my back.

Immediately, I let Felix go. My mind started to clear. The prick of that knife had been enough to jar me free of that horrible trance. I could think again. Underneath my tunic, I could feel my mother's necklace burning hot against my skin again.

My hands were shaking as I started to raise them in surrender. Before I could speak, a big boot kicked me to the ground. Someone started roughly tying my hands behind my back, binding me up like a prisoner. Fear poured over my body like ice water.

I could sense incredible strength in the arm that yanked me to my feet. The other students still gathered around all looked at me with different expressions of horror, fear, and awe. Some of them were checking on Lyon. He was sitting up and moving. I was so relieved that he was alive, even if his face was a pulverized bloody mess. I hadn't killed him, and that was enough to make me thank the fates.

Felix was standing a few feet away, rubbing his arm. I couldn't bring myself to meet his gaze. I was so ashamed and disgusted with myself. I had never intended for the fight to get this bad. I hadn't wanted to hurt Lyon like that.

"Who let this piece of filth into our midst?" The man holding my arms shook me violently and roared. He sounded like an angry bear. It terrified me. Even though I couldn't see him, I could sense his size and incredible strength just by the way his massive hand gripped me. The other students looked afraid of him, too. Their eyes were wide, and some of them were even slipping away into the dark.

"Commander Rayken has betrayed us by letting this creature into our brotherhood," he rumbled. "But it's easily fixed. Pay attention, all you little mutts. Let me teach you something useful. This is how you sever a demon's spine without getting any blood on your sleeves."

I felt the point of a knife press hard against the back of my neck, and hot breath against the tips of my pointed ears. I trembled, and squeezed my eyes shut.

"Lieutenant Thrane." My knees almost buckled with relief when I heard Jace's voice. "That avian belongs to me. I'm going to have to ask you to let him go."

I opened my eyes, and he was standing right in front of me. Jace was looking at the mess I'd made with the same eerily blank expression he always wore. It wasn't comforting at all, but at least he wasn't going to let Lieutenant Thrane—whoever that was—butcher me like a spring calf in front of the whole academy.

"This *thing* isn't an avian," Thrane snarled ferociously. He squeezed my arm so hard I was sure it would snap in half. "Or have these months away from the battlefront made you forget what the enemy looks like? Here, let me remind you." He grabbed a fistful of my hair and jerked my head around to look at the crowd.

Jace stared at me for a few uncomfortable moments before he spoke. "I'm very aware of what he looks like. I'm his instructor. Now let him go. I won't ask you again." His voice was so calm it gave me chills. He still hadn't made any expression, but I could see something like cold fire burning in his eyes. It chilled me to the bone.

Almost all of the other students had found a chance to slip away by the time Lieutenant Thrane finally let me go. I stumbled and almost tripped, but Felix caught me. He started untying my hands while the two lieutenants continued to argue. Thrane's voice boomed like a dragon's roar, and when I finally got a glimpse of him, my stomach turned to mush.

Thrane was a huge man. He towered over everyone like a mountain of muscle. His body was so bulky that he barely had a neck. He had a long, scraggly black beard, but no hair on his head at all. His eyes were as black as pitch, and they darted back and forth between Jace and me like he was looking for a chance to strike at one or both of us.

I swallowed hard. My whole body was still shaking. I couldn't tell if it was from fear or because I was still coming down off whatever had made me go crazy like that. Standing under the inferno of Thrane's glare, I could sense how much he hated me. He leered down at me, flexing his huge hands like he was imagining what it would feel like to break my neck. I held my breath and waited to see what he'd do. Finally, Thrane made a snarling sound and stormed away. Apparently, he wasn't willing to fight Jace over the chance to kill me—at least, not yet.

"What's wrong with you?" Felix whispered as he finished untying my hands. "First you challenge Lyon to fight, then you try to crack my arm off?"

"I-I don't know," I stammered as I rubbed my wrists. Thrane had tied them so tight that it left deep red marks and bruises behind.

"You scared me to death." Felix grumbled. He smacked me on the back of the head. "Don't do that again, idiot."

"I'm sorry. I didn't mean to. I couldn't control myself. I couldn't stop it." I didn't know how else to explain it to him. I didn't even understand it myself.

"It's battle fever," Jace interrupted suddenly. I almost jumped out of my skin when I saw he was standing so close, listening to us. "The elves call it *kulunai*, or something like that."

I wanted to duck away, or hang my head in shame. I knew there was going to be some kind of punishment for this. Still, hearing Jace talk about it like he understood caught me completely off guard. I couldn't look away. I'd never heard of battle fever before.

"It's brought on by pain and adrenaline," he continued. "It's some kind of self-defense response. I've only ever seen it in adults on the battlefield. I don't think the kids are capable of it."

Felix let out an uneasy sigh when he sized me up

again. "That explains why it's never happened before. Right, Jae?"

I couldn't speak. I was too humiliated and shaken up. All I could do was nod.

"I've heard rumors that the adults induce it before battle in some kind of ceremony. Who knows how much truth there is to that." Jace started to stroll away from us. As he passed me, I let myself hope that he might actually let me go without any punishment.

Then he slapped me hard across the cheek. It made my whole jaw hurt. He'd never hit me before, and it felt like someone had taken a plank of wood to my face. Normally, I would have been terrified or hurt that he would slap me like that. But after everything I'd done, I knew I deserved it.

"Don't do that again," he warned me in a deep growling voice. "You have to control it. You don't realize how lucky you are; Thrane will not forgive you a second time."

I didn't say it out loud—I was too busy rubbing my cheek because it was stinging like it was on fire—but I knew Thrane hadn't forgiven me at all. He wasn't willing to fight Jace in order to get to me. Jace had saved my life.

"Who was that other student you were fighting with?" he demanded.

Felix piped up first, so I kept my mouth shut. I knew he was eager to tattle on Lyon the first chance he got. "Lyon Cromwell. He's your third student, sir."

Jace's eyes narrowed. "What?"

"Yes, sir. Lyon Cromwell, son of Duke Cromwell. He arrived this morning. He was supposed to be cleaning tack with us today, but he never showed up to help."

"Is that so?" Jace's tone deepened, and he turned his

cold eyes back on me. "Well, it seems you three need some encouragement in order to act like soldiers. Lucky for you, I'm very good at providing that kind of … *encouragement*."

Felix and I cringed at the same time. We knew what kind of encouragement he was talking about. Tomorrow was going to hurt.

"We're not finished with the saddles yet, sir," Felix said. "Being shorthanded put us way behind."

Jace had already started walking away. But Felix's comment made him stop and glance back at us. He gave us a hard, disapproving frown. "Hurry and finish them, then. But clean yourself up first." He gestured to my face. I'd forgotten all about the few good punches Lyon had scored on my nose. It was still bleeding a little.

Once Jace was out of earshot and we were alone, Felix let out a string of curses. I was still too overwhelmed to be angry. Between not getting any sleep because of my nightmares, worrying about running into Katty again, figuring out that rumor about Sile, and hiding all these secrets about my strange abilities, I didn't have room for anything else. My head felt like it was going to pop. I couldn't take it.

I took off toward the tack room. Before I could get to the door, a mountain of blue scales dropped from the sky and landed right before me. Mavrik chirped with concern as he lowered his head. I could barely concentrate. I was still shaking. He pushed his snout against my chest, and I leaned against him.

"I can't take much more of this." I muttered as I ran my hands over his scaly head.

Mavrik gave me a low growl. He could sense what I was thinking, and I guess he didn't like it. I was beginning

to think maybe this wasn't the place for me, after all. So much was happening. I felt out of control. I couldn't even trust myself anymore. At any moment, I might snap like that again and end up hurting someone I cared about. How could I live with that? Jace told me to control it as though I actually could. But how could he understand? He was a human.

"You better not be going off to pout," Felix called after me. I could hear him running to catch up. "I'm fine. I'm not even angry. So don't worry about it."

I stood there frozen as I watched the green colors of concern Mavrik sent swirling through my brain. I was still thinking about leaving. How could I ever hope to keep my promise to protect my friends if I was going to end up being dangerous to them? I couldn't trust myself to fight next to Felix if there was a chance I might turn on him at any second.

"I'm not stupid, you know." Felix was walking up behind me. "I know when something's bothering you. You've got circles under your eyes like you haven't been sleeping. So what is it? What else aren't you telling me?"

I shut my eyes tightly and pushed Mavrik's head away. I didn't want to tell him about my nightmares. It was embarrassing and it made me feel weak. They were just dreams. "It's nothing."

"Liar. Quit being such a girl and confess. What's going on?" He slapped a hand down on my shoulder so hard it almost knocked me over. "You know you can trust me. I'm not going to judge you."

I bit down hard on the inside of my cheek. As much as I wanted to tell him everything, I couldn't. I was turning into some kind of monster, and I didn't deserve to be here anymore.

"I can't." I snapped at him. "Just stay away from me."

"Why? Because you think I'm afraid of you now? Nice try, kid. You'll have to do worse than break my arm if you want to scare me." He stepped into my path and crossed his arms. "Jaevid, come on. I can see that you're struggling. You can't carry all this on your own."

I was determined not to cave. I wouldn't give in, not this time. "I don't have a choice," I told him.

His expression fell some. He looked hurt. For a few minutes, we stood there silently until it was awkward.

Finally, he nodded and stepped out of my way. "Fine. Have it your way. You want to be the cool loner, so be it."

I didn't want to be a loner. There was nothing cool about it. I hated knowing I had hurt Felix by shutting him out like that. I needed him to be my friend like before. But Sile had warned me about saying too much, and now I was starting to understand why. There were things about myself—dangerous things—that I wasn't even aware of yet. In order to protect him, I had to keep this stuff to myself. If someone like Thrane figured out that I was turning into some kind of mutant halfbreed sorcerer, then I couldn't let Felix be guilty by association. He'd defend me to the bitter end, even when I didn't deserve it.

The days leading up to training passed slowly, and

each one was more miserable than the last. Felix didn't talk to me at all. He wouldn't even look at me. I'd never been so lonely in my life. I knew he was just sulking. It was probably killing him, too. But I wasn't going to give up now; it was much safer for him to keep his distance from me.

My nightmares continued every night without fail. As soon as I closed my eyes, I was pulled into that same vision. I fought it as hard as I could. It never helped at all. All I wanted was a few hours of sleep. The dream played over and over again in my head, startling me awake every time. I always woke up in a cold sweat with those eerie words ringing in my ears:

"*Return it.*"

After he was released from the infirmary with a broken nose, Lyon joined us in our early morning training drills. He struggled with the running because his old instructor had never required him to do anything like that. Jace spent a lot of extra time "encouraging" him.

The closer we got to the start of training, the more ruthless Jace was about our morning routine. He yelled until it felt like my eardrums were sore. One day, he even came out with a bullwhip while we were struggling through an hour of push-ups. If we slowed down at all, he cracked it in the air. He was incredibly accurate with it. He could pop it right at the tip of my nose. It never actually hit me, but I could practically taste the leather in my teeth.

After finishing our morning drills, the three of us worked through cleaning saddles. It took us hours to finish, but no one ever said a word. Felix was still sulking, so he wouldn't talk to me. Lyon looked terrified of both of us, and he never said a word. His face was bruised up, thanks to me. I felt really bad about that, but I couldn't bring myself to apologize. I couldn't find the will to try talking to either of them, not that they would have answered. It was depressing to work for so long in total silence.

In the dining hall, I sat by myself. It was painful to watch Felix sitting with the other avians, laughing and carrying on like always. The gnawing sense of loneliness in my chest wore on me. It was getting harder and harder to cope. I didn't want to be here anymore. I started thinking about leaving altogether, but I knew Sile would probably hunt me down to the ends of the earth if I gave up. He'd spent a lot of money and risked his honor and good name for me to be here.

The day before training, I got word that my gear was finally finished. It had taken a lot longer than I expected, especially since none of my stuff was that intricate. But after morning drills, Jace gave me permission to go and pick up everything before I started to work on cleaning saddles.

I went alone to pick up my armor first. I waited while the blacksmith brought it out piece by piece, laying everything out on a worktable so I could inspect it. He'd wrapped it all in rags to protect it.

About the same time I started unwrapping it, the blacksmith spoke up. "Took a little longer after you made those changes."

"Changes?" I held up one of the gauntlets. It was definitely the traditional style I'd chosen, but there were a lot more grooves cut into it than before. As I unwrapped each piece of my new armor, I noticed more and more of those same beautiful details. All the bolts holding it together were plated in gold. The breastplate was accented

with grooves and etchings. The armor was much more ornate than I had asked for.

The helmet was the most detailed of all. There was a snarling dragon's head engraved on both sides of it, so that it looked like my face was coming out of its mouth. The engraved lines of the design had been inlaid with gold, so it shimmered in the light. It was beautiful, but definitely not what I'd ordered.

"I didn't ask for any of this," I said.

The blacksmith scowled at me. He dug through his box of paperwork until he found my forms, and shoved them at me roughly. The first few pages looked exactly how I remembered, but on the last page there was big paragraph scribbled asking for all the extra details. I knew that handwriting right away.

"It's already been paid for," the blacksmith grumbled.

I scowled at the paper. I had to fight the urge to crumple it up in anger. "It's okay," I managed to growl through my teeth. "I must have forgotten. I'll take it."

The blacksmith wrapped all the pieces back up for me, placing them carefully in a big canvas bag. I slung it over my shoulder and carried it away toward the tackmaster. I already had suspicions burning in my brain before I ever got there.

And I was right.

My saddle order had been changed as well. Instead of the plain saddle I had ordered, someone had gone right behind me and added details. They'd also paid extra for them. The saddle was beyond beautiful. It was made of dark, chocolate brown and black leather. The buckles were layered with an extra layer of brass so that they shimmered to match the gold details on my armor. The sides were engraved with intricate scrollwork like vines, images of dragons, and something that looked suspiciously like a turtle. The seat was padded with layers of soft deer hide, and the handles were made from engraved milky white ivory.

Even with the extra money I'd had leftover, there was no way I could have afforded something like this. I had only seen my father make a saddle this nice a few times in my life, and always for some high ranking official like a general. I was so shocked that I forgot to get upset about it.

Mavrik stretched out obediently on the ground when I asked him to let me fit the saddle to his back. He made a big show of yawning and groaning as I put it on, testing the fit of all the straps. It was perfect. The brown leather looked almost red against his dusky blue scales. And the black leather picked up on the onyx color of his horns. It didn't look like a saddle at all—it looked like a part of him. The sight of it made me smile.

Mavrik shifted and squirmed, testing the fit before he finally gave me a chirp of approval.

"It's good?" I asked him.

He answered with a blast of hot, stinking dragon breath in my face as he yawned again. I took that as a "yes."

"Fine, then. Try not to bang it up, will you? I can't afford to replace it." I patted his neck and sent him off. After I cleared everything with the tackmaster and thanked him for his work, I didn't waste any more time around the armories.

I owed someone a piece of my mind.

Felix was sitting outside the dormitory, picking food out of his teeth after breakfast. A few other avians were standing around talking to him, but they cleared out as soon as they saw me coming. I guess I had made an impression after all.

I took the bag of armor off my back and sat it on the ground between us. "Why did you do that?" I demanded.

Felix glared at my shadow. He wouldn't look up at me, and he didn't say a word. That stubborn, rich idiot. I'd recognized his handwriting on those order forms immediately.

I was getting really tired of his sulking act. "You know I can't pay you back for this. That saddle probably cost more than I would at the slave market."

"You're not paying me back," Felix snapped suddenly. "So don't even try. It was supposed to be a gift."

"Why?"

He finally met my gaze with stubborn fury in his eyes. "Because even though you're being stupid, you're still my friend. Because you're a dragonrider, and there's an expectation of how we should look when we go into battle. And because when you die, you'll be buried in that armor, and it shouldn't look like a rusted out tin bucket. You deserve better than that. Do I need any other reasons?"

I choked on my frustration. I couldn't even get a word out.

"I get why you're doing this. You think you're doing me a favor by keeping me in the dark. Don't you realize I know the risks of being around you?" Felix's body language relaxed some as he let out a heavy sigh. He started scratching at the back of his head. "I understand all that, and I don't care. If you're going down, then I'm going down with you. That's the way it is."

"But—" I started to object until he cut me off.

"Oh give it up, will you? If you're not ready to tell me

what's really going on with you, then fine. I guess that's your business. But quit trying to protect me. It's weird and annoying."

For some reason, I had to smile. I knew Felix pretty well. He never liked admitting when he was wrong about anything. This seemed like his way of letting me know he felt bad about pushing me for information. He would let me keep my secrets for now.

"Fine. Quit buying me stuff behind my back." I added.

When Felix looked up at me again, he was finally grinning. The tension in the air was gone. Things were back to normal again. It felt like a weight had been lifted off me.

He stood up, and punched my arm. "That's the worst thank you I've ever heard."

fifteen

Working through tack detail duties was so much easier now that Felix and I were back on speaking terms. Lyon never said a word, but he showed up and helped out as usual. I still felt a nagging sense of guilt whenever I looked at him. Lyon's blue, battered nose was wrapped up in gauze that went all the way around his head. I'd overheard some of the other avians joking that he would probably have a crooked nose for the rest of his life. I'd never meant for that to happen, and he seemed genuinely terrified of both of us now. I decided to try to find the right moment to apologize to him—preferably when Felix wasn't there to heckle me for it.

After we finished up with tack detail, there was still plenty of daylight left. It was the last day before the official start of training, so the academy was full of people. Craftsmen were packing up to leave in the morning. Instructors were showing the new fledglings where they ' d to go on their first day. There were dragons eve., vhere. Some circled overhead, riding in the updrafts or chasing each other. Others lounged on the ground, napping in groups like lazy housecats. More were climbing the walls and preening their scales, or basking in the last few rays of sunlight. There was so much energy in the air that it felt contagious. Sure, my brain was a scrambled, exhausted mess, but I was still excited for the first call to arms in the morning. I was ready to get started.

On our way out of the tack room, Felix started poking my shoulder excitedly. "Hey, let's go for a ride. We haven't flown together since last year, and you need to test out that new saddle."

I tried to resist. I'd already gotten in trouble with Jace twice. I wasn't looking to test how many chances he'd give me. "Will Jace get angry if we go without his permission?"

"Maybe not. I mean, we're not fledglings anymore. We can handle it if something goes wrong." Felix was a champion when it came to bargaining with me. He knew I wanted to fly as badly as he did. It didn't take much to convince me.

"Okay, fine." I stopped and glanced back. Lyon was still in the tack room pretending to put things away. He always did that. I guess it was so he would have an excuse not to walk out with us. "What about him?"

"Forget him." Felix scoffed and started climbing the stairs up to the Roost.

But I couldn't forget him. He was supposed to be our third man, now. He was our partner in training. It was bad enough his old lackeys from last year had abandoned him. If we shunned him, he'd be alone. I knew what alone felt like.

"Lyon," I called out to him.

He flinched, and looked over at me with wide eyes. His face was pasty white with fear, like he might suddenly bolt if I made a wrong move.

"We're going out for a flight. You should come, too."

Lyon stood there, motionless. He didn't say anything. We stared at each other for a long time, and finally I decided he wasn't going to answer me at all. I cleared my throat and took a step back toward the stairs.

"Well, if you change your mind, you should come find us," I said. I left him in the tack room and ran up the stairs after Felix.

Mavrik growled and chirped with excitement when I came into his stall. He chattered and grumbled anxiously while I strapped on some of my new armor. I didn't dress out fully since this was just a pleasure ride. I slipped the chestplate over my head and buckled it into place, then tightened the shiny vambraces and gauntlets over my arms. The palms of the gauntlets were coated in a thick layer of rubbery resin that made it easy to grip the saddle handles. I slipped the helmet over my head, tapping a finger on the long glass slit cut across the front so I could see without the wind blowing in my eyes.

I could tell this armor had been made with much more care and precision than the stuff I had worn last year. It fit snuggly, but it was so much lighter and more comfortable. It was made to fit me, and something about it felt right.

"Nice. It looks good," Felix muttered from the doorway. He was dressed out in a few pieces of his own armor. His was different than mine, with a much sleeker style. The metal had been stained to look almost golden brown, and there was a crest of black horsehair on the top of his helmet.

I gave him a thumbs up. "Fits good, too."

"Glad to hear it. I'll take the lead, if you don't mind." He chuckled and waved before going back to his own stall.

I smirked at Mavrik. He eagerly crawled to the edge of his stall and looked out to the steep drop below. I could see his armored sides moving in and out with his excited breaths. His powerful hind legs were coiled, ready to leap into the sky. The setting sunlight shimmered over his blue scales.

"He can take the lead," I muttered as I ran my hand over my dragon's side. I could feel the power of his muscles underneath his thick hide. "But let's see if he can keep it."

As I climbed into the saddle and got myself buckled in, Mavrik let out a booming roar. He didn't give me a second's chance to prepare. When the last strap was in place, he dove headlong out of his stall and we went rocketing toward the ground. Out of the corner of my eye, I saw Nova and Felix doing the same thing. We spiraled down like two bolts of lightning, and at the last second, our dragons flared and caught the wind with their powerful wings.

We soared into the sky, sailing on the winds like two armored kites. I could barely make out the sound of Felix laughing as he urged Nova to go faster, taking the lead as we left the academy behind. I could see other riders flying in pairs or groups all around us. Some flew high, scraping the clouds like they wanted to get a glimpse of the stars. Others were doing low passes, or weaving dangerously close to the steep cliffs.

The minute I got a deep breath of the free air in my

lungs, I felt all the stress and worry in my mind melt away. None of it seemed that important anymore. I could fly away and leave it all behind. When we flew like this, I had a hard time telling which feelings were mine and which were Mavrik's—not that it mattered. When we flew, it was like our souls touched, and the spark could be seen for miles and miles.

Felix and Nova flew considerably fast, but they were no match for our speed. Mavrik caught up to them quickly. We zipped past, and rolled over into another steep dive. Nova chased us, and we started doing spirals and rolls as fast as we could. We flew up, punching holes through the clouds and getting a glimpse of the first few evening stars before we stalled and started falling. The freefall was incredible, and Mavrik roared with delight as we plummeted back toward the ground.

When we were all winded and exhausted, we landed on a nearby cliff to rest. The sun was beginning to slip down behind the distant ocean. From where we were sitting, we could barely make out the surface of the water, glittering like a mirror on the horizon. The cliff gave us a really great view of the academy, which stood out on the valley floor like a big stone circle. The dark shapes of dragons flew all around it.

I sat on the edge of the cliff with my legs dangling over the drop. Mavrik was crouched beside me, still panting with his mouth open. On the other side of me, Felix was drinking from a canteen he'd clipped to his saddle. Nova was preening her brown and golden scales. Everything between us felt calm. It felt right.

"Where did you get Nova, anyway?" I didn't know why I'd never thought to ask him that before. "Did she choose you?"

Felix wiped his chin and handed me the canteen so I could drink, too. "No, of course not. I bought her when she was a hatchling. That's the way it usually goes, these days. It's like when people breed horses, or dogs. Whoever owns the female pays a siring fee for a male to come and, well, you know. When she lays her eggs, people start bidding to get one of the hatchlings. The highest bidder gets first choice."

"And she was your first choice?" I looked up at Nova. I could see why he would choose her. She was big, for a female. She had beautiful markings, and there was definitely something regal about her.

"She was the dominant of the clutch. When dragons hatch, there's always a dominant baby. Just like with eagles, you know? There's always one that's bigger and stronger. They call it the dominant hatchling. Nova came out of her egg squawking like she owned the place, and she showed me her teeth when I tried to touch her. I can't explain it. I knew she was the one I wanted, even if she didn't like me. I knew I could win her over." Felix laughed and winked at me. "I'm great with girls."

I rolled my eyes. "I'm not sure that applies to dragons."

"Well, does she like me?" he asked.

"What do you mean?"

Felix arched a brow at me curiously. "I mean, you can talk to animals, right? So ask her if she likes me."

I eyed Nova uncomfortably. I'd never tried to talk to another dragon other than Mavrik except for Icarus. That hadn't ended so well for the rider. Besides, Mavrik was the only one who had been able to talk back to me.

"I-I'll try," I stammered and got to my feet. I started walking toward Nova.

As soon as I got close she turned her big head around

to look right at me. Her intelligent, dark green eyes studied me. I swallowed back my fear, and reached a hand out toward her. She shied back, her pupils narrowing with distrust. I'd never tried to touch her before.

I started searching through my mind like before, looking for that quiet warmth that spread over my body. I felt her presence in that warmth, like a ripple on a pond. I could feel Mavrik, too, but his presence was so familiar to me now it was like second nature. Still, letting my guard down so I could sense these things gave me chills. My ability was getting stronger. I could focus faster. My fingertips buzzed and tingled with energy.

"It's okay," I said softly. "You can feel me, too, right? You know I won't hurt you. I just want to talk."

Behind me, Mavrik gave her some encouraging chirps.

Nova looked hesitant, but finally she pushed her snout against my hand. I could feel the blast of her strong breaths against my chest.

I couldn't keep myself from smiling. "You can understand me, can't you?"

She made a low, chattering noise. Her wise eyes focused directly into mine. It was silent except for the wind.

Then it happened.

Felix's dragon, Nova, spoke back to me.

It hit me like a tidal wave. It wasn't words, just like Mavrik didn't speak to me with words. It was a rush of emotion that poured into my thoughts like a dam had broken inside me. I saw visions, flashes of moments, and they blurred through my mind so quickly that I could barely understand all of it. But one thing kept leaping out, gripping me so that it stuck in my brain like a thorn: Danger was coming.

There was a strong sense of impending doom, like she knew something terrible was going to happen. I tried to ask her what it was. Even though I couldn't get a word out, she seemed to understand my question. She was reading my thoughts like Mavrik did.

But I didn't understand her answer. It was too jumbled; a curious mixture of images and feelings like a tangled mess of string. I cringed as I felt something familiar surge through our minds—that sense of chaos I'd felt from the wolves and mountain cat. I was starting to hate that feeling. It frustrated me, and dulled my senses. But now, thanks to Nova, I understood something new about it. The animals were afraid of this chaos that was trying to possess them. They could sense it coming, but they couldn't do anything to stop it.

Finally, Nova settled on one image. She showed me a deep, dark pit surrounded by trees. It was like a cavern in the earth that went straight down. There was a staircase overgrown with roots carved into the side of the cave that went spiraling around and around down into the dark. I didn't even realize that it really felt like I was standing there on the edge of the pit, until I almost tripped and fell in. Then I got that weird, panicked sensation like I was about to fall. It seemed so real.

Then I heard a voice. A voice echoed up from that dark place, and filled every corner of my mind.

"Return it."

Feelings of anxiety and genuine fear for my life surged through my body. I jerked away from Nova. The instant I took my hand away from her snout, my mind went quiet. The images and emotions were gone. Everything was calm.

Nova was still looking at me, her head canted to

the side like she didn't know why I had stopped our communication all of a sudden. I noticed my nose had started to bleed a little. My heart was pounding in my ears.

"Are you okay?" Felix rushed over. "What happened?"

I choked. My hands were shaking again. I got that cold, clammy feeling like I was going to pass out. Then my knees started to buckle.

Felix caught me before I hit the ground. He helped me sit down, and propped me up against the side of the cliff. He and the dragons gathered around, looking at me with concern.

"Just breathe. You're fine." Felix patted my shoulder roughly. "What happened? What did you see?"

My heart was still beating out of control. "I'm not sure," I managed to answer. "She *answered* me."

"Answered?" He looked confused. "Of course she did. Don't they all answer you?"

I shook my head and tried to wipe the blood off my nose. "Only Mavrik. Most animals seem to understand me, but he's the only one who has ever communicated back. But she answered me."

Felix started to look pale. "What did she say?"

I hesitated. Telling him what she showed me would definitely lead to questions. I would end up having to tell him everything. Well, almost everything. I hadn't told him anything about my dreams, but I couldn't deny that my repeating nightmare was somehow connected to whatever Nova had shown me. That voice that had spoken to me from the depths of that cavern—it was my mother's voice. There was no mistaking it.

I guess Felix could see me struggling, trying to decide what to tell him. He let out a sigh of frustration and sat down beside me. He leaned against the side of the cliff, rested his hands on his knees, and stared off into the sunset.

"You remember that time last year when you asked me why I wanted to be friends with you?" He said. "We had just gotten into a huge fistfight with Lyon and his buddies. You had been beaten to a pulp again, like always. I honestly didn't know if we could even win that fight. We were outnumbered. I guess it's a good thing we're both either too stupid or too stubborn to know when to run, huh?"

I'd been beaten up more times than I could count. That was a general side effect of being born a halfbreed. Even Lyon had found multiple opportunities to pulverize me. But I knew exactly which fight he was talking about. "You must be a lot more stupid than I am, though, since you still want to be friends with me even after everything that's happened."

"Probably. But I'm okay with that." He smirked. "We work best when we work together. Haven't you figured that out by now?" Felix looked over at me, and I knew he was right. Neither one of us would have survived last year if we hadn't been together. He needed me watching his back every bit as badly as I needed him watching mine.

"Fine." I surrendered. "But if you give me that look again like I'm turning into some evil gray elf monster … "

He laughed so loud it almost made me have a heart attack. "You already did that once, right? And I survived, arm and all."

"That's not what I meant." My ears were starting to sizzle with embarrassment.

Felix punched my shoulder. I punched him back. We were both going to have permanent bruises on our arms.

"I know what you meant. I already said I'm not gonna judge you. So relax and fess up."

By the time I finished telling Felix about the dreams I was having, the sun had set and it was almost dark. I couldn't bring myself to watch his reaction, but whenever he said something or asked a question, I could hear how serious he was. Something about my dream had him worried.

"Jaevid, did anyone ever tell you how this war got started?" Felix asked as we stood up. We started checking our saddles one more time, just to be sure nothing had bent or come loose during our last flight. We had to get back to the academy soon, or Jace would come looking for us.

"No." To be honest, it had never really mattered to me before. I assumed it was a problem a lot bigger and older than I was. I didn't see how knowing the details would make any difference.

Felix got quiet. The look on his face was intense. He started rubbing his chin, scratching at the beard that was starting to grow in. Finally, he started to tell the story.

"I mean, after twenty years or so, the details are muddy. Truth gets mixed with rumors. Pretty soon, it's hard to tell what's true and what's not," he said. "But the way I've always heard it was that the gray elves struck first. They launched an attack against our northern border, started burning villages and killing townsfolk. The royal family was traveling up there and got caught in the crossfire. Only the king survived—if you can even call it that. His whole body was so badly burned and mutilated that to this day, he wears a mask and long baggy robes to hide the scars. They say his face was almost burned completely off by shrike venom. He doesn't come to balls or parties unless he has to. People rarely see him outside the castle. They say his whole mind has been consumed by the desire to win this war at all costs, not that I blame him. Look at what it's done to him, and to his people. Anyone would want justice for something like that. That's why he hates gray elves so much."

I tried to think of what to say or how to respond. Nothing would come out. I stood frozen, staring at Felix. And he stared right back at me with a haunted look in his eyes. I knew we were both wondering the same thing.

"I'm dreaming about something that happened twenty years ago?" I forced myself to ask. I wanted to make sure this wasn't some kind of twisted Felix-style prank. He was totally capable of doing something like that just to watch me squirm. It was basically his favorite hobby.

Felix frowned and looked away. "No. Don't be ridiculous. That's not possible. It's a coincidence."

I was starting to panic. If he wasn't joking, then why was I dreaming about something like that? "But, Felix, the details are the same!"

He turned away and picked up his helmet. "No, they're not. You said the king died in your dream, right? Well he's not dead. I've seen him myself. He came to one of our solstice parties once. I was a kid then, but I remember it. He was definitely there, and definitely alive."

"Then why would I dream something like that? And why do I keep dreaming it every night?" I crossed my arms. I was ready to argue this until my ears bled, or until it made sense. Whichever came first.

"Maybe you overheard someone talking about it and you forgot." Felix shrugged off all my questions and crammed his helmet down onto his head. "I knew you weren't sleeping. You've got bags under your eyes big enough to store gear in. Don't let something like this distract you, much less keep you from sleeping. You can't afford to lose your focus now."

I knew I had never heard anything about this before, but I wasn't getting anywhere with Felix. I wasn't even finished telling him everything, yet. "I heard my mom's voice when I talked with Nova. She said the same thing: Return it. And she showed me a place with a cavern that went straight down into the ground."

"I've never heard of a place like that." His voice echoed from inside his helmet. "And return what? You haven't stolen anything, right?"

"No, of course not." I put my helmet on, too. "I don't know what she's talking about."

"It's probably some old memory of your mom that you've forgotten until now. That's all. Look, I've got something back at the dorm that'll help you sleep. You need it, especially tonight. Tomorrow is the first day of training, remember?" Felix gave me a thumbs up as he settled himself into the saddle. "They're only dreams. You're over thinking this. Not everything is a conspiracy, Jae."

I nodded. I didn't see how I had much of a choice. Not sleeping was killing me slowly, and tomorrow was guaranteed to be one of the hardest days of my life. Felix was right about that, at least. I couldn't afford to get too distracted. But as for the dreams ... I didn't agree. It couldn't just be a coincidence. I wasn't that lucky.

Once we landed back at the Roost, I took off Mavrik's saddle and carried it down to the tack room to be stored with all the others. It was nice to walk in there and know that tomorrow we wouldn't be on tack detail anymore. Someone else would be cleaning and checking the saddles. Sure, we'd have to take another turn at it eventually, but not for a while.

Felix bumped into me as he came in carrying his gear. "So that was You're worried about some crazy dreams?"

My stomach squirmed nervously. "Not just that. There's something else I've wanted to ask you about. I heard a rumor."

"About me?" He looked amused, maybe even a little excited.

"No, about Sile."

Felix's expression fell. "What about him?"

"Do you know a lot about him? About his past?" I knew Sile liked his privacy. What little I had found out about him was probably more than anyone else knew. But then, dragonriders liked to talk—especially about each other. Someone was bound to know something. Felix prided himself on being involved in as much gossip as possible. Wanting to be involved in everyone else's business must have been a side effect of being born a noble.

"I know some. He's been on the battlefront lots of times, and most of the other instructors really respect him. His kill-count is in the hundreds. They say he and Valla were a real terror in combat back in the day." He put his saddle down next to mine and started staring off into space. "He was supposed to be a crack-shot with a bow. I heard he could take out the eye of a deer from a hundred yards away, while flying. Most riders wouldn't even bother with a bow, you know. It's not a good weapon for us because most people can't make accurate shots in flight. The wind and speed are too much."

"Have you ever heard about him going into Luntharda?" I asked quickly before I could lose my nerve.

Felix paused. Slowly, he turned around to face me. "No one goes into Luntharda. Not unless they have a death wish. If the gray elves don't kill you, the forest definitely will."

I started telling him everything Mr. Crookin had told me about how Sile had supposedly abandoned his men, gone into the forest alone, and come back without a scratch. It sounded unbelievable, even to me. I'd never seen Luntharda for myself. Based on what I had read in my studies as a fledgling, I understood how dangerous it was. There were monsters and vicious beasts at every turn. The idea that anyone could survive it alone was crazy.

"I've never heard any of this," Felix replied. "It sounds made up. Sile may be a little unstable, but he's not insane. It has to be a lie."

"It isn't," someone interrupted.

We both looked back to see Lyon standing in the doorway of the tack room. He kept his head down, like he was trying to hide the fact that his nose was still basically being held together by gauze. "It's true," he mumbled.

Felix puffed up defiantly. "Yeah, right. Like you'd know anything about it."

"I would," Lyon snapped. It surprised me. I couldn't believe he was still willing to stand up to Felix, even after what I had done to him. "You know who my dad was. And my grandfather, too. I'm a third generation dragonrider. And I've heard this story before."

I took an eager step toward him. It was a stupid thing to do. It shouldn't have surprised me that he flinched and started backing away. He was terrified of me.

Immediately, I stopped and raised my hands to show him that I wasn't going to hurt him. "I just want to know the story. Do you know what really happened?"

Lyon glanced back and forth between Felix and me, like he was trying to figure out if it was safe to stick around. At last, he started to talk. "It was at the beginning of the war, I think. My dad flew in the same legion as Lieutenant Derrick. They weren't friends, but you know how it is; everyone knows everyone." He shrugged and fidgeted nervously. "I heard my dad talking about it once. He was pretty out of it that night. He'd been out till late with some of his old war buddies. They were telling stories. They talked about a skirmish they got into with some shrikes right outside the forest."

"Shrikes?" I stopped him long enough to ask. Felix had said that word, too, but I didn't know what it meant.

"Is it a happy place, this private little world you live in? Seriously, get a clue." Lyon scoffed like I was being intentionally stupid. "Shrikes are our enemy. We aren't the only ones who fly. The gray elves ride on their own monsters. We call them shrikes."

"They're brutal monsters, too," Felix chimed in. "Small, quick as the devil, and almost impossible to see. Their bite is extra nasty. It's got some kind of poison in it that rots your skin away. The gray elves tip their arrows and blades in the stuff, too, so that if you get shot … it's more likely to kill you."

Both of them were silent, looking at me and waiting for my reaction. I wasn't sure what to do with that information. I'd never known we would actually be fighting enemies in the air. I didn't even know what a shrike looked like, let alone that I was going to be fighting them soon.

When I didn't speak up, Lyon rolled his eyes and continued. "Anyway. The story was that they were mixed up in a skirmish with a few shrikes. Things weren't going so great. But in the middle of the fight, Sile lands and starts going into the forest. No one could stop him because they were locked in combat. Dad said he strolled into Luntharda like he was out for an afternoon walk. A few days later, he showed up back at the citadel. He didn't have a scratch on him. No one knew what happened to him, or how he managed to come out of there alive. The captains and colonels interrogated him, but it didn't make any difference. He never said a word. They said it was like he was under some kind of spell. Like he was in a trance. He wouldn't talk to anyone about what happened. That's why they took him off the frontlines and sent him here to be an instructor."

"It had to be some kind of torture," Felix said quietly. "Something the gray elves did to him to keep him from talking."

Chills swept over me. I was trying to process it all. Felix seemed to be doing the same. He was frowning so hard it put lines on his forehead. I was so busy watching him and letting that new information sink in, that I didn't even notice Lyon was staring at me until he spoke.

"I came to make sure you weren't late for curfew." Lyon was already starting to walk away. "So hurry up. It's already dark, and I'm not running any extra laps tomorrow. And some guy came by our room looking for you, Jaevid. He left something for you. He said you'd be expecting it."

Felix and I exchanged a look. Since when did Lyon check up on us? I was starting to worry I was hallucinating, but then I saw Felix start to grin. Nope, I was definitely not imagining it. Usually Lyon called me halfbreed. But tonight, he had used my name.

sixteen

I waited until Lyon and Felix were asleep to unwrap the scimitar. Bren had carefully bundled it up in a soft cloth, and left a note thanking me for saving them again. As I unwrapped it, my hands shook with excitement. I could see the faint glow of the metal in the candlelight. It was the most beautiful weapon I had ever seen.

Bren had fixed everything, even the carvings on the side of the blade that had almost been rubbed completely off. I still couldn't understand what they said, though. They were written in another language. The blade shimmered. The polished bronze looked like gold. The ivory shone like pearl. The soft leather grip felt comfortable in my hand, and the metal hummed a beautiful note as I drew it from the scabbard.

I ran my thumb over the emblem on the pommel. The head of a stag stared back at me. Bren had said it was the symbol of gray elf royalty. My mind was still processing everything I'd heard that day. It was a lot to take in. But knowing that the rumor about Sile was true, that he had been into Luntharda, made my thoughts churn. He was definitely hiding something. His kidnapping last year, my place here as a dragonrider, the dreams—somehow, it was all connected. I just had to figure out how.

I put the scimitar away. I wrapped it back up in the cloth and tucked it under my bed where I hoped no one else would find it. I had a feeling that if anyone else knew I was carrying around a blade with the gray elf symbol on it, they wouldn't be as calm about it as Bren was. Now was not the time to be pushing my luck. Now was the time for sleeping.

Felix had already given me a tiny square of folded paper before he went to bed. He called it a sleeping remedy, and d me to pour it into some water and drink it all. If it worked, he promised he could get more. So I went to the washroom and took it. The white powder wrapped inside the paper tasted horrible. It was so bitter it made my eyes water. But I choked it down.

I wasn't sure the remedy was even working until I got back to our room. While I was changing out of my clothes, the room started to spin. My head got fuzzy. I barely made it to my bed before I collapsed. I was still wearing one of my shoes, but I couldn't get my arms and legs to cooperate long enough to take it off. And then, I didn't care.

Sleep overtook me, and the next thing I knew, it was morning. For the first time in a while, there were no dreams or nightmares. That remedy, whatever it was, had definitely worked.

I knew it was morning because a boot hit me in the

head. That was the way Felix usually woke me up when I was running behind. He had a good aim.

"Get up, moron!" Felix barked at me.

I pushed myself up from the bed. That's when I realized my face was cold and sticky. I had been drooling in my sleep.

Lyon and Felix heckled me the whole time while I got dressed. They were already outfitted and ready to go, so I guess I deserved it for lagging behind. It was still dark outside as we hurried out of the dormitory to meet Jace outside the academy walls. He was waiting for us, armed with that bullwhip he liked so much.

We ran until we were all soaked with sweat. We did push-ups and sit-ups until my bones ached. Jace cracked his whip, shouting out the names of different stances, parries, and strikes. If one of us got it wrong, he was right there in two seconds to yell at all of us until our ears were ringing. Then we had to start over and do it all again.

We were the first ones to drag our saddles out of the tack room that morning. We saddled up, strapped on our armor, and took off into the first few breaths of twilight. It was the first time I had ever seen Jace and Lyon's dragons, but I didn't have much time to admire them.

Jace's dragon was a sleek gray male with faint markings that were only visible if you were standing close. The color of his scales looked like smoke in the pale light of dawn. That, Felix told me, was partly what had earned him his name. They called him Ghost not only because of his color, but also because he flew so fast you were likely to be dead, engulfed in dragon flame, before you even realized he had flown over.

It was the first time I had seen a dragon up close who had been in combat recently. It must have been for

Felix, too, because he was full of awe and admiration. He pointed out the intricate striped grooves that looked like they had been engraved onto the horns on Ghost's head. I'd never seen that on another dragon before. Or at least, I'd never taken the time to notice it.

"It's his kill count," Felix announced. His eyes were shining like he could barely contain his excitement. "A notch for every gray elf rider he's brought down. Look at them all!"

After that, looking at the engraved stripes gave me a strange, nauseous sensation in my stomach. It reminded me that Jace wasn't just an instructor. He was a soldier. He had killed people—lots of them judging by the amount of notches on his dragon's horns.

Ghost wasn't the only one with those marks, though. Lyon's dragon was a much older male named Demos. He had notches going down every inch of the long horns on his head. He was big dragon, closer to Nova's size than any of the others, and apparently had a bad temper. It made me wonder if dragons picked up on the bad habits of their riders over time. His scales were a burnt orange color, and he had black stripes like a cat all over his body. According to Felix, Demos had been in combat more times than any of the rest of us. Lyon's father and grandfather had both ridden him into battle. That explained all the notches.

Jace gave us hand signals in the air, directing us to break off into pairs and fly our usual drills. Felix and Lyon flew together in a pair, with Felix in lead. I took up the position of following Jace. Dragonriders called it being a "wing end" because I was supposed to stay in formation, right behind Ghost's left wing, as we flew through our drill patterns.

I had already flown these drills before. It wasn't

supposed to be anything new. But right away, I figured out why Jace had paired us together. Ghost was fast—*unbelievably* fast. I doubted Nova or Demos could ever keep up with him. When he poured on the speed, I gave Mavrik a mental nudge to follow.

At first, we could keep pace, but as Jace started whipping through spins and spirals, Mavrik started lagging behind. He was huffing and puffing, beating his wings harder than I'd ever seen him just to keep Ghost in our sight. I heard him growling, and I could sense his frustration. It made me angrier than I expected. We had always been the fastest. Falling so far behind made our drills sloppy and frantic, and each passing second made me more and more aggravated. I was every bit as mad about it as Mavrik was.

By the time we landed, Mavrik was furious that he had been outdone. I was bitter about it, too. Still, I didn't put on a show about it the way he did. Mavrik bared his teeth, snapping at the air as I dismounted. I could tell he wanted to challenge Ghost again, but the gray dragon ignored him as Jace and the others landed nearby.

I expected Jace to say something to me about how sloppy the drills had been. After all, we'd been scrambling to keep up the whole time. I was braced for the inevitable chewing-out I deserved as he walked past us. But he didn't even look at me.

I was stunned. Jace had outright ignored me! Surprisingly, that hurt even worse than being yelled at. It stuck in my pride like a splinter. I hated it. Sure, I had been ignored and even pitied plenty of times when I was floundering through ground combat training. But I had never been a disappointment in the air. It was like Jace was so disgusted with our performance that he wasn't even going to acknowledge how bad it was.

Being disregarded like that lit a raging fire in my chest. I looked at Mavrik. He was bristled and hissing, swishing his tail bitterly. I nodded and clenched my teeth. Next time. We would be better next time. I wasn't going to get shown up like that again.

Jace gave us all a short pep talk about keeping our morale up before he dismissed us. He passed out our new avian uniforms, and gave us our schedule. It was basically the reverse of last year. Instead of starting the day with combat training, we would be attending classes on survival techniques, orienteering, and battle planning until lunch. After the noon break, we would assemble at the gymnasium for combat training that would last for the rest of the day.

I raised my hand to ask, "What about interrogation training? I thought that started this year."

Jace smirked like he found my enthusiasm hilarious and cute. "It's coming. But you're not ready for that, yet."

I was still so angry about the flying at breakfast that I couldn't force myself to eat much. It was a stupid thing to get so upset about. I knew that. I still couldn't help it. I had never had much to be proud of. Our speed had always been our advantage, something about us that was special, and now ... it wasn't.

The dormitory was alive with activity as the sun began to rise. We hurried through our morning baths, fighting our way through the other avians who were trying to do the same thing. We got dressed in our new uniforms, grabbed our stacks of maps, and filed down toward the breaking dome with everyone else. The horns on the academy walls began to blare, giving the call to arms. That was our signal to report in for our morning brief.

I can't explain what it was like to stand with all the other dragonriders of Blybrig Academy. But overwhelming would probably be the best place to start. I stood with Felix on one side, and Lyon on the other, lined up according to our rank in the breaking dome. We stood at attention even before the command was called, and we didn't talk to each other. Last year, I hadn't really understood what I was doing there, or what would happen to me. But now, things were different. I was starting to understand my place here. I knew I had an objective, and that was to survive.

Dressed out in our black tunics and pants, with our navy blue cloaks brushing at our heels, and the king's golden eagle pinned around our necks, I knew we looked intimidating to the younger riders. It made me want to stand up a little taller, to put on my fiercest face. I wanted to look capable. I wanted to be a standard that someone could strive for.

Before us, Commander Rayken and the other officers were assembling. They were all dressed out in their formal armor, wearing swords at their hips, and talking in low voices. I recognized many of them. Jace was there, frowning like always. Lieutenant Morrig glanced my way for a second, and then did a double take when he realized who I was. He had been my combat instructor last year.

Even though it wasn't appropriate, I wanted to thank him for putting up with me. Lieutenant Morrig had worked hard to find something I could do when it came to hand-to-hand combat. Not many others would have even bothered, especially considering how I had looked back then. When we locked gazes, I gave him a small nod. I wanted him to know he hadn't wasted his time on me. I wouldn't be a disappointment this year.

Lieutenant Thrane's glare caught my attention next. He was standing off to the side, away from the other instructors, with his burly arms bulging like two giant, overstuffed sausages. His dark eyes were narrowed right at me. I could practically taste the cold pressure of his presence. Even after Commander Rayken started calling everyone to attention, he kept glaring at me like he hoped the heat of his wrath might make me burst into flame. Thankfully, it didn't.

"Welcome to Blybrig Academy. For some of you, this is your first time to stand in our midst. For others, you are already a part of our brotherhood and understood the importance of what lies ahead of you this year," Commander Rayken started with basically the same speech as last year. Then he started telling a brief history of dragonriders. It hadn't meant all that much to me as a fledgling, but now the history interested me a lot more. Now I was a part of it.

"There are only a few savage beasts upon this earth that share a bond with man: dogs, horses, ... women," he paused. Some of the other instructors snickered and elbowed each other. I guess that was supposed to be a joke. "But greatest amongst these is the dragon. His kind first came to us in our darkest hour, when foreign enemies struck our soil with intent to destroy and enslave us. When we were faced with the greatest foe our kingdom had ever known, one who dared to call himself God Bane. Upon the smoldering field of battle, the first dragon chose a humble infantryman to be his rider. Their strengths and desires were united, bonded for life. They became an image of hope to others, who began to look to the sky as they prayed for victory. More dragons came from their nests far on the eastern coast and followed that example, choosing men of merit and strength as their riders. That was how our mighty brotherhood was formed. We were born from the ashes of devastation, to rise and bring the flames of war upon any enemy who would try to invade our beloved kingdom."

Commander Rayken paused again and looked across our company. No one said a word. "Time has indeed changed us. The ways of old have become a distant memory. But you are all here for that same purpose. The reason for our existence has not changed. We fight and die as one, as brothers, as dragonriders." He saluted, clasping a fist over his breastplate. "For his majesty's honor!"

We all responded without hesitation, snapping a fist over our chests and mimicking that gesture with a shout. That's when I realized my pulse was racing. The sense of purpose that surged through my veins was overwhelming. When I glanced beside me, I saw that Felix looked flushed, too. His face was the picture of fierce determination.

After we were dismissed, we split up according to our classes and started making our way out of the dome. Felix, Lyon, and I were assigned to a survival class first. I was already excited when we hit the door. The huge, sloping room had seats all the way around it like an amphitheatre. We sat together, listening as the instructor stood at the center of the room and explained what we would be learning.

"If you are shot down in Luntharda, or find yourself a prisoner of the gray elves, you will most likely die," the instructor said sharply. A few students shifted uncomfortably in their seats. "If you do survive, it won't be because of your sword or fighting techniques. It will be because of what you learn here, in this classroom.

Survivors pay attention. Survivors listen, learn, and remember. My name is Lieutenant Haprick. Welcome."

I swallowed hard. I didn't feel very welcome. Panicked was more like it. I quickly made a mental note never to zone out during this class. It wasn't hard, though, because most of what he talked about was interesting.

After his introduction, Lieutenant Haprick launched right into listing off exactly what we would be given in our saddlebags to help us survive a worst-case scenario. He had a table set up in the center of the room with a bag exactly like the one we would all be issued. He called it a "go-bag" because in the event of an emergency, we had to grab it and go. We all scrambled to take notes as he took each item out, one by one, and quickly demonstrated how to use it.

The first item was a thick candle made from beef fat. He explained that it would provide light, but it could also be eaten if you were ever in a situation where you were starving. Next was a piece of flint, which he intended to teach us to use in order to light a fire. There was a small sewing kit for treating wounds or mending clothes, several spools of gauze, and a small round tin of an herbal salve that would keep open wounds from getting infected. He went on to list a lot of other things like rope, a knife, a canteen, and snare wire. I lost count, and it took all my focus to keep up with him while taking notes. He said he would teach us more about each item, how to use it, and what to do if we lost it. Then and only then would we be getting go-bags of our own.

"These are tools," he insisted. "Not trinkets or toys. Only once you understand their use and respect their value can you be trusted with them."

Our next class was about memorizing maps. This, at

least, was very familiar to us. Last year, Felix had struggled some when it came to memorizing maps. He groaned and slouched in his seat when we were given the same assignments as last year. We would have to duplicate a map of the kingdom down to the very last detail. I hadn't struggled with it that much, so I was confident. Sile had shown us how to divide the maps up into quadrants, and memorize them one by one, to make things easier.

A little before lunch, we finally shambled into our last class of the morning. Battle planning sounded boring, but we had only gotten a small taste of it last year. This year, the instructor promised to present us with problems and battles that we had to present calculated plans for. It looked a lot more difficult than I was expecting.

"An effective plan is half the battle, boys." The instructor, Lieutenant Graul, gave a deep, throaty laugh. "Otherwise we'd all be buzzing around randomly, just as liable to kill our own men as the enemy."

When morning classes ended, we were all dismissed to have lunch. We stood in line, got our ration of food, and sat down at our usual place at the end of one of the long dining tables. Felix was staring down at his food with a glazed look in his eyes. Lyon was swirling a fork in his potatoes. I was starving, as usual, but my head felt like it was going to explode. This was only the first day, and already it seemed like there was a mountain of knowledge looming over me.

"I don't know if I can do this," Felix admitted.

The rest of us looked up at him. I was surprised to hear him sound so defeated already.

"It won't be so bad once we get into it." I tried to sound confident. "It seems like a lot because we just started. It'll get better."

He grumbled angrily, and started stuffing food in his mouth. I couldn't understand most of what he said, but I did catch the words, "I hate maps." The rest was probably a string of curses.

After lunch, we had a few spare minutes to shed our formal cloaks and put on our vambraces and sword belts before combat training. I tucked Beckah's handkerchief into its usual place against my arm, and followed Felix and Lyon to the gymnasium.

I assumed Lieutenant Morrig would be instructing us again. After all, he'd done a good job last year. But as we joined the rest of the avians flocking into the building, I heard a voice that made my insides turn to jelly.

Lieutenant Thrane was standing in the center of the gymnasium, his bulging arms crossed, and his huge bald head wrinkled in a scowl. He was looking at the crowd of students filing in like he was searching for someone. I got the immediate sense that the person he was looking for was most likely me.

Thrane wasn't alone. Jace and Morrig were standing there, as well. There were a lot more avian students than fledglings, so Morrig probably needed the extra help. As soon as we were all inside, Morrig called us to attention and began doling out orders. He divided is into three large groups and announced that we would be working in stations. After two hours at one station, the groups would switch until we had all visited each one.

Station one was basic sword dueling with Jace. Station two was for learning dual wielding with two weapons or with a shield with Morrig. And finally, station three—which was bound to be my favorite—was grappling and barehanded combat with Thrane. All three sounded like they were going to be unpleasant. I was determined not to think about it too much.

I had a lot to prove. Last year, things hadn't gone so well in combat training. Being half the size of everyone else in my class hadn't helped. But that wasn't the case anymore. Now, I was one of the tallest. I knew this was my chance. My performance here would decide the fate of my friends and myself when it came time for the battle scenario. So I clenched my teeth, and did my best not to look at Thrane.

Lyon, Felix, and I were grouped together with twenty other avians and sent to station one. After retrieving a wooden practice sword from the armory room, Jace lined us up in a grid, and unfurled his long, leather whip. He stalked back and forth in front of us like a prowling jungle cat, staring down every student he passed.

"What you did last year was child's play. You are not children anymore. You are men. And you will be held accountable for not knowing your maneuvers. Be glad that it is just the taste of a whip that is your punishment, and not the bite of an enemy's blade." Jace spoke so calmly that it made me nervous. His eyes scanned us as though he were looking for weakness. "Now, show me an opening stance!"

The gymnasium filled with the sound of shouts, of grunts, of Jace snapping his bullwhip, and Thrane bellowing out orders like an angry bear. The first time someone slipped up, it was an avian standing right in front of me. I saw it happen. Jace called a parry maneuver, and the student moved into the wrong stance. In an instant, Jace was there, looming right in his face and demanding to know why he couldn't do something so simple. Then came the crack of the whip. The student screamed. None of us dared to move.

"Now, do it again." Jace snarled. His eyes locked with mine, and I felt my stomach do a back flip. "No mistakes."

Jace had threatened us with that whip before. He was good at popping it right in front of our noses if we stumbled, but he'd never actually used it. It made me realize that practice was officially over. This was the real deal now. And the consequences were going to be just as real.

A few other students got to taste of Jace's whip before the two hours were up, but thankfully I wasn't one of them. Someone blew a horn to signal it was time to switch stations, and we moved toward the other side of the room where Morrig was waiting. He didn't have a whip, but that didn't make me feel any safer.

Morrig had us pair up and form two long lines facing each other. First, he demonstrated new maneuvers with two weapons, and then we all began drilling. Once he felt we were getting a good grasp on it, he started teaching us how to fight with a shield on one arm. I was reminded again that even though I had grown, I still lacked the sheer bulk of most young men my size. The shield was heavy, and I had a hard time lifting it to shoulder-height like I was supposed to.

"It is not only for protection," Morrig said as he strolled down our lines, watching us perform the maneuvers over and over. "A shield can be a weapon of brute force. It can allow you to advance in close enough to your enemy to catch them off guard. Do not treat it as a burden. Treat it as an extension of yourself, just like your sword."

I tried. My arms were already aching, and raising the heavy metal shield was about all I could manage. I could barely lift it, much less whirl it around. But I didn't want my weakness to show. I pushed myself until I had nothing left. Finally, the horn blew. It was time to switch stations again.

With sweat running down my face and dripping off my chin, I looked over at station three. Thrane was staring right at me. I saw him lick the front of his teeth like a hungry wolf. It was like he was waiting and hoping I would snap again so he would have a good excuse to kill me.

I was determined not to give him that satisfaction.

We put our weapons away before we went to his station. My heart was still pounding in my ears as I lined up between Lyon and Felix. The rest of our group did the same, waiting for Thrane to give us orders.

He walked through our group, sizing us up one by one. When he stopped right next to me and stood there, so close that I could smell his breath. It took everything I had not to look up at him. I knew that's what he wanted. We were at attention. We weren't supposed to move. Thrane was trying to provoke me. I could feel the hate and rage rolling off him like bad body odor. So I picked a spot on the wall straight ahead of me and focused on it.

"All right, ladies," Thrane sneered. He was so close that his voice rustled my hair. "I'm supposed to teach you how to fight like men. Some of you have already proven that you can't, even against each other. I've seen you slapping each other around like little girls. It's pathetic. You want to break someone's arm? This is how you do it."

Before anyone could react, he snatched Lyon by the collar of his shirt. Thrane spun him around, twisting him like a ragdoll and giving his arm a sudden, violent jerk. Lyon's arm made a horrible crunching sound. He started screaming in pain.

When Thrane let him go, Lyon fell into a heap on the ground, clutching his arm. He was still crying out in agony, and a few other avians lurched forward like they wanted to help him. But Thrane raised a hand to stop them. His eyes settled back on me with a vicious smile. This wasn't about Lyon. This was about *me*. He wanted a reaction. He wanted to set off my battle fever again.

The sound of Lyon's screams set my blood on fire. As horrible as it might seem, the fact that he had attacked Lyon instead of Felix was probably the only thing that saved me in that moment. If it were Felix lying there, clutching his arm and sobbing, I don't think I could have held it together. But I managed to keep my composure.

I didn't move. I didn't blink. I kept my eyes fixed on Thrane, and neither of us spoke. I poured as much of my anger into my gaze as I could, like a silent promise. One day, I would make him pay for this. I could be patient. I could wait for the right moment. Until then, I would endure anything he threw at me.

The continuing sound of Lyon's cries made the rest of the gymnasium stop their training. They all gathered around us, eager to see what was happening. Even Morrig and Jace came over, pushing their way through the crowd to see what was wrong.

"Couldn't contain yourself for even five minutes?" Jace snapped at Thrane as he pushed past him. "You stupid barbarian."

Thrane shot Jace a glare like he might decide to hit him. It seemed like they already had some bad blood between them. "I don't see how it's any of your business, pretty boy."

"He's my student. That makes it my business. If you

can't be professional, then I'll take this to Rayken and have you formally dismissed back to the frontlines, with or without a wing end." Jace crouched down next to Lyon and began inspecting his arm. "You broke it. Looks like a compound fracture. Do you even realize what that means? He's done. He can't fly like this. And he certainly can't train."

"He was useless anyways. Look at him. His face all plastered together like a broken baby doll. A kid like that won't last two seconds on the front lines. I did him a favor." Thrane let out a cold, booming laugh. Nobody laughed with him. "Don't tell me you're worried because his daddy will be upset? This is avian training. Accidents happen."

"Yes. Accidents *do* happen." Jace cut Thrane a promising look that made the big, burly man hesitate for a second. Even though Thrane was easily twice Jace's size, I got the feeling that if it ever did come down to a fight … size wouldn't be much of an advantage for him. Jace could be every bit as brutal and merciless.

I couldn't focus on combat training after that. Jace and Thrane left to take Lyon to the infirmary. An injury like that would mean Lyon couldn't train anymore. But maybe, if he kept up his training on his own, he could try again as an avian next year.

Morrig had no choice but to put us all in a big block formation and run through the same basic sword maneuvers over and over. My mind wandered, and I felt overwhelmed by guilt. Lyon's career might be over just like that. And it was my fault. If I hadn't challenged him to that first fight, he never would have been a target for Thrane.

When training was over for the day, I found a shady

spot on the front steps of the dormitory and collapsed. I leaned against the cool stone, and watched the dragons circling overhead like giant, scaly vultures. Everyone else was going in for dinner, but I didn't feel like eating.

I felt the toe of someone's boot nudge me. "Hey," Felix said. "Get up. We need to eat and study."

I cracked an eye open to stare up at him. "How can you eat? Didn't you see what happened?"

Felix's expression was tense. He had his hands in his pockets, and a serious frown on his lips. "I saw it. But that's the way things are now. We're not fledglings anymore, Jae. The instructors are going to knock us around."

I slumped forward to hang my head and rest my elbows on my knees. "That had nothing to do with training, and you know it. It was personal. It was a threat. Thrane is trying to provoke me into attacking him."

"So don't attack him." Felix shrugged. "Seems simple to me."

I gave him as much of a glare as I could muster. "Right. It's simple now. But will it be simple when he does something like that to you?"

We stared at each other for a few minutes without saying anything. At last, Felix sighed loudly and came to sit down next to me. "You think I can't handle getting my arm broken?"

"I'm not sure *I* can't handle it," I told him. "If I have to watch that happen to you, I don't think I'll be able to stop myself. You saw how I was before. If I get battle fever again, I might kill him."

Felix smirked. "Cocky, aren't you? You really think you could kill someone like Thrane?"

I rolled my eyes. His sense of humor was exasperating

sometimes. "I don't know."

"Look, I get it, okay? You feel guilty. But it wasn't your fault. It could have just as easily been anyone else. Lyon was in the wrong place at the wrong time, as usual. And if you ask me, he had this coming to him sooner or later." He patted my shoulder roughly. "Don't blame yourself."

"What if Thrane does something like that to me?" I asked him. "Could you handle it? Could you stand there and watch him break my arm?"

Felix's eyes got distant. I saw his demeanor change from his usual happy-go-lucky self, to someone much more serious. It made him look older, and not in a good way. He squeezed my shoulder. "I don't know. Let's hope it doesn't come to that."

seventeen

My intentions started out great. I was going to apologize before it was too late. But as I stepped out into the cool midnight wind, I started to think—and that's usually when things go wrong for me.

I was only holding one last secret back from Felix. He knew about everything else, including my weird nightmares. What he didn't know was that a few weeks ago, I had been able to heal Sile's wife with my bare hands. I wasn't sure how I had done it, or if I could even do it again. Sile had warned me not do it again, and I assumed that was because doing it had almost killed me before. I knew he probably didn't want me to risk my life like that again, or that someone might catch me doing it. But as I wal' alone toward the infirmary, I knew I was about to disobey Sile's warning.

I was going to try to heal Lyon.

His injuries were my fault. It was only fair that I should do everything I could to make it right. Sure, it might kill me. Or I might turn into an old man if it triggered another growth spurt. But I couldn't let his career end like this. It wasn't right. And as far as I knew, I was the only one who could do anything about it.

The infirmary was dark when I opened the door. Only a few candles burned in the hallways, casting heavy shadows into empty rooms. Only one medic was still awake. He was sitting at Lyon's bedside reading what looked like a letter.

"Come to pay your friend a visit?" he asked when he noticed me standing in the doorway. "You should come back tomorrow. He's sleeping now. You should be, too."

I started to get nervous. "I-I want to talk to him now, if that's okay. I know it's past curfew, but this is the first chance I've gotten to come by."

The medic was an old, heavy-set man. He looked at me for a minute, scratching his chin through his curly white beard. "Very well," he sighed at last, and pulled a wooden pipe out of his pocket. "I could use a break for a smoke. Try not to get him too worked up. Poor lad had quite a shock."

I slipped into the room as the medic left. I waited until I heard him go outside, then I quietly closed the door to Lyon's room. If I was going to do this, I didn't want anyone else to see it.

The sound of our voices must have woken Lyon up, because before I could turn around I heard him speak. "Why are you here?"

I faced him and tried not to stare. It was hard, though. Lyon was lying on a small bed, covered in a white sheet up to his chin. His arm was splinted and wrapped up in a thick layer of bandaging, and he had fresh dressings on his nose as well. There were dark circles under his eyes, and his cheeks were swollen like he'd been crying. Overall, Lyon looked awful.

"I came to apologize," I finally managed to say.

"For what?" He sounded confused.

"For what happened with Thrane. It's my fault. It should have been me, not you. I'm the one he really wants to hurt." The words came spilling out of my mouth so fast I couldn't stop them. "I never wanted this to happen. If I could take it all back, I would."

Lyon was quiet for a few minutes. The silence was awkward, and I didn't know if I should explain what I wanted to do … or just do it and let him figure it out for himself.

"I don't get you," he muttered. He almost sounded angry. "Why would you apologize to me? Why would you even care what I think?"

His questions caught me off guard. I wasn't sure how to answer. But before I could try, he started talking again.

"You know you'll never really be one of us. You'll always be the odd man out. There's always going to be people like Thrane, doing whatever they can to break you. They're all waiting for you to make a wrong move. And still you don't leave. You just keep trying. It doesn't make any sense. Why? Why are you doing this?" Usually, that kind of speech from Lyon would have been filled with as much hatred and sarcasm as possible. Now he looked confused instead.

I sat down in the chair at his bedside and stared down at the floor. "I wonder that, too, sometimes. I want to watch Felix's back the way he watches mine. That used to be my reason. Now I'm endangering him and everyone else by being here."

"So are you just trying to prove that you aren't a traitor?" he asked again.

"No." I shook my head. "I don't have anything to prove. I'm here because this is where I'm meant to be. I believe that Mavrik chose me for a reason. Whatever that reason is, I have to stay here and figure it out. Even if that means being a danger to the people I want to protect."

"Yeah, right." He snorted like he didn't believe me. "Like you would ever want to protect *me*. I'm not stupid, you know. We're not friends."

I looked at him right in the eye. "I would protect you. And I will."

Lyon flashed me a skeptical glare. "Why? After everything I've done to you, why would you want to do anything for me?"

"Because I can. And because you need me to, even if you don't like me," I said. "I know you're alone now. Your friends from last year—they don't come around you anymore."

I watched Lyon's eyes get watery and his cheeks got red. He bit his lip and looked away, like he was trying to fight back tears. "It's got nothing to do with you, Jaevid," he managed to mumble. "It's not your problem."

I couldn't help but smile a little. "You can call me Jae, you know."

He shot me another glare. "Only your friends call you that."

"Yeah." I shrugged. "I know."

Lyon fell silent again. We stared at each other in the dim light of the candle burning on the bedside table. Finally, I knew the time had come. It was now or never. I didn't want to lose my nerve or risk that the medic might come back.

I stood up and went to his bedside. "I'm going to do something really, really stupid." It seemed like a good idea to give him a fair warning in case, you know, I died.

Lyon looked nervous. "What?"

I was nervous, too. I couldn't keep myself from shaking as I reached to lay my hands on his broken arm. "I'm going to tell you something, and it's up to you if you want to turn me in to the instructors or not. If you do, I'll probably get shipped off to a prison camp right away. Or Thrane will save them the trouble and kill me. No one, not even Jace could do anything to stop it."

I took a deep breath. Lyon was probably the last person in the world I should have been trusting with a secret like this. But if it actually worked, he was going to figure it out anyway. "You already know I can talk to animals."

He nodded a little. "Yeah, I remember. Like with the paludix turtle last year."

"Well. That's not all I can do." I swallowed hard. "I can heal people, too."

Lyon's mouth fell open.

"Felix doesn't know. No one else does. Well, except for Sile. That's the other reason I came." I looked down at his broken arm. "I'm going to fix it."

"W-will it hurt?" He started stammering. His eyes were wide and afraid. "It hurt so much when they set it. I-I can't go through that again."

I shook my head slightly. "I don't think so."

Part of me knew I should warn him that doing this might kill me. But he already looked terrified. So I kept that to myself, and gathered my courage. These strange abilities I had were getting stronger. It was getting easier and easier to talk to animals. I barely even had to concentrate to talk to Mavrik. And now I could even feel Nova's thoughts if I focused hard enough.

It was now or never. I had to try.

With my hands resting on his arm, I knelt down at Lyon's bedside. I closed my eyes, and looked for that warmth in the back of my mind. I felt it there, tingling like a chill that wanted to spread all over my scalp. I felt the pressure settle on my chest, making it harder to breathe.

My ears began ringing. All around me, the room started to slip away. That little bit of warmth in my mind turned into heat, and it spread all over my body. It was creeping over my skin and making my palms feel like they were on fire. I got the sense like time was slowing down, that the room was spinning, and the pressure on my chest became so intense that I could barely breathe at all. I wanted to panic. The room spun faster, and my vision started to blur.

"No." My body jolted suddenly as I heard my mother's voice in my mind. *"Do not lose focus."*

I braced myself. The room's spinning slowed a little. The heat on my palms burned like I was sticking my hands into a roaring fire. I clenched my teeth to keep from screaming.

When I had healed Sile's wife, it had felt like something inside me snapped. This time, it wasn't like that. This felt like a slow, agonizing tearing sensation in my chest. Like someone was slowly ripping my lungs apart. I couldn't breathe, but I didn't give up. Next to me, I heard Lyon whimper. I felt him try to pull away, so I gripped his arm harder.

Then the tearing sensation stopped. I could breathe again.

My body was suddenly so weak I couldn't keep myself from falling backwards. I landed on the floor, and I stared up at the ceiling. My ears were still ringing so loudly I could barely hear Lyon calling my name.

Then he slapped me across the face.

It jarred me. The ringing stopped, and I could hear him more clearly. Lyon was crouched on the floor beside me, shaking my shoulders. "Wake up, you idiot! You better not die over a stupid broken arm!"

I blinked, and looked at him. Every inch of my body was numb and tingly. I felt so exhausted I could barely twitch a finger, but I managed to ask, "Did it work?"

Lyon hesitated. He looked down at his arm, which was still wrapped up in bandages. Then, without warning, he began ripping them off. He tore through all the layers of gauze, and held his bare arm up to the light. I watched him wiggle his fingers, and run his hand over the smooth, unmarked skin on his forearm.

His arm was completely healed. There wasn't even a scar. It didn't look like it had ever been broken.

Lyon's eyes were as big as saucers when he stared down at me. "What are you?" I heard him whisper.

I was too tired to say anything, even though the answer was simple. I had absolutely no idea what I was. But one thing was certain: I was getting stronger.

The last thing I remembered was Lyon pulling one of my arms over his shoulders so he could drag me to my feet. I must have passed out after that because the next thing I knew, I was lying back in my bed in our dorm room. I bolted up right in bed, and it made Felix scream with surprise. He'd been preparing to throw another shoe at me like he did every morning. Apparently, I had startled him.

"Geez!" He started yelling. "Who the heck wakes up like that? What's wrong with you?"

I ducked as a boot went soaring past my head. Before I could yell back at him, the door to our room opened. Jace was standing there, and he was frowning harder than usual. Felix and I exchanged a quick, panicked glance, like we were silently asking one another who he was here for.

"You." Jace pointed right at me. "Come with me."

He waited right outside the door while I cleaned myself up. I was still wearing my clothes from yesterday. They stank from sweat, so I changed quickly and started for the door.

Felix caught me by the arm on my way out. Our eyes met, and he didn't have to say anything to get his point across. He wanted to know what was going on, and if I would be okay. I wasn't sure. I smiled so he wouldn't worry.

Jace didn't speak as I came out into the hall to meet him. He curled a finger at me, and started walking. I followed him out into the early morning air. A thick fog had settled over the academy, and something about it made Jace seem even more dangerous than usual. His long dark cape rolled off his shoulders and licked at his heels. All I could see was the back of his head, but I knew he was probably scowling like an angry wolf.

Jace had a way of looking at everyone that way—like he was a predator about to strike. Anywhere else, that was probably a terrible way to look at people. No one wanted to be friendly with someone who seemed like they might suddenly bite your head off. However, I had a feeling that on the battlefield, men like Jace were exactly the kind of people you wanted fighting on your side.

He didn't slow down until we reached the doors of the infirmary. By then, my stomach was doing nervous flips. Through the gloom, I could see two figures already standing there waiting for us. The old medic had his arms crossed, and he was looking at me with a hard frown. Beside him, Lyon had a stubborn glare on his face. His hands were clenched into fists at his sides, and he made a point never to look me in the eye.

"Is this the one?" Jace asked sharply.

The medic nodded.

Lyon didn't say a word.

Jace turned on me with a look of wrath in his eyes that was downright terrifying. Still, I didn't let him see me shake. I was learning better than to cringe away from him when he glared at me like that. I was a soldier now. Soldiers didn't cringe.

"Tell me what you did," he demanded. "Tell me now."

"I told you already, he didn't do anything!" Lyon tried to interject. Jace didn't pay him any attention.

When I didn't answer right away, Jace took an aggressive step toward me. He met me nose-to-nose, since we were about the same height now. His cold, dark eyes locked onto mine, like he was silently daring me to lie to him. "Tell me," he repeated.

"I don't know," I managed to say, although I knew that answer wasn't going to fly far with him. "I'm not sure how it works. I don't know why I can do it. I just … can."

"Is it because you're a halfbreed?" The old medic was still scowling at me suspiciously. "Because of your elf blood?"

I shook my head. "I don't know. If you're asking me if a gray elf trained me to do it, then the answer is no. I've never seen anyone else do it."

Jace looked like he sincerely wanted to hit me. Instead, he backed off and turned away from us. I could hear him cursing furiously under his breath.

"Listen, I may not be a dragonrider, but I understand a threat when I see one," the medic said. There was resignation in his voice. "What he did is nothing short of a miracle, but it's not a threat to anyone. Quite the opposite, actually."

Jace didn't answer, and the silence became very tense.

Lyon flashed me an apologetic expression.

I nodded back at him. It wasn't his fault. I should have been more careful with my planning.

"I owed him a favor. I promised him I would look out for you, if anything happened. But Sile never, ever mentioned anything about this." Jace started to rant, muttering under his breath like a madman. "What am I supposed to do with you now?"

I flinched. Deep down I knew the answer. I had to leave. If Thrane found out what I could do, it would be all the excuse he needed to finally have his way. Miracle or not, any form of a gray elf doing any kind of magic was not going to be okay with the other instructors here. Thrane would finally have a good reason to kill me that no one else would argue with.

"Now hold on a minute, Lieutenant Rordin." The medic stepped forward and put his hand on my shoulder.

"So far, we are the only ones who know about this, correct? So it ends with us. We won't speak another word about it."

"Are you being intentionally dense?" Jace growled. "Everyone in that gymnasium saw his arm get broken. Do you expect them to believe it just got better on its own overnight?"

"They saw what they *thought* was my arm getting broken," Lyon piped up suddenly. He had a confident grin on his face.

We all turned to look at him.

I'd never considered lying to be a valuable skill. But the way Lyon did it—well, I don't know how it could be called anything else. It was his craft. Some men made saddles, others painted beautiful artwork. Lyon told superb lies.

"No one except us knows it for sure," he said. "So we say I got better. It was dislocated, not broken like we thought. No one else has to know anything about it."

"Thrane will want an explanation." Jace didn't sound convinced. "You can bet he was sure he broke it. He won't believe otherwise."

"Then he can come to me." The medic patted my shoulder roughly. "As good as he is at breaking bones, he isn't a medic. If he wants to talk specifics, send him to me. I've dealt with him before. Don't give him credit for brains he doesn't have."

I slowly started to realize that these men were rallying around me. They were actually trying to find a way to keep my abilities a secret from everyone else. It made me uneasy, especially since I didn't even know the medic. People didn't usually do kind things for me just because they could. I felt my face get hot with embarrassment.

The medic must have noticed me blushing, because he started to chuckle. "Make sure no one suspects you. In your case, my boy, any attention from Thrane will be negative attention, I'm afraid. Try to keep out of his way."

I nodded. When I looked up again, my eyes met Jace's. He still didn't look happy. I knew I had a lot of explaining to do, and I wasn't sure where to start. But I had to try. "Lieutenant Rordin, I—"

"Are you with us?" Jace interrupted.

His question caught me off guard. "I don't understand, sir."

"Do you understand that you are here to be a part of something greater than yourself? The people of this kingdom assume that we fight for them, for the kingdom, and whoever is wearing the crown. But you will learn quickly that kings and politics don't mean anything when you are faced with the battlefront. You fight for the man next to you. You bleed for your brothers, because they would do the same for you. Our brotherhood, your peers and instructors, they have to be more important to you than your own vendettas." Jace snapped in a bitter voice. "So I'm asking you, are you with us? Or is there something else that is more important to you?"

I swallowed hard. I don't know why, but I immediately looked over at Lyon. If you had asked me last year if I was willing to lay down my life for him, well, I probably would have said no. Now things were changing. I was changing. And as far as I could tell, this was only the beginning. While we struggled together, we were all learning that petty differences didn't matter. What mattered was our loyalty to one another. Protecting each other against any enemy. Trusting each other in times when one slip up could cost everyone dearly.

As I looked back at Jace, I felt a strange sense of calm come over me. I saw the same glare in his eyes, and this time ... I understood it. This wasn't just a job to him. He wasn't being harsh, or ill tempered when he glared at everyone. He was giving this mission the best of his dedication because there were lives at stake—our lives and his.

From now on, I knew I had to do the same thing. "I'm with you," I said.

"To the death?" He narrowed his eyes.

"If it comes to that." I gave him a firm nod. "But don't think for a minute that if it comes down to choosing between revealing my abilities to the others and saving someone, that I won't make the obvious choice."

Jace *smiled*.

Okay, so it wasn't actually a smile. More like a challenging smirk. But it was the closest I'd ever seen him come to one. It gave me the creeps.

He glanced me up and down, and made a snorting sound. "Nice of you to finally show up, avian," he quipped. "Fear is useless to me, so maybe you'll finally be of some value."

eighteen

Lyon, Jace, and I left the infirmary together. It was still dark as we went outside the academy walls for our usual morning routine. No one said a word, even when Felix ran up to meet us. He was still sending me questioning looks. I knew I would have to confess to him sooner or later. He'd never let it go otherwise, and patience wasn't exactly one of his better qualities. But for now, I was going to need to tread carefully. The less he knew, the better. Someday, when Thrane was out of the picture—or at least not in a good position to break anyone's arms—I would be able to level with him completely.

As the days began to blur by, I discovered that my talk with Jace had put a new fire in my veins. I muscled through running laps and intervals of strength training exercises, but I didn't feel defeated. Each day, I could tell I was growing stronger. Each day, I felt less and less like a victim, and more like a soldier.

Of course, Jace was as ruthless as ever. He made us do one-handed and knuckle push-ups. A few times, he even had us run laps with bags full of rocks on our backs. He growled out commands as we ran through our new combat moves over and over. He was always armed with that whip in case we messed up. For some reason, the sound of it cracking in the cool air, only inches from my nose, didn't scare me anymore. I could hear his words ringing in my head. *"Fear is useless."* Those words made me push myself even harder.

My confidence always started to fade once we started for the Roost, saddled up our dragons, and strapped on our armor. By the time we took to the air each morning, the sun was finally rising. It turned the horizon pale pink, and like clockwork I could feel my ears start to burn with frustration under my helmet.

Jace always paired us together, and immediately poured on the speed. He went streaking through the sky like a gray comet, and Mavrik and I flailed around while trying to keep up. It was an absolute battle. I couldn't even match anything he did much less outdo him. All the speed and agility I had felt so confident about was basically useless to me now.

Every day, I landed several minutes behind him. I was so angry I could have spit dragon fire myself. Jace ignored me altogether, like I was invisible because my efforts were so pathetic, and I left morning drills ready to punch the first person that crossed my path.

One day, I couldn't take it anymore. As soon as Jace was out of sight, I ripped off my helmet and threw it as hard as I could.

"Feel better now, you big baby?" Felix was smirking

at me.

"Just shut up. You try competing with that every day. You haven't had to fly with him even once." I glared at him and stormed away to get my helmet.

Felix crossed his arm and swaggered after me, like he was enjoying watching me throw a tantrum. "That's exactly your problem, dummy. Quit trying to compete with him and try learning for a change. Watch what he does, how he moves. That's the point of all this, you know. He's obviously grooming you."

I picked up my helmet and dusted it off. Thankfully it wasn't scratched. "Grooming me for what? Public humiliation?"

Felix rolled his eyes. "To be his wing end. Don't you know? When young seasoned lieutenants like him come back from the battlefront to teach, it's usually because they lost their old wing end or lead in battle. Look, you already know we always fly in pairs. Seasoned lieutenants have a choice if they lose their partner. They can either pair up with another seasoned lieutenant, if there's one available that they want to work with, or they can pick up a new graduate like one of us to be their wing end. Sile must have told him about your speed. That's why he always flies with you. It's common knowledge that out of all the dragonriders, Jace and Ghost are the fastest pair. Jace is auditioning you because you might be the only other pair that can actually keep up with him. He's waiting to see if you can handle being his wing end or not."

I felt downright stupid for not realizing that myself. I glared down at my helmet, and thought about throwing it again. How had I not seen it? It was so simple. It had been staring me right in the face the whole time. This had to be the reason Jace was ignoring me. I hadn't done anything worth acknowledging yet.

But that was going to change. I slammed my helmet down onto my head and turned around to get back on Mavrik's back.

"What about breakfast?" Felix called after me. "We've still got a day full of training, you know. You should be resting."

I swung my leg over the saddle and started buckling myself in. Mavrik shifted and flexed beneath me, spreading his wings wide. He understood my thoughts; we had work to do.

I gave Felix a thumbs up to let him know I was okay. "I'll rest when I'm dead."

Mavrik and I went over the drills again until I had no choice but to put my gear away and go to class. I barely had enough time to put on a clean shirt and sprint to the auditorium before the instructor began. I threw myself into the seat between Felix and Lyon. They both stared at me while I sat there, gasping for breath.

After a few minutes, Felix leaned over to whisper, "You smell horrible."

I shrugged. "Who cares?"

"I do. I have to sit by you," he muttered.

We settled in to listen to the lecture. Hours passed, and my stomach started to ache. Skipping breakfast was a bad idea. I couldn't pay attention, and my belly was growling so loudly I was sure everyone else could hear it.

Then I felt someone nudge my knee. Lyon glanced my way from where he sat on my other side. He bumped my knee again to get my attention. I watched his eyes track down, gesturing under the table. He passed me something wrapped up in a napkin, making sure no one else saw. It was a big square of cornbread leftover from breakfast.

When I looked back up to thank him, Lyon was staring diligently toward the instructor like nothing had happened. I didn't even want to imagine the punishment I would get if I got caught eating in class, but I was too hungry to care. I snuck bites of the cornbread until it was gone.

That was how my new morning routine started. I flew and trained right up until I barely had enough time to race to class. Felix complained about how bad I smelled. Lyon snuck me scraps so I didn't cave in from hunger. Then at lunch, I wolfed down as much food as possible before it was time for combat training.

The first time Thrane spotted Lyon back in the lineup, I had to fight to keep from smirking. The look on his face was a priceless mixture of shock and total confusion. It didn't take him two seconds to snap an accusing glare in my direction, though. He suspected me right away. I saw him pull Jace aside and the two men argued in hushed voices. Thrane pointed at Lyon and me. I could read the wild rage in his body language easily. Jace waved a hand at Thrane dismissively. He was playing it off like Lyon's injury hadn't been as serious as everyone thought.

Our plan was working. Sure, Thrane suspected something, but no one else did. It helped that he had basically established himself as a barbaric, overly aggressive idiot by breaking Lyon's arm in the first place. Basically everyone thought he was crazy now, even the other instructors.

Crazy or not, Thrane had a new hatred for me. He made each day at his training station a special slice of agony. His favorite teaching technique was what he called a "drill-down." He had us all line up in a big circle with one person standing in the center. The student in the middle sparred with everyone standing around him one-by-one. Win or lose, he stayed in the center of that circle until he'd fought all nineteen of the other avians in our group. It sounds easy, but nineteen fights back-to-back like that is nothing short of torture. Each person fights differently, has different strengths and weaknesses, and exhaustion makes you want to be careless and clumsy. That can be deadly when you're facing a fresh opponent every time.

Of course, I was usually the first one in the middle of the circle, so everyone I fought was *especially* fresh. I lost a lot of fights at first, and Thrane got to call me an assortment of creative racial slurs. But as the weeks passed, I started to get stronger. I didn't lose as many fights. My reflexes became faster. My body was changing and I was actually starting to gain a few pounds of muscle. Thrane's special attention was actually doing me more good than bad. I knew it was purely by accident. He was probably hoping I would break under the pressure, but I was beginning to thrive instead.

I lost all track of time as the months ran together. Our schedule intensified, and I was more and more thankful to have the sleeping remedy Felix offered. I took it every night, and I didn't have any more nightmares. There were no more sleepless nights, no more waking up in cold sweats.

The only reminder of time passing was the change in temperature. As the summer settled in, I was reminded why they called this valley the Devil's Cup. It was a desert, after all. The heat was so intense during the day that it made the horizon look like bubbling liquid. Fortunately, the bulk of our outdoor work happened before the sun ever rose.

The seasons were the least of my worries as I chased Ghost's tail through the twilight skies every morning. Felix's advice was burning in my brain like it had been branded there. I didn't try to compete with Jace anymore. I watched every move he and Ghost made, and tried to copy it. I made a mental note of very twist and turn, every wing beat, and precisely how he responded to the air around us. I memorized his patterns, and soon, I was able to predict them.

Our flights improved almost immediately. All the extra work was paying off. After a few weeks, I could keep him in my sights. Then after a few months, I could keep my position off his left wingtip like I was supposed to.

The first time I landed right beside him in perfect formation, Jace finally acknowledged me. He glanced me up and down, nodded, and told me that one of my first turns wasn't tight enough. That was the first recognition I had ever gotten from him, and my heart soared higher than any dragon could fly. I felt unstoppable, and with that new confidence came a willingness to take risks.

One of those risks was writing a letter to my brother. I wasn't even sure he would ever receive it. I'd heard how rough things were on the battlefronts. I wasn't even sure he was alive, but I still wanted him to know what was happening. I wished him well, let him know I was staying at the house, and told him he would be welcome whenever he wanted to visit. I hesitated to tell him about the scimitar I had taken from his room. I wasn't sure if he would appreciate me going through his things like that, but then, he had given me the house along with everything in it. If he wanted it, surely he would have said something. I decided not to bring it up.

I wrote another letter. This one was to Beckah. It took me a lot longer to come up with things to say to her that didn't sound stupid. I told her a little about training … but mostly I admitted how much I missed her and how I wished I was back at the beach in Saltmarsh with her. I crammed the rest of Sile's leftover money into the envelope, too.

I tried to keep the letter to Beckah a secret from Felix. Apparently he could smell my embarrassment like a bloodhound. He waited until the worst possible moment to tease me about it, though. While we were sitting down at lunch with the rest of our group from combat training class, he cleared his throat and glanced up at me with that scheming twinkle in his eyes. My blood ran cold.

"So, were you asking her to the officer's ball?" Felix asked casually.

The mention of a girl got the attention of everyone at the table. All eyes immediately turned to me, and I glared at him. "No."

"Oh?" I saw that sadistic glint of pleasure in his smile. "So you don't mind if I ask her, then?"

I gripped my fork so tightly it turned my knuckles white. I debated lunging over the table to throttle him. The thought of him asking Beckah to the ball, even out of spite, made me furious.

"Who?" Lyon asked, glancing between us curiously.

Felix was still grinning as he leaned back in his chair, making a big show of this so that it would be as embarrassing as possible for me. "Believe it or not, Jae is in love with an instructor's daughter."

A chorus of excited noises went up from the crowd

sitting around us. I wanted to crawl under the table. My face was so hot it made my eyelids tingle.

"You aim high." Lyon snorted and went back to his mashed potatoes. He clearly still had no faith in my ability to have a romantic relationship with anyone.

"Oh it gets better," Felix went on. "She gave him a love token before training. Isn't that right, Jae?"

I didn't answer, and I didn't dare to move. The last thing I wanted was to betray the fact that I was actually carrying it around with me. Felix would have pinned me down to take it from me just so he could parade it around in front of everyone.

"Maybe this will be the year he finally kisses a girl and becomes a man." Felix batted his eyes at me sarcastically and pretended to wipe away a tear. "Kids—they grow up so fast."

Another avian sitting behind me clapped a hand on my shoulder and laughed. "We'll be rooting for you. But is her dad really an instructor? Better not let him catch you."

"Better make sure you make your move fast. If she's good looking, you know those infantrymen will be all over her," Lyon murmured with a mouthful of food.

"He's right. She's pretty cute." Felix pointed his fork at me. "You might have some competition."

My stomach started to churn and suddenly I lost my appetite. I hadn't considered that someone else might try to compete with me for her. My eyes wandered around at the crowd of older, much more eligible avians sitting around me. They would all be looking for a girl at the ball, too.

"Just make sure you're the first person to ask her to dance." Another avian chuckled and jostled me as he walked by. "That way you have her attention right away."

I shuddered at the thought of dancing. Beckah had tried to teach me some last year, but that was so long ago I barely remembered any of it. Well, except for stepping on her toes several times. "I'm not a very good dancer."

"You can't be as bad at that as you are at sparring," Felix teased.

Everyone else laughed.

I didn't.

"Seriously? You don't know how to dance?" Felix's smile faded. He was starting to look genuinely concerned.

I shook my head. "Who would have taught me something like that?" No way was I going to tell him Beckah had tried. The last thing I wanted to do was give him anything else to tease me about.

"The ball is still a few months away. You've got time to learn." Lyon shrugged like it was nothing.

"When do I have time for that? I'm already training nonstop from the moment my eyes open every morning," I grumbled. The idea of losing Beckah over something stupid like not knowing how to dance made me frustrated and angry.

"Calm down. It isn't the end of the world." Felix was still grinning at me, sitting kicked back in his chair with his arms crossed. He was the picture of confidence, as usual. "You've made a lot of progress with Jace lately, right? You can afford to back off the extra flight training a few times a week. Lyon and I will work on teaching you to dance."

"Don't volunteer me for that!" Lyon's face went red.

Felix glanced at him coolly, "Why not? We need a third person. Who else is going to play the girl?"

Lyon fumed. His eyes were smoldering. "Why not

you? You guys act like an old married couple anyway."

"I'm too manly to play a girl. Besides, you're the shortest," Felix retorted quickly. "And you whine like a girl, so it'll be very realistic."

Laughter erupted around us. Lyon looked embarrassed enough to puke. His face was a frightening shade of red, and he was glaring daggers at Felix. I decided if it did come down to a fight, I was going to stand back and watch this time. These two might never get along, but at least their arguments didn't come to blows anymore.

Even though I was still learning about Lyon, it didn't take me very long to figure out that he was a stubborn hothead. Felix was stubborn, too, which was why I knew they would probably never see eye to eye. As long as they didn't kill each other, I decided it was better to stay out of the way and let them duke it out on their own. Playing referee with them only prolonged the inevitable.

I was hoping they were just kidding about teaching me to dance. I was dead wrong about that, though. The next morning, after another perfect landing in formation with Jace, Felix caught me by the arm and gave me that scary, scheming grin.

"Ready?" He looked a little too excited for my comfort.

"We are not doing this, Felix. It isn't a big deal. I don't have to dance with her," I whispered. The whole time, I was watching Lyon glare at us out of the corner of his eye, like he knew what was about to happen. "I didn't even ask her to the ball."

"Idiot! Why not?" Felix slapped me hard on the back. "Write her again and ask her. And yes, this is a big deal. You're a dragonrider. You're expected to know how to dance as well as you fight. It's not all about swords and wearing strings of fallen enemies' ears around your neck, you know."

I stared at him in horror. "Who is wearing ears around their neck?" For some reason, the only person I could envision doing something like that was Thrane. Yeah, he definitely seemed like the type to make jewelry out of his fallen enemies.

He waved off my question. "That's beside the point. Jae, I am going to teach you something that will take you a lot further in life than sword fighting or air combat techniques ever will. Something that has saved men's lives and reputations countless times. Something invaluable. Something more precious than the finest gold or rarest gems. Something that will have duchesses and queens falling at your feet."

"And what is that?"

He smirked at me and winked. "Charm."

"You want to teach Jae to be charming? That'll be the day." Lyon snickered.

I scowled at them. "Shouldn't be very hard, if you two manage to pass for charming. You both eat like hogs and fight like wild animals."

Felix shook his head. "Sure, we can be like that around each other. But being at a ball will be different. You'll see, Jae. There's a code for how you have to act around girls if you want to get anywhere. It's like a game. And believe me, as dragonriders, we are expected to always win."

nineteen

For the record, I didn't enjoy Lyon playing the girl any more than he did. In fact, Felix was the only one who seemed to be enjoying that arrangement. He kept coming up with new, creative ways to tease us the entire time as I staggered through leading the dances. I was too flustered by the complicated footwork to pay much attention to his taunting, but Lyon's face stayed so red I was afraid he was going to start bleeding from the ears.

Three mornings a week, after our laps and drills were finished, I tolerated being teased while Felix coached me through different line dances and waltzes. Lyon and I refused to make eye contact as I was forced to hold his hand and, even worse, his hip. The first time Felix actually got us to stand in a waltz pose together, he burst into laughter. Lyon snapped. They punched each other for a few minutes, and I considered leaving the room and walking off the nearest cliff. It seemed better than having to hold Lyon like that ever again.

I still had a shred of dignity left, though. I was learning to dance, and Felix insisted I was getting better. It gave me some hope that maybe I wouldn't completely embarrass myself at the ball.

"Lyon dances like a three legged cow," he assured me. "So it'll be easier with a real girl. They're much lighter, and more graceful. And a lot less ugly."

Lyon cursed under his breath. "Oh right, well excuse me for not dancing like a girl." We only had a few weeks left before the ball, and I knew he was probably just as ready as I was for this dance class to end.

"Remember what I said about greetings and introductions. Confidence. Eye contact. Charm. It's a state of mind." Felix snapped his fingers at Lyon like he was summoning a pet dog. "Let's run through it one more time."

Lyon sputtered a few more curses as he stomped toward me. I tried to visualize Beckah standing in his place with her warm smile and deep green eyes. It was nearly impossible, though. Lyon was definitely a boy. And this was definitely the most embarrassing thing I'd ever done in my life.

As soon as we had gone through our awkward bows and stepped into an opening dance pose, the dorm room door to our room burst open. I was holding onto Lyon's waist and hand, as usual, and he was pretending to hold up a dress. We both froze, too stunned to react.

Jace was standing in the doorway. He looked at all of us, his brows raised and his expression completely blank.

My last shred of dignity withered and died.

"When you're finished with … whatever this is, I

need to see the lot of you downstairs to be measured for your formal uniforms." Jace managed to say, although he sounded a little hoarse. I could have sworn I saw him suppressing a smile. "Hurry up."

The door shut, and I died a little inside. Lyon shoved away from me. Judging by the shade of red his head was turning, he was too angry and embarrassed to speak. I couldn't say anything, either.

The only person who could make a sound was Felix. He was laughing so hard he was choking. He fell down on the floor, gripping his sides. I had to step over him in order to get out of the room. Lyon followed me, but he kept his distance. I couldn't blame him for that.

"You think he will tell any of the girls at the ball about this?" I heard Lyon mutter from behind me.

I glanced back at him. That hadn't even crossed my mind. "He better not. I know where he sleeps."

Lyon met my gaze and sighed. "You know, I used to envy you. Felix's family is the most powerful in the kingdom, next to the royal family. I thought it must be nice to have friends in such high places."

"And how do you feel about that now?" I couldn't resist smiling.

"I'm wondering how you've managed to survive him this long." Lyon actually laughed. He sped up to walk beside me down the stairs.

Felix caught up with us halfway, still snickering under his breath as he draped his arms over both of our shoulders.

The dining hall was filled with chatter when we arrived. Avians and instructors were rushing around like crazy, taking measurements and placing orders with the tailors who had set up work areas at different ends of the long dining tables. Felix drifted away to talk as soon as we entered the crowd. He disappeared, leaving us to hold a spot in line until it was our turn to get measured.

"Morning classes are canceled today," he announced. He sounded really excited about it. "Some kind of emergency meeting for all the instructors. Some of the guys are planning on taking a joyride. We should go, too."

Lyon shrugged. "As long as the instructors don't mind."

"What's the meeting about?" I had a feeling Felix was holding out information. He loved gossip too much not to find out all the details he could.

"They're keeping it a secret, but rumor is it has something to do with the battle scenario this year." Felix gave me a funny look. "Maybe even something about crazed animals."

My stomach twisted into a knot. I looked away, diving headfirst into worry as I waited to be measured for my uniform. If they were calling meetings about it, did that mean things were getting worse? I cringed at the thought. I was worried about Beckah and the rest of Sile's family. I knew I had to write her another letter as soon as possible. I had to warn them.

After we were measured, the three of us filed out to the Roost and saddled up with a handful of other avians. We took off and spent the rest of the morning goofing around in the air. It was nice to ride for pleasure instead of chasing Jace's tail. But as much fun as it was to swoop through spirals and launch pretend attack runs on Felix and Nova, I couldn't get into it. My head was in a fog because of what Felix had said. I kept looking back at the academy and wondering what was happening in that meeting. Not knowing was killing me. I couldn't shake the sense that I was somehow *entitled* to know.

That feeling didn't go away even after we landed and started toward the gymnasium for combat training. As we started lining up, Felix elbowed me to get my attention. He was staring at me like he was concerned.

"You all right?" He whispered.

I wasn't sure what to say, or how to explain how I felt. I shook my head a little, and we both snapped to attention as the instructors arrived to start the class. Jace and Morrig walked in together, talking quietly until they split off to manage their separate stations.

Thrane was a bigger jerk than usual when we got to his station. He made us do drill-downs, and of course, I was the first one in the middle of the circle. We had progressed to using practice weapons now, and were learning to fight against multiple enemies who were also armed. Sometimes, we even had to start without one and hopefully steal one off someone we sparred by disarming them mid-fight.

I was expecting to get that kind of treatment when Thrane stuck me in the middle of the drill-down circle first. One by one, the other students in my group moved in to attack me. I disarmed my first opponent in a matter of seconds, catching him totally off guard and twisting his arm until he dropped his sword. The pent up frustration about the meeting must have made me space out, because before I knew it, all the fights were over and I had sparred with everyone else in the circle.

I had won every fight, and I wasn't even sweating.

Thrane pushed through the circle, his dark eyes glittering suspiciously as he eyed me up and down. "You must be feeling proud of yourself," he growled.

I stared back at him. He didn't scare me anymore, and I wasn't stupid enough to answer that comment.

Thrane moved in closer, invading my space until I could see the little pink veins on his eyeballs. Standing that close gave me a real appreciation for how big he was. His neck was thicker around than my leg. His breath blasted on my face as he started to laugh. It was like standing nose-to-nose with a fully grown bear.

"Pick someone," he commanded.

I blinked in confusion. I couldn't stop myself from glancing behind him, catching Felix and Lyon's faces in the crowd. They looked worried. This was new to all of us.

"You act like my training is boring to you. You think you're a soldier, now?" A wicked smile spread over Thrane's face, showing off his horrible, crooked teeth. "So let's see it. Pick someone, or I will."

Panic made my throat seize up. I couldn't speak. I didn't know what to do. Once again, I looked past him at the rest of the guys in my group.

Lyon was looking right at me. When our eyes met, I could read the determination in his gaze. He gave me a nod.

I knew I didn't have a choice. If Thrane was going to make me do something terrible to anyone, it had to be Lyon. He was the only one who knew about my healing power. He was the only one I could fix without risking revealing my abilities to everyone. He must have known that, too, because when I hesitated, he glared at me and mouthed two words, "Hurry up."

I pointed at Lyon. He stepped out of the crowd and started walking toward us. Suddenly, Thrane spun and grabbed Lyon by the hair. He pushed him down to his knees in front of me, jerking his head back so that we were forced to look at each other.

"Break his arm." Thrane snarled at me like an angry wolf.

I didn't dare to move an inch.

"A soldier does what is necessary. He doesn't feel pain or guilt in combat. So break his arm, or fight me." He rumbled again.

There was no good option. I didn't want to hurt Lyon, but I definitely didn't want to fight Thrane. It wasn't even that I didn't think I could win. Maybe I could win, but I didn't trust myself not to fall victim to battle fever again in order to do it. I knew that was what Thrane really wanted.

"Tick tock, halfbreed." Thrane was giving me another toothy, evil smile. "I'm about to make the choice for you. Don't act like you don't have a killer instinct. We've already seen that you do. So let's see it again. Let's see if you can handle being a soldier."

"We can't keep doing this," Jace said. He was standing over Lyon's bed in our dorm room, checking both of his forearms. They were freshly healed.

I sat, propped up in a chair at his bedside, wiping the cold sweat from my face with a rag. After healing Lyon's arms three days in a row, I was able to do it without losing consciousness anymore. I still got a little nauseous, but it wasn't anything I couldn't handle. That might have made me a little proud, since my abilities were obviously coming more easily to me now, except that keeping this a secret was getting more and more impossible.

People were starting to suspect—people that mattered. Thrane already suspected that I was up to something, but he didn't have any proof. At least, not yet. Now the other avians were talking. Felix was asking questions, and sulking when no one would give him a straight answer. Lyon was spreading the rumor that he and I were faking it every time Thrane called me out and demanded that I prove myself. The others seemed to like that, like it was some kind of elaborate prank we were playing, but I knew we couldn't keep this charade up for much longer. And Thrane was probably counting on that.

"What other choice is there?" I buried my face in the rag. I was starting to blame Jace for not intervening to stop this. "It's that or I fight him, which is exactly what he wants. Just tell him to stop it."

Jace scowled at me. "I'm not his superior, and by healing Lyon, we're taking away any evidence that he's doing anything wrong in the first place."

"Something has to be done," I insisted. "Lyon can't keep doing this."

"Don't talk about me like I'm not here," Lyon muttered. He looked as frustrated as the rest of us. "I can handle it."

Watching Lyon go through this pain every day was beginning to wear me down. I definitely had a new respect for him. He had the best tolerance for pain I'd ever seen. I had broken his arms four days in a row, and he had yet to even second guess stepping up and basically volunteering for it. He was going through a lot just to save my reputation.

"We should be counting ourselves lucky that he is letting you pick Lyon every time." Jace sighed and moved away from the bed, staring at the door like he was deep in thought. "I suspect that isn't by accident, though. He's hoping to attract attention and suspicion."

"Well, he's doing an excellent job of it." I frowned down at my shoes. "Felix knows this has something to do with me. It's only a matter of time before he figures it out."

The silence was awkward as we all stared at one another. The question of what to do hung in the air, but no one had the answer. Even after Jace retired to his own quarters, and Felix came back to the dorm with dinner for us, I couldn't shake off my worries. I wasn't in the mood to eat, so I went ahead and settled into bed. It didn't even dawn on me that I had forgotten to take Felix's sleeping remedy until I felt sleep suck me down into the darkness of another nightmare.

When I opened my eyes, I was back in the old house my mother and I had shared. It stunned me to see it, even in a dream. Just like before, everything looked the same as when I left it. It even smelled the same. But I didn't get to enjoy the nostalgia for very long.

I was sitting in an old chair beside my mother's bed. She was lying there, looking so fragile that I was afraid to touch her. It brought back all the pain of what had definitely been the worst time of my life. When my mother got sick, she lost the light in her eyes. That was something I knew I would never forget, no matter how much I wanted to.

My mother turned her head to smile at me from her

pillow. She was so thin, and her lips and eyelids were a strange purplish color. I could see little beads of sweat on her brow from the fever.

"You have to be strong, dulcu." Her voice was weak and soft.

Like in the other dreams, I couldn't make myself move at all. I couldn't touch her, or hold her hand, or wipe the sweat away from her face. It made my heart hurt even more.

"Mom." I started pleading with her. "What's happening to me? I can speak to animals. I can heal people. What's happening to me?"

Her smile started to fade as her eyes became distant. "We always remember our ancestors," she started to whisper. "Always, even after they are gone. It keeps us bonded. It draws our spirits together like reeds in a basket."

"Mom?" Nothing she said made any sense to me.

"Listen to them, dulcu. Listen and be strong." Her eyes widened. Her face twisted up like she was about to start screaming, but she never made a sound. The darkness swallowed me up again, wiping away everything and dropping me back on that muddy, snowbound road.

The dream of the gray elf warrior murdering the royal family began to play out before me again. I struggled to move. I did everything I could to will it away, and force myself to wake up. Nothing worked. I was trapped in that repeating nightmare, just like before.

I saw the lone Maldobarian guard standing with his sword in hand, facing the murdering gray elf with no hope of winning. I saw them draw, stepping into combat. This time, thanks to my training, I could appreciate more of the logistics behind their footwork and strikes.

I held my breath as the gray elf moved in for the kill. Everything he did was so deliberate. It was smooth, calculated, and completely flawless—from the way he gripped his weapons, to the way he measured his steps. Nothing was left to chance. I shuddered to think of what he would do to the guard, who could barely stand because of his wounds.

The dream started to collapse on itself again. The only thing I could think about, the only thing I could hear, was that gray elf's voice ringing in my head like a tolling bell.

"What would you do to save your own life?"

twenty

The nightmares were back. No matter how much of Felix's sleeping remedy I took, I couldn't get any relief. Every night I woke up drenched in a cold sweat with my heart pounding in my ears. Sometimes the pendant around my neck would burn like it was on fire, and other times I gasped awake alone in the dark feeling cold and terrified. After that, I couldn't go back to sleep at all.

I tried not to let it affect my performance in training, but I knew the lack of sleep was starting to show. Even I could see the baggy circles under my eyes growing darker by the day whenever I saw my reflection. I was always tired, and it was hard to stay awake and pay attention in class.

Whenever we were in front of instructors, I tried not to let my fatigue show. I didn't want anyone, especially Jace, to think I wasn't on top of my game. But Thrane seemed to pick up on it right away. It was almost like he could sense I was closer than ever to finally snapping and giving him the fight he wanted. As much as I tried to put up a tough front, he pushed me harder than ever, just waiting for me to break.

The days dragged on, and the rest of the academy began buzzing about the annual officer's ball. I was looking forward to it, too, but having those nightmares made it hard to think about anything else. When the others started going on about who would be there, or where the ball was going to be held this year, I always seemed to space out. A few of my classmates actually noticed, and asked me if I was okay. I sloughed off their remarks, and tried to make it seem like I was just studying late at night.

I couldn't fool Felix, though. He saw right through it, and he seemed to take it personally that the sleeping remedy wasn't working on me anymore.

"Maybe you've built up a tolerance to it," he suggested.

I shrugged. I was digging through a pile of new uniforms Jace had brought to our room. The tailor had stitched our initials into each of the pieces, so it was easy to arrange them into three piles for Felix, Lyon, and myself.

"Have you talked to the medic? You're pretty chummy with him, right?" he asked, and I could feel the sting of accusation in that question. Whatever was going on between Lyon and me, Felix knew it had something to do with the medic.

I shook my head. "Why would I? It's not a medical problem, Felix." I sighed and rubbed my eyes. They felt itchy and tired. "There's nothing he could do about it anyway."

Felix was quiet again. He was sitting on his bed with his legs crossed and his arms folded behind his head. I could feel his eyes on me, like he was trying to find some clue about what was going on.

"You're immy with Lyon, too." He baited me. Lyon was still taking a bath, so he wasn't there to back up my story.

I tried to keep my voice steady. I didn't want Felix to know how nervous his questions made me. It was hard enough to watch Lyon lie to him, but it was almost impossible for me to fool him. "Why wouldn't I be? He's part of our team."

Felix snorted. "Team? What team is that?"

"You know, Jace's team." I said.

"We're not a team, Jae. Not yet, anyways. We might not even get sent to the same post after this. You know that, right? We may never see each other again." I knew he was trying to twist my feelings so I would spill all my secrets. He wanted to make me feel bad—and he was doing an excellent job of it.

"I'm always going to be watching your back, Felix. It doesn't matter if we're posted on opposite ends of the kingdom." I reminded him.

I heard the bed creak as he sat up. "Right. Just like you've got Lyon's back, right?" He snapped at me angrily.

I turned around to frown at him. "Don't tell me you're actually jealous because I'm friends with him now?"

Felix snorted again and glared at the floor. "I don't understand how you can be friends with someone like him. Think of everything he's done. He beat you up multiple times last year. I even had to save you from him once. Don't you remember that? He probably would have killed you if I hadn't shown up. He's said horrible things about you, even this year. He betrayed us and left us to die at the prison camp. How can you trust anything he says? How can you trust him more than me?"

Words didn't come to me right away. It was hard to explain, and I wasn't that great with words to begin with. "Do you think I should hate him?" I finally asked.

Felix raised his eyes up to stare back at me. "I don't see how you can't."

I nodded. "Should I hate everyone who's ever done something bad to me? Even if they were sorry for it later?"

"You know that's not what I mean." His eyes narrowed. "Lyon's proven over and over that he's nothing but a coward. He can't be trusted. You're making a mistake by sharing secrets with him."

"Maybe you're right. Maybe he will betray me, and maybe I'll end up wishing I hadn't given him any more chances." I took a deep, uneasy breath. "I think I'd rather give someone a chance to prove me wrong, than live under the assumption that no one can change."

The door opened suddenly, and Lyon came stumbling into the room. He was struggling to carry three brand new pairs of black uniform boots. "Look!" He announced proudly, dropping two of the boots as he tried to shut the door. "They're already polished and everything!"

While Lyon fumbled around, Felix and I kept glaring at each other in silence. I knew he might never understand. He was stubborn that way. But I needed him to trust me. And more than that, I needed him to respect me enough to let me make this kind of a choice on my own. If I got burned, it wouldn't be his fault.

The academy fell silent as we settled in for the night. I stayed awake long after the others fell asleep, twirling my mother's necklace between my fingers and watching the shadows from the moonlight move across the ceiling. I was afraid of what I would see if I closed my eyes.

By the time dawn finally broke, I had managed to sneak in a few short spurts of sleep. It was enough to keep me from crashing, although it didn't do anything to help the circles under my eyes. The academy started waking up. Noise came from the hallways outside our door as people fought for their turn in the baths.

I sat up on the edge of my bed, staring at the stack of clean new uniforms I had set out the night before. Today was the day. Tonight, I might see Beckah again. My stomach squirmed nervously as I reached to pull her handkerchief out of my pocket. I ran my thumb over the stitching of the two dragons. Seeing it always made me smile, no matter how bad things seemed.

"Rise and shine, kids!" Felix shouted as he bounded out of bed. It almost made me have a heart attack.

Lyon basically fell out of his bed with surprise. He came up cursing and sputtering, looking for something to throw at Felix.

"Tonight is the big night. Tonight, we wine, dine, and dance until dawn!" Felix patted my head roughly as he walked past, gathering up his towel and soap. "So comb your hair. Shave your chin—except for you, Jae. We all know you can't grow a beard. Gray elves can't grow body hair, right? I guess that applies to halfbreeds, too. Such a shame. The ladies love beards."

I glared at him.

"Ooh, watch it. You don't want your face to get stuck that way just in time to scare all the girls away. You look like an angry old buzzard with those circles under your eyes." He laughed. His sunny mood was really grating on my nerves this early in the morning. "Come on, show a little enthusiasm! Tonight, you'll be dining at my house, after all."

"Your family is hosting the ball?" Lyon perked up.

Felix grinned smugly. "That's right. It was supposed to be a surprise. You guys have no idea what you're in for."

"But what about your dad?" I asked. "I thought he was sick?"

"A lesson about nobles, Jae," he said with a smirk. "We are never too sick to throw a party."

Lyon laughed like that was a good joke. "What he means is, when it comes to showing up the other noble families, there's nothing they won't do."

"Absolutely." Felix had a mischievous twinkle in his eyes that was a little scary. "Dad would have thrown this ball from his coffin. Besides, Mom's been writing me and asking for ideas. We've got a guest list two miles long and enough wine and ale to float a ship. My whole estate has been preparing for this night for the past two months. Trust me, this will be a night to remember."

We left the dormitory with our saddle bags crammed full and slung over our shoulders. All our new uniform pieces were packed and ready. Every buckle and button was polished to perfection. I had even taken the time to trim my hair a little, so the ends didn't look as frayed.

Felix teased me about it, of course. He kept poking fun at me about not having to shave, like it was a big deal or something.

The sun wasn't even up, but the Roost was already packed with people moving their dragons in and out of stalls when we arrived. A few groups had already taken off, and were catching the first few bursts of chilly morning air. Jace was waiting for us beside Ghost, and he started shouting at us to hurry up the second we got there.

With our armor strapped on, our bags tied down, and our dragons saddled, the four of us took off in formation toward the rising sun. Jace flew in the front, leading the way for the rest of us like a big flock of geese going south for the winter. It took all day to fly across the kingdom, past the royal city of Halfax, to the eastern shores where Felix's family lived.

The estate of Duke Farrow was so big I could see it even from miles away. Except for the royal castle, I had never seen a place that big before. As we swooped down through the clouds, the sunlight caught off the hundreds and hundreds of gothic-styled arched windows. It looked kind of like a massive cathedral made out of pearly white stone, perched high on a rocky cliff overlooking the cold eastern sea below. I counted a dozen spires of different shapes and sizes rising up toward the sky, flying blue and gold banners with the king's eagle stitched on them.

Ahead of me, Felix turned around to give me a thumbs up. Jace even let him take the lead as we started our descent into one of the big grassy courtyards where other dragonriders were taking turns landing and unloading their gear.

The closer we got to the cliffs and the sea, the more excited Mavrik got. I could feel his heart pounding against my legs, even through the thick saddle padding. His big nostrils puffed as he scented the air. His bright yellow eyes darted around, and he chirped at the other dragons. They all chirped back excitedly.

"It must remind them of home," Lyon muttered once we landed. Demos was giving him a hard time, squirming around like he was eager to get back in the air.

"What do you mean?" I asked.

"They come from the highland cliffs further north, up the coast. Didn't you know? It's not that far from here." Lyon pointed toward the ocean. "The land rises and creates these massive, steep cliffs that drop hundreds of feet into the sea. That's where wild dragons nest."

I tried to envision that. It wasn't hard to imagine that many dragons, not when I spent my time around so many of them every day. But as soon as I started trying to picture it in my mind, Mavrik took over. He changed the image, showing me what it was really like. A huge stone cliff face that went on for miles and miles, jutting straight up out of the dark, foaming ocean. Dragons flew, catching the strong winds in their powerful wings, and building their nests on the narrow ledges. They ate fish from the sea, or flew many miles inland for larger game to bring back for their hatchlings. The roaring sound of the waves pounding against the rock was constant, and the rich smell of cold, deep ocean water filled my lungs. It was hard to tell which was just a picture coming from Mavrik's mind, and which was real.

"Beautiful," I murmured.

Mavrik crowed with agreement. I grabbed my bag off his back and stepped out of the way as he took off, filling his wings with air that smelled like home to him. It made me smile.

The closer we got to Felix's house, the bigger it seemed to get. The gates had to be at last twenty feet tall, and were plated with bronze that shone like gold in the light of the setting sun. All the courtyards and pathways were paved with white cobblestones. Felix told us it was limestone straight out of the heart of this kingdom.

"It's the oldest castle in Maldobar," he said. "My family was one of the first to settle here, hundreds of years ago."

The inside of the estate was even grander and more beautiful than the outside. Two massive mahogany doors were opened to welcome guests into a foyer that was at least the size of the breaking dome. The vaulted ceilings were detailed with dark stained wood. Huge iron chandeliers sent candlelight sparkling over white marble floors, and enormous hearths in every room roared with fires. There were paintings and elaborate tapestries hanging on all the walls, depicting all the years of Felix's family history. All the furniture was made of polished wood, silk, and animal furs. It looked expensive, but welcoming and comfortable. The arched windows were adorned in wreaths made from holly, pine needles, and the rugged-looking flowers that grew in this area. It made the castle smell as good as it looked, and put me at ease right away. The whole place managed to be incredibly lavish without seeming untouchable. It felt warm and inviting—well, as far as noble estates go, anyway.

As Felix led the way through the estate, guiding us down long hallways lined with portraits, we passed more servants and maids than I could count. They all wore similar blue and white uniforms with gold aprons and ties. They smiled at us as we passed, but when they spotted Felix, they quickly bowed or curtsied to him and asked him if they could help carry his things. He kept waving them off, telling them that he could manage it on his own.

"I was hoping maybe I had been away long enough they wouldn't recognize me," Felix complained as he opened the door to his chambers. Apparently, we were staying in his wing of the estate tonight.

Jace made a sarcastic sound in his throat. "Good luck with that. You look too much like your mother."

Felix stared at him, looking a little nervous. "How do you know that?"

"Because I tried to get her to elope with me. It was at a ball just like this. She was young and beautiful. I begged her to fly away with me," Jace answered bluntly. He didn't even give Felix a second glance, like it wasn't a big deal.

No one was ready for that, especially not Felix. I don't think any of us realized that was Jace's bizarre attempt at a joke until *he* started laughing. Even then, I was afraid to assume anything.

"It's refreshing to have such gullible students," Jace chuckled as he patted Felix's shoulder roughly.

For a few seconds, Felix looked like he was going to throw up. He managed to suck it up, and crack a smirk as Jace wandered away to explore our housing for the night. As soon as he was out of sight, though, the three of us all shared a horrified moment of silence.

"You think he was serious?" Lyon whispered.

Felix shot him a poisonous look. "Shut up. Don't even say things like that. My mother is a saint."

I couldn't help but laugh, which promptly got me punched in the arm.

Felix's chambers were bigger than my entire house. I

understood now why he had insisted it would be fine for me to stay with him during the interlude; he basically had a small city's worth of rooms all to himself. He had his own library, four or five different bedrooms, balconies, parlors, and a washroom that could have comfortably bathed a dozen people at once.

"Make yourselves at home," he said casually as he threw his bags down on a sofa and started for a buffet table in the corner of the room that was stacked with silver platters of desserts. Seeing them reminded me of Beckah, and my stomach squirmed nervously again. I wondered if she was already here, waiting somewhere in this huge castle.

Everyone split up as soon as we got settled, rushing around to get ready as quickly as possible. I wiped the sweat off my neck and face with a warm washcloth, and went to work trying to braid my hair. I knew there was no way I would ever get it to look as good as when Beckah did it, but I wanted to try. After a few minutes of tying it in knots, though, I finally gave it up and brushed it back into a long ponytail.

Felix had given each of us our own room in his chambers. While we were cleaning up, a small army of servants had come in and set out all our belongings for us. I found my uniform, armor, boots, and weaponry laid out perfectly on the bed. It even looked like they had taken the time to polish my breastplate and vambraces again.

Seeing all that fancy stuff made me anxious, but I took my time getting dressed. My formal uniform pants were black and made of more expensive cotton. They had a blue line down each side of the leg that was trimmed in gold. The blue tunic was made to match, with black and gold stripes down the sides of the arms, and a high collar that fastened with a gold button. There were gold plates on the shoulders with special clasps for the thin breastplate that buckled against my chest.

The breastplate wasn't made to be worn in actual battle. The metal was way too thin, and it was plated in silver with intricate gold detailing in the shape of the king's eagle with swords and spears in its claws. The vambraces were made the same way; to be comfortable and light, but beautiful. The servants had polished them all until they shimmered like mirrors.

I laced up my tall black riding boots, and buckled my long black cloak onto the gold plates on my shoulders so that it hung down my back and barely brushed the floor. When I stepped to the mirror to make sure everything was straight, I barely recognized myself. I looked older, more mature, and except for the pointed ears and ash-colored hair ... I actually looked like a dragonrider.

"Not bad," Felix called from the doorway. He was already dressed in the same thing I was wearing. "Are you ready for this?"

"Sure," I lied.

He laughed. "I seriously doubt that. Just remember what I taught you. This is a show, Jae. It's all a game. And if you want to win, you have to have two things."

I followed him out of the room. We walked side by side toward the main parlor where we were supposed to meet up with Lyon and Jace. "Oh? Remind me what they are again?"

He smirked at me with that familiar cunning light in his eyes. I had figured out a long time ago what that look meant. He had girls on the brain. He tossed his feathery blond hair out of his eyes and chuckled. "Charm and confidence."

Duke Farrow had opened up three of the estate's huge ballrooms for the ball. They sparkled with dazzling décor, and roared with the sound of laughter and music. The air was filled with the smell of pine needles, flowers, and food. Hundreds of men in uniform, infantrymen and dragonriders, gathered to watch the nobles arriving through the front entryway. Carriages were lined up one after another, pulled by horses with ribbons tied in their manes and tails. Each carriage was given an introduction before the doors were opened and a few fledgling students rushed to help the noble ladies and gentlemen out.

Felix was right, it really was a show. The ladies were wearing gowns made out of silk, velvet, or expensively embroidered cotton. They had flowers or ribbons in their hair, and expensive jewelry on their necks and wrists. They laughed, giggled, and waved at some of the other dragonriders as they arrived. A lot of them seemed to recognize Felix.

I'd never seen anything like this up close—I mean, girls like this had never visited the gray elf ghetto or my father's house. My mother had never owned a dress like that, and she certainly didn't have any jewelry with big gems and crystals like these girls were wearing. At first, I stared at each one that walked past us. I couldn't help it.

Then Felix elbowed me again. "Not charming, Jae.

Quit gawking. And close your mouth."

I swallowed hard and tried to remember some of the stuff he had taught me before. I guess I wasn't naturally a very charming person. The best I could manage was a smile that must have looked as disturbing as it felt, because the girls all gave me strange looks as they walked past. Being charming came so naturally to Felix, though. I watched him wave at the girls. He even winked at some of them, and it always made them blush.

As soon as the introductions were finished, and the last of the carriages were emptied, Felix's mother stood up at the front of the room and gave a welcoming speech. I decided Jace must have been joking about Felix looking like his mother, because they didn't favo much at all. Her eyes seemed sad and exhausted. She wished us all a good evening, and offered a toast up to her husband who wouldn't be able to join us because of his illness.

As soon as his mother's speech was over, Felix vanished like a racehorse after the starting gun. He practically vaporized into the crowd, and the next time I caught a glimpse of him, he was standing in the middle of a big group of girls.

Anyone else probably would have been upset about being left behind like that. I guess I was a little shocked he bolted so quickly, but I knew better than to think that Felix was going to coach me through tonight. He had his own agenda, and nothing was going to get in the way of that.

"I'd give my left arm for some of his connections," Lyon murmured next to me. He was watching Felix with envy written all over his face.

"I'd give my right arm for some of his confidence," I added.

Lyon laughed. "He's got plenty of that to go around. So where's your girl? Didn't she come?"

I glanced back at the open doorway that led out the front entrance. There were still carriages arriving, a few guests running late, but no sign of Beckah. I tried to convince myself there was still hope that she might come. I'd never gotten up the nerve to write another letter to her and ask her about coming. I was starting to worry that maybe I should have. Maybe she had been expecting it, or even waiting for it, and I had failed to deliver.

Lyon patted my shoulder. I guess he could tell my hopes were hanging by a thread. "She's probably just running behind. It's a long ride out here."

I nodded but I didn't feel any better. After all, Beckah probably was going to come by carriage—not when she had a set of wings that would take her wherever she wanted to go.

The ball got underway, and I mixed with the other guests about as well as oil and water. Lyon stuck close by me most of the time, except when he got the nerve up to ask a girl to dance, and I felt bad for holding him back. He didn't have much trouble getting girls to notice him. He wasn't as tall as some of the infantrymen, but he was still a dragonrider with a noble pedigree. Felix had been right about our armor attracting more attention. The girls definitely gravitated toward dragonriders over everyone else, and I got the impression right away that the infantrymen had a big chip on their shoulders about it.

Lyon at least had the good taste to wait his turn, though. Felix on the other hand, treated the infantrymen like they were invisible, or faceless obstacles in his way, whenever there was a girl he wanted to dance with. Several times, I felt my heart starting to pound because I was so sure one of the infantrymen was going to finally lose his self-control and start a fight. That was not something I wanted to deal with tonight, but I was obligated by the bonds of friendship to have Felix's back in a fight … even if he was the one being a jerk.

The armor didn't help me much, though. Any girl that got close to me took one look at my pointed ears, and made an immediate sprint in the opposite direction. It shouldn't have surprised me, let alone gotten under my skin. But after about the fourth time of finally working up the nerve to ask someone to dance, only to have them run away like I was carrying some kind of deadly disease, I was beginning to ask myself why I even bothered.

"Have a drink," Lyon said as he handed me a glass of wine. "You look like you need it."

"Tell me this is almost over," I groaned. I'd never tried wine before, so I didn't think much about it before turning up the glass and drinking it all at once. That was a horrible mistake. The strong drink made my stomach ache immediately.

Lyon snickered as he watched me choke. "You're the only dragonrider I know who hates parties."

"Probably because I'm the only halfbreed you know." I shot him a glare.

He nodded in agreement. "You need to dance at least once, though. Want me to pull a bait and switch for you?"

"And what is that, exactly?" I couldn't help but sound suspicious.

"You know, ask a girl to dance, then come up with an excuse to leave, and suggest you dance with her instead. That way she can't say no, and you get some face time with at least one girl tonight." Lyon shrugged like this was a completely normal tactic.

I frowned as I glanced around the room again. I looked at all the noble girls in their expensive dresses, hanging on the arms of men who were probably better worth their time and effort. Men who had something to offer, and who didn't have to explain why they had pointed ears. As much as I hated feeling sorry for myself, this was getting depressing.

"No, don't worry about it." I sighed. "I think I'll go sit outside and get some air. Have fun."

I smiled at Lyon and punched his arm the way Felix and I always did to one another. He didn't seem to get it, though. I left him standing in one of the ballrooms as I moved through the crowds, looking for the doorway that led out onto a balcony.

When I finally found one that wasn't as crowded, I took a seat on a marble bench and let the cool night air wash over me. The balcony had an impressive view of some of the estate's gardens. There were little pathways leading away into the dark, lit by candles inside glass globes. Beautiful fountains filled the silence with the sound of burbling water.

I leaned forward to let my elbows rest on my knees, and stared down at the floor. Underneath all my fine clothes and polished armor, I was still a halfbreed. I was still a coward, and I felt like an idiot for thinking this might go differently. What had I really been expecting, anyway? I couldn't even answer that question for my own peace of mind.

"It doesn't·look like you're having very much fun," someone spoke to me. It startled me because it was a girl's voice, but what I saw when I looked up left me at a loss for words.

Beckah was standing only a few feet away, looking more beautiful than I'd ever dreamed. She was wearing a long black and gold dress with sleeves that dragged the ground. Her hair was fixed up in a gold pin shaped like a bird's wing, and her sea green eyes were outlined with something like charcoal that made them stand out even more. I'd never seen anything like that, even on the other girls.

She must have noticed me staring because she started to blush and look away. "It's called kohl," she said. "Momma says it's all the rage in the eastern courts. She thinks I'll start some kind of fashion craze by wearing it here. What do you think?"

I was still having a hard time remembering how to talk. It was definitely Beckah. It was her voice, her smile, and her mannerisms. But the girl in front of me looked so different. She was a little taller, more slender, and seemed so elegant without even trying. It made me acutely aware of how awkward I was as I stumbled to my feet.

Her brow crinkled slightly, and she looked worried. "You don't like it?"

"I do!" I finally forced out words. They came out way too loud, though, and a few people standing nearby stared at us. I was so embarrassed.

Beckah giggled. "Why are you sitting out here all by yourself? Where's Felix?"

It was hard enough just to look at her when she smiled at me like that. But when she reached out to touch my arm, I almost jerked away from her for fear I'd do something to mess up how great she looked.

"He's … somewhere." I tried to explain. "You know how he is. This is his paradise."

She nodded, and slipped her arm through mine.

When she looked up at me again, she was standing so close I could smell her perfume. It made my head spin. "Well, I've found you now. So don't leave me. I'm so nervous I'm going to trip on my stupid dress. I told Momma it was way too flashy, but she never listens."

"Y-you look really pretty," I managed to croak.

She flashed me a disbelieving glance. "What's the matter with you?"

I could have written her a complete textbook full of answers to that question. But the simplest explanation was the truest. "I didn't think you were coming."

"So you sat out here moping by yourself? Don't be ridiculous. This is supposed to be your debut." She arched a brow. "Besides, I promised you last year we would dance together, didn't I? Did you think I forgot?"

I swallowed hard. "I thought a lot of things."

She slid her hand down to grasp mine tightly. "Don't doubt me, silly knight. I hope you haven't promised to dance with anyone else because now you're all mine."

Beckah had held my hand plenty of times before. Usually, it made me feel more courageous. This time wasn't like that at all. My palms were sweaty and clammy. I didn't know what to say to her, or how to look at her, or what I should do next. This time, I realized that I was crazy, insanely, and completely in love with her.

"Let's dance," she said excitedly.

I would have agreed to anything she said at that point. She could have suggested we go walking barefoot over red hot coals, and I would have tripped all over myself to get my boots off. Ballroom dancing wasn't much different, though. Or at least, that's how it seemed to me.

As I led Beckah to the dance floor, I started noticing how the other men were looking at her. Infantrymen and nobles started grinning after they glanced her up and down. I didn't like the glint I saw in their eyes one bit. Other dragonriders, even some of my avian peers, got that same hungry look on their faces, too. It made me squeeze her hand tighter, and pull on her slightly so that we walked close together. I didn't want anyone else getting any ideas about talking to her.

I wanted them all to know that she belonged to me.

The instant the dance started, panic made me forget almost everything I had learned with Felix and Lyon. Fortunately, Beckah was well acquainted with my sad attempts at dancing. She eased me into it, and smiled like she was having the time of her life. The more she grinned, the more confident I got, and the better my dancing became. I forgot about everyone else there. It was just me and her, and no one else mattered. By the end of the dance, I was trying the more daring steps that were a lot more complicated.

"You've been practicing, haven't you? Who else have you been dancing with?" she teased as the song finally ended and we left the dance floor.

I was happy to go to my grave without ever answering that question.

Beckah squeezed my arm a little and leaned in close to whisper, "Look, everyone's staring at us!"

She was right about that, but I knew better than to think any of them were actually looking at me. Well, at least not for the same reason they were looking at her. They were all wondering what we were doing together, a beautiful girl and a halfbreed.

"Let's go for a walk in the gardens," she suggested as we made our way back outside.

I started to suggest I get her something to drink first,

since Felix had advised me that this was a charming thing to do, when someone I didn't recognize stepped into our path.

They were infantrymen. I did know that much. Their matching uniforms were telling enough, and they were looking at Beckah with expressions that reminded me of the wolves I had fought in the mountain pass. It was a predatory look that put me on guard immediately.

"If you're finished with her, how about letting someone else take a turn?" The one standing at the front of their group spoke to me without ever looking my way. He seemed older than me, and he had a lot of medals pinned to his uniform that probably meant he had been in combat multiple times.

I was immediately at war with myself. I didn't want to share her with anyone. But Felix had advised me about this kind of situation. The chivalrous thing to do was to step aside, and let it go, even if I outranked them—which I did, since ˙ ˙s a dragonrider. It was good manners.

I cleared my throat so that he was forced to look at me. For the first time, I felt thoroughly pleased that I was a lot taller than someone else. It made me feel more powerful for some reason. "I'll allow it." I kept my tone as dry as possible. "So long as you remember to address me as sir next time, soldier."

That stung him. I could feel it in the air, like a fog of anger rolling off the infantryman's back. I knew it had to be embarrassing for him to be talked down to by a dragonrider in front of his buddies, let alone a halfbreed. For an instant, I saw wrath in his eyes. I wondered if he would actually try to fight me, and I was actually kind of hoping for it.

Thankfully, he didn't. He clenched his teeth, and

managed a "Yes, sir" before offering Beckah his arm. She took it, but I could tell she was reluctant about it. She glanced at me with a worried expression, and I tried to reassure her with as much of a smile as I could manage.

"I'll be waiting right here," I promised.

They walked back toward the dance floor together, and it took everything I had to stand there and watch. Felix hadn't mentioned anything about how angry it would make me to see her dancing with someone else. The longer they danced, the more frustrated I got. I had to stop myself from stepping in and stopping it. After the song was half over, I decided I was going to need another glass of wine if I was going to survive the second half without punching anyone. I went to grab one off a servant's tray, and returned to my spot immediately.

But when I got there, I didn't see them anymore. In fact, I didn't see them on the dance floor at all.

They were gone.

My blood started boiling. I was seeing red as I shoved my glass into the hands of the nearest stranger without ever taking a sip. I started combing the crowds, looking through every ballroom for Beckah. The more I looked, the more desperate I got, and the more I started to panic. She was gone. There wasn't any sign of her or that scheming infantryman anywhere.

Lyon caught me by the arm as I flew into the last of the three ballrooms. "Hey, what's going on? Are you okay?"

I didn't know where to begin. There wasn't time to explain it all. All I could do was look at him and growl, "He took her. I can't find her anywhere."

Lyon's eyes widened. "Who?"

I was too angry to speak. I shook my head and stormed

off to start searching again. Lyon fell in step beside me, abandoning the group of noble girls he had been talking to. "You need to calm down, Jae." He warned. "You're going to lose it and this is the worst possible place for that. She's got to be here. She didn't just vanish. Have you checked the gardens?"

twenty-one

Lyon was right. As soon as we started searching the candle-lit paths that led into the gardens, I could hear Beckah's voice screaming. The sound of the music and roar of the crowds in the ballrooms had drowned it out while I was inside. But in the quiet of the outside air, I heard her right away. My pulse raced even faster, and I started running and calling her name.

Lyon hesitated to leave the ballroom. He shouted about going to find Felix, but I wasn't going to wait for reinforcements. I knew he was worried I might lose it again and launch headlong into battle fever. At that point, though, I actually wanted to. I wanted to hurt these soldiers for ever thinking they could lay a hand on Beckah. I wanted to do a lot worse than break a few arms.

But I started noticing something strange the closer we got to the sound of her voice. Beckah wasn't screaming in terror or pain. She was screaming in rage. In fact, the only sounds of panic I heard were coming from men.

When I burst through a line of hedges, the last thing I expected to see was Beckah pinning a guy to the ground in a complex choke hold—but that's exactly what was happening. The three other infantrymen who had been following their ringleader when he asked to dance with her were lying nearby, groaning in pain.

"Say it! Say it you piece of filth!" Beckah screamed again, tightening her choke hold on the soldier who was struggling to get free. "You think you can force yourself on any girl you want? Well, you picked the wrong girl this time! Now, say it!"

"U-u-uncle!" He managed to gasp.

She let him go, and he sucked in a desperate breath. He started clawing at the ground, frantically trying to get away from her. I was the last thing he expected to see when he finally got to his feet. He turned to run from her and smacked right into my chest. The infantryman bounced off me, completely stunned, and I took that opportunity to get a little revenge of my own.

I hit him. I punched him across the face as hard as I could. I felt his nose break as it met my knuckles, and he crumpled to the ground to join the rest of his buddies.

For a few seconds, Beckah and I just sat there looking at each other. Her hair was falling out of the gold pin, and there was dirt smudged on her cheek. Her dress was rumpled and her eyes were wild. But in that moment, I had never seen her look more beautiful.

Lyon ruined my moment of awe. He and Felix broke through the hedges behind me, and skidded to a halt to stare in awe at the mess.

"What did you do?" Lyon gasped as he surveyed the

damage. "How did you beat them all so fast?"

I didn't know what to say. But before I could think of anything, Beckah interrupted. She got up and ran toward me, throwing her arms around my waist and beginning to make desperate crying noises.

"He saved me! He beat them all!" She sobbed.

I was stunned.

Lyon and Felix were, too, but for a completely different reason. They seemed to actually believe her.

"We need to get out of here before they wake up. Is she all right?" Felix grabbed my shoulder and started pulling me away.

Beckah laid her head against my chest and trembled. "I was so scared," she sniffled. "They ruined my hair. And my dress."

While Felix started checking the infantrymen to make sure I hadn't hurt anyone important, I unclipped my cloak and put it around her shoulders. Our eyes met for a moment, and I knew without a doubt that she was just acting. I could read it in her face, even if she had the others fooled. She might have been upset, but she wasn't really crying. In fact, she looked more embarrassed than anything else.

Lyon left us once we got far enough away from Beckah's unconscious victims to give him peace of mind. He didn't want to be anywhere nearby when someone found them, or they started waking up. I didn't blame him at all for that.

Felix stuck around a little longer, though. He kept apologizing to Beckah like it was his fault she'd been attacked. I guess he felt guilty because it had happened at his house. She told him over and over that she was fine, thanks to me, and promised she didn't blame him for it at all.

"I'm so glad you're okay." Felix sighed, looking relieved. "Well, I'll leave you two alone. Try not to kill anyone, Jae." He gave me a strange little grin as he left us sitting together on a stone bench in the garden.

It was awkward. At first, we couldn't even look at one another. I didn't know what else to do, so I started trying to wipe the dirt off her face with the handkerchief she'd made for me. Her fake crying had made the kohl around her eyes run down her cheeks, too.

As I wiped her face, Beckah sat there and stared at me. She almost looked afraid, like I might get angry at her and start shouting. I wasn't sure if I should be angry or not. She had fought all those trained soldiers by herself, and I was still trying to wrap my mind around that. I was so relieved that she was okay—that was the most important thing.

Finally, I had to ask, "What just happened?"

She dropped her eyes away from mine as though she were embarrassed or ashamed. She pulled the pin out of her hair so that it all fell down over her shoulders. I could see worry on her expression, like she didn't want to tell me.

"It's okay." I took her hand gently and tried to give her a reassu , smile. "I'm not going to tell anyone. You know that."

"Dad's been teaching me to fight," she confessed. "Please, you can't tell a soul. No one can know. Promise me you won't tell. If anyone found out, they would arrest me for impersonating a soldier."

My first reaction was anger, which wasn't what I was expecting. I wasn't angry at her, though. I was angry at Sile. He had acted all high and mighty a few months ago, insisting that Beckah could never be a dragonrider even if she had been chosen by the king drake. But now he was teaching her to fight?

"What do you mean he's been teaching you? Why would he—?" I was furious.

Beckah frowned dangerously. "I have just as much right as you do."

"That's not what I mean." I shook my head. "He was so against this before. He wouldn't listen to me about it. What changed his mind?"

She let out a small sigh, and her frown melted away. My stomach did a nervous backflip as she leaned and put her head against my shoulder. I saw her hands shaking some as she fidgeted with the gold pin she'd been wearing in her hair. I hadn't even noticed it before. Now I could see the thick calluses on her palms and fingers. I had those same marks on my hands. They were marks that could only come from learning swordplay.

"He was against it," she answered quietly. I could hear something different in her voice when she talked about Sile. She had always acted a little childish around him, which I assumed was a father-daughter thing. Now when she mentioned him, she sat up straighter and her face became serious. She wasn't calling him "daddy" anymore.

"I think he still is," she continued. "Things are starting to happen, Jae. Dad said you probably wouldn't know. He said they like to keep students in the academy sheltered so you don't worry about anything but your training."

I got a sick feeling that I knew what this was about a few seconds before she said it.

"There's something wrong with the animals in the kingdom. They're turning on people. More and more of them every day. It's much worse the closer you get to the northern border," she said. "At first it was only predators like wolves or bears. Now people are getting attacked by their own horses, dogs, even flocks of birds. It's like nature is starting to go crazy. Dad can't deny that something is coming, and whether he likes it or not, I'm a part of it now. Icarus chose me to fight with him. It's what I have to do. I can't explain it."

"So you've been training." I had to say it out loud so I could believe it.

"I'm good at it, too," she added. I could hear a smile in her voice. "I'm not as heavy as you big boys, but I move a lot faster. I'm also good with a bow, just like Dad was. I think he's actually impressed."

As much as I wanted to be happy for her, I couldn't be. I didn't want Beckah to fight. I didn't want her to get hurt. That sudden rage when I thought the infantrymen might be hurting her was eye opening to me. It had pushed me right to the brink of my sanity, and the thought of her being in real combat made me downright nauseous.

"Are you okay, Jae?" she asked.

I shook my head. "I don't know how to feel about any of this."

"Because I'm a girl?" Once again, she gave me a meaningful glare. I could hear bitterness in her voice.

"Because you mean more to me than anyone else," I clarified. "If anything happened to you, I don't think I could stand it."

It must have caught her off guard because her mouth opened slightly, but no sound came out. She started fidgeting with that hairpin again. "Nothing's going to happen to me. I'm very careful."

"You just fought a bunch of infantrymen twice your

size," I reminded her. "And you did it while wearing a party dress and the biggest ball in the kingdom. There are literally hundreds of people here, Beckah."

"I won, though." She started giggling proudly.

I didn't think it was that funny, though. "You could have been hurt. Or what if someone else had seen you?"

Before I could put my defenses up, Beckah leaned in and batted her eyes at me. If she was trying to charm me so I didn't get angry with her, it worked brilliantly. Her smile was very distracting. I couldn't help but smile back. And when she put one of her hands on my face and started touching my ears, I knew I was probably blushing like crazy.

The urge to kiss her rose up in my chest like a tidal wave. It was impossible to look at her without my eyes wandering down to her lips. She must have noticed because she started blushing, too.

"No one else saw." She mumbled. Her fingertips tickled the point of my ear. "I have to do this, Jae. It's okay. I'm not scared. I bet I could even beat you in a duel now."

I was entranced. I couldn't even move. "P-probably." I stammered without thinking.

It made her laugh and she leaned against my shoulder again. "I missed you a lot. I bet you didn't even miss me at all."

"That's not true! I've thought about you every day!" I was trying to make up my mind about kissing her. I didn't know how to do something like that. I didn't know if I should ask her permission, or do it and hope she didn't hit me for it.

"Is that why you look so tired?"

I knew she was just teasing me. But those words

wiped all the thoughts of kissing right out of my mind. I hadn't told her anything about my dreams. Felix was so sure there was nothing strange about them. Thinking about all those sleepless nights spent drenched in sweat and terror gave me chills. I looked away, and tried not to let her see the embarrassment on my face. It didn't work.

"Jae? What's wrong?" She leaned in closer to stare into my eyes.

I shook my head. I didn't trust myself to speak without telling her everything.

She put her hand in mine again and squeezed it tightly. "Come on, tough guy. You can tell me."

As I started describing my nightmares to her, I realized that I actually *wanted* to tell her. It was a relief to tell someone I knew wouldn't slough me off or treat me like a potential traitor. I described all my dreams from the time they started, even the parts with my mother in them. Beckah listened, and she kept holding my hand so tightly it made my hands even sweatier.

"Even the sleeping remedy doesn't work anymore," I finished. "I can't sleep for more than a few hours before the nightmares start, and no matter how hard I fight, I can't stop them."

I leaned over to put my head in my hands so I could rub my forehead. Talking about the nightmares made me feel anxious. I could see them so clearly in my mind, even now. It gave me a headache.

Beckah put a hand on my back and started rubbing my shoulders. It immediately made me feel more relaxed. "You've been trying so hard," she cooed.

"It doesn't matter. I'm barely holding it together." I muttered. "I can't keep fighting them much longer. It's driving me crazy."

Her hand stopped moving on my back. I glanced over at her. She was staring back at me with a serious expression, looking wild and powerful with the wind in her hair.

"So stop fighting them," she suggested suddenly.

"What do you mean?" The idea alone made me nervous. I was afraid of what I might see if I surrendered to those dreams. I hadn't actually witnessed the gray elf warrior killing that guard yet, but I knew it was coming. It had to be. And for some reason it felt like I might die with him if I actually saw it happen.

"It's just a dream, Jae," she said like she could read my thoughts. "It can't hurt you. You can sense that something is coming, too, can't you? Like the animals can? You're a part of it. We both are. This could be some kind of warning, or a clue to what's going on. You need to pay attention to it. You need to quit fighting it, and try to listen instead."

Moments like that reminded me why I needed her in my life so badly. She was so much smarter than I was. She saw things I couldn't. Fate didn't scare her. She was the bravest person I knew, and the only reason I was still clinging to my sanity. I needed her to be at my side forever—and that realization was as crippling as it was amazing.

I was about to tell her that. I wanted her to know exactly how much she meant to me. I wanted her to know that I loved her more than anyone. Just as soon as I got up the nerve, she spoke first.

"When you see me again on the battlefield, you can't let anyone know who I am. You have to pretend you don't know me." She looked at me firmly.

I choked out loud. "What do you mean 'on the

battlefield?' You're not actually thinking of going to war, are you?"

Beckah's expression never changed. "Why else would I be training to fight, Jae? To fend off wild animals? Dad can handle that himself. No, I'm fighting for the same reason you are. I'll do whatever it takes to protect the people I care about."

Anger stirred up in my chest like a storm. I couldn't believe what I was hearing. It was one thing for her to learn to fend off a few infantry thugs, but it was a completely different issue for her to actually show upon a battlefield and fight an enemy that would kill her without a second thought. I didn't want that.

"You can't do this." I glared at her. "You'll be killed. You aren't ready for the battlefront. You have no idea what you're getting into."

She snapped an angry scowl back at me, like I'd just insulted her in the worst possible way. "It's not your decision to make. I'm no less prepared than you are."

"That's what I'm trying to tell you! I've been training for over a year," I tried to reason with her. "And I'm still not ready. You'll be killed! And then what am I supposed to do? How am I supposed to live with that?"

She didn't answer.

Beckah stood up and started walking away into the gardens. Overhead, I heard the familiar sound of huge wing beats booming in the air. I saw a ripple in the night sky as Icarus's black body blotted out the stars.

Before disappeared into the garden, Beckah stopped and looked back at me. Her long dark hair blew around her face. I couldn't tell if she was angry at me, or really sad.

"My dad wanted me to tell you to prepare yourself.

He said the next few months are going to be the hardest you've ever faced," Beckah said. "But I know you'll make it. I believe in you, Jae. I always have."

I was at a loss for words. When our eyes met, I saw that sad look on her face more clearly, and it tore at my heart. I couldn't stay angry at her. I loved her too much.

"I'll see you again." She promised.

I wanted to believe that. I wanted to tell her how I felt, but that moment slipped through my fingers and was gone in an instant. She sent me one more smile, and disappeared into the night. In the distance, I heard Icarus's bellowing roar like a rumble of thunder.

After I pulled myself together, I started back toward the party alone. Things were still lively inside. People were laughing, drinking, and dancing under the light that sparkled off the polished marble floors. Music filled the air. All the guests seemed to be in good spirits. Every now and then, I caught a glimpse of Lyon or Felix roaming through the crowds with girls hanging onto their arms. It looked like they were having a good time, too.

I finally made up my mind to try to rejoin them. Sure, I knew I was probably about to get shot down cold again, but this was as good a time as any to get some revenge on Felix for embarrassing me all the time. I couldn't pass that up.

The sound of someone crying stopped me in my tracks before I ever got back into the ballroom. I could barely hear it over the music, and I almost shrugged it off. But then I was sure; it definitely sounded like a girl was crying somewhere nearby.

I didn't see her right away. She was hiding behind a giant porcelain flower pot right beside the doorway. But when I peeked around to see what the noise was about, she gasped in surprise. She looked as shocked to see me as I was to see her.

I didn't recognize her. At least, not at first. But when she tried to smile at me, I knew it had to be Julianna Lacroix. I remembered Felix saying something about her teeth being big. They were, I guess, but it wasn't like she was ugly. She had coppery colored hair, and warm brown eyes that were red from crying.

"I-I'm okay." She sniffled and kept trying to smile even though there were tears in her eyes. I was not an expert on how the female brain worked, but she definitely did not look okay.

"Are you sure?" I came a little closer to get a better look at her. Part of me was worried maybe she'd been attacked by some infantrymen the same way Beckah had. I glanced around for any possible culprits. There was no one else nearby.

Julianna had squeezed herself into a tiny corner between the outside wall and the flower pot, like she was trying to hide. I squatted down so that I could be eye-level with her. The instant I asked her that question, she started to cry again. It was that real, frantic kind of girl-crying that makes us men spin into a state of panic because we don't know how to fix it.

Remembering Felix's intense training on how to be

charming, I took out my handkerchief. It had a little bit of dirt and kohl on it from when I had wiped Beckah's face, but I didn't know what else to do. I couldn't leave her there like that. She was obviously miserable. I felt sorry for her.

"Here, take this." I offered her the handkerchief and tried to smile at her in a non-creepy way. "It's okay. Just try to calm down. Are you hurt?"

"I-I'm okay. I promise." Julianna took my handkerchief and immediately started blowing her nose. I made a mental note not to use it myself until it had been washed.

"Do you want to talk about it?" That seemed like a safe question to me.

She sniffled some more as she dabbed at her eyes. "No one will dance with me. Not even the lowest ranking soldiers. They laugh and give me all these excuses." The more she talked, the more she cried, and soon she was sobbing again. "I know it's because I'm such a horrible dancer. I know I'm terrible. It's useless. I hate parties like this!"

I remembered everything Felix had said about this girl and how she accidentally spat on people all the time when she talked. He had warned all the other avians at our dining table not to dance with her because she was awkward. It had annoyed me at the time, but now it made me feel bad for her. I knew what it was like to be teased and unwanted.

"I'm not a good dancer either," I said as I sat down beside her.

She blinked at me like she was surprised. "But I saw you earlier. You were dancing with that girl in the black dress. You looked so beautiful together."

"Yeah, well, that was only because I had to practice with some of the other guys in my class for weeks," I confessed. "Those were basically all the dance moves I know. Good thing she didn't ask for another one, huh?"

I heard her laugh. It was weird since she still had tears in her eyes, but at least she was smiling now. "You mean ... you really danced with other boys to learn?" She started laughing harder, and covering her mouth with her hand. "I-I'm sorry! That's just so funny!"

I smirked and nodded in agreement. It was funny. And I was glad she was laughing now instead of crying her eyes out. I started telling her about how Felix made Lyon and I practice as dance partners, and how Jace had walked in on us once while we were doing a romantic waltz pose. By the end of my story, Julianna was giggling so hard her cheeks were red.

"I guess we're both awkward dancers, then." She sighed and handed my handkerchief back.

I shrugged as I stuck it back in my pocket. "Maybe. But that doesn't mean we can't have fun. Do you want to dance?"

Julianna looked hesitant. "You're sure you want to? Even if I trip or step on your feet?"

"Sure. As long as you don't care that I'm a halfbreed." I chuckled.

She smiled at me brightly, and bobbed her head up and down. "Okay! Let's dance!"

I stood up and helped her crawl out of her hiding place behind the flower pot. She was pretty tall for a girl, probably even taller than most of the men, but there weren't many people around who were taller than I was. I still towered over her, and she seemed to like that because I kept catching her looking up at me with these strange little smiles.

When we stepped into the ballroom, she leaned over to whisper, "You know, I didn't know halfbreeds could be so handsome."

I tried not to blush. Felix had warned me that it wasn't very charming to act like a kid. I had to be cool and confident. "Thanks."

"Are you courting that girl? The one you were dancing with before?" She asked as I led her out onto the dance floor. "It's just, well, you two looked so happy together. Everyone else was making comments because, um, because you're a … "

She didn't have to finish. I knew what she meant. "Because I'm a halfbreed. It's okay. I'm used to it."

"Right." She nibbled at her lip as she stared up at me. We started slowly moving through a few simple dance steps. "So, are you courting her?"

I wasn't sure how to answer that. Technically, I wasn't. The problem was asking Sile if I could. According to Felix, I had to get her father's permission, and somehow I seriously doubted Sile would ever allow that. I distinctly remembered him threatening to rip my ears off if I messed with her.

"No," I finally answered.

"But you want to be. I can tell. It's written all over your face." Julianna let out a sigh as she gave me a weird, misty-eyed smile. "It's forbidden love, right? That's so romantic!"

It took all my brainpower to keep from turning beet red again. "Right. Something like that."

"You should tell her how you feel," she insisted. "It's always better to be honest, even if it's difficult."

I swallowed hard and tripped over my own feet.

Thinking about it made me nervous. "It's too late for that. I think I already blew my chance to tell her."

Julianna smiled brightly. "It's never too late to tell someone you love them."

We both tripped and stumbled a lot while we danced through three or four songs together, but it was fun. A lot more fun than dancing with Lyon, anyway. She didn't spit on me at all, even though I probably deserved it since I accidentally stepped on her feet at least ten times. I couldn't figure out what Felix had against her. In my opinion, however little it counted, I thought she was kinda great.

When we finished dancing, she started introducing me to some of her noble friends. They didn't look very interested in getting to know a halfbreed. In fact, most of them looked terrified. But the fact that she was trying meant a lot.

As soon as Julianna started telling them about my forbidden romance with the mysterious beauty in the black dress, all the girls lit up like torches. Suddenly, they were all interested in knowing every single detail, even though none of them had recognized Beckah. They didn't know who she was, and I decided not to tell them. The last thing I needed was Sile showing up in the dead of night to beat me senseless because he'd heard through the grapevine that I was having a secret romance with his daughter.

"Isn't it wonderful?" Julianna giggled with excitement. "It's like a fairy tale! She might even be a princess. Her makeup was pretty exotic, wasn't it?"

The other noble girls ate up that idea like expensive dessert. They gossiped and laughed, whispering things and looking at me out of the corner of their eyes. It made me nervous because of the way they were all blushing and staring. I had no idea what kinds of things they were saying about me, and something told me I didn't want to know.

It didn't take long for that much female excitement in one area to attract Felix, Lyon, and some of the other avian students from my combat training group. They gathered around to join the conversation. Felix was quick to introduce himself as my best friend, and that made the girls even more excited because now I was associated with the resident celebrity.

Now that I had found a niche, the ball was a lot more fun. We took turns dancing, and the girls seemed understanding about how horribly I danced compared to the other men. They told me it was adorable, which I figured was about as much of a compliment as I could hope for. Felix always had a different girl on his arm every time I turned around. He changed partners almost as quickly as he drank glasses of wine. The more he drank, the louder he got, and less he cared about how many infantrymen he insulted on his way around the ballrooms.

It didn't take long for things to deteriorate to a full on drunken mess. Some dancing was still going on, but a lot of couples had broken off and left to find a quiet spot to be alone. Lyon and Felix had teamed up to challenge a few of the other infantrymen to arm-wrestling contests. Well, it started with arm-wrestling, then it quickly devolved to other pointless feats of strength.

The girls seemed to enjoy the show. Those that were left were talking loudly and giggling, hanging on the arms of whichever man had won their loyalty for the evening. For me, that was Julianna. She stuck at my side and held onto my arm, which I didn't mind. I didn't think she was expecting anything from me since she knew about my feelings for Beckah.

But I was wrong about that.

She asked me to walk her to the restroom so she could refresh her makeup. It probably should have seemed strange to me, especially since I had already picked up on the way the other girls always seemed to go together in pairs or groups to do that kind of thing. But I was so distracted by watching Felix arm-wrestle a soldier who was twice his size, I didn't think twice about it.

I led her out of the ballroom and down a hallway, still trying to catch a glimpse of the showdown going on at the arm-wrestling table even as we left. I was expecting Julianna to go on and leave me to wait for her. But she didn't. Instead, she grabbed the collar of my tunic, pulled me down toward her, and kissed me on the mouth.

It only lasted about two seconds before I managed to pry her off me and hold her at arm's length so she couldn't try it again. "What are you doing?"

"I just wanted to see what it was like," she said with a dreamy-eyed smile. "I've never kissed a dragonrider before."

"I-I'm sorry, Julianna." I struggled to keep my voice quiet. "You know I'm in love with someone else."

She eyed me sheepishly. "I know. But she left you here alone, didn't she? Don't you like me? Even a little bit? No one else has to know. I won't tell a soul."

"No. I can't do that." I kept a firm hold on her shoulders. Sure, it was a little tempting. I was a guy, not a saint. The way I felt about Beckah kept me from wanting to do that with anyone else. She was the only girl I wanted to kiss.

We exchanged an awkward moment of silence,

staring at one another. She kept smiling like she was waiting for me to surrender to that foggy look in her eyes. I was waiting for her to give it up so I could go back to the ballroom and forget this had ever happened.

"You really do love her, don't you?" Julianna finally sighed and took a step back. "I guess that's a good thing. It isn't fair, though."

I was relieved. "Please don't try that again."

"Fine, I won't." She agreed reluctantly. "But tell me one thing. That was your first kiss, wasn't it?"

"Uh," I started to answer. I didn't want to admit that it had been. Felix acted like that wasn't something I was supposed to be proud of.

She seemed to know just because of my reaction. She smiled a little and patted my arm. "I'm sorry. You were saving it for her, weren't you? Well, don't worry about it. You didn't kiss me back, so it doesn't count."

"It doesn't?" I wasn't so sure Beckah would see it that way.

Julianna nodded. "Oh, of course. Besides, you can blame it all on me. Tell her I forced you."

Technically she had forced me, so that wasn't exactly a lie. Regardless, I decided I was going to take this to my grave. No one needed to know—especially not Beckah.

When we returned to the party, things had gotten even more rowdy. A huge crowd was gathered on the balcony, pushing and shoving to see something going on outside. I held onto Julianna's hand so she didn't get swept away, and muscled my way to the front. I had my suspicions that this had something to do with Felix, and of course, it did.

Felix was in a fight with a much older man. In fact, it looked like the same big burly soldier he was going to arm wrestle when I left. They had taken their disagreement down into the gardens, and were duking it out on a patch of grass right below the balcony. The man was dressed like a high-ranking infantryman, and it looked like he had the upper hand at the moment. Felix was pinned underneath him, taking blow after blow while the older soldier punched his face in.

Julianna gasped and turned away to hide her face against my shoulder. "That's horrible! I can't watch!"

Fury rose up inside me like a roaring fire. Felix was such an idiot, picking a fight with someone like that when he was too drunk to win. I was going to have to clean up this mess before he got beaten up so badly he couldn't go back to training.

I led Julianna to the edge of the balcony and planted her hands on the railing. "Stay here," I commanded.

She nodded frantically. "But what are you going to do?"

I had a crazy thought. It was stupid, really. But no one was ever going to remember me for doing the sensible thing in a moment like this. I pressed out with my thoughts, calling to Mavrik in my mind, as I shoved my way through the crowd. I found a servant with a tray of liquor bottles. I snatched up two of the bottles and started back for the railing.

I heard a few people scream my name, probably Lyon and Julianna, as I jumped up on the stone railing of the balcony overlooking the garden. It was about a ten foot drop to the spot below where Felix was still losing the fight. I waited, listening, and when I felt the buzzing presence of a familiar dragon ringing in my mind, I threw one of the alcohol bottles into the air as hard and far as I could.

Dragon flame erupted into the night sky. Mavrik spat a burst of venom that made the bottle explode into a shower of fire. The fight immediately came to a stop. People screamed and backed away at first. Then, they all started *clapping*. I guess they thought it was some kind of show.

I took that opportunity to throw the second bottle. Mavrik swooped down again, the air humming over his wings, and ignited the second bottle. It sent fire showering down over the dewy grass. While everyone was distracted, I ran down the steps toward the garden.

My plan had worked. The older soldier wasn't hitting Felix anymore. He was too busy trying to put out a fire on his shirt sleeve. He didn't even notice me until I grabbed him by the collar and drug him off my friend.

When he saw who it was—or rather, when he noticed I was a halfbreed—he started to throw random punches at me. He was too drunk to aim well enough to hit me, though. I dodged his blows easily, and tossed him face-first into a nearby water fountain. Water splashed everywhere, and he came up dripping and gasping for breath.

"Fight's over," I growled at him. "So cool off."

I turned around to find Felix struggling to get his feet. His cheeks were swollen and his nose was bleeding from being punched in the face so many times, but he looked like he was going to be fine. At least, fine enough to take a swim. I grabbed him by the collar, and threw him into the water fountain, too.

"You jerk!" He yelled as he came up for air. "What was that for? I thought you were on my side!"

"Sober up. You're embarrassing us all and acting like an idiot," I snapped as I glared at him.

That shut him up. He stood knee-deep in the water fountain, soaked to the bone, staring at me with his mouth hanging open.

I got a round of applause as I climbed the stairs back to the balcony. Julianna hugged me, which was weird, and it took me a while to pluck her arms off from around my neck. I wasn't used to being accepted by anyone, let alone a court full of noble guests. Normally they would have treated me like a filthy rat. But it was nice to see them all smiling at me. I kind of enjoyed it.

"Nice one!" Lyon laughed as he patted my shoulder roughly. "They'll be talking about this for years!"

"I hope not." I stole a quick glance at Felix as he struggled to climb out of the water fountain. "I don't think his ego could take it."

twenty-two

The party finally ended as the sun began to rise over the ocean. Nobles staggered to their suites in the duke's castle, or were escorted to their carriages to start the long journey home. The ballrooms and gardens were eerily quiet and empty. They were also a complete wreck, and servants were already beginning the long process of getting them cleaned up again.

Lyon and Jace didn't waste any time retreating to their rooms to sleep off the night's excitement. I was exhausted, too, but I couldn't calm down enough to try sleeping just yet. My exchange with Beckah had me contemplating how I should handle my dreams. I was starting to wonder if she was right. Fighting these nightmares wasn't getting me anywhere. Maybe if I listened to them, I would finally get some answers.

I was in a daze as I changed out of my formal uniform

and into some casual clothes. I started looking for a quiet place where I could sit and think. That's when I found Felix.

He was standing alone on one of the balconies attached to his wing of the castle. His shoulders were hunched as he leaned against the tall stone railing, staring into the glare of the rising sun. His face was bruised up from his fight with the infantryman., and his formal uniform still looked damp from his swim in the fountain.

When he noticed me staring at him, Felix let out a heavy sigh. "I'm not mad at you, if that's what you're worried about."

I walked over to stand next to him. "I'm sorry about throwing you," I said.

He shrugged. "I deserved it. We're fine. Besides, everyone seemed to like your little fire show."

"Why did you get so drunk?" I dared to ask. "You could have gotten seriously hurt. That guy looked like he wanted to kill you."

Felix's eyes closed slowly. He hung his head, and wouldn't look up. "I got called away from the party for a few minutes last night," he replied. "I guess you were outside beating those infantrymen to a pulp."

I could hear some kind of tension in his voice. It was strange, though. It didn't sound like anger or frustration. It was disturbing, and I wasn't sure how to respond.

"Why? Did something happen?" I dared to ask.

He laughed hoarsely, but it was an eerie, humorless sound. It gave me chills. "I guess you could say that."

We stood there in silence for a few minutes, listening to the distant roar of the waves against the cliffs. The sun was warm on my face, and it made the tops of the waves look like ripples of light. Seagulls made lonely cries as they rode the strong winds. The cold sea air cut right through my clothes and chilled me to the bone. I could only imagine that Felix was freezing since his clothes were wet.

"My dad died last night," he said at last.

I couldn't believe what I was hearing. It didn't seem possible. No one had said anything about anyone dying last night.

Felix didn't look up. "Mom called for me not long after the ball started. She said it had just happened, but not to tell anyone. She didn't want to ruin the party. She wouldn't even let me see him. She made me go back, so no one would suspect anything was wrong."

His voice cracked and I saw his shoulders tense up. His jaw clenched. He was trying to keep it in.

"Can you go see him now? I'll go with you, if you want," I offered.

"What's the point?" He frowned harder. There was a quiet rage in his eyes. "He never liked me, anyway. I was always a disappointment to him."

Without thinking, I put my hand on Felix's shoulder. I could sense his pain and grief. It shocked me how intensely those emotions surged through me, resonating in my mind almost like the way Mavrik used images to speak to me. It made my heart surge with shared grief, and without realizing it, I started squeezing his shoulder really hard.

"That kinda hurts, dummy." Felix was looking at me curiously.

I snatched my hand away. I felt the coldness of the air rush back over me suddenly. "Sorry," I muttered.

Felix looked away again. He stared out toward the sea with the wind blowing in his shaggy hair. "Anyway, now I have to decide if I'm going to stay here and take over the estate, or return to the academy."

I didn't want Felix to stay here, plain and simple. We had started this journey through training together, and I wanted to finish it that way. But I couldn't tell him what to do. It was his life, and I knew I had no right to impose my selfish opinions on him.

"What do you think I should do?" he asked without ever looking away from the horizon. I was surprised, and a little suspicious he could read my thoughts. "I know you well enough by now to be able to tell when you have something on your mind. So just say it and quit making all those weird faces at me."

I joined him in watching the waves. "I can't tell you what to do, Felix. It's your life, and your choice. So do whatever you think is best, and I'll support that."

He didn't reply.

"But if you want my honest opinion," I added. "I think you have to at least ask yourself if you would regret quitting or not."

He nodded a little, although he still didn't say anything. I didn't blame him for that. He had a lot to think about now. As of this morning, he was heir to everything we were looking at. All this land, the castle, and the towns inside the Farrow estate belonged to him. Felix was a duke now, and he was going to have to deal with that eventually.

It was late in the afternoon when we finally got packed up and ready to make the long flight back to the academy. Jace said we could have given it another day, since we would have a short break when we got back, but we were all ready to get back to work. So after lunch, we loaded all our gear, checked our saddles, and took off toward the western coast.

Felix left with us.

We didn't arrive back at Blybrig until well after dark. Other riders were still coming in, taking their time putting their dragons to bed in the Roost, and hanging up their saddles in the tack room. I stuck closer to Felix than usual. He didn't talk much at all, not even to the instructors who kept giving him compliments on how great the ball was. He wasn't his usual smiling self, not that I expected him to be.

I didn't ask him about deciding to come back to training, either. I knew he had his own reasons, and I wasn't going to assume that anything I had said made a difference when it came down to making that choice. I was glad he came back, though. I couldn't imagine returning to the academy without him.

We were given a few days of rest before training started up again, and even then, it seemed unusually calm. Even Thrane had backed off his game a little bit, and didn't torment me as much as usual. All the instructors were acting kind of tense, and even though no one said it, I had a feeling it was because of what was happening with the animals in the kingdom.

As the interlude approached, that tension only got stronger. Rumors started filtering in about more and more attacks. A flock of birds had slaughtered a whole family on an open road near the royal city. Horses were throwing off their riders and trampling them to death for no reason. Wolves, mountain cats, and bears were roaming the cities without fear. Even a farmer outside of Mithangol had been trampled to death by his cows.

"It's like the whole world is going crazy," Felix muttered as we stood outside the dormitory.

We were watching the last of the fledgling students take off. It had taken almost a full week for all of them to clear out of the dormitory. Last year, Felix, Lyon, and I had left with them for a three-month break in training while the avians were put in their battle scenario. This year, all we could do was watch.

"I hear they're worried about the dragons turning on us next," Lyon murmured like he was afraid someone might hear.

"I don't suppose you could talk to any of them and make sure they're not about to go homicidal?" Felix sent me a sarcastic smirk.

So far, no dragons had been effected. At least, not that I could tell. "I think they're just as scared as we are. These animals aren't doing this on purpose. The ones I interacted with couldn't even answer me when I tried to call to them. It was like they were possessed by something."

"Possessed? By what?" Lyon stared at me with wide, haunted eyes.

"I'm not sure," I answered. "It felt like chaos."

Felix made a groaning noise. "Great. Well that's peachy. No wonder the instructors are on edge. If the chaos is spreading, then putting us on the Canrack Islands could be like throwing us in a meat grinder."

I shuddered at the thought. It was almost time. We had two months of intensive interrogation training left, and then the battle scenario. The anxiety was so thick in the air, it literally made me nauseous.

"They won't let us go unless they're sure it's safe, right?" Lyon fidgeted nervously.

No one answered him. I wanted to believe the instructors wouldn't toss us to the wolves like that—literally. Except this was supposed to be the most intense training we ever endured. It would make or break us. So maybe it wouldn't matter. They might send us there regardless.

"We have to be prepared." Felix let out a noisy sigh. "Nothing else we can do but hang on, and brace for whatever comes our way."

Those words rang in my ears like a reminder. Ever since we'd gotten back, I had been trying to follow Beckah's advice about my dreams. I was trying, but it wasn't going well so far. Every night when I got into bed, it felt like I was bracing for impact. Watching that scene play out crippled me with fear, and it always made the dream start to fracture and fall apart. I didn't know how I could overcome that, except that maybe eventually I would get used to seeing people being butchered mercilessly like that. If I saw it enough times, then it wouldn't scare me anymore. I didn't want to get used to something like that, though. I didn't want to end up like Thrane, who actually seemed to enjoy watching other people suffer.

The next morning, the call to arms sounded earlier than usual, and we all gathered in the breaking dome. With all the fledglings gone, our group was smaller, but far more serious than usual. The instructors stood before us as we got into a block formation, and none of them looked pleased. Commander Rayken addressed us the same way he always did, giving a short speech on the glory of the dragonriders and how we should all be proud to be standing in this company. I was eager for him to get to the point.

"By now I'm sure you have all heard the rumors circulating about the mysterious animal attacks happening throughout our kingdom," Rayken said with a grim expression. "No doubt, you are all wondering if this will have any effect on your training. I'm here to tell you that as of now, it doesn't change anything. There have been no reports of attacks in our immediate area, so for the time being, we are going to carry on as normal."

A few of the instructors, including Jace, shifted uncomfortably. They didn't look happy with that decision. It made me nervous to see that they weren't all in agreement about this.

"Some of you already know how things will progress from here, but for those of you who don't, listen up." Rayken continued. He didn't seem eager to dwell on the topic of the animal attacks any longer than was necessary. "As of right now, everything changes. You are being groomed for the frontlines of combat, and we expect a premium level of performance from every single one of you. There will be no more scheduled morning calls. No more scheduled meals. You are guaranteed nothing, and expected to be prepared for everything. As of this moment, you are no longer boys in training. You are men. You are soldiers. Everything you do will decide whether or not you graduate and join your brothers in battle."

Commander Rayken went on like that for almost an hour. He explained that we were going to be issued our go-bags with all our survival gear in them, and we were expected to have them ready to go at a moment's notice. Our combat training would be intensified, and for the first time, we would be learning complex aerial attacks using dragon fire. Very little time would be spent in the classroom, and no day would be the same. That comfortable rhythm of class, food, and rest was officially over.

It was a lot to take in. Everyone looked slightly rattled when we were finally dismissed. We filed toward the dormitory, and lined up in the dining hall to be issued our go-bags. Each bag was exactly the same, and I recognized the tools from our survival training class. There were a few new items, though. There was a thick, coarse brown cloak tied up in a bundle. It was plain and felt like there were several layers of some kind of padding inside, so it was pretty heavy.

"It's waterproof," Felix announced as he unrolled his and tied it around his shoulders to test the fit. "It's for camouflage on the ground, I guess. Or you could use it to make a small shelter."

We spent the rest of the day sorting through our bags, and standing in line for more new gear. We were issued thicker boots with steel toes made into the leather. We were also given our shields, daggers, and a generic-looking sword.

"These are just basic weapons," Jace explained as he showed us how to wear our shields slung over our backs comfortably when we weren't using them. "You'll get to choose something more specific to your style later on. But for now, everyone is given the same thing so there are no unfair advantages during the battle scenario."

As he spoke, Jace and I locked eyes for a few seconds. I had an unfair advantage, and we both knew it. He didn't have to say anything to get his warning across. His glare said it all. I wasn't supposed to use any of my abilities during the battle scenario. Trouble was, I didn't know if I was going to be able to follow those orders in the heat of combat.

When Jace stared at me like that, as though he were expecting some kind of acknowledgement, I had no choice but to look away. I couldn't promise him anything. Especially not when there was a chance things go could wrong. If our dragons started turning on us, I would be forced to act. I wouldn't hesitate, and he was going to have to make his own peace with that.

No one really said much as we ate dinner that night. Felix was staring silently down at his food. Lyon was using his fork to arrange his peas into a pyramid. I was thinking about the animals, my nightmares, and the million other things I had to worry about now.

We were all shocked when the table flinched, and Jace sat down with us with a tray of food. He *never* ate with us. He was an instructor. He always ate at their table at the head of the room, or by himself.

"It's like dining with corpses," he muttered as he started cutting his meat into neat little squares. "You should eat. You'll regret it later, if you don't."

Everyone was staring at him in surprise.

"S-sir." Felix was the first one to get up the nerve to say anything to him. "We're all worried. You know, about the battle scenario."

"Because of the animals?" Jace didn't even look up from his food.

The rest of us exchanged a wide-eyed glance at one another. Our silence was as much of a yes as we could muster.

"Forget about that. It's irrelevant," Jace said with a cheek full of potatoes. "The Canrack Islands are the most hostile territory this side of Luntharda. That's the reason we have the battle scenarios there. The purpose of all this training isn't to beat you senseless or watch you writhe in pain for our own amusement. Our objective is to prepare you to endure and survive what you'll be facing later. The environment on the Canrack Islands is the most comparable to Luntharda. Even some of the trees and animals are the same. It's the best place to test you. And it's extremely dangerous, even if the animals aren't going berserk."

That was not comforting at all. In fact, Lyon looked like he might throw up from anxiety.

Jace looked up at us suddenly, his cold eyes as piercing as sword points. "Does that frighten you?"

No one answered.

"It shouldn't." His voice snapped over us, making me sit up straighter like I was standing at attention. "You are dragonriders, and we are bred to fight things that make other men stand paralyzed in terror. We are the kingdom's last hope. Remember that. No matter what awaits you on any battlefield, you have been prepared to handle it."

His words were inspiring, but I wasn't satisfied. As everyone else finished, or gave up on eating, I sat there across the table from Jace and waited for the room to clear. Finally, we were the last ones left.

Jace was taking his time eating, but he didn't waste any time getting to the point once we were alone. "You need to think long and hard about what you're going to do if things do go wrong."

I clenched my fists. "I have, sir. People have questioned my reasons for fighting on the side of humans from the very beginning, and my answer has always been the same. I fight for my friends. That's it. And there's nothing anyone can do to me that will make me too afraid to do whatever I can to help my brothers."

A strange, disturbing smirk curled up Jace's lips. He looked at me, twirling his fork thoughtfully between his fingers. "Brave to the point of stupidity," he said like he was quoting someone. I had a feeling I knew who it was. "Sile told me I would like you. I didn't expect him to be right, though. You've surprised me at every turn."

His eyes darkened then, and he calmly placed his fork back down on the table. "But I fear that bravery is about to be tested. I pushed for Rayken to postpone this year's battle scenario. There's no need to let you all be butchered for the sake of tradition, not when you may be needed very soon to protect cities and villages from being overrun by their own livestock."

" … But you just said that it shouldn't matter what's going on. You said we are prepared to handle it." I was totally confused, and a little upset to hear him contradicting himself like this. It seemed like he was lying to everyone to keep them calm.

Jace shrugged. "Morale is everything, avian. Wars are won and lost before anyone ever sets foot on the battlefield. Broken spirits lead to broken bones."

"You shouldn't have lied to us," I dared to sound defiant. Sure, his reasoning made sense, but it still didn't sit right with me.

"So it would be better to send them all into the jungle completely terrified?" he countered.

I frowned. "No, I guess not."

"Few of us live to see things get this bad. And those who do can't help but feel hopeless and afraid, even if they are supposed to be the ones standing firm and fearless. But you need great darkness in order to see great light."

Jace stared at me from across the table. His expression was hard to read, and his dark eyes burned with something I couldn't understand. "Don't let the darkness shake you. I believe the world is about to witness something incredible. I believe we are all about to watch you shine. The question is, are you ready for it?"

twenty-three

I wasn't ready. As much as I wanted to believe I was prepared for what was coming, there was no way anyone could have been. The months leading up to the battle scenario were just as terrible as everyone had promised they would be, and then some.

There was no set schedule. That probably doesn't sound like such a bad thing. But after you've lived in a constant state of routine for so long, not having any idea what's coming next is like living in the constant state of drowning. I could barely keep my head above water.

Sometimes the call to arms sounded at the normal time, and we got up, dressed, and started our aerial combat training with our dragons. We still had a lot to learn when it came to attacking targets on the ground and using our flame against the enemy without hurting any of our own forces. Some of the maneuvers were extremely difficult, and we switched up partners daily, so I was never able to get used to anyone else's style.

But then, on other days, the battle horn would blare in the darkness long before the sun ever rose. The eerie, panicked sound of it made me bolt upright in bed. My whole body tingled like there was ice in my veins. We all scrambled to put on our armor, grab our go-bags, and get our dragons saddled as quickly as possible. The instructors gave us a brief mock-scenario of a battle, and we had to fly specific attack patterns to do mock attack runs. It was supposed to simulate how things would be once we were put on the real battlefront.

Sometimes, they would mix the two days. We would be sitting calmly, listening to an instructor give us a lecture about some of the dangerous plants and animals in Luntharda, and then the battle horn would blare. Immediately, everyone bolted into action, rushing to get to the Roost.

I figured out right away that falling behind was not a good idea. The first time I was a little late coming to the Roost, I felt the bite of something across my back. It didn't hurt that badly at first, but then the pain hit me like someone was holding a white-hot branding iron against my skin. Jace had popped me across the shoulders with his whip, and it set my back on fire. The pain brought me to my knees instantly, and I could barely breathe. When I checked under my shirt later, I realized I had a huge black and purple welt where the tail of the whip had snapped over my back. It took days for the swelling to go down enough for me to sleep on my back comfortably.

The closer we came to the battle scenario, the more intense training became ... and the more I started to wonder if my nerves were finally going to start snapping.

We were called by the battle horn in the dead of night, or even after we had only been asleep for a few hours. The scenarios the instructors gave us were getting more and more difficult. Our attacks had to be precise and synchronized. We barely had time to sleep, much less eat or study. If you didn't know something, forgot some of your gear, or were too slow to respond, you got to taste of an instructor's whip. We were all being pushed to the limit, our noses shoved into the molten gears of war to see if we could handle the fire.

Then the interrogation training started. All my other training at Blybrig Academy had been difficult from the very start. I'd spent days with all my muscles aching, drenched in sweat, and feeling like I was going to drop at any moment. But interrogation training was, by far, the most horrible thing that had ever happened to me. There was no comparison to anything else I had been through so far.

I was already exhausted, starving, and in a constant state of panic because I was terrified I was forgetting something. It was impossible to ever feel relaxed or confident. Lying awake in my bed, I strained to hear the sound of the battle horn. Every second felt like an eternity, and my brain played tricks on me, making me believe I was hearing things that weren't there.

Then the door to our dorm room burst open. Six or seven instructors filed in, all wearing wooden masks that covered their faces. I couldn't tell who any of them were, and I was terrified that one of them might be Thrane. They dragged us out of bed, and tied our hands behind our backs before shoving us out into the hallway. I caught a glimpse of Lyon before they slammed a burlap sack over my head; he looked completely terrified.

They herded us down the stairs and out into the night, and forced us to walk for what felt like an eternity. Then someone kicked me in the back and I went flying forward, landing on my knees and face. Someone else ripped the bag off my head, and grabbed me by my hair.

When my vision cleared, I was finally able to see who was standing over me. Lieutenant Haprick, from our survival training class, leered down at me through the holes in the wooden mask. I knew it was him. I could tell by the color of his eyes and the shape of his body against the pale starlight. I was so relieved I actually smiled. He probably didn't understand why, or took it as sarcasm, which was also probably why I got another lash from a whip across my back. But honestly, I was just so glad it wasn't Thrane.

They ripped us out of bed like that at random. Sometimes, it happened every night for a week straight. Then other times, they would only do it once every few days. We never knew when it was coming, and we never knew what to expect once we got there. Usually, we were bound up and dragged into the night, only to get beaten or whipped until we were too weak to scream. Instructors wearing those wooden masks would demand to know our names, or where our forces were hiding. We were not supposed to say a single word. That was the whole point of this training. We had to be steady and keep our mouths shut no matter what the enemy did to us. We couldn't betray our brothers, even if we were threatened with death.

We seemed to be holding our own fairly well. That is, until they started singling members out. The first night they only took Felix out of our room, and left Lyon and I to sit there and stare at each other in the dark, I was so stunned I couldn't speak. Neither of us made a single sound until morning. When they finally brought Felix back, he was a little bruised up, but he said they mostly made him walk around all night. Lyon and I were actually the ones being tested. If we had made a scene, we were going to get a meaningful taste of Jace's whip.

"We've got to make a pact," I insisted as we gulped down a quick meal the next morning. "If Thrane comes after one of us—"

"—you mean *when* Thrane comes after one of us," Lyon interrupted.

I nodded grimly. "Right. Well, when he does, we can't let anything he does or says break us down. Even if the others in our group start losing it, we have to stand together. Thrane is going to be looking at us even harder at the battle scenario. There won't be any more reason for the other instructors to stop him from coming after us."

"Are you thinking he's going to use the battle scenario as an excuse to finally attack you?" Felix sounded tense.

"I hope so." My answer made both of them stare at me in surprise. I shrugged and kept eating. "Better me than you. I can take whatever he dishes out. But I don't want either of you to suffer any more because of me, so when he does come for me, don't try to intervene."

"Because you don't think you can stop the battle fever? Even after everything he's done so far?" Lyon asked. It was easy to read the concern in his tone. After all, he had been Thrane's primary target until now.

I hated admitting to that kink in my armor, but there was no avoiding it. "Yeah," I replied, and tried not to look at Felix. He still didn't know about my healing abilities, but I knew it was only a matter of time now. He was already starting to figure out that it had something to do with my other strange powers.

"I think you should practice with your powers," Felix announced suddenly.

Lyon and I swapped an uncomfortable glance.

"Seriously, I do." He pointed his fork at me accusingly. "If something does go wrong on Canrack, and we get into a spot where the only thing standing between us and getting crushed by a bunch of angry forest creatures is you, then I want you to be on top of your game. No more desperate last minute saves. I want the full-force of your weirdness to be ready to go at a moment's notice."

"When am I supposed to practice?" I scowled at him. "The instructors watch our every move. And we never know when they are going to sound the battle horn."

Felix's frown hardened. "I don't know, but you need to figure out something. We're running out of time."

I knew he was right. As uncomfortable as it was to admit I had these abilities, they might be our lifeline in a bad situation. I needed to be ready. There wouldn't be time for foul-ups and second chances.

The only time there was to do that kind of experimentation was during training. It wasn't ideal, but I didn't have much of a choice. Not with Thrane and the other instructors breathing down my neck, beating me senseless in the middle of the night, or shouting commands.

I started out as gently as I could. I held conversations with Mavrik and Nova in my mind while we flew through aerial drills. I gave Nova simple instructions, like getting her to do spirals or breathe flame even when Felix hadn't asked her to, and then I watched to see if she obeyed. When she did, I started to get more confident. I started talking with other dragons, too. Demos was a stubborn, arrogant jerk if I'd ever seen one, but he was also the most experienced out of all the dragons when it came to actual aerial warfare. I took his advice on maneuvers when he showed me how he thought the scenarios were going to play out, and most of the time, he was right.

Having the dragons all whispering in my mind with their endless stream of images and colors was very distracting. Thankfully, the more I did it, the easier it became to balance what I saw in my mind with what was happening around me. It was like having eyes everywhere at once. It gave me an edge, and it was completely undetectable to all the other dragonriders.

I started talking to the birds next. There weren't many wild animals around in the Devil's Cup. That was part of the reason they had put the academy there in the first place; it was remote and there wasn't much you could accidentally burn down except for a few prickly shrubs. But there were birds and small animals. I started calling them to our dorm room window, which bothered Felix a lot. Apparently, he didn't like birds.

My powers were definitely growing. I didn't even have to concentrate at all to talk to Mavrik anymore, and it was starting to become that way with the other dragons, too. Mavrik's presence was always the loudest in my mind, though, and our bond was getting stronger by the day. I asked him repeatedly about what was going on with the animals. His answer was always the same. He showed me the same scene Nova had of a place in the forest, and a moss-covered staircase leading down into the dark. I could sense his anxiety and fear. The other dragons gave off that same sense as well. They knew what was happening. They could feel something bad coming, and they were every bit as helpless to stop it as the other wild animals.

"If it comes down to it," I told Mavrik as I sat in his stall, scratching his head after a day full of training. "If you have to choose between leaving me behind and saving yourself from that chaos, don't sacrifice yourself for me. That wasn't part of our deal."

He growled with discontent, and shot me a dirty look.

"Hey, I don't like it any more than you do, big guy. But I would rather stand and fight alone than watch you turn on me because that chaos had possessed you." I scratched that special place right behind his ear, and he couldn't help but purr. "I know you want to protect me. I want to do the same for you."

Mavrik lifted his head. His big yellow eyes stared down at me. When the moonlight reflected off of them, it almost looked like they were glowing. He pushed his massive snout against my chest and let out a deep sigh. Hues of blue and yellow swirled in my brain.

"I know," I said as I ran my hand over his scaly head. "I'm scared, too."

I could feel the instructors' eyes on me, burning holes in my back with their stares. Across from me, Felix was poised for the attack. I could barely see his eyes over the top of his shield. Sweat ran down the sides of my face, dripping off my chin. All around us, the other avians were shouting, but it just sounded like muffled noise. They cheered us on, trying to distract us or tempt us into making a careless mistake.

This was the last day of training. It was the final test before we packed our things and left for the Canrack Islands. We had spent all day in the battle dome under the glare of firelight from the big bronze braziers burning all the way around the arena floor. Early in the morning we had drawn names to see who we would be dueling for our final sparring match. This match would be judged be all the instructors, and we were encouraged to win ... at all costs.

I wasn't stupid enough to believe that I had been paired with Felix by chance. I knew Jace was probably responsible for it. Felix was the only avian who actually posed a challenge to me in the sparring ring anymore. He was consistently perfect in form, and he hit with so much strength it made my teeth rattle every time our blades locked. He was a lot more muscular than I was, with easily twice as much brute strength, but he couldn't match my speed. I had to use that, and the fact that I was taller and my arms were a lot longer than his, to strike from a distance before he could defend.

After nearly an hour, though, I was beginning to get tired. No one else had dueled for this long. What started out as a small crowd of our peers gathering around to watch had now grown into a full-blown mob. I didn't dare stop to check, but it seemed like the whole academy had gathered to watch us.

Felix dove at me again, letting out a roar of frustration as he swung his sword. It hummed through the air, coming down against my blades as I parried. For a brief moment, I regretted not picking a shield instead of two blades. It was way too late to be thinking about that now, though. The force of the impact made my bones creak. I saw him rear back, preparing to use his shield as a weapon while we were so close together.

I quickly dodged, sidestepped, and made a wild strike at his arm. I didn't expect it to work, but Felix must have been getting tired, too. His reactions were becoming more sluggish. That big shield was weighing him down. I felt my blade hit something solid and snap it.

It was one of the straps on his shield that held it onto his arm.

The big sheet of bronze clattered into the dirt, and Felix spun to face me. He bared his teeth, and made another wild dive with his sword swung wide. I spread my stance, and prepared to take him on. Without his shield, he would be a lot easier to deal with.

At least, that's what I was hoping.

Our strikes were furious and fast. We moved through technique after technique, testing each other at every turn for any possible weakness. The roaring of the crowd grew louder.

Then I got the hilt of one of my blades locked perfectly with his. I'd tried that same maneuver at least a dozen times already, and he had evaded it effortlessly. This time, I saw panic in his eyes. I twisted my sword, and jerked his sword out of his hands. It went skidding across the dirt to the other side of the arena, far out of his reach.

The crowd went silent.

Felix stood back, his chest heaving as he panted for breath. He watched me, his eyes narrowed like he was waiting for me to end this. The duel was technically over.

Or it should have been, anyway. I had disarmed him. I had won. All I had to do was make that final strike and force him to surrender.

It seemed too easy. Felix's strength wasn't spent. He still had fight in his eyes. I knew in a real battle, he wouldn't have surrendered just because he didn't have weapon. Felix didn't know when to quit—he was stubborn like that.

"Finish it!" Someone shouted from the crowd.

I snapped a punishing glare to the hundreds of eyes watching us. "Stay out of this!" I shouted so loud it echoed off the dome's ceiling.

Felix was still staring at me. He squinted his eyes a little, canting his head to the side like he was trying to figure out what I was going to do. The expression of pure shock on his face was priceless when I suddenly threw down both of my blades and balled my fists, assuming a fighting stance.

A dark smile spread across Felix's face. "What, all that wasn't enough for you?" He chuckled. "You really think you can beat me hand-to-hand?"

I curled a finger at him slowly, taunting him in to fight me. "I think I can."

Felix didn't need much encouragement when it came to diving into a fistfight. That kind of combat was his specialty. He ran for me at full speed. The crowd exploded into cheering again. We met in the middle of the arena, and Felix stunned me with a barbaric right hook to the stomach.

We fought until our knuckles bled. I still couldn't match his strength, but I still had speed on my side. When he finally managed to knock me down with a leg sweep, I did everything I could to stay out of his grappling hold.

I knew if he managed to get an arm or a leg around my neck, it was over. I wouldn't be able to bre k free.

As I reached the end of my stamina, I started to make stupid, desperate choices. A risky attempt at a complicated pin cost me big time. Felix managed to twist me around and mash my face into the dirt with his elbow.

"You know, I'm kinda used to being surprised by your crazy decisions. But this is especially stupid, even for you." He growled at me, putting his face close to mine so no one else could hear. "You've already won this. What are you trying to prove?"

"That Thrane better be prepared when he comes after me," I answered with a mouthful of dirt. "I want him to know I'm not easy to kill!"

"Well, you picked a dumb way to do it," he snarled as he grabbed a handful of my hair and used it to lift my head far enough to slip an arm around my neck. "You've never beaten me hand-to-hand before. And you never will!"

I didn't know what else to do. Felix was right, it was stupid to challenge him like this. I couldn't afford to lose. In a moment of wild desperation, I threw my head back against his and head-butted him as hard as I could.

It was like my brains were scrambled the instant our skulls hit. His grip on my neck loosened, and I pushed off the ground to flip us over. The crowds were screaming so loudly that it was disorienting. The lights of the braziers seemed to be spinning around me as I tried to crawl away from him.

When I looked back, Felix was on his hands and knees. He was dazed, too. At first, I thought he might get to his feet and use that moment to claim the upper hand. But he didn't. Instead, he slowly raised his head and looked at me. I saw him smirk for the briefest second, wink, and fall over onto his side.

Felix didn move again. The crowd started to count. When they got to ten, the victory was mine. I had beaten Felix in armed combat and hand-to-hand.

Except, I knew I hadn't. Felix did a pretty good job of acting when Jace went over to see about him. He played it off like my head-butt had knocked him out. But I knew better. That smirk and wink was his way of letting me know he was throwing the match for my sake. He was doing it so I didn't look weak in front of Thrane and the other instructors.

For some reason, that really made me angry. I knew why he'd done it. It made perfect sense. I had gotten in way over my head by challenging him to a fistfight like that. Still, being treated like some helpless little kid was annoying. We were too old for that now. I wasn't a kid anymore, and this wasn't a game.

This was war.

twenty-four

The morning of the battle scenario was colder than usual. A thick fog had settled over the academy, making the morning seem darker as we gathered our gear and moved to the Roost. Lyon, Felix, and I walked together with the rest of the avians in our class. No one spoke. The silence was intense, and I knew I wasn't the only one dreading what was waiting for us later that day.

As we filed into the Roost, a few instructors stood waiting at the door. They were handing out folded pieces of paper sealed with wax. They told us to go ahead and get our dragons ready, but we weren't supposed to read what was on the paper until the battle horn sounded. Then we were officially dismissed to move out.

My hands shook with restlessness as I checked my saddle. Mavrik could sense my worry. I knew he was nervous, too. I could feel his strong sides shuddering slightly as he trembled with that anxious energy. According to Jace, the dragons wouldn't be able to help us once we reached the island. They would drop us off, and wouldn't be set loose to pick us up again until the scenario was over.

I was dressed in my full armor, sitting on my saddle, looking down over my dragon's large head through the glass-covered slit in my helmet. Outside the Roost, I could see the skyline beginning to turn purple and orange as the sun rose over the mountain peaks.

Together, Mavrik and I waited. I was clenching my teeth to keep them from chattering. The paper rattled in my hands, and I thought about sneaking a peek at what was on it.

Then the battle horn sounded.

Frantically, I ripped open the wax seal and started reading the paper. Written on it was our scenario, a brief set of instructions, and a map of where we were supposed to land on the Canrack Islands. Our first objective was to land in a small clearing near the center of the island. There was a stone fortress, sort of like an outpost, positioned nearby. That was our destination.

The paper didn't say anything about it, but I had a feeling that was where the interrogation was going to take place. It did say that we would be set loose on the island to find our way to the beach, where our dragons would be picking us up. We were going to have to prove that we could survive the jungle, even after being beaten and tortured.

I heard the thundering roar of the other dragons as they began to take off. It took me a few minutes to finally pry my eyes off the paper. I was second guessing everything. This was going to be horrible, just like Sile had promised. I didn't want to go through it. I wasn't sure I was strong enough, or if I had enough training. I didn't know if Thrane was going to try to kill me, using the battle scenario as an excuse. I didn't know if any of us would even make it out alive.

Mavrik sent me an image. In my mind, I saw Beckah on the night of the ball. She had seemed so sure about her own destiny. I envied that about her. She was strong, wise, and beautiful in a way I only barely understood. Jace had called me brave before, but what little courage I had was nothing next to hers.

Thinking about her made me more aware of the lump under my vambrace where I still had her handkerchief hidden. Felix had reminded me not to take anything with me I couldn't stand to lose. I had left my mother's necklace beside my bed, but I couldn't leave Beckah's token behind. Having it with me gave me strength, and reminded me that there were things still worth fighting for.

Underneath all my fear and doubt, I knew Beckah was right. I was here for a reason—the same reason she was training. Giving up was not an option. Felix and Lyon were going to that island, and they might need me. There was no other choice. I had to protect the people I cared about.

Mavrik let out his own booming cry as he leapt into the sky. We caught the rush of cool morning wind, and turned west toward the sea. As we soared up above the fog, I saw other dragons and riders flying all around us. I started looking for my friends, and when I couldn't find them, I reached out with my thoughts. I called to Nova and Demos, asking them to come closer.

I heard Nova's roar from over my shoulder. When I

looked back, Felix was giving me angry hand signals.

Quit steering for me, he gestured.

I smirked under my helmet.

We flew in formation toward the sea. After several hours, the air started to smell more and more like salt. In the distance, I could see big, dark spots rising up on the horizon. The islands were like droplets of green in an endless blue sea. The largest was where we were supposed to find the clearing and make our way to the fortress.

It was easy to find the clearing. The rest of the island was covered in jungle so dense, it looked like a quilt of rustling leaves. It was so thick you couldn't see anything below the canopy. The clearing obviously had been man-made by cutting down some of the trees, and I could see the sandy-colored stone of the fortress peeking out between some of the branches not far away.

I gestured to Lyon and Felix to hang back and circle while the other avians landed, dismounted, and sent their dragons away. We were the last ones to touch down. I hurried to unload my go-bag, buckle my helmet to the saddle, and clip my sword to my hip. As soon as I was finished, I gave Mavrik a gruff pat on the neck.

He stared down at me. I could sense his worry and fear. He didn't want to leave me and honestly, I didn't want him to go.

"Go on," I pushed against his head. "I'll be fine. If anything happens, I'll call you."

Mavrik growled at me, but he didn't argue. He puffed an angry snort, blasting my face with his hot breath, and then took off to join the other dragons who were returning to the Roost.

Felix dismounted next. I waited for him in the clearing, and then we stood together while Lyon took his turn. Dressed in our brown cloaks and carrying our bags and weapons, we probably looked prepared. But deep down I knew we weren't. We were like lambs being led to the slaughter.

"Remember our deal," I said as soon as Demos took off.

Lyon and Felix stared back at me with wide, worried eyes. They both nodded.

"We can't stay close to one another. They already know we're friends, so they'll probably try to use that against us. But any doubt we can give them would work to our advantage. Once we're let back into the jungle, we need to find each other. We have a better chance of surviving if we work together to get back to the beach." I looked around the clearing and picked a tree nearby. It was taller than the others. "When they let us go, let's meet there. Okay?"

Once again, they nodded. One by one, we broke off and started for the fortress alone. I waited to go last, watching Felix's back as he marched off into the trees. When it was my turn to go, I was so caught up in staring at the jungle around me it wasn't hard to let my thoughts wander for a second. Jace had said this place was a lot like Luntharda, and seeing it gave me strange chills.

There were huge ferns everywhere with fronds as tall as I was. The tree trunks were covered in moss and vines, and the canopy over head was so thick that almost no sunlight made it down to the forest floor. It was almost like the branches of the trees had woven together to make a living basket. Strange sounds came from everywhere, but I didn't see any animals. I tried to press outward with my thoughts to see if I could sense them.

Then something hit me on the back of the head.

Everything went dark.

When I started to wake up, I could feel that my hands were tied behind my back. I also realized that I was completely naked. All my gear and all my clothes were gone. Overall, not a good way to start a day of training.

I forced my eyes open and squinted into the sunlight. Immediately, I saw the familiar sand-colored stone of the fortress. I rolled over onto my side. The back of my head was hurting from where I'd been hit, and I could hear others moving around nearby. There were other avians sitting all around me, stripped down and tied up like I was.

"What's going on?" I rasped as I sat up and started testing my bonds. Whoever had tied my hands had done a great job. I couldn't slip free.

"Shut up," a familiar voice growled at me. It sent anger burning through my veins about a second before I felt him grab a fistful of my hair. I glared into Thrane's eyes as he forced me to look at him. "Welcome to Hell, demon. You should feel right at home."

I didn't answer.

He let me go and slung me back down on the ground. I waited until he had moved away to sit back up again. All around me, the other avians were sitting in a circle. Everyone was tied up the same way while a few instructors, including Thrane, stood guard over us. I saw more instructors stripping down the few remaining students, and taking their gear into the fortress's only building.

The compound wasn't much. The center building was only two storeys tall, and it had no windows that I could see. All around us was a stacked stone wall that was at least twenty feet high, with only one gate that led out into the dark jungle. The tree branches spread out and almost completely covered the compound, even though there were no trees inside the walls.

We were sitting in an empty dirt courtyard. The only other thing standing was a tall wooden post that stuck straight up out of the ground. I hadn't seen anything like it before, but it didn't take a genius to figure out what it was. If the old blood splattered around it wasn't evidence enough, then the shackles hanging from the top of it made it pretty clear what that post was used for. It was a whipping post.

When the last of us had been captured, the instructors made us all get up at once. We were marched into the fortress in a line, which was completely humiliating. No one wants to walk around naked like that. Anyone who tried to step out of line or run was immediately punished, usually with a punch to the face.

I can't go into much detail about what happened in that compound. Some things just shouldn't be said. What I can say is that Sile's warnings about this training didn't come anywhere near how bad it actually was. Not even the interrogation training could compare.

After what must have been several days, I started wondering if I would live to see the sky again. They kept us in the dark as much as possible so that we lost track of time. But worse than that, they kept us alone. The cells they crammed us into were so tiny I couldn't stand up straight. There wasn't enough room to sit with your legs straight, either, so it was impossible to find a way to sleep or even be comfortable. It was a miserable, cold, dark, stone box.

The first time I heard someone break down, I was terrified it was Felix or Lyon, but I couldn't tell because of how the voices echoed off everything. I heard someone crying and screaming hysterically, begging to be let out. I wanted to yell back at them, to remind them to keep quiet. I heard the instructors take him out of his cell. I heard them beat him until he was quiet. Then they threw him back in his cell.

A few others broke down like that. Each time, I covered my ears and tried not to hear it. I was afraid it would be one of my friends or that I'd hear them call out to me for help. But there was no refuge in the silence because when it was quiet, you were reminded of how hungry and thirsty you were. At first, they didn't feed us at all. Then they let us out into the courtyard and threw a few rations out, so that we had to fight for them. I didn't fight very hard, though. Something about the way Thrane was watching us fight, like he was enjoying it way too much, made me suspicious.

In the end, I was glad I hadn't tried to get any of the food. The ones who did were doubly rewarded with a turn at the whipping post. Five lashes in exchange for those few bites of food.

Eventually, they did give us our clothes back. By that time, I was so filthy from scrounging around in the dirt that I hated to' put anything on without bathing. There wasn't much choice, though. It was better than being naked.

Once we were all sufficiently weak from hunger, thirst, and the psychological torment of being trapped in a windowless, dark cell for days … the actual interrogation finally began.

They pulled us out into the courtyard one by one. They beat us. They yelled, and demanded information. They even promised food or freedom if we talked.

When it was my turn, I knew Thrane would be there even before I saw his big ugly face leering down at me. My hands were still tied behind my back, and my body was so weak from dehydration I wasn't sure I could survive one of his beatings. But I did.

Afterwards, my face was so bruised it felt like raw meat, but I was alive and I still had all my teeth. I knew that was probably because of Jace. He had been there the whole time, standing off to the side and watching with that cold look in his eyes. He didn't seem to care when Thrane hit me, but I let myself hope that if it went too far—if Thrane actually tried to kill me—then Jace would intervene. I think the fact that I didn't break down and talk actually surprised them. I got a little pleasure out of that as I limped back to my cell.

In the end, we never knew who talked and who didn't. We never saw one another. At least, not until everyone had taken several turns. Then it was time for a different approach.

We were all herded back into the courtyard like cattle and made to stand in lines. As I looked around, I noticed everyone else looked about as bad as I felt. Every one of us had been bruised up badly, although some were worse than others. I searched the faces of the other avians, but I couldn't find Felix or Lyon. I was kind of glad about that. I didn't want to feel anything. It was safer not to feel until this was over.

The instructors started pulling us out one by one to interrogate us in front of everyone. They picked on the weaker students first, trying to see who would react. I was surprised that I didn't get called out ... that is, until I realized it was only because Thrane had something *extra* special in store for me.

"That one." Thrane turned his nasty smile in my direction and pointed. "Take him to the post."

My stomach twisted painfully. I couldn't help but look back at the whipping post. It was spattered with fresh blood now. Fear immediately made my legs feel even weaker. I started having radical thoughts about trying to run, or fighting back. I didn't think I could handle a beating like that, not without having a full mental breakdown in front of everyone. I was so tired, so hungry, and in so much pain from the beatings I'd already taken. The thought of the lash of that whip over my skin—it was unbearable.

But I didn't have a choice. I had to go. This was the moment Sile had warned me about; the moment when my strength would truly be tested.

"We don't want him to get lonely up there, do we? Nah, of course not. Send that one, too. They seem real fond of each other already." Thrane laughed hoarsely as he pointed to someone else.

I knew I shouldn't look. I didn't want to see who it was. It was better not to see, to let it all roll off and stare at the ground. But I couldn't help it. As one of the instructors shackled me to the post with my arms above my head, I looked up to see who else they were pulling from the group.

Felix was looking right back at me. His face was so battered I barely recognized him. The instant our eyes met, I knew what was about to happen.

We stared at one another as they shackled him on the other side of the post so that we were forced to look into each other's eyes. I knew he had to be thinking the same thing I was: Thrane knew about us. He had been waiting all this time for the perfect moment to finally break me by using the one person who could push me over the edge. I was not ready for this, and I could already feel my sanity starting to slip through my fingers.

"You seem to like taking the fall for this piece of filth." Thrane walked up to Felix, curling a long, braided leather whip around his arm. "Did you think I wouldn't notice? Maybe the others didn't, but I know a con when I see one. You threw that fight for this demon. I'll admit, I was a little surprised. They say you're a high noble. Well, that may be, but I'm willing to bet your blood is red just like everyone else's. I guess we'll find out, won't we?"

My heart was pounding in my ears so loudly I could barely hear anything else. I clenched my teeth and started to twist my hands in my shackles. Immediately, Felix's expression changed.

He glared at me fiercely and shook his head.

Thrane grabbed my chin suddenly, jerking my eyes away from Felix so that I had to stare back at him. "The beating stops when you talk. You've fooled everyone else here into thinking you're one of us, but you don't fool me. I've seen your kind. I've watched your people butcher my brothers like cattle. It's time you show these people whose side you're really on, demon. Until then, watch him bleed for you."

There was no way to win this situation—not in my eyes. If I kept my mouth shut, I was betraying my whole purpose for being here by letting Felix suffer. If I talked, I was proving that I couldn't be trusted. Thrane had me cornered, and there was no way out. Somehow, I'd walked right into his trap.

I started pulling against my shackles as they cut Felix's shirt off his back. He was still looking straight at me. Even though he didn't seem afraid, I couldn't calm down. I fought the iron chains with all my might.

"Stop it," Felix whispered suddenly. Behind him, I could see Thrane unfurling his whip. "We had a deal."

I stopped struggling long enough to whisper back, "He's going to kill you!"

Felix sent me one of his typical, carefree grins. He opened his mouth to speak, but he never got the words out.

The whip cracked in the air.

It cracked over, and over, and over. Each time, Felix yelled, and his whole body jerked violently against the chains. His blood ran down his legs to drip onto the ground at our feet. His head sagged to his chest, and his knees had buckled so that he was basically dangling by the shackles on his wrists. I could hear him struggling to breathe. I was terrified he'd stop, that any one of those haggard breaths might be his last.

But the lashes kept coming. Even after Felix stopped screaming altogether, as though he didn't even have the strength to make a sound anymore. The metallic smell of his blood hung in the air. It made me sick with rage. Thrane curled that whip again and again, smiling at me the whole time.

I hated myself for not stopping this. I hated Felix for not letting me. I hated Thrane because there was nothing I wanted more than to rip his heart right out of his chest. I hated Jace for not intervening. Didn't he see what was happening? This wasn't training. This was torture.

Another instructor beside Thrane was keeping count of the lashes. It was the only other sound other than the awful sound of that whip cracking in the air.

"Twenty-two. Twenty-three. Twenty-four ... "

I squeezed my eyes shut. I let my head sag to my

chest. Deep inside me, something was starting to rise up. It was a familiar burning heat, like someone had poured dragon venom into my veins. Before, I had always tried to fight it. I'd been so afraid of it, or of what would happen if I lost control. But now I had no reason to be afraid. I didn't have any reason to resist it.

So I surrendered.

Immediately, my mind snapped into focus. Strength bloomed through my body despite the pain, hunger, and thirst. None of it mattered anymore as I raised my head, and stared past Felix's slumped body to where Thrane was standing.

I wanted to kill him, and nothing was going to stop me.

I didn't even notice the way the post was beginning to sprout branches. At least, not until I felt the ground move under my feet. The post was coming to life. It was sprouting roots that dove into the earth around our feet. It was growing branches and leaves in a matter of seconds.

I heard the others starting to scream, but that sound only stoked the fire in my chest. I could feel the post now. It wasn't just wood anymore. It was a living thing, and it would obey me.

I commanded it to set us free. Immediately, a branch began twisting round the thick iron chains and squeezing them like a boa constrictor.

The chains snapped.

Felix was badly hurt. He couldn't even stand. As soon as his chains were broken, he started to fall. I caught him long enough to make sure he made it to the ground without cracking his head. Then I set my eyes upon Thrane.

Thrane was terrified. Everyone else was, too. They

were running, yelling, or standing in awe as the whipping post grew bigger, turning into a large tree in the middle of the courtyard. But none of that mattered to me.

"You will pay with your blood," I snarled at Thrane. I barely recognized my own voice. I sounded like some kind of a growling beast.

Thrane was fumbling around, trying to figure out how to fend me off. He drew back his whip, and lashed it at me.

I caught it in the air and let it wrap around my forearm. Then I pulled on it hard enough to make him loose his footing. Thrane fell to his knees.

He started frantically grasping for his sword. His expression of fear changed to rage and hatred. When he got to his feet, he started toward me, bellowing like a maniac. He raised his sword, ready to cut me in half.

The heat in my chest suddenly swelled. It spread throughout my body, blazing out to every finger and toe like a roaring inferno. It sent such a jolt through me that my legs buckled. I was on my knees, but I wasn't surrendering.

I was just getting started.

Thrane took three steps before the ground beneath him started to rumble and move. Three huge vines erupted out of the soil around him. They wrapped around his arms and legs, snagging him like giant tentacles. He started to scream as they lifted him into the air.

"End it," I heard myself snarl.

A splinter of doubt pierced my chest, but I couldn't stop it. The rage had overtaken me. It was battle fever— the *kulunai*. Thrane was getting what he wanted, a lot more than he bargained for, and precisely what he deserved.

A flex of my hand made the vines all squeeze at once. There was a nasty crunching sound, and Thrane's screams went silent. I felt it as he died, almost like I was crushing a glass ornament in my hands. It was shattered completely, and there was no way to repair it.

Suddenly, something struck me. It hit me hard in the chest, right at my shoulder. I looked down, surprised to see the shaft of an arrow sticking out of my body. It didn't hurt, though. The battle fever prevented me from feeling anything but the boiling fire in my body. I immediately stood up and started looking around for the person who had shot me. They were the next threat that had to be dealt with.

I saw Jace. He was slowly drawing another arrow back. He stood only a few yards away, his expression just as brutally wrathful as though he were facing down someone he truly hated.

I was confused. I knew his face, even through the haze of the battle fever. I didn't understand why he was shooting at me. But when he fired again, hitting me in the side, I felt the fires of my own fury start to rise again. It didn't matter who he was, then. He was a threat that needed to be dealt with, and that was all I cared about.

"No!" Someone yelled. I was sure I had heard that voice before.

Lyon burst from the ranks of panicking avians and threw himself in between us. He was facing me, his eyes wide and desperate. "Jae, you have to stop," he yelled again. "You have to stop this right now! Thrane is dead! It's over!"

The roaring fires in my veins start to fizzle—until I felt the pain of the arrows in my body. That sensation spun me back into the battle fever in a matter of seconds.

"Get out of the way," I growled at him.

Lyon didn't move. He stood between Jace and I, his arms spread wide, staring me down. Behind him, I could still see Jace, and he had another arrow notched and ready to fly.

"No. I won't let you do it." Lyon said. I saw his chin tremble some, like he was trying not to lose his nerve. "Are you with us?"

That question struck a chord. It roused a memory I had almost forgotten. Someone had asked me that before, but I couldn't remember who. The battle fever made everything seem so out of control.

"Answer me! Are you with us?" Lyon shouted louder.

Coolness washed over me so suddenly that actually gave me chills. The fire within me died, reduced to ashes as the battle fever left my body. Before my legs buckled again, I managed to answer.

"Always."

I wasn't expecting any kindness, not after what I'd done. Part of me was okay with whatever they chose to do with me. I wasn't going to beg for my life, not when I was so obviously guilty. I was a murderer, and I couldn't ask for mercy when I hadn't shown any myself. So I let myself slip away, sleeping off the exhaustion from using so much of my power, and hoped that I would never wake up.

Maybe they'd just behead me in my sleep. I didn't want to face Felix, Lyon, or Jace again, anyway.

As the haze of fatigue finally cleared from my mind, I woke up in the darkness of a prison cell. The wounds left by Jace's arrows had been bandaged, but they still hurt. Thankfully, it didn't seem like he had been shooting to kill me, because they were nothing more than flesh wounds.

As I started to get my bearings, I realized there were voices speaking loudly nearby. One of them sounded like Lyon.

"He's the only one who can do it. Let him show you!" Lyon was pleading. "He's done it to me dozens of times already!"

"He's telling the truth," Jace insisted. "I've seen it myself."

"That ... that *thing* cannot be trusted! He almost turned on you, too!" I heard someone arguing. He was joined by a few other voices, all grumbling in agreement.

"But he didn't," Jace countered. He sounded as calm and collected as ever. "It was my mistake. I struck him first. If I hadn't presented myself as a threat, he wouldn't have even considered me one. You saw how Lyon was able to talk him down. He was rational because he didn't perceive Lyon as a threat."

"Don't be a fool, Lieutenant Rordin," someone else snarled in defiance. "We've all seen these creatures when the battle fever possesses them! We've witnessed firsthand what they are capable of! They are not rational!"

No one spoke for a moment. I didn't move from where I was lying on my back, staring up into the darkness of my prison cell. Then Jace said something that made me go numb.

"I don't think it was battle fever." He sounded very solemn. "I know we suspected that after the first incident with Lyon. It certainly seemed the likely explanation, considering his heritage. But now, having witnessed what else he can do, I think this is something else. You all saw how his eyes glowed. You saw how his teeth turned to fangs, and how he made those plants obey him. I've never seen that before from battle fever—or from any gray elf, for that matter. Whatever he did—whatever he is—it's something we've never encountered before."

Once again there was silence.

All I could do was lie there and try to comprehend what Jace had said. My eyes had glowed? And my teeth had turned to fangs? I poked at them with my tongue to be sure, but they didn't feel any different from normal now.

"So what exactly are we dealing with?" Another voice asked. It sounded like Liuetenant Haprick. I was too dazed to be sure. "Surely you aren't thinking he could be some sort of pagan gray elf deity?"

Lyon snorted. "Jae's not a god. He'd tell you that himself if you asked him."

"Regardless of what he is, there's no reason we shouldn't let him save his friend. Everything he did was for that same purpose, and his ability to heal has never provoked a violent attack before," Jace said. "Besides, I don't see any other choice. We can't escape even to send out a distress call. If we don't act soon, Felix will die of infection. I can't let that happen. It's my fault he's in this state. Thrane took things too far, and I didn't stop him in time."

Hearing that got me on my feet in an instant. I walked to the iron bars at the front of my cell. A small group of instructors and avians stood close by, huddling together under the light of a single torch.

"Let me save him," I begged. "Please."

My words made everyone, including Jace and Lyon, jump in surprise. They all turned to face me. I could see the fear in their eyes. It made me realize I was more alone now than I'd ever been before. Now, they all saw me as a potential threat.

"What are you? How do we know we can trust you?" Lieutenant Haprick demanded.

My shoulders sagged. "I don't know. And I don't know how to prove to you that I don't want to hurt anyone else."

"Well, you've done more than that." Jace sighed and took a step toward me. "After your little outburst, it's like the whole island has gone mad. We can't even get out of the compound now. The few of us who have tried were killed in minutes, before they could even reach the wall."

I stared at him, trying to understand everything he said. "The plants?"

"And animals," Lyon added. "It's unbelievable, Jae. Remember how you woke up that ancient turtle everyone thought was extinct? There are monsters outside right now no one has ever seen before. They didn't even know creatures like that lived on this island. They attack anyone who dares to step foot outside the door."

"Because of me?" I swallowed hard.

Jace's expression said it all. It really was my fault. "We can't even send anyone out to call for help. We're trapped here. Our supplies won't last a week. But Felix's wounds will kill him long before hunger and thirst do."

I frowned at them as hard as I could. "Then let me out. I have to heal him. If you let me do that much, then

I will call the dragons back here for you. You won't have to send anyone else outside."

Lieutenant Haprick's brows rose in surprise. "Are you bargaining with us?"

I narrowed my eyes at him. "Yes. And as far as I can tell, it's the best option you've got. You don't even have to take me with you when the dragons come. Leave me here to die alone, if it makes you feel better."

"Jae, that's not—" Lyon started to protest.

"They won't trust me again after this, right? Then it's better if I stay." I snapped at him.

"There's no way the dragons can pick us up here." Jace started rubbing his chin thoughtfully. "The forest has completely invaded the compound. The canopy is too thick for them to land. We have to get to the beach."

"Maybe he can talk to the trees?" Lyon suggested. "You know, get them to move or something?"

Lieutenant Haprick scoffed, "Do you even hear yourselves? Talking to trees?! This is ridiculous!"

"No, what's ridiculous is letting everyone here die on principle because you don't understand what I am. You don't have to like me. You don't even have to trust me. You have to let me try. I'm the only chance you've got to escape this place." I growled at them. "So let me out. Now."

twenty-five

Felix was in bad shape. When I entered the small, dimly lit room where they had him resting, the smell of infection hit me like a rock to the forehead. It was a disgusting, sickly-sweet smell that made me gag.

Felix was lying on his side facing the door. His back was wrapped in bandages that were soaked with blood. Jace had already warned me about that. They were out of medical supplies, so they were trying to reuse what little they had on hand.

A small audience of instructors and avians were gathered in the doorway, but they didn't follow me into the room as I went to kneel down at Felix's bedside. They all kept a safe distance from me now, as though they were afraid I would snap and go crazy again. I couldn't blame them for that.

"You know, when I said I wanted to see what amazing, unexpected thing you were going to do next, this is definitely not what I had in mind." Felix opened his eyes slowly and stared right at me. His voice sounded weak, but his usual sense of humor was still there.

I had to smile back at him, even if it felt like it might be the last time we ever spoke like this. "Too late to back out on me now, though. Right?"

He smiled faintly. His forehead was dripping with sweat from fever, and I could see the pain in his eyes. He was suffering.

"As if any of your weirdness would scare me off at this point." He grabbed one of my shoulders roughly and squeezed it. "I know you've always kept secrets from me, which I guess was your way of trying to protect me, but I'd rather be remembered as the friend of a weird halfbreed than a duke who only cared about his reputation."

"After this, neither of us will have much of a reputation left to defend," I managed to whisper. "I'm so sorry, Felix."

He smiled again, and punched my arm with a little bit of that strength I'd always envied. "Don't be. We're family, Jae. Maybe not literally, but you're the closest thing to a real brother I've ever had."

"I know." Somehow, I was able to smile back at him. "Which is why no sacrifice I make for you will ever be enough to repay you for everything you've done for me. So shut up and let me heal you. I'm going to do something else amazing after this, and I know you won't want to miss it."

No one said a word as I placed my hands on his back. I could feel how his body was burning up with infection. I could feel his pain, and how the subtle glow of his spirit was growing weaker. It flickered and struggled like a candle slowly smothering without air. Jace was right. If I didn't heal him, he might not last another two days.

I let my power flow. It surged through my body so

suddenly that it made me flinch. Never had this ability come so effortlessly to me. It felt more natural and calm than ever before, seeping out of my body and washing over his like a cleansing water.

I heard Felix suck in a sharp breath. I felt him go tense as my power took hold of him. In the doorway, the others were whispering, or gasping in awe. Only Lyon seemed to be able to keep his composure. He just looked on with a firm, confident gaze.

When it was finished, I took my hands away and backed up a few steps. Felix stirred on the bed. He was panting for breath, and staring at me with eyes so wide I thought he might scream in alarm. Instead, he started to sit up. His body was shaking, but I knew that was normal. It would take a few minutes for my power to finally leave his body.

Jace immediately rushed into the room to help him. Lyon followed and started peeling away the old bloody bandages from his back. Underneath was nothing but a few faint scars. The wounds, fever, and infection were all gone. Felix was perfectly healed.

The others rushed in to see, stumbling and climbing all over each other to touch his back like they thought it might be some kind of trick. One by one, they slowly turned to face me. Their faces stared at me with haunted expressions.

I bowed my head in submission. "Now, please let me try to save the rest of you."

"We've only managed to stand out there for a few minutes at most before the animals start to converge," Jace explained as he led me to a small balcony on the backside of the complex. "This is the only way out other than the main entrance."

"A few seconds is all I'll need." I nodded as I walked quickly after him.

After my attempts to call back the dragons from inside the fort had failed, the instructors had given everyone back their armor and sword. But before I went diving out the main gate to try anything radical, I needed to do a test run. I hadn't forgotten about my encounter with the wolves and mountain cat. The chaos that had possessed them had also made them deaf to my voice. If that was the case here, then that might explain why I couldn't get my calls to reach out beyond the canopy. All my power might be useless, which basically meant we were doomed.

"And if it doesn't work?" Jace asked as he stopped at the heavy wooden door that led out onto the balcony. He pulled a big iron key out of his pocket and started to unlock it.

"Then we'll have no choice but to take our chances in the jungle. It's that or die here, right?" I said as I pressed a hand against the wound on my shoulder. It still hurt, but at least it wasn't infected. "You can cover me with your bow, right? Without shooting me this time?"

Jace snorted and shot me a poisonous glare. "Just do whatever it is you do, avian, and leave the rest to me." He grasped the door handle and let out an anxious breath. "Ready?"

"I never am," I muttered as I braced myself. I gave him a countdown with my fingers. On three, Jace opened the door and I stepped out onto the balcony.

The sunlight filtering through the leaves cast everything in a greenish glow. Jace hadn't been exaggerating. The jungle had swallowed the compound completely. Vines and moss covered all the walls. Fully mature trees were growing everywhere, even knocking over portions of the wall to make way for their swelling trunks and branches. Strange flowers bloomed in every color imaginable, and some were so big I could have used one of their petals as a blanket. The air was thick and humid, and it smelled richly of soil.

Being on the second story put me right in the midst of the branches. They were so big I could have walked on them easily, but I stayed on the small balcony with the door right behind me. I wasn't feeling confident enough yet to venture very far away from it.

"All this … is because of me?" I heard myself ask.

"Apparently. Whatever you did before started some kind of chain reaction." Jace grumbled from behind me. "Hurry up. You're pressing our luck here."

I forced myself to focus. Jace was right. Apparently two instructors had already tried this and ended up paying the ultimate price for their bravery. I clenched my teeth and took a few more steps away from the door, stopping to look up through the interlocking limbs of the trees. I reached out to them with my thoughts, gently at first but with growing intensity. I commanded them to recede, to move away from the compound.

All I got was silence.

I shut my eyes and tried to focus harder. I tried to visualize what I wanted them to do. That's when I got my first little taste of something foul and all too familiar.

Chaos stung my mind and scrambled my thoughts.

The balcony flinched under my feet. I heard a piercing, screeching sound that sent a cold pang of alarm through my body. I had heard that sound before, but only in my nightmares.

"Jaevid," Jace growled my name like a warning.

When I opened my eyes, I saw it. I knew what it was right away, even though I had never actually seen one in person. Felix had told me about the creatures gray elves rode on; monsters that were supposed to be the natural archenemy of dragons.

Crouched before me on a thick tree limb, only a dozen yards away, was a shrike. It was as terrifying as it was beautiful. All I could do for a moment was stare at it, completely in awe.

The shrike was about the size of a small horse, though its shape was more like a six-legged cat. It had a long, flowing spine, robust shoulders and haunches, and a slender tail. Its entire body was covered in tiny scales that reflected the jungle like shards of a broken mirror. It was extremely lean, with a bony-looking exterior and a long tapered snout. Its sleek wings were made of nearly transparent feathers that almost looked like they were made of purplish tinted glass. Its eyes glowed like sunlight through leaves, focused right on me.

I immediately understood why Felix and Lyon had seemed so afraid of these creatures. It was difficult to differentiate where the shrike's body began and ended unless it was moving. It blended in so perfectly with the jungle around it. Its bony jaws were lined with teeth like a crocodile's that were about as long as my index finger. There were also claws on each of its toes that were long and curled like an eagle's talons.

I could sense the shrike's strength, speed, and power

just by looking at it. It was a wild, brutally vicious creature. But something about it was incredibly beautiful. Even so, its presence in my mind was tossed amidst the chaos. I tried to talk to it anyway. I tried to ask it to acknowledge me, to see if it really was possessed.

It acknowledged me, all right.

The shrike snapped its jaws and let out a blood-curdling snarl. Its body rippled with raw, brutal strength, and the sunlight danced off its mirror-like scales as it sprang at me, jaws open wide for the kill.

An arrow zipped past my head, hitting the shrike in the chest. It screamed with pain and rage, and kept right on coming. It moved so unbelievably fast, I barely had time to think, much less react. At the last second, I frantically dove out of the way. As the shrike barreled past me, one of its razor-sharp claws caught my face. I could feel it tearing through my skin, cutting to the bone.

"Get in here!" Jace yelled.

I scrambled back toward the door and held it shut as he locked it again. While the shrike clawed at the door, we both stood there panting and staring at each other in shock. That had been way too close.

"My power isn't working," I managed to rasp. I could feel the hot, wet sensation of blood running down my face. "I couldn't talk to it at all. I couldn't even get my voice out past the trees. They're acting like a cage, keeping the chaos trapped in."

Jace scowled. "You must not be doing it right. It worked before. And your eyes didn't glow like last time."

"I can't let it go that far again." I glared back at him with fresh blood running down my face. As much as I hated to admit it, I couldn't control my reactions very well in that state. Battle fever or not, it seemed too dangerous. What good would it do to hold the forest at bay if I killed all my friends in the process?

"What other options do you think we have? If you don't do this, we're all dead anyway," he roared back at me so loudly it made me cringe. "We only have enough water left to last us three days at most. If we don't get off this island, we will all die here in this god-forsaken place."

The door rattled again as the shrike clawed at it from the outside. The terrible noises it made sounded like the feral scream of a cat mixed with an eagle's cry. Hearing it made me wonder what other horrors would be waiting for us in the jungle if I did try to lead everyone to the beach.

"Fine," I answered at last. "But swear to me if I start to turn against you again, you won't hesitate to put an arrow in my skull. No more flesh wounds. You might not get a second shot."

Jace's mouth pinched up like he'd tasted something sour, but he agreed. "If it comes to that."

The silence between us was awkward as we returned downstairs to the large open room where everyone else was gathered. The large doorway of the main entrance was barricaded with every piece of furniture in the compound, and all the supplies left were piled in a corner. There wasn't much left. The food was already almost gone, but more importantly, we only had a few barrels of fresh drinking water.

The rest of our group looked up with grim, haunted faces as Jace and I came down the stairs. I was holding a rag against my face to stop the bleeding. The cut was deep, and it had narrowly missed my eye, but Jace insisted it would be fine. His expression told me otherwise, but

I knew better than to complain. Thanks to Thrane, and everyone's efforts to save Felix, most of our medical supplies were probably gone.

As we entered the main room, the instructors and avians gathered there stared at me with a mixture of fear and hope. I hated that I didn't have better news for them. All I could do was shake my head.

Immediately, I sensed the morale in the room start to crumble.

"No dragons. No moving the trees. So I guess we try the jungle, then?" Felix spoke up as he came to meet us. "We should leave soon, before everyone's too weak from hunger to make the hike."

"This is suicide," another avian murmured nearby.

I wanted to agree with him, but for the sake of the rest of the group, I tried to sound confident. "If we are fast and silent, we might be able to make it through without causing much of a disturbance. I'll go out first in case we encounter anything. Jace and the instructors should form a barrier with all the other students in the center."

Felix crossed his arms stubbornly, "Yeah, right. Look at you; you've already almost lost your head to one of those monsters. I'm not letting you offer yourself up like some kind of martyr. I'm walking right beside you."

"Me too," Lyon agreed as he came to stand right next to Felix.

I stared at them and wondered if it was even worth trying to argue. I decided against it. Felix was too stubborn and Lyon would ride his coattails to the bitter end. Besides, having them both close by actually made me more confident. It was a stupid thing to hope for, but I was thinking maybe if either of them got into real danger, then my power would grow strong enough to make sure nothing from the jungle would come close.

"All right, let's get everyone up." Jace clapped a hand on my shoulder as he brushed by us.

He started rousing everyone and giving commands, and Felix joined him. I stood back and watched as the instructors advised everyone to have their weapons at the ready. Anyone with even a little skill at archery was encouraged to carry a bow and quiver. They poured what was left of our water into as many canteens as they could find, and started passing out our go-bags.

I was relieved to be reunited with the rest of my belongings. I found Beckah's handkerchief and carefully tucked it back under my vambrace without getting any blood on it. Of course, the only thing missing were my medical supplies, which had most likely been scavenged.

"Here," I heard Felix say right before he started roughly tying something around my head. One of my eyes went dark as he started wrapping cloth over the wound on my face like an eye patch. It was a piece he'd apparently cut off his cloak. "Jace said it was a scratch. Lucky for you it wasn't a bite. No venom in the claws. If it'd bit you, your whole face would start rotting off."

I looked at him with my uncovered eye, but I didn't know what to say except, "Thanks."

He shrugged. "It's better than watching you bleed all over the place. Good thing it missed your eye, huh?"

I wasn't ready to call myself lucky, yet. With my bag slung over one shoulder, I stood in front of the main entrance while a group of instructors moved their makeshift barricade out of the way. My heart was pounding, and I was beginning to question myself again. Willingly surrendering to that power for only a few seconds had weakened me so much before. I wondered if

I could last the entire hike to the beach.

"It's seven miles to the beach," Felix announced. "If we don't get lost."

I sighed and drew my sword as the last piece of debris was cleared out of the way. "We won't. Getting lost is the least of our worries, anyway. There's still an angry shrike out there."

Felix chuckled and punched my arm so hard it almost knocked me over because I wasn't ready for it. "There's always something right? Shrike in a jungle full of killer plants, king drake and a prison camp full of angry guards—what's the difference?"

I punched him back as hard as I could. "Right. Just another work day for us."

"Not going to run away this time, are you?" Felix teased Lyon.

I didn't find it that funny, and neither did Lyon. He'd come over to stand with us, and kept staring at the ground while his face turned red. He didn't try to tease Felix back or defend himself. It was an awkward subject for all of us now.

We all fell silent as two instructors started working the crank that opened the big iron-gilded doors enough for us to slip out. The hinges groaned and creaked, and green light poured in. The rich jungle air flowed through the open doors, and I took a deep breath. I let it fill my lungs. Somehow, it made my body seem lighter and stronger. It was more refreshing to me than normal air.

Felix, Lyon, and I went out first. They both stared around with their mouths hanging open in silent awe at how the jungle had reclaimed the compound in only a short time. It was barely even recognizable. The sight made Felix draw his sword.

While the others followed us out, I kept my good eye and both ears alert for a shrike. In the dim light, I knew it would be hard to see until it was much too late because of its scales. But I had another, better way of detecting it. I let my mind reach out, spreading my senses over the area around us. If anything besides plants and trees got too close, I would know about it.

"All right, weirdo," Felix said as he poked me with his elbow and destroyed my concentration. "Do your thing."

I shot him a glare. "I was trying, idiot. Be quiet."

I couldn't risk him messing me up again, so I took a few steps away before I tried again. Slowly bowing my head to my chest, I let my eyes roll closed and my thoughts slowly fade into silence. I searched through my body for that fire. When I couldn't find it, I started to panic. I started to doubt myself again, and wonder if I wouldn't be able to do it at all.

Then I felt a hand rest on my shoulder. It was strong and warm, and it filled me with confidence. It soothed my worries and quietened all my doubts. My mind drifted back to that horrible moment when I thought Felix was going to die right in front of me at the whipping post, and found that fire flickering deep in my memories. It started to burn brighter, blazing outward through my chest and sizzling through my arms and legs.

When I looked to see who had touched me, but there was no one there. Felix and Lyon were still standing a few yards away, helping the others get into a block formation. For a moment, doubt started to leak back into my mind. I was confused and a little afraid.

"*Don't be afraid,*" my mother's voice whispered in my mind.

The heat inside me surged even brighter then, and

set my heart ablaze. I wasn't alone. Somehow, she was with me. And whatever I was turning into, she didn't want me to fight it. She didn't want me to be afraid of it. Realizing that gave me courage. It gave me confidence that everything would be okay because this wasn't a mistake—I was supposed to be this way.

My body shuddered with the sudden wave of power. My mind broke into that state of eerie, perfect calm. Everything seemed to move in slow motion around me. I could see it all, the jungle with its many wonders, like it was a disobedient child. And I was here to deliver a well-deserved spanking.

"Let's go." My voice had become that strange, growling tone again. I knew by the way the others were looking at me that the eye they could see must have been glowing again. Tracing my tongue over my teeth, I could feel that my incisors on top and bottom had become long and pointed like animal fangs.

Now wasn't the time to be worried about that. I started into the jungle with Felix and Lyon on either side of me. The others followed a few steps behind, their weapons at the ready.

The foliage swallowed us like a green maze. It was disorienting at first because there was no horizon or sunlight to determine direction. But it didn't confuse me for long. I could feel the sea, or rather, I could sense the point in the distance where the forest ended even though it was a long way off. That was the direction I led everyone.

It didn't take five minutes for the first threat to show itself. The instant I knew something was approaching, I stopped dead in my tracks. The feeling of pressure coming from whatever was headed our way made me shudder, and made my aura of power ripple. Whatever was coming, it was large and strong.

Felix and Lyon stopped on either side of me. I could sense their fe. It wasn't the first time I could remember feeling a person's emotions like that. I remembered the morning after the officer's ball, when I had been able to glimpse a little of Felix's grief over his father. A simple touch on the shoulder had allowed me to tap into his feelings. I was doing the same thing now, except I didn't have to touch any of them.

At that moment, though, I was too distracted to think about their feelings much. My bigger concern was coming towards us with booming footsteps that echoed from the dense trees. The sound of them seemed to come from everywhere at once, and I could feel the ground flinching under my boots.

"Look there!" Felix shouted suddenly.

A monster nearly ten feet tall lumbered into our path, bringing with it a stench that reminded me of the paludix turtle. It was the smell of old, rotting leaves, fermented swamp water, and decaying plants. Not something you'd want to run into on purpose. But this creature definitely was *not* a turtle. In fact, it looked more like a giant wolf. Its fur was so matted with leaves, sticks, and mud that it almost seemed to be made out of the jungle itself. Its white eyes flickered like bog fires in the dim light, and it was starting right at us.

As soon as it saw us, the beast stopped. I could hear its deep, growling breaths. Slowly, its snout start to wrinkle, showing us giant yellow fangs. I could sense the chaos rolling off the monster's body like a poisonous smog. It hit my nostrils and made the fire in my body blaze with fury. For whatever reason, feeling this creature turn against me filled me with unspeakable anger. It was like being betrayed by a family member I had trusted. I refused to stand for it.

The beast started hunkering down with intent to strike. I felt my irritation grow in response. Felix tried to stop me as I started walking toward it, but I jerked away from him.

"No," I commanded the monster. My voice sounded bizarre, like a mismatched chorus of different languages all speaking at once.

The beast growled so loudly it made the earth tremble. Its flickering eyes were fixed on me, and I raised a hand toward it, letting it feel the heat of my power like a silent warning. I didn't want to fight. I only wanted the respect I deserved.

"You will regret your disobedience," I promised.

The monster bristled, the matted fur raising along its neck and back. Chaos resonated so deeply inside it, entangling with its free will like a knotted ball of string. I knew it would attack no matter what I said. There was no reasoning with it.

With a twist of my wrist, the earth began to shift. Vines burst from the ground like before, growing to be as thick as a man's arm, and wrapping around the monster's legs and neck. It fought, snarling and biting as it tried to get free. But for every vine it broke, three more grew in its place until the creature was pinned against the ground. It let out a howl of frustration.

The other dragonriders behind me didn't make a sound. They all stared like they weren't sure what to be more afraid of: me or the monster I'd just brought down.

I stepped toward the pinned beast. It stared back at me through the fog of that chaos and the vines that were holding its head to the ground like a hundred giant pythons. I could sense its panic and rage. I knew even though I had established my dominance, if I let that creature go now, it would still try to attack us rather than flee. I couldn't allow that.

So I drove my sword into its skull.

Immediately, the beast's energy began to fade away, taking that sense of mindless fury with it. It drew one last, rasping breath, and finally lay still and soundless.

Behind me, Lyon was whispering, "He just killed a rotwolf with one blow."

I snapped a punishing gaze back at him. The death of this animal was not something to celebrate. Feeling its life slip away gave me the same sense of despair as when I had killed Thrane. Even in my anger, seeing a life be crushed was like watching someone smash a glass sculpture into bits. It wasn't fixable. It wasn't something you could ever duplicate again. It was destroyed forever, and I was to blame.

Suddenly, my legs started to feel weak and numb. I stumbled, and Felix rushed up to catch me. I noticed my nose was bleeding. We still had a long way to go … and I was already beginning to feel the effects of using so much of my power. I wasn't sure I would make it seven minutes, let alone seven miles.

It was time to do something radical again—before I was too weak to do anything at all.

I pushed away from Felix and widened my stance, gripping my sword in both hands and raising it high above my head. I threw my head back, looking to the trees overhead, but pressing all my thoughts and power into the ground under my feet. The vines seemed to be my most obedient tool. I could use them easily. So I would use them as much as I possibly could to save my dragonrider brothers.

I plunged my sword down into the ground with all my might, and at the same time, poured every ounce of my will into the earth with it. The ground began to rumble. The trees groaned. The wind howled around me, and a wave of wild energy spread out through every inch of the island.

Vines burst from the ground again on each side of me. But instead of a few, or a dozen, it was hundreds—maybe even thousands. Some were normal-sized, others were as big as tree trunks. They snaked across the ground, compiling and weaving together to create a living barrier around us. They continued on into the forest, mixing with the trunks and branches of the trees, and forming a protective tunnel that led away into the jungle. It was seven miles long, and would take my brothers all the way to the beach.

My whole body shook with exhaustion as I pulled my blade from the soil. I could barely grip it, and I tried not to let it show. The others stared at my creation. They stared at me, too.

"Go," I said without looking back. "This will take you safely to the beach."

The instructors didn't stop to ask any questions. I guess they had seen enough miracles already to obey me. They herded the rest of my avian peers toward the tunnel, making a wide berth around me as they hurried past.

Felix, Lyon, and Jace didn't follow them. They stood around me, but no one seemed ready to say why. I waited for someone to give me an explanation, searching the faces of my friends one by one. I could sense their apprehension, their awe, and their fear. They were afraid of me, even if none of them were ready to admit that.

"We aren't leaving without you," Lyon finally said.

"Don't be stupid," I snarled at him angrily. Didn't he realize I was doing all of this for them? If they didn't go, then all my efforts were for nothing. "I've served my purpose. Go with them. *Now!*"

"Knock it off," Felix growled back at me. "We've come this far together. We won't let them throw you in some prison camp. You have to trust us."

I laughed darkly, and all the voices mixed with mine laughed, too. "You honestly think there is any prison in the world that can hold me now?"

That made them all look a little pale.

"I am master here. This is where I belong." I turned a wrathful glare to Felix.

"Okay, master, but you're bleeding from the ears now, too. You have to stop. You're killing yourself." Felix took a fearless step toward me.

I touched one of my ears, and saw that he was right. Blood was dripping from both of them. That rattled me. I dropped my sword and staggered back away from them. Through the flames of power burning inside me, I had a moment of clarity. I knew Felix was right. I had to stop.

It was harder to call back the flames this time. They burned so freely through my body, filling me with that intoxicating heat and power. Getting it under control was as much a fight as calling it out had been. The fire didn't want to be contained. It wanted to burn forever, even if it consumed and killed me in the process.

A sudden screeching cry made us all look up at once. I knew that sound just as well as they did, and it stoked that roaring fire in my chest all over again. It was a shrike.

"Time to go," Jace ordered as he drew an arrow

from his quiver. "Grab him, and let's go!" His voice was drowned out by another screech, and then another, and another. One shrike was bad enough, but now it sounded like we were facing a whole flock of them.

Felix threw my arm over his shoulder and started dragging me into my tunnel of vines with them. We ran, or in my case staggered, as fast as we could over the ferns, rocks, roots, and fallen trees. Being in the vine tunnel made things darker than usual, and after tripping all over ourselves for a few minutes, Jace finally stopped and tore open his go-bag. He pulled out his candle and lit it. Felix and Lyon did the same. Then we started running again.

"They're following us," I said as lifted my good eye to the ceiling of the vine-tunnel. I could feel them there, beyond the barrier I had created. They moved so quickly, flying through the twisted arms of the trees with more speed and agility than a dragon could ever dream of.

"How many?" Jace demanded.

"Four on the outside." I answered. "They're looking for a way in. Two are already in the tunnel, chasing us. They're too wary of me to come closer, but not for much longer." My body was starting to fail me in more ways than one. My legs were completely numb, and I was beginning to have trouble breathing. It reminded me of that horrible coma-like state I had been put in when I'd healed Sile's wife. That must have come from pushing myself too far.

Jace cursed, and we kept running. I held on for as long as I could, but about a half a mile from the end of the tunnel, I couldn't take another step. I crumpled to the ground, bringing Felix down with me. My ears were ringing so loudly that everything else was muffled. The fire suddenly snuffed out leaving me limp, drained, and completely useless. I couldn't move at all.

Felix hooked his arms around my chest and tried to drag me. It didn't work. The ground wasn't flat and smooth. It was the jungle, after all. The soil was wet and spongy, riddled with all kinds of snags and roots. He only made it a few feet before he tripped and fell, almost landing on top of me.

"I won't leave him!" I heard Felix roar in frustration.

"There's no choice!" Jace bellowed back.

From down the tunnel, I heard the screeching of the shrikes coming closer now. I couldn't defend my friends anymore. Bits of bark and wood started falling from the ceiling of the tunnel, raining down upon us. The shrikes on the outside were using their venom-laced teeth to gnaw through the vine tunnel.

We were out of time. And I was out of miracles.

I was busy making peace with my demise when I felt something prick at my mind. Even in my paralyzed state, something familiar reached me through the numbness and exhaustion. It was a presence I knew all too well, and the last one in the world I thought would ever find me here. It was a presence so great, so old and powerful, not even the canopy of the jungle could keep it from reaching me.

There was an explosion from overhead. Felix, Lyon, and Jace dove for cover. I still couldn't move my body, so I kept lying there, staring up into the dark with my one uncovered eye, and hoping someone would remember to drag me out of the way before I got crushed or eaten.

I needed to make a noise. They were looking for us, and when my power was snuffed out so suddenly, they had lost track of me. But I knew that this was our last hope. They had to find us, or it was all over.

I called upon all the power I had left. Even if it killed me, I knew it might save my friends. It took every ounce of my will to call out with my thoughts, *Here. I'm here.*

His answer was a roar like the eruption of a volcano.

Icarus dropped through the canopy like a boiling inferno, bathing the forest in his dragon fire and smashing the trees with his giant wings. He was big enough to crush his way down, making a path through the foliage and a hole in my vine tunnel. Sunlight poured down over us.

Icarus's show didn't last. He couldn't stay on the ground, and just as violently as he arrived, he started wriggling free of the branches and bursting back up into the air. The shrikes emerged from the forest again, four in all, and started to attack us.

I fought with all my might to get up, but I couldn't even wiggle a finger. A shrike made a vicious lunge at me. I couldn't move to fight, let alone flee. I thought I was dead for sure until an arrow caught it in the head … right between the eyes. It dropped dead immediately.

Everyone was still getting up. Felix had his sword in his hand. Jace was scrambling to get his bow ready. Even Lyon was running toward me, sword in hand, shouting my name. He skidded to a stop right beside me, crouching down and taking up a defensive stance like he was going to protect me while the others fought.

But only one person was doing any real fighting.

From up in the trees, arrows rained down with deadly accuracy. Two caught another shrike in the back of the skull, killing it just as instantly as the first. I caught of glimpse of her stepping along the tree branches like a phantom. I couldn't see her face since she was wearing a helmet, but I knew it was her. Beckah was fighting with us.

And she was starting to make us look bad.

When she ran out of arrows, she dropped from the trees into a crouch and drew a pair of long, slender scimitars from a sheath on her back. Her body was completely covered in sleek black battle armor that was painted with six sets of golden angel wings on the helmet, chest, back, forearms, legs, and feet. Her face was completely covered. To look at her, no one ever would have known it was a girl under all that armor. She'd grown so much she really looked like a small, skinny young man.

Beckah may have looked like a knight, but she fought like a demon. Her strikes were so fast, I knew I wouldn't have been able to keep up with them. She never missed. She never hesitated. And she killed all the shrikes who attacked her in less than five minutes, making it look like child's play.

Everything was quiet except for the crackle of burning dragon venom still smoldering on a few of the trees. Beckah stood over her last kill with her blades dripping with blood. Slowly, she turned to look at us through her helmet's small eye slits.

Jace, Felix, and Lyon were speechless. They hadn't even moved, or tried to help her fight at all. It was over before they could find their weapons and figure out what was going on.

"W-who are you?" Lyon stammered in awe.

"Seraph," she answered in a deep, hoarse tone. She must have been trying to make her voice sound like a man's.

Just as she was turning away, placing her blades back on the sheath across her back, something rustled behind us. I couldn't move or look to see what it was. But I saw Beckah whip around suddenly, ripping her scimitars back out again.

There was a gory, crunching sound.

Someone let out a garbled scream, and out of the corner of my eye, I saw Lyon crumple to the ground. There was a shrike on him, digging its teeth into the back of his neck.

Beckah sprang back into action before anyone else. She moved out of sight like a black shadow, but I could still hear the sounds of combat and the dying screech of the shrike. It must have been slinking around in the dark, waiting for the perfect time to attack. With my body drained of all its strength and power, I couldn't even sense the shrike let alone warn any of them.

The others started shouting in panic. I couldn't see Lyon. I couldn't tell if he was still alive. All my abilities had completely fizzled out, so I couldn't even try to sense if he was there or not. Pure panic coursed through my body as I lay helpless because of how much of my power I had already used. With all that remained of my physical strength, I was able to turn my head enough to see where Lyon was lying only a few feet away.

They were trying to stop the bleeding. Jace was pumping on his chest and breathing into his mouth. But Lyon already had a distant expression on his face. His eyes were glazed over, and his skin looked pale.

Lyon was dead.

twenty-six

Everyone was complaining about the rain. Sitting in the dining hall, I listened to the chatter of my peers as they enjoyed their dinner. It was our last meal together before graduation. Tomorrow, at first light, we were going to be sent off to the royal city of Halfax to officially be sworn into the king's service. What would follow would be a grand celebration, and then we would learn where our next assignment would take us. But everyone was worried that the rain might slow us down.

Felix sat right beside me. He hadn't left me alone for days except to attend Lyon's funeral. Of course, I hadn't been invited. It was only for nobles and close friends. But I wrote a long letter of apology to Lyon to be burned on his funeral pyre. Felix agreed to take it, even though I still hadn't spoken to him. I hadn't really spoken to anyone, though. There was a lot I needed to sort out before I felt like talking about it.

First of all, it was still sinking in that I wasn't about to be shipped off to a prison camp or locked in a dungeon. The instructors and avians from the battle scenario hadn't spoken a word about anything I had done on the island. They all acted like nothing bizarre had happened at all, apart from things going awry when a few animals went crazy. They had blamed it all—including Thrane's death—on the jungle coming alive and attacking us. Commander Rayken wasn't even suspicious of me.

After a few days of hanging in suspense, waiting for the doors to burst open and elite guards to slap shackles on my wrists, I started to wonder if it ha all just been a nightmare. I was thinking that again, hoping that somehow it had been another one of my horrible dreams. Then I glanced to my other side where Lyon usually sat, and that stupid hope came crashing down around my ears. His seat was empty. Lyon was gone, and he wasn't coming back. He was dead because I hadn't been strong enough to keep my own power under control.

I knew Felix would be furious if he knew I was thinking those kinds of things. I couldn't help it. I was the only one who could have healed his injuries. I could have saved him. Instead I made a stupid tunnel out of vines that had nearly put me into another coma. It had taken days for me to be able to move normally again, and in that time, I could only lie there while everyone else grieved and mourned for my friend.

My other worry was about Beckah. I hadn't seen or heard from her since she had appeared to save us on the island. The other riders were talking about her plenty, though. They didn't know it was a girl under that helmet, but everyone was very impressed with a knight who had been able to take control of Icarus and could fight so well without ever setting foot in the academy. Rumors were flying about the mystery knight's real identity, and some people were even suggesting it might be the King of Maldobar himself.

"Nah, the king is way too old for that. You should have seen this guy. He had to be young to be that fast. He called himself Seraph," Felix explained.

He was telling the story again to a table full of our peers. When he glanced my way, our eyes met, and I knew he was keeping the rumor going on purpose. He knew who was really under that armor, thanks to me. I'd already told him about Beckah being chosen as a dragonrider, and I knew he wasn't stupid enough to believe it was anyone except her.

I waited until after dinner to finally ask the question that was driving me crazy. "Why are you keeping her secret?"

Felix closed the door to our dorm room and sat down on the edge of his bed. Behind him, Lyon's bed was still empty and untouched—exactly the way he had left it before the battle scenario.

"Because there may come a time when we need her help again." He sighed and rubbed his forehead. "So you've decided to talk now?"

I sat down on my bed across from him. "I'm trying to understand what happened … and why no one has arrested me yet."

Felix snorted like that was a bad joke. "No one is going to say a word about it, Jae. You saved us. Monster or maniac, those guys don't care what you are as long as you're on our side. And you proved that a hundred times over. No one would have made it off that island if you hadn't intervened. They know that. I know it. You just aren't ready to admit it, yet."

"I'm a halfbreed. They used to care a lot about that," I reminded him coldly.

"Things change. Sometimes even people change, too. Since you came here last year, you've made everyone second guess what they thought about halfbreeds." He sighed and shook his head. "As much as I hate to admit it, you were right about Lyon. He was able to change, and I didn't want to let myself see it. Now it's too late and I'll feel like a jerk forever."

"Not forever," I said.

Felix shook his head. "I wasn't going to tell you about this. I wasn't even close friends with him like you were, but hearing it made me sick. When I went to his funeral, I saw his father and grandfather standing in their old dragonrider armor. I went up to talk to them, since they were both pretty famous before they retired, and as soon as I got close enough to hear them talking ... it all started to make sense."

"What made sense?" I stared at him.

"Why Lyon ran that night at the prison camp. Why he was so mean to you, and why he seemed to hate me so much before. His dad and grandfather were talking about how Lyon was such a disappointment to them. I couldn't believe it," he said, and as he spoke, his voice started to shake with emotion. I saw rage filling his eyes. "At first, I thought I was imagining it, or that maybe they were talking about someone else. But they were standing there, over his funeral pyre, talking about how he'd never been cut out to be a dragonrider. They said they never understood before why he didn't want to go to the academy in the first place. Now, they said they saw it was because he couldn't handle it. They called him weak for not trying harder, and said it was better that he never stepped foot on the battlefield."

Felix had to stop and calm down. He was so furious he was clenching his fists so hard that his knuckles turned white. "For me it was the opposite, you know. I wanted this so badly, even though my parents didn't approve. Lyon didn't want to be a dragonrider. He must've been terrified the whole time. I'm sure knocking you around when you were little probably made him feel like he actually belonged here. It probably made him feel braver and stronger."

"Probably," I agreed.

"I wanted to punch them both in the neck for talking about him like that," Felix snarled. He was clenching his teeth. "But I stood there and realized I was just as guilty as they were. I hated him, Jae. I wanted an excuse to beat him up all the time. And I'm not saying what he did to you was right, but … "

"It's okay. I understand." I started rubbing at my face. My fingers traced over the stitches on my forehead and cheek. The medic had done the best he could fixing my face from where the shrike had scratched me, but he said it would definitely leave a scar. A memory etched into my skin.

"Where do we go from here?" Felix asked. When I looked at him again, he was staring at me with the most haunted expression on his face.

"I'm going wherever they send me," I told him. "I guess you have to decide again whether or not you're going to stay with the dragonriders or go be a duke."

He pressed his lips together into a frown. "That's not what I meant. I'm already a duke. My mom signed the estate over to me, and I gave her permission to act in my place when I'm not there. I'm going with you to war, Jae."

"Then what do you mean?"

"I mean, Lyon is dead, the animals and plants are conspiring to kill us all, and you're turning into some kind of vine-wielding forest deity. What do we do now?" He asked again. "What's happening to the world?"

I stopped to think about that. While I decided how to answer, I reached under the mattress of my bed and took out the scimitar Bren had restored for me. I ran my thumb over the elven crest on the pommel, the head of a stag engraved in the shimmering metal.

Felix stared down at it with wide eyes, and I could see his reflection in the side of the polished sheath. "Where did you get that?"

"I think I was supposed to find this." I sat the blade down on the bed beside me, and started digging under my mattress again. I pulled out the bone-carved necklace my mother had given me and put it back around my neck. It felt good to have the familiar weight of that talisman against my chest again. "I think I've been missing a lot of things I was supposed to find. Answers that have been staring me in the face all this time."

"Answers? To what?"

I started unlacing my boots and unbuckling my belt, changing into my night clothes. "To the same questions we've all been asking ourselves since the first time I called to Mavrik. What am I? Why do I have these powers? What am I meant to do with them?"

Felix shifted uncomfortably, and eyed me skeptically. "And you think you know how to figure all that out now?"

"Maybe not all of it, but I think I know where to

start." I crawled into bed and held the scimitar against my chest. "Goodnight, Felix."

I could sense him scowling at me. It was like a familiar stink in the air. He didn't like vague answers, but I wanted to wait until I was sure before I shared it with him. Beckah had suggested I listen to my dreams, and now I was beginning to believe she was right. I needed answers. And so far, my dreams held the only person in the world who could give them to me.

I stood on the muddy road. Around me was the snowy valley, white-crested mountains, and the looming wall of trees I knew was Luntharda. The air was so cold it made me gasp, and the sunlight sparkled over the snowdrifts. Before, when I saw this place in my dreams, it had always filled me with fear because I knew what was coming. I clenched my teeth and tried to control my emotions.

I wasn't going to be afraid. I was determined to see it all, to the bitter end.

"It's just a dream," I reminded myself out loud.

"No, not a dream," a familiar voice spoke softly. "A memory."

I looked, surprised to see a new figure standing right next to me. It was my mother.

She was much shorter than I was, giving me a real appreciation for how petite her people usually were, and how different I was by comparison. Her silver hair was flowing down her back, and her strange eyes reflected the blue sky, making them shine like aquamarines. Her clothes were strange and exotic. She was draped in one long ivory sheet of silk dotted with stitching of green vines and purple flowers. It was wrapped around her like some kind of ancient goddess, and there was a golden band in her hair made to look like rose vines twisted together. She looked ageless and powerful, and it surprised me. I'd never seen my mother look like that.

"But I don't remember any of this," I argued with her.

She smiled without ever looking back at me. "I never said they were your memories, dulcu. Now hush. I cannot stay with you much longer. My presence draws his attention."

I obeyed and turned my gaze to the road again. I stood beside my mother in the muddy road, prepared to face what was going to happen next. Neither of us said a word as we waited. In the distance, I heard a horse whinny. Anxiety started to swirl through my brain as the carriage and company of guards approached. Knowing what was about to happen made dread turn my stomach sour.

The gray elf warrior appeared, just like before. When he spoke, I noticed my mother's expression was hardening. Her eyes seemed to darken with frustration and disapproval, and when he drew his blade and started to slaughter the guards, she turned her face away. There were tears in her eyes.

I couldn't comfort her. I couldn't even move except to turn my head around some, so I watched the battle again. Emotion swelled in my chest with every passing second. Overhead, I heard the familiar screech of a shrike. I could see its shadow blur over the ground as it flew around us. Each swing of the gray elf's blade made my heart pound painfully. He dragged the king out of the carriage like before, and murdered him first. Nothing about the scene seemed different this time, though. I had seen it play out so many times, after all. I wanted it to be over.

But then something caught my eye.

The glimmer of sunlight off metal made me look at the king again. He lay on his stomach in the mud, motionless and dead, but there was something sticking out from under his cloak. It was the hilt of a blade.

My heart hit the back of my throat so hard I couldn't catch my breath.

I knew that blade. I knew it because I was the one carrying it now. It was my scimitar, the one with the elven crest on the pommel. It had belonged to the King of Maldobar!

Beckah's words resonated in my mind like an echo, reminding me why I had to pay attention. All my anxiety melted away. She was right, I had been missing things because I was too afraid to watch. Emotion had clouded my sight, and my own fear had pulled the dream apart.

I braced myself, setting my eyes upon the gray elf warrior. He moved like a predator over the bodies of the people he had murdered. His sneer was ruthless, and he cut his eyes right past me to look as the wounded guard, the only survivor, stood up shakily with his sword in hand.

The guard could barely keep a grip on his own weapon. Blood made his hands slick, and there was a deep gash on his leg that would definitely be deadly if it were left untreated. But I could see him fix his eyes upon the gray elf through the slit in his helmet. Something about him was so familiar, and I studied him over and over trying to figure out why. I still couldn't see enough of his face to recognize him, though.

"Aren't you brave?" The gray elf warrior taunted, spinning his strange white blade like it was weightless. "Tell me, little soldier, just how brave are you? What would you do to save your own life?"

I saw the guard brace for the attack, squaring his stance and preparing to stand and fight. My heart was beating out of control, and every fiber of my being cried out to let me step in and stop this. But I knew better now. It wasn't real. I had to watch. I had to see and understand.

The gray elf lunged like a panther, crossing the distance between them as the guard raised his sword and prepared to defend. They collided in combat, locking blades and pressing in to test each other's strength.

"You are made of tougher stuff than the rest of these fools," the gray elf purred with approval, grinning from ear to ear. "You might be very useful indeed." He twisted his stance in the blink of an eye, easily dropping the guard to the ground by kicking his already wounded leg.

The guard scrambled to get away. It was no good. The gray elf planted a foot on his chest to pin him down, and lowered the tip of his sword until it barely touched the guard's throat. He was caught with no choice but to lie there, staring death in the eye.

"Perhaps destroying such bravery and strength would be a waste, even if you are only a human. Why don't we make a bargain, you and I? You want to live, and I need an errand boy. You see, there's something that belongs to me hidden away in that forest. An artifact my people call the god stone," the gray elf said as he pressed his blade a little harder against the guard's throat. "Bring it to me, and not only will I spare your life, but I will reward you handsomely. Betray me, and I will hunt you down to the ends of the earth, along with everyone you have ever cared for. You will watch your entire family, your friends and loved ones, all pay the price for your disloyalty."

I waited in horrified silence. I couldn't imagine the gray elf would ever keep his word, or that the guard would even agree to help this murderer. Everything about this was wrong.

"Swear to me," the guard rasped from under his helmet. "Swear that you will not lay a hand on my family, if I agree."

The gray elf's grin widened. His eyes glittered maliciously, like a spider eyeing a fly caught in its web. "I swear it on the god stone."

A hot, buzzing sensation pricked at the back of my mind. It made me shiver at those words.

"Then I agree." The guard reached for the point of the blade at his throat and pushed it away. He started to get up, limping on his wounded leg and meeting the gray elf's gaze with a bitter, defiant glare.

I recognized that glare an instant before he started taking off his helmet. It fell from his hand, and my heart fell with it. The helmet made a sound like an empty metal bucket when it hit the ground and rolled away.

The guard brushed a hand through his hair, and turned so that he was looking right in my direction. I could see his face. He was scowling toward me with the same harrowing look in his eyes I had seen a thousand times before.

I knew exactly who he was.

twenty-seven

I couldn't eat breakfast. The sight of food made me even sicker, as though all my insides were rotting away. I sat with my eyes squeezed shut, trying to see anything but the image that was burned into my mind like it had been branded there. It was the face of someone I knew, someone I had thought I understood. Now I knew I was only beginning to truly understand the truth—the ugly, despicable, awful truth.

Felix elbowed me as he got up, letting me know it was time to go. We had to leave for the graduation ceremony soon. My mind was hazy as we gathered up our bags again, put on our armor, and saddled our dragons. Only the graduating avians were allowed to leave, which amounted to about twenty of us in all. The rest were either too wounded, or hadn't performed well enough to pass. They would have to wear another stripe and try again next year. I should have been proud to be one of the students who had been given the honor of graduating, but all I felt was complete disgust with myself. I had been so blind for so long, and the truth had been staring me right in the face.

A few instructors, including Jace, had volunteered to go with us as chaperones. I was surprised to see him standing in Mavrik's stall when I came in. My former instructor was standing there, already dressed in his armor, casually chewing a piece of straw. He glanced at me, and frowned down at the scimitar hanging off my belt.

"Interesting choice of weapon," he mumbled. "Some would call that heresy, or even treason."

"Are you going to ask me whose side I'm on again?" I snapped with as much defiance as I dared. I walked past him and started buckling my bags onto Mavrik's back.

Jace snorted. "No. I came here to ask if you wanted to be my wing end."

I froze. Slowly, I turned around to make sure I wasn't hallucinating. "You still want to fight with me? Even after what you've seen me do?"

"Actually, I'm surprised I'm the only one who's asked you. I guess the others are waiting until after you graduate. Lucky me for getting to you first." He smirked and nodded toward Mavrik. "You two are the only ones to ever be able to keep up with Ghost and me. My last partner couldn't keep in formation. That's why he got killed. You think you can handle being my wing end?"

I debated pinching myself to make sure this was really happening. But I didn't want to run the risk of looking like an idiot, so I nodded. "Only if you think you can handle my occasional weirdness."

Jace's smirk widened, and it was starting to freak me out. Smiling came about as naturally to him as it did to a hungry wolf. "I'm counting on it. After all, we're the only ones who stand any chance in an aerial skirmish with shrikes. Being able to talk to Ghost and anticipate his moves makes you my number one choice."

Thinking about shrikes made me sick all over again. I went back to buckling down my gear and put my helmet on. "So, I guess that will put us on the frontlines?"

"To the worst parts of them, in fact. We'll be going to Northwatch. We deploy from here in five days. That should give you time to get things squared away at home—that is, unless you planned on getting married before you leave." Jace stopped on his way out the door and gave me an expectant look. "Were you?"

I was so glad I already had my helmet on so he couldn't see me blush. "No, sir."

He made a grunting sound, like he approved. "Good. Then don't be late. And quit calling me sir; I'm not your instructor anymore."

The closer we got to Halfax, the heavier the secret I was carrying became. It threatened to break me, to send me spiraling into a reckless rage that would more than likely get me killed. I struggled to keep it together and remain calm. There was still so much uncertainty. My mother had told me I was watching a memory instead of a dream, but wasn't she merely a dream, too? She had died a long time ago, and I was certain about that. How could I trust what I saw in my dreams wasn't a trick of my own mind? Felix had seemed so sure that the real king wasn't dead. I knew he would never lie to me, especially not about something like that.

We started our final descent to the royal city, and I could hear music even several hundred feet in the air. I could see the streets around the castle were filled with people coming to welcome us. As we got closer, Jace took the lead and brought us to a wide, open courtyard in the middle of a beautiful garden right in the middle of the city. There was enough room for all of us to land together, and people cheered as we arrived. They threw so many flowers and petals that it looked like colorful snow.

"Keep your helmets on," Jace warned us as we all dismounted.

Dressed in our finest armor, with sweeping black capes buckled over our shoulders, we followed him as he led the way down a white stone path that wound through the city. The path led all the way up to the front gates of the castle. Everywhere we went, people were clamoring to see us. Girls threw handkerchiefs. Kids waved flags with the king's eagle on them. I saw lots of them with their faces painted to look like dragons. It was a huge celebration, but I was almost too anxious to enjoy it.

"Why can't we take our helmets off?" I whispered to Felix. He was walking right next to me, waving to the crowd and drinking in all the adoring looks the girls were giving us.

"For you, idiot." He winked at me through the eye slit in his helmet.

I frowned. Right away I knew Jace was trying to shield me from any more discrimination. He didn't want the crowds to see I was a halfbreed, probably because he was concerned they wouldn't accept me. But I was not in the mood to be coddled like some child who might get his feelings hurt. I did have some pride left.

I ripped my helmet off and stuck it under my arm. A few people standing nearby gasped so loud I could actually hear them over the noise. They stared at me in complete horror. A young girl screamed.

Jace whipped around and glared like he might actually punch me. "What are you doing?"

I glared back at him. "They'll find out sooner or later. I can't change what I am, so either they will learn to accept me, or they won't. Either way, it isn't my problem."

Felix took off his helmet, too. He was grinning and laughing when he draped an arm over my shoulder. That made even more people gasp in horror. "He's right. Let's have a good time."

When he took off his helmet, I could see Jace's nostrils were flared like an angry dragon about to breathe fire. But he didn't say anything else about it. He kept walking toward the castle gates, and we followed while we waved to the crowd.

People were definitely staring at me. Most of them didn't look happy. They probably had never seen a halfbreed before, and definitely not one wearing a dragonrider's armor. But nothing they said could touch me now, though.

I looked through all the unfamiliar faces, and didn't see a single person I knew. There were no gray elves in the audience, either. They were all locked away in the poor ghetto where I had lived with my mother, only a few blocks away from where I was standing at that moment. Thinking about it made my insides twist painfully.

The king was waiting for us at the front steps of the castle. The huge gates were open wide to let everyone inside the perfectly manicured courtyard. People poured in by the hundreds. Banners hung off every roof and gable, and garlands of roses adorned either side of the walkway leading up to the front steps. Guards in gleaming armor stood at attention, their swords drawn in a parade stance as we passed.

But I couldn't look at anyone, or anything, except the king. He was at the top of the staircase that swept up from the courtyard to the front doors. There were six elite guards on either side of him, all wearing those white masks I remembered all too well. The sight of them made my chest burn dangerously again, and I clenched my fists to keep from lashing out. I reminded myself over and over that I had no proof. There was no evidence except for a dream and a coincidence. That wasn't nearly enough for me to do or say anything.

Felix had been telling the truth when he said the king looked pitiful. He was small, bent over like an old man, and every inch of his body was covered—even his face. He wore a porcelain mask painted in blue, red, and gold. It looked regal, and was supposedly hiding the gruesome scars of his battle with a shrike.

One by one, we each went up the stairs alone to meet the king. Felix went ahead of me. He knelt at the king's feet, kissed the royal signet ring on his hand, and swore an oath to be obedient until death. Then they took off his old black cloak, and put a new blue and gold one in its place.

Suddenly, it was my turn.

As I walked past Jace, he muttered, "Don't look him in the eye. Keep your head down. And for kingdom's sake, don't do anything stupid."

I didn't answer. I was wondering what, exactly, he meant by "stupid." Tripping, maybe? Or drawing my sword and ramming it through the so-called king's chest before his elite guards could save him? Both were definitely stupid, and entirely possible for me at that point.

At the top of the staircase, I decided to follow Jace's advice. I kept my head bowed, and my eyes on my boots as I knelt before the king. Being close to him made my heart beat loudly in my ears. Over and over, I reminded myself that there was no proof. It was a dream. I couldn't do anything based on a dream.

The king's hand appeared in front of my face. It was covered in a white glove, and there was a big golden signet ring on his middle finger with the shape of an eagle engraved on it. My soul burned as I kissed it. The metal tasted bitter.

"This is the first time a halfbreed has ever knelt at my feet." The king spoke in a hoarse, gravelly voice that made his words hard to understand. "How did you become a dragonrider?"

I couldn't help myself. Slowly, I looked up and met the king's eyes through the holes in his mask. They were bloodshot, and their color reminded me of cracked amber glass.

"I was chosen," I said.

The king didn't reply. He stood there, staring back at me until I lowered my eyes again. Then he went on with the ceremony like nothing had happened. He spoke the oath, and the words passed over my ears like white-hot flames. "Do you swear yourself to the service of the kingdom of Maldobar? To protect it and its people with every bit of your strength, even unto your dying breath? And do you swear yourself to the service of its king, to honor and obey him in all things without hesitation?"

I hesitated. I was thinking about doing one of those stupid things Jace had warned me about. Then I bit my tongue, and squeezed my eyes shut. "I swear."

The elite guards removed my old black cloak, and clasped the blue and gold one onto my shoulder armor. It was made of expensive silk, and the neck was trimmed with white fox fur. When I stood, there was a reluctant round of applause, and I went back down the steps feeling like I had just sold my soul to a demon.

I didn't smile. I didn't wave. This wasn't something to be happy about, much less proud of.

When everyone in our group, except the two instructors, had gone up to take their oath, the crowds erupted in cheering and applause. Music and laughter filled the air. People rushed in upon us, eager to meet the newest dragonriders to join the ranks.

Not many people came close to me. Only a few brave souls dared to smile and bow, or offer me a handshake. But I could sense their apprehension and disapproval when they did. The only ones who didn't give me that kind of greeting were the children. They didn't seem to care what I looked like, and a few of them rushed up to stare at me and ask me weird questions, like how heavy my shield was, before darting away.

The sunset drove the people out of the streets, but it didn't put a stop to the festivities. The castle wasn't open to us, but every single shop and home in Halfax was. Felix was set on going from tavern to tavern until he was too drunk to stand up. The others seemed to like that idea, but I had other plans for the evening. I followed them to the first few taverns, watching as they laughed and eager citizens bought drinks for them and thanked them for their service.

"We'll be getting our first lieutenant's pay soon!" Felix chuckled. He had that mischievous glint in his eyes. "Better drink up while it's free, and before some woman comes along and gets her hands on your money!"

I smiled at him. It was good to see him in high spirits again. I was beginning to realize he hid a lot under that cunning, dangerously charming smile—all the things he didn't want anyone else to see. I didn't know how to put up that kind of a barrier, not when all of my emotions smoldered so near the surface.

I waited until it was very late. We were on our fifth tavern, and I knew everyone was too distracted to realize I wasn't drinking. When I saw a good chance, I ducked out the back door of the tavern and walked the dark alleyways with my helmet still under my arm. I let my feet guide me, taking me on familiar secret paths I hadn't taken in years.

There was a hole in the wooden wall that separated the elven ghetto from the rest of the city. When I was little, I had used it to sneak in and out so I could run errands for my mom. But now I was way too big to fit through it anymore. That wasn't about to stop me, though. I pried the boards apart with my bare hands, and managed to squirm through the gap even with my armor on.

Beyond that fence, it was like stepping into another world. There was no light except for the moon and stars because it was well past curfew. The narrow dirt streets were empty. Trash was scattered everywhere. The wooden shacks leaned in all directions, looking more like piles of debris that had been raked together than something anyone would want to live in.

I passed several city guards on night patrol as I walked the dark, filthy streets of the ghetto. They stared at me, but as soon as they saw my armor, they hurried on their way and never said a word. Halfbreed or not, I was out of their reach now.

I walked past the old shack my mother and I had shared for so many years. Seeing how little it had changed put a pain in my chest like I'd been stabbed. I wanted to go inside and touch the things that had once been my entire world. But there was light coming from inside, and shadows were moving past the windows. Another family was living there now. So I stared at it for a moment before continuing on.

My feet carried me to a place I had almost forgotten. On the far edge of the ghetto, closest to the castle, there was a skinny, three-storey building that backed right up against the perimeter fence. The old gray elf woman who had lived in the shack beside it had made herself a lattice out of scrap wood, and she always grew flower vines on it in the springtime. I had used that lattice as a way to climb up to the roof of the building a few times, when I was feeling especially brave. You couldn't beat the view from up there.

The climb might have been easier because of my height, but my armor definitely made up for that. I clambered up to the flat stone roof, and sat on the edge like I had when I was little. I could see all the lights of the city stretching out around me. I could see the castle bathed in the light of a thousand torches. Overhead, the stars glittered beyond my ability to count.

This place still made me feel as small and forgotten as it had years ago. Once, that feeling had been so frustrating to me. Now, it was a nice change of pace. It felt good to be out of the spotlight for once.

"You're missing your own party, you know."

I jumped to my feet, turning around at the sound of a soft, feminine voice coming from behind me. Beckah was standing with her long dark hair spilling over her shoulders. In the glow of the city lights, I could see her smiling at me. It was more beautiful to me than all the stars hanging over our heads. It made my world move, and pulled toward her like an ocean tide.

"Sorry, I should have said something sooner. But I saw you sneaking away, and I wanted to see where you'd go." She started nibbling on her bottom lip.

I couldn't speak. I just ran to her and hugged her as hard as I could.

Beckah hugged me back. She put her arms around my waist, and buried her face against my breastplate.

For a long time, we stood there holding each other without ever saying a word. Finally, she pulled back so she could trace her fingers over the scar on my face. I saw her expression change, as though seeing it made her feel guilty.

"Does it hurt?" she whispered. "I'm so sorry. I should have gotten there sooner."

I took her hands and squeezed them firmly. "I can live with a few scars. You saved our lives, Beckah. That's the only thing that matters."

"I saw you lying there like you were dead. I was afraid I was too late. You were so pale, and you weren't moving, and—" She choked on her words. I saw her eyes welling up with tears, even though she was trying to smile at me.

"I'm so glad I wasn't too late. I love you, Jae. I can't lose you."

I had been resisting doing stupid things all evening. Eventually, I was bound to slip up. When she told me that, I didn't even think about it. I grabbed her face and kissed her as hard as I could.

She gasped, and at first she was stiff. I was beginning to think this might be a mistake. I might be about to get punched in the face by a girl half my size. But then I felt her put her arms around my neck.

She kissed me back.

We sat together as the first light of dawn started to turn the skyline pink, slowly melting away the stars. I had an arm around her, and she was leaning against my side while holding my hand. It was the best feeling in the world.

"I'll be going to Northwatch," I told her. "Jace asked me to be his wing end."

She smiled strangely as she wriggled her hand down into my vambrace and pulled out the handkerchief she had stitched for me. Seeing it made her cheeks turn pink. "You carry it with you?"

I laughed. "You told me to!"

Beckah stuck her tongue out at me. "Do you always do what girls tell you? I heard you already kissed someone else before me."

Panic hit me right in the chest so hard I literally wheezed out loud. I stared at her and tried to think of how to explain. But when I tried, no sound would come out.

Then she started giggling. "Look at your face! You look like a fish gasping for air!"

"H-how did you know about that?" I managed to ask.

"I-It's not what you think! Julianna practically attacked me!"

Beckah smirked and pinched my nose playfully. "Oh stop it, I know that already. Gossip travels fast, especially about a noble girl tackling a halfbreed like that. I wish I could have seen your face. But I bet you looked just like you do now." She started laughing again.

I still wasn't sure if it was safe to laugh with her or not. I gave a few careful chuckles and tried to remember how to breathe normally. "I thought you would be upset about that."

"Upset because some other girl kissed you?" She rolled her eyes. "Oh please. If I were going to be upset with anyone, it would be her not you. She's gone around telling everyone how you rejected her and broke her heart because you're in love with some mystery girl. But it was my fault, anyway. I shouldn't have left you alone at the ball. If I had stayed, it never would have happened."

I put a hand over my face to cover my embarrassment. "She promised she wouldn't tell anyone ... "

"Only a man would believe something like that," Beckah quipped. "Women tell each other everything, Jae."

I filed that crucial information away for future reference. "Well, I'm sorry. I should've realized what she was up to."

Beckah smiled and planted a kiss on my cheek. "Don't worry about it. You're so naïve when it comes to girls, but it's really cute. And you're all mine now."

We sat in silence again, watching the sunrise. I was trying to figure out if being called cute was a good thing or not. She seemed happy and content. The morning light shining in her eyes made them sparkle. I could see all the freckles on her cheeks.

I hated to ruin the moment. I wanted this to last forever. But there was something I had to tell her, and I was running out of time. Soon, Felix and the others would come looking for me. Then I'd have to head back to the academy and prepare to deploy to Northwatch.

"Beckah." I squeezed her hand to get her attention.

She looked at me with that blissful smile still on her lips.

"I took your advice. I paid more attention to my dreams," I started to explain. Anxiety and bitterness made my hands shake, and I watched her smile start to fade away.

"What did you see?" she asked quietly.

I didn't know where to begin. So I told her everything I could think of as quickly as I could. I told her every detail of my dream, from beginning right up until the guard had taken off his helmet. I showed her the scimitar with the elven royal crest on the pommel, and explained how I had found it hidden in my half-brother's room. I told her how the dream, the gray elf warrior had made a deal with the guard to let him live, but in exchange he had to take something from the forest. But not just anything. No, he only wanted the god stone.

Beckah listened. She studied me and the scimitar, and waited for me to give her that last piece of the puzzle. "The guard," she pressed when I didn't offer it up quickly enough. "You said he seemed familiar somehow. Do you have any idea who he is?"

"Yes," I answered through clenched teeth. "Before the dream ended, I saw his face."

"Who?" She was staring up at me with wide eyes and gripping my hand so hard it cut off my circulation.

"Who is it?"

I hated the answer because if it was actually true, then I was just as responsible as he was. I hated seeing his face whenever I closed my eyes. It took all my self-control to keep from shouting as I glared at the royal castle.

"The guard in my dream, the traitor who made a deal with that murderer and stole the god stone from Luntharda," I growled furiously, " ... is my father."

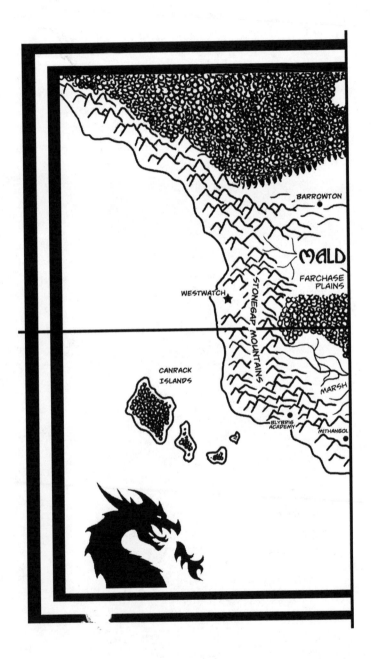

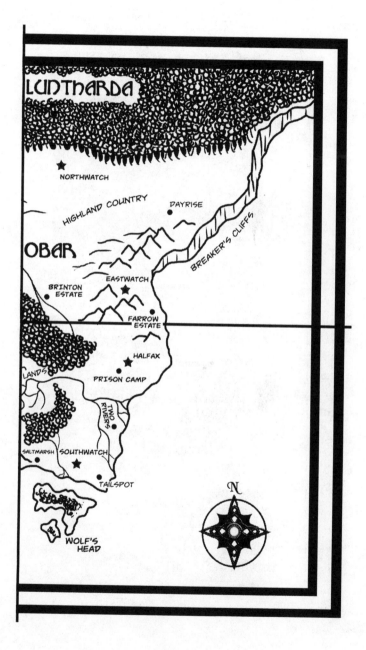

LUNTHARDA

NORTHWATCH

HIGHLAND COUNTRY

DAYRISE

OBAR

BREAKER'S CLIFFS

EASTWATCH

BRINTON
ESTATE

FARROW
ESTATE

HALFAX

PRISON CAMP

LANDS

TWO
RIVERS

SALTMARSH SOUTHWATCH

TAILSPOT

WOLF'S
HEAD

N

Nicole Conway

Nicole is the author of the children's fantasy series, THE DRAGONRIDER CHRONICLES, about a young boy's journey into manhood as he trains to become a dragonrider.

Originally from a small town in North Alabama, Nicole moves frequently due to her husband's career as a pilot for the United States Air Force. She has previously worked as a freelance and graphic artist for promotional companies, but has now embraced writing as a full-time occupation.

Visit her online at
http://anconway422.wix.com/anconway

OTHER MONTH9BOOKS TITLES YOU MIGHT
LIKE

AVIAN
TRAITOR
THE THREE THORNS

Find more awesome Teen books at http://www.
Month9Books.com

Connect with Month9Books online:

Facebook: www.Facebook.com/Month9Books
Twitter: https://twitter.com/Month9Books
You Tube: www.youtube.com/user/Month9Books
Blog: www.month9booksblog.com
Instagram: https://instagram.com/month9books
Request review copies via publicity@month9books.com

DRAGONRIDER CHRONICLES 1

Fledgling

NICOLE CONWAY

THE
BROTHERHOOD
AND THE
SHIELD
THE THREE THORNS

MICHAEL GIBNEY